Readers everywhere are loving each
of the stand-alone books in
the popular Beach House series...

THE BEACH HOUSE

"When I turned the last page of *The Beach House,* I sighed. I didn't want it to end. I wanted to know more about these ladies. But, oh, what a satisfying read—one of the best of the year."

Ane Mulligan, Atlanta

"I wasn't familiar with Sally John before reading *The Beach House*.... She writes an enthralling story with fully developed characters that are experiencing the problems that many women of faith face daily. And she does it with warmth, realism, and sensitivity. The four friends, an intriguing beach house, and two men of God are frosting to this delicious novel.... It's a wonderful story that is guaranteed to leave you with the knowledge that God has a plan for all of us."

Armchair Interviews, Minnesota

"What Christian fiction often aims at but struggles to do, John seems to accomplish with ease. This conversational style not only keeps the reader turning pages but also empowers readers to consider and listen for spiritual solutions to their own problems.... Fans of women's contemporary Christian fiction will find *The Beach House* a satisfying read."

Cherri Vanover and Kim Peterson for www.readerviews.com

CASTLES IN THE SAND

"Once in a very long time, a book comes along that has the ability to touch hearts, change lives, and inspire hope. *Castles in the Sand* is one such book. It is not just another beach read, as one would guess by looking at the cover, but a profound, inspiring read of a family torn apart and the long road home.... The characters in this book feel true to life, and really became real people and friends to me before I finished it. I laughed, cried, and felt for Drake, Susan, Kenzie, and all involved with them. The book, which comes from a Christian publisher, intertwines faith-based aspects without becoming preachy or overdone as so many inspirational books are. I found *Castles in the Sand* to be a very well-rounded read; just be sure to keep a box of tissues handy!"

Shaley Melchior for www.readerviews.com

"*Castles in the Sand* is a riveting novel of God's mercy when our very foundations crumble, and in this reviewer's opinion, it is destined to be an award-winner....Sally John has earned a permanent place as a favorite author of mine."

Ane Mulligan, Atlanta

Beach Dreams

Trish Perry

HARVEST HOUSE PUBLISHERS

EUGENE, OREGON

Per

Cover by Garborg Design Works, Savage, Minnesota

Cover photo © Derek Latta / iStockphoto

Back cover author photo © Sarah Huntington

Trish Perry: Published in association with the literary agent of Hartline Literary Agency, Pittsburgh, PA.

This is a work of fiction. Names, characters, places, and incidents are products of the author's imagination or are used fictitiously. Any resemblance to actual persons, living or dead, or to events or locales, is entirely coincidental.

BEACH DREAMS
Copyright © 2008 by Trish Perry
Published by Harvest House Publishers
Eugene, Oregon 97402
www.harvesthousepublishers.com

Library of Congress Cataloging-in-Publication Data

Perry, Trish, 1954-
Beach dreams / Trish Perry.
   p. cm.—(The beach house series ; bk. 3)
ISBN-13: 978-0-7369-2446-7 (pbk.)
ISBN-10: 0-7369-2446-9 (pbk.)
   1. Young women—Fiction. 2. Mothers—Death—Fiction. 3. Seaside resorts—Fiction. 4. San Diego (Calif.)—
Fiction. 5. Psychological fiction. I. Title.
PS3616.E7947B43 2008
813.'6—dc22

                                                    2008011785

Printed in the United States of America

08 09 10 11 12 13 14 15 16 / RDM-NI / 10 9 8 7 6 5 4 3 2 1

*For my daughter, Stevie,
and Tucker, my son.*

You are the greatest miracles of my life.

Acknowledgments

I give my deepest thanks to the following people for influencing my life and this book.

Tamela Hancock Murray for always having time for me, especially this past year.

Nick Harrison and Kim Moore for working so hard to make my books better.

Harvest House Publishers for being such an excellent family of people with whom to work.

My readers, especially those who have taken time to give me feedback or post reviews. Your messages absolutely make my day and inspire me to keep going.

Vie Herlocker, Mike Calkin, Betsy Dill, and Gwen Hancock for hanging together and critiquing, even as we scatter across the country.

Eileen Milnes, Stephanie Zullinger, the Saturday Night Girls, and all of my friends at Cornerstone Chapel in Leesburg, Virginia, for many prayers and much support.

My friends at American Christian Fiction Writers and Capital Christian Writers, two amazing sources of camaraderie, inspiration, and support.

My friends in the Open Book Club, for some of the best evenings and laughs ever.

Gwen Hancock for her help with my diabetes questions.

Donna Hawley for her expertise with regard to personal training.

Lynn Lees for helping me weed through all of that British slang.

Wendy Driscoll for her constant prayer. I know you're out there, girl!

Barb Turnbaugh and Michelle Sutton for their heartfelt friendship and encouragement. You two are gifts.

Bryce, Ali, Luke, Shelby, Sara, and Hunter, for being such wonderful, promising people. I love you and miss you.

Charles, Lilian, John, Donna, and Chris Hawley, my loving parents and sibs, for always being there for me.

Stevie, Tucker, and Bronx, for making me laugh and utterly adore life.

My precious Lord Jesus, for being the reason I do this.

Beach Dreams Characters

Tiffany LeBoeuf ~
> Personal trainer from Northern Virginia, 29, currently unemployed.

Jeremy Beckett ~
> Elementary schoolteacher from Northern Virginia, 30, boyfriend of Eve Danfield.

Eve Danfield ~
> Jeremy's girlfriend, 28, paralegal from Washington, D.C.

Orville LeBoeuf ~
> Tiffany's father, 57, truck driver and volunteer firefighter from Florence, South Carolina.

Sean Beckett ~
> Jeremy's father, 60, civil servant from Bristol, England.

Vera Beckett ~
> Sean's new wife, 52, shop owner from Bristol, England.

Ren Young ~
> Friend of Jeremy's and Tiff's, 30, elementary schoolteacher from Northern Virginia.

Kara Richardson ~
> Friend of Jeremy's and Tiff's, 30, personal trainer from Northern Virginia.

Therefore, if anyone is in Christ, he is a new creation;
the old has gone, the new has come! (2 Corinthians 5:17 NIV)

One

March 11, Northern Virginia

Tiffany lugged her suitcase up the three steps of the airport shuttle bus. If she hadn't packed the case herself, she'd be suspicious of its contents. It felt as if it were full of cinder blocks.

The March air hung colder here in Northern Virginia than it had in South Carolina. Yet Tiffany perspired with the effort to carve out a spot for herself and her luggage in the shuttle. Every spot was filled, jammed with people eager to get to their cars. Evening rush hour at Dulles Airport—never one of Tiffany's favorite situations.

She lurched backward and might have fallen when the bus took off, but there was nowhere to fall. Everyone on board groaned when the bus crawled to a stop for even more passengers in front of the American Airlines exit.

Oh, man. They were all getting on through the back door, where she stood sandwiched between a woman with an over zealous fondness for perfume and a man wearing too little deodorant.

The new passengers entered with a cold whoosh. There were only three of them, but three too many as far as Tiffany was concerned. She looked down to make sure no one stepped on her Moschino slingbacks. Why did she do stupid things like this? Why didn't she wear sneakers when she flew, like normal people?

She closed her eyes briefly. She was doing it again. Complaining about her circumstances, which really weren't all that bad. For the past

9

six months—ever since she came to Christ—she kept catching herself like this. With an exhale she determined to upgrade her attitude starting now. *Appreciate, girl, appreciate.*

When she lifted her eyes, they fell on the most attractive man she'd ever seen, especially this close. The cramped quarters forced him to stand within kissing distance of her.

Thank You, Lord!

He and Tiffany looked directly into each other's eyes—there was really nowhere else to look at the moment. He topped her in height by a few inches, despite her heels. The bus took off, and the quick forward movement shoved them against each other. They each grabbed at the hand rail and offered one-word apologies to the other.

Oh, mercy, did she hear an English accent? Maybe. And she was a sucker for an accent. There was something familiar about him. What was it? Had they met? Or was it just because he looked like Jude Law? Or Jude Law's even cuter brother.

Dear Lord, is it okay for me to talk with You about stuff like this? My goodness, he's so close I can tell he has really excellent skin. And the perfect amount of five-o'clock shadow. Is that bad of me to notice? Am I a horrible Christian for absolutely loving this moment?

She tried to sneak a casual peek at his ring hand, but the handrail obscured her view. Oh, wait, now, that was the wrong hand. But his ring hand was blocked by other people.

She glanced back up and saw him studying her with his crystal blue eyes. He looked quickly away, but then he playfully looked back at her, sideways.

She laughed, maybe a little too loudly. Embarrassed and reluctant to look at him again, she trained her eyes on his warm brown sports jacket. And his white shirt appeared freshly starched, even this late in the day. Six months ago, she would have made an unabashed comment to get things rolling with this guy. Where was the old Tiffany?

Me again, Lord. I cannot believe I'm getting shy. Me. The biggest flirt ever. This is Your doing, isn't it?

The man next to him asked the time. Mr. Gorgeous looked up at the handrail to read his watch. Hmm. A watch on his right wrist? That usually signaled a left-hander. Maybe he was creative. An artist. An actor.

Would you look at those eyelashes? And yes, he said the time—six thirty—in a distinctly British accent.

Wow, it really was hot in there.

The shuttle stopped at the first parking lot. Ah good, the cool air would help. And now people would get off and she could check out his ring finger.

As he rolled his luggage out of the way, she saw. Single. She smiled.

He smiled back. Friendly; not particularly flirtatious. He smelled like soap and spice.

And then he stepped off the bus.

He stepped off the bus!

She knew her disappointment was obvious, but she couldn't help it. She realized she had already mapped out some wonderful plans for the two of them. She'd accompany him to his next gallery opening. To his opening night performance. Anywhere!

He turned to face the shuttle before it pulled away. She saw him look for her. When their eyes met, he smiled again, but with a hint of sadness. It was a smile that said, "What a pity." Then he nodded once in her direction, as if he were saying goodbye.

She actually raised her hand in a resigned wave.

Okay, Lord, that was not fun. You and I both know I decided to trust in You about everything, especially men. And I'm going to try to be good. But that one right there? I'm going to need a whole lot of help, if You're going to parade many more like that in front of me.

She sighed and watched for her stop. She was home. It was time to focus on getting her life back in order.

Two

Three days later, Tiffany stood outside Ledo's Pizza, a hungry grumble in her stomach and a hint of dusk in the sky. In one swift moment, she kicked her flat tire, broke her stiletto heel, and gave voice to the thought floating through her mind.

"Maybe coming back here wasn't such a great idea, after all."

But she immediately regretted her negative words. No, that wasn't the attitude she wanted to adopt, was it?

She had made it this far. She had moved back into her condo and restarted all of her services and utilities. She had put in a call about her old job at the gym. Tomorrow she would touch base with some of the people she left behind when Mama's cancer got so bad.

During those five sad months, she had noticed it: South Carolina didn't feel like home anymore. Even with Daddy still there.

This was home. Northern Virginia was home, and Tiffany had missed living here. She was surprised at how much she missed her...friends?

Yeah. Friends. Kara and Ren had sent flowers and the sweetest condolence cards to Daddy and her while she was away. They would even have come for Mama's service if Kara's wedding wasn't the same week and Ren's pregnancy wasn't so far along. Considering they had barely met Mama, their intentions said "friends" to Tiffany.

She smiled at that and sallied forth, hobbling like a peg-legged pirate on her broken Biba pump. She walked into Ledo's, where the lights were dimmed for the dinner crowd. That unmistakable aroma—bread, garlic, oregano, and burnt cheese—made her stomach growl again. She had planned to grab dinner, even before the tire blew. Maybe someone here would help her change the flat.

She reached the front counter and stopped in her tracks. Wasn't *he* just the one for the job? The guy behind the counter focused on the cash register, his pale brown hair soft against his forehead. He looked more than friendly; he was one red-hot pizza man. Tiffany didn't even have to try to smile at him; he brought her mood up several notches just standing there.

When he turned his attention to her, she saw a visible lift in his mood as well.

Then it seemed to hit them both at once.

Mr. Gorgeous from the shuttle bus. The Jude Law look-alike. He worked in a pizza joint? She would never have placed him in this environment. He *had* smelled spicy, but not garlic and basil. So much for galleries and stage performances.

He seemed slightly embarrassed, but he quickly recovered.

"Fancy a pizza, love?"

Were they not going to mention the shuttle-bus incident?

Seeing him for a second time triggered something else in Tiffany's mind. She felt like she had met him—actually been introduced to him—somewhere before the shuttle bus. The gears in her rewind machine worked quickly. Had they dated? No, no way. She'd never dated a pizza man. Plus, she would definitely have recognized him on the bus if they had dated in the past. But her stomach tightened, and the pieces of her memory fell into place.

"Miss?" He had a polite question in his expression.

Shoot, she'd just been staring at him, glassy-eyed. She ordered the first thing she saw on the menu behind him. "I'll have the Hawaiian pizza, small. Please."

"Righto." He jotted her order down, and she felt minor frustration with him. Wasn't he going to say anything about the other evening?

"Hawaiian pizza." He looked up at her and smiled. "I always thought that was an odd combination."

"What?" Tiffany frowned and focused for a moment on what she ordered. Hawaiian pizza. Yeesh. She hated ham. "Oh, hold the ham, okay?"

He gave her a nod and jotted again. Fantastic forearms. "Right, then. So...hmm." He glanced up, looking confused. "I have to say that sounds rather more odd than the original. You just want a pineapple-and-cheese pizza, is that it?"

"Ew. No. Hold the pineapple too." She grimaced. She was an idiot.

"Ah..." He altered the order form again. "You want a Hawaiian pizza, hold the ham, hold the pineapple. The cheese, apparently, stands alone. Do I have it, now?"

She would have found him annoying, but that accent was so charming, and he had the slightest grin on his face. She was reminded of his sideways glance in the bus. She couldn't help but laugh. "Just a plain pizza, okay?"

His eyes crinkled, and Tiffany's stomach did a little flip. Too, too cute. She paid him and saw him considering her. He cocked his head before he spoke.

"I think you were on the Dulles shuttle the other night, yeah?"

Finally! "Yeah. I wasn't sure if you recognized me or not."

He retrieved her change from the register and spoke without looking up. "You have rather unforgettably blue eyes."

A blush ran all the way up to her ears, especially when he gave her the change and she felt the warmth of his hand.

She was blushing? What had the good Lord done to her?

"Wow, what a nice thing to say. Thanks. But, um, I feel like we were introduced sometime in the past. I'm not sure when—"

A woman's tired voice interrupted them.

"Hey, Jeremy, could you please come help me carry this tray of pasta dishes when you have a second?"

Tiffany turned her head, blinked once slowly, and opened her eyes and mouth in shock. "Ren!"

The immensely pregnant woman looked just as amazed as Tiffany when she turned in answer to her name.

"Tiffany?" Then her expression brightened, and she came as close to hugging Tiffany as she could, considering the size of her belly. She smelled like a pizza oven. "Are you back home now, or just visiting? And, oh, I'm so sorry about your mom. Did you get our card? The flowers? Oh, don't answer that; we were just so sorry everything happened over the Christmas break and during Kara's wedding. We—Hey, what's with your shoe?"

Tiffany glanced down. She'd already gotten used to favoring her right side and had nearly forgotten. "Broke it. Kicking my flat tire. Outside."

Ren heaved a commiserating sigh. "Not your day, is it?" She glanced into the dining area, which seemed full of an inordinate number of kids with their parents.

The guy from the shuttle bus—Jeremy—had quietly gone after that tray for Ren. Tiffany heard his voice above the din of all those families clamoring for their orders.

Ren adjusted the short green apron over her belly. "Let me go help Jeremy with those entrees and I'll be right back. Sit!" She gestured toward some chairs for waiting patrons and took off.

Tiffany obeyed, but she was totally confused. Now she knew why that adorable Jeremy looked familiar. He worked with Ren; she had heard Ren and Kara talking about him in the past. But Ren and Jeremy were schoolteachers. Tiffany was sure of that. She felt like she inhabited some alternate universe, watching them serve pizza and pasta to the masses, especially with the once-svelte Ren waddling like an emperor penguin in baggy drawers.

Then the *other* memory hit her. A slow seep of acid started in her stomach. She had met Jeremy when she worked at the gym. He was a member. Just as she had done on the bus the other night, she immediately saw a big neon "Gorgeous!" sign over his head the moment she met him. But something she said back then turned him off. She remembered seeing it in his eyes—from appreciation to disdain in a few easy words. And she hadn't crossed paths with him since.

Here he came back again. Tiffany sat up and tried to look like someone who wouldn't *think* of saying anything mean or stupid.

But it was too late. He must have remembered too.

"Right, I'll see how your order's doing." He passed her. A kind smile on his face, but he appeared determined to avoid her eyes. Wow. What a difference one little memory made.

Now he was very polite. But very *not* interested. Whatever she had done or said before, it had oozed into his mind as the acid had her stomach.

"So, how are you holding up, Tiffany?" Ren eased herself down in the seat next to her and drew her attention away from the kitchen and Jeremy. Sympathy was clear in Ren's small smile. "Everything happened so quickly with your mom, didn't it?" She placed a hand on Tiffany's knee.

Despite all the kindness shown to Tiffany and her dad over the past several months, she still found it difficult to be comfortable with most physical gestures of affection. She didn't like that about herself. She willed her knee not to tense up under Ren's hand.

"I still can't talk about Mama very well." She stared at her lap.

After a quick pat Ren moved her hand away. "That's okay. Don't talk about her if it hurts too much. I can't imagine your pain. But...I never got the chance to tell you something."

Tiffany looked at her and saw respect in her eyes.

"Your leaving here to spend those last few months with your mom? So loving, Tiffany." And then Ren must have sensed that Tiffany couldn't talk without crying, because she swiftly changed the subject. "So has your health been all right through all of this?"

"The diabetes?" Tiffany shrugged. "Pretty much the same. No better, no worse. It's just a way of life, and as long as I get my shots on time, I'm fine."

Ren tucked a long stray lock of her dark hair back into her ponytail. "I'll bet you never expected to see Jeremy and me working at Ledo's, huh?"

Tiffany gave her a weak smile. "Yeah, what's up with that?"

"School fundraiser. Most of the people working tonight are teachers from our school. We're working for free, and Ledo's is contributing fifty percent of the night's profits to the school. A bunch of the clientele tonight is from our school."

Tiffany's eyes wandered to Ren's massive stomach. "I can't believe they're letting you work here like that!"

"Why not?" Ren laughed and gently rested her hand on top of her tummy. "I'm pregnant, not radioactive."

"But you're huge!"

Ren looked down and smiled at her abdomen. "Twin girls."

Tiffany's cell phone rang, and she looked at the ID. "Oh, good. It's the gym about my job."

"You mind if I stay here awhile?" Ren pressed her hands against the small of her back.

"No, stay. This shouldn't take long." She answered the call. "Hi, Mickey. Thanks for calling back so soon."

But as he began to speak and she heard the frown in Mickey's voice, her own spirits fell.

"But I left to care for my dying mother, Mickey!" Tiffany said. "Do they know why I left?" *Don't cry. Do not cry.*

Tiffany glanced at Ren but had to look away. Those kind eyes were going to break her down right in the middle of this restaurant. She finished the call with Mickey and stared at the wine-colored carpet, willing her heart to slow down.

A couple of waiters passed by on their way to the kitchen. Ren broke the silence. "How can I help, Tiffany?"

Tiffany looked at her. "They replaced me. I don't have a job."

Ren sighed. "Oh, Tiffany. That's not right." After a pause, she began again. "Listen, Tru and I don't have much, but we could help you out financially for a while—"

"Oh, no, that's not really a problem." Tiffany couldn't help the little rush of appreciation she felt. "Thanks, though. Mama left me a little money." She frowned. "I took the job for granted, that's all. I'm a little disoriented."

"But there are other gyms, right?"

Tiffany nodded. "Sure, sure. I just need to get my thoughts together. I've been so distracted by my mom and then making sure Daddy was going to be okay when I left. He's been so lonely. I've just had a lot on my mind and wasn't expecting my circumstances here to change. And I do have my mortgage on the condo, so I—"

As if given an electric shock, Ren sat upright and gasped. "Tiffany! I know what you should do!"

Her enthusiasm made Tiffany chuckle. "You do, huh?"

"Absolutely!" Ren put her hand on Tiffany's arm, and this time the gesture didn't bother Tiffany. "You should take a couple of weeks at the beach house."

"The what? What's the beach house?"

Ren sighed and looked up with a dreamy expression. "Mission Beach.

In San Diego. Tru and I spent a fantastic week there a couple of months ago, and I've been raving about it ever since."

"Fancy, is it?"

Ren snorted in laughter. "Not exactly. Compared to the houses around it, it's the ugly-but-lovable child in the group."

"Then what's the big deal?"

"Did I mention it's in *San Diego?* Come on! Gorgeous weather every day. The locals are cool. The guy who lives next door is this charming Scot—you'll love him—and the house is right on the beach, and—" She stopped to take and expel an ecstatic breath. "You've just got to go, Tiffany."

Tiffany raised her eyebrows and cocked her head.

"To get your thoughts together, like you said."

Tiffany laughed. "What, are you on commission with the rental company or something?"

She was suddenly aware of someone behind the counter.

Jeremy patted the top of the pizza box he held. "One plain pizza, ready to go." His behavior was still friendly but distant. Yes, he had obviously recalled their brief meeting in the gym all those months ago.

"Hey, Jeremy," Ren said. "Tiffany's got a flat tire waiting for her out there. Do you think you could be a gent and change it for her?"

Tiffany looked quickly from Ren to Jeremy. Man, nothing like putting him on the spot.

He hesitated for only a second or two. He untied the chef's apron from his waist. "Righto." He picked up Tiffany's pizza, came out from behind the counter, and gestured for Tiffany to leave ahead of him. "After you."

Tiffany harrumphed inwardly. He *might* have been after her, had he not remembered who she was. Everything had seemed so romantic for those few minutes on the bus. Now she had to suffer the consequences of her own bad behavior of the past. And what should it matter, anyway? She needed to focus on getting a job, not a boyfriend.

She stepped in front of him, and her heel finally fell completely off her shoe. With the sudden, four-inch drop to the floor, she nearly lost her balance. The spastic jerk she did with her other leg and both her arms kept her upright but thoroughly goofy looking. As an added bonus, she punched Jeremy in the chest with her elbow when she jerked her arm back.

"Oh, I'm so sorry!" She turned to catch him grimacing, teeth clenched. He rubbed the center of his chest.

He quickly regained his composure. "Not a problem. Really."

Ren said, "You'd better get those shoes off, Tiffany, before you hurt yourself."

"Yeah." Tiffany bent down abruptly, which Jeremy obviously hadn't expected. He only took one step forward, but that was enough to bang into Tiffany's backside and send her further off balance and falling forward.

Jeremy cried out something that *may* have been a British swear word.

When he lunged to catch her, he put his entire body into it and simply furthered her momentum. The two of them sailed forward in graceless symmetry, like two geese coming in for a landing. They finally stopped by crashing, face first and momentarily entangled, against the opposite wall. It was as if a tightly strung catapult had launched them as one. Neither was significantly hurt, because Tiffany's upended pizza box formed a cushion between them and the wall.

"Blasted twit!" Jeremy straightened up and unsuccessfully tried to catch the pizza box. It fell, half-opened, to the floor.

"Well, I don't think I'm *totally* to blame for this!" Tiffany yanked off her shoes. She nearly started crying, so she charged out of the restaurant. Before the door closed, she heard a sputtering attempt at communication from Jeremy, along with Ren's admonition to him.

She tiptoed gingerly across the cool asphalt, trying to avoid anything that might hurt her feet. She had been through enough today.

Jeremy ran out behind her. "Tiff!"

She quickly dabbed away a few tears, stiffening her posture in the process.

"I didn't mean *you* were the twit," he called.

She turned to face him.

Jeremy rubbed the back of his neck. It was almost too dark to tell, but Tiffany thought he might be blushing.

"I was talking about myself. I should have watched where I was going." After a resigned sigh, he put his hand out to her. "Truce?"

Accepting apologies was not something Tiff had much experience with. But she was working on that—along with what seemed like a thousand other things. She took his warm hand and shook it. "Truce." She opened her car, threw her broken shoes inside, and retrieved her gym sneakers. Great. She would be elegance personified, wearing these with her little black pencil skirt.

He smiled. "I believe I owe you a Hawaiian pizza, hold the ham and pineapple. Why don't you go back in and order another, my treat. I'll get this tire changed while you wait. And tell Ren we've kissed and made up. She's worried."

Tiffany refrained from making a bold comment about the kissing and making up—yet another thing she was working on. And God seemed to be lending a hand in that area, too, with all the doggone blushing and shyness she kept experiencing.

"Thanks." She gave him her keys and turned to tiptoe back to Ledo's, her sneakers dangling from her hand. She suddenly felt happy. Hopeful. And far more confident. She might be unemployed, but coming home may have been a blessing after all.

She looked over her shoulder and couldn't help but exercise her most innocently flirtatious eyelash flutter. "You need a ride home after slaving away here? I'd love to return the favor."

He opened the trunk of her Corolla, matched her smile, and brought her mood swiftly back to earth.

"No worries. I've got it covered. My girlfriend's due here any moment."

Three

Tiffany wasn't quite back in the restaurant before Jeremy chanced a quick glance in her direction.

She was trouble, that one. Their moment on the bus the other night had been quite fun, but he had Eve to consider. He shouldn't have flirted.

Anyway, once he had seen her and Ren embrace minutes earlier, he remembered meeting Tiffany at the gym last year. Straight away, she had said something cruelly sarcastic to their friend Kara, who worked at the gym with Tiffany. And then she had given him a sexy smile of conspiracy. As if he'd been so impressed with her looks that he would turn on Kara and share in deriding her. In that, she'd not only insulted Kara, but him as well.

She *was* stunning, he'd give her that. That brilliant auburn hair of hers was like something out of a TV advertisement for shampoo or hair color. And he'd admit he wasn't above being astoundingly impressed with women based solely on their looks. Or even just their legs. She did have lovely legs—

He suddenly noticed he wasn't doing a thing but standing in the parking lot gazing into space, the village half-wit. And it would be dark soon. He looked at the flat on Tiffany's car.

"Righto." He opened the trunk, relieved to find he didn't need to remove much in order to get to the spare. Just one of those bins the post office uses to hold your mail—empty—and a couple of books. After a furtive peek toward Ledo's, he checked the titles.

The Secret of Beautiful Skin. He frowned. The subtitle was about antiaging. Blimey, she wasn't even thirty. He could tell these things. He was no expert, but he had noticed his girlfriend Eve's perfect skin immediately. Tiffany's was almost as lovely, except for that frown mark between her brows.

Jeremy picked up the second book. *Jesus Is Enough: Love, Hope, and Comfort in the Storms of Life.* He lifted his eyebrows. This was more than skin deep, eh? He couldn't help wondering what recent storms had been torrential enough to drive a girl like Tiffany to reading an entire book about them.

"Jeremy, what are you doing?"

He dropped the book and shot upright, banging his head on the trunk door.

"Blast!" He rubbed at his head and looked at his girlfriend, Eve, who didn't react sympathetically to his obvious pain.

"Whose car is this?" She spoke in her ever-gentle voice, but he sensed disapproval. Either she felt he'd invaded someone's privacy (which he had), or she felt he had involved himself with someone she'd rather he avoid. That, too, was highly likely.

"Sorry, love. I'm getting Tiffany's spare tire and jack. She's had—"

"Tiffany?"

He hesitated. He almost said "sorry" again before realizing he had already apologized for...well, for banging his head on the trunk door, apparently. Why did he feel so defensive?

"You haven't met Tiffany yet. I barely know her myself." He cocked his head toward Ledo's. "She's waiting in there. A coworker of Kara's. A friend of Ren's. She's just come back to Leesburg after being, uh, somewhere else. For several months, I gather."

Eve gave him a sweet smile, and he leaned forward to give her a peck on the cheek. She smelled lovely, like powder and blossoms.

"That's so like you, Jeremy, to do the chivalrous thing."

He smiled in response.

Her eyes were such a gentle, muted shade of blue. Considerably softer than the intense blue he had noticed in Tiffany's eyes.

Everything about Eve was light—silky, Nordic blonde hair, skin like honey-tinged cream. Even her demeanor was airy and graceful, the result of ballet training as an adolescent, she once told Jeremy.

He pulled Tiffany's spare tire free from the trunk and saw Eve glance down and straighten her soft pink cardigan. She wore it over a matching top as if it were a dainty cape, held together by a single pearl button at the neck, her slender arms left free of the sleeves. She looked like she'd just walked out of a country club.

She spoke without looking up at him. "And in a way, you're letting me play a small role in your gracious gesture."

"How's that, love?"

She pointed at his shirt and pants, which the tire had already smudged. "We'll have to change our plans for the evening. I certainly wouldn't ask you to go out in public all dirty like that. So that will be my little contribution to...Tiffany, right? My tiny sacrifice?"

Jeremy grinned. "Not to worry, love. I brought a change of clothes for tonight anyway. I didn't want to take a chance, working with all that pizza and pasta in there."

Eve put her hands on her slender hips and smiled. "Well, you're just the smartest man ever!" She touched his cheek and gave him a quick kiss. "Do you mind if I go in and say hi to Ren? Maybe meet Tiffany?"

"Brilliant idea." Jeremy kneeled on the ground and set up the jack. "I'll be in shortly."

She gave him a parting smile before walking toward the restaurant.

Jeremy watched her for a moment before turning back to the jack. She really was so lovely. Elegant, ladylike, smart, and absolutely smashing looking. He felt he could be happy with her.

But he did wonder for a moment, why—despite not having exerted himself yet—he had already broken out in such an intense sweat.

Four

Tiffany watched Ren waddle out of the kitchen, hand a tray to another server, and finally look her way. Hands on hips, Ren spoke like a TV announcer.

"Cheese pizza—the sequel—coming soon." She smiled. "And the manager says it's on the house."

Tiffany frowned at that. "But won't I be cutting into your school's fundraising profits? I don't mind paying again. I feel like it was my fault, all that stupid stumbling and pizza smashing."

Ren did a double take at her. Tiffany knew instantly she had surprised Ren by thinking of the school's welfare ahead of her own. She had seen that reaction several times recently, when she'd shown the slightest kindness to people who knew her. Admittedly, she had tried harder since becoming a Christian, but she couldn't believe her previous reputation stunk that bad. She looked at Ren with indignation.

"What? Can't I be fair once in a while without people thinking I've finally overtaken my evil twin? Does everyone still only think of me as selfish and demanding?"

Before Ren could respond, a soft voice spoke behind Tiffany.

"Ah, there you are, Ren. Holding down the fort, are you? While my poor Jeremy toils away in the mucky parking lot? Such hard workers."

"Hey, Eve." Ren gave a little wave to the woman.

Tiffany winced and turned, surmising who this must be. Oh great, the woman was the spitting image of the perfect porcelain doll Daddy brought home from Germany when she was a kid. So delicate she seemed viewed through gauze. And Tiffany recognized that sweater set she wore. Michael Kors. Delectable.

Ren peeked into the dining area. "There's not much of a fort to hold down right now, actually. The crowd's thinning. And my shift is ending soon. So is Jeremy's. But I guess you know that, with your being here to get him and all. I mean, I'm guessing that's why you're here. Unless you wanted to order something. Did you want to—oh, what am I saying, you two are probably going out to eat, right?"

Tiffany studied Ren. She was babbling just a little. Why?

Ren met eyes with her, and Tiffany read relief in them. "Tiffany! I should introduce you two. Tiffany, this is Eve…uh, Eve—"

"Danfield." Eve extended a pale, slender arm and placed her cool fingers in Tiffany's palm.

Angelina Jolie arms. Never lifted a barbell in her life. Tiffany closed her hand gently around Eve's and tried to exude as much femininity as she could. She was painfully aware of the calluses on her palms from pressing weights last week without using her gloves. Not to mention the well-worn sneakers that finished off her klutzy ensemble.

"And this is my friend, Tiffany LeBoeuf," Ren said. "She's just moved back home after spending the past—what was it, Tiffany, five months? In South Carolina with her mom—"

Ren stopped abruptly, as if she had said too much.

Tiffany smiled at Ren categorizing her as a friend. That was nice. And that little boost gave her all the confidence she needed for the moment. She turned to Eve, her smile softening with genuine sadness.

"Nice to meet you, Eve. Yes, I was with my folks, down in Florence. My mom…I lost her to cancer. She died just before Christmas."

Open surprise crossed Eve's face. "I'm so sorry! I had no idea. Jeremy didn't say—"

"I don't think Jeremy knows." Tiffany gently shook her head. "He and I don't really know each other." She glanced at Ren. "We just have mutual friends."

Jeremy walked back in, patting dust from his pants legs. "Right, that's got it for you, Tiff. Soon as we get you another pizza, you'll be set. You ordered another, yeah?" He handed Tiffany's keys to her.

She appreciated the change in subject. She grinned at him. He really was such a cutie-pie, but she tried not to seem flirtatious. "Thanks. Yeah, and the manager is giving it to me free, isn't that nice? So thanks for the offer to pay, but that won't be necessary." She cocked her head. "You know, that's the second time you've called me Tiff. I kind of like that." She looked at Ren. "What do you think? Tiff?"

Ren nodded once. "Suits you."

Jeremy assessed her. "Absolutely."

Eve cleared her throat.

Jeremy started and swiftly put his arm around Eve, prompting her to pull away from him.

"Jeremy Beckett! You're filthy! And I don't have a change of clothes with me." She seemed to catch herself after that, darting a look at Tiffany and Ren before forcing a light, nervous laugh.

"Egad, I'm sorry." Jeremy looked at his dirty hands. He stepped behind Eve and checked the back of her sweater. "All's well. Not a speck, I promise. Look here, I'll go change." He checked his watch and spoke to Ren. "We're finished here, yeah? It's eight."

Ren nodded. "The late crew is on board for the last two hours."

"Small cheese pizza's up." The manager emerged from the kitchen with a box in his hands. He set it down and headed back into the kitchen.

"Thanks, Freddie." Ren stepped behind the counter, drew a soda from the fountain, and removed her apron. "That's yours, Tiffany. Tiff."

Jeremy passed the counter on his way to the kitchen. Tiffany spoke with mock authority. "Step away from that pizza, son."

Jeremy looked back at her and laughed. He seemed pleasantly surprised by her humor.

He put his hands up, surrendering to Tiffany's authority, a twinkle in his eyes. Then he glanced in Eve's direction and stopped fooling around. "Be right with you, love." He turned and disappeared into the kitchen.

Ren touched Tiffany's shoulder. "Do you have to head right home? Tru's going to be a few minutes before picking me up." She sank into a chair at a small table near the front counter. "Thought I'd take a load off and have a soda."

Tiffany, feeling the onset of a headache, pressed her fingertips against her temples before she took the pizza box and joined Ren. "Actually, I need to eat something right away, so the company would be great." She opened the pizza box and looked over at Eve. "Want to share a pizza?"

"No thanks." Still, she sat at the table. She was close enough that Tiffany recognized her perfume. Estee Lauder's Beautiful, one of Tiffany's favorites. Eve smiled at them both. "Perhaps I'll join you until my man is ready."

Tiffany returned the smile and fought her judgmental nature. *My poor Jeremy. My man.* Was Eve sweet or possessive? Sounded a little controlling.

Whoops. Maybe she needed to fight the judgmental thing harder. She would probably be just as controlling if Jeremy were hers.

Anyway, it had been quite some time since Tiffany had had a boyfriend long enough to even consider him "hers." And it wasn't just because of the months tending to Mama. Before that she had dated too many men to remember, and none of them ever came to anything deep or serious. And talk about bad judgment. She had done some really shameful things in those days. She tried not to cringe, recalling her horrible decisions before—

"Tiff? Are you all right?"

Ren and Eve were both looking at her with concern. At least Ren—who had spoken—looked concerned. Eve's expression bordered on scorn.

Tiffany had been on autopilot while her mind wandered into her past. She had frozen in thought, her mouth wrapped around an oversized slab of pizza, with a sneer of self-derision on her face.

"Ah, no. Tastes bad, does it?" Jeremy had walked out of the kitchen just in time to catch her. Now he looked more like the hottie from the airport shuttle, fresh and handsome in a grey sports jacket and pale blue jeans. And she sat there stuffing pizza in her face, wearing a pit-bull snarl and sweaty gym shoes and sitting next to his perfect porcelain girlfriend in her fabulous Michael Kors sweater set.

Yeah. Tasted really bad.

Ren pushed her drink toward Tiffany. "Sugar free, Tiff."

She grabbed it and drank too soon, sending some of it up her nose. She fought valiantly—but unsuccessfully—to subdue the pained expression she held for several tearful seconds. After a deep breath and an absolutely necessary but subtle burp, she looked at them. They had become horribly silent, so she spoke without much thought.

"No, no, the pizza's fine. I was just a little disgusted with myself, that's all."

Silent stares. Clearly, no one knew the proper response to her comment.

"I mean, I just remembered back before, back when I, how I used to…"

Nope. There was no save here. She briefly closed her eyes, gave her head a quick shake, and flipped the issue away with her hand. "Never mind. I'm fine. Pizza's fine." She forced a resigned smile and spoke to Eve. "Nice meeting you, Eve. Hope you guys have fun tonight." She looked at Jeremy. "Thanks so much for fixing my tire."

"My pleasure. You have a good night, too, yeah?"

But she saw a hint of pity in his expression. Is that what that was? Pity? That was just so downhill from the "if only" expression he gave her when her shuttle bus pulled away the other night.

She threw a flash of haughtiness at him and caught him looking confused before she glanced away.

He spoke haltingly. "I…I guess I'll see you at work Monday then, Ren."

Once he and Eve left, Ren tapped Tiff's hand. "So why did you get ticked off at him just now?"

"What? I'm not ticked off."

Ren chuckled and ate a small piece of burnt cheese from the edge of Tiff's pizza. "The two of you looked like actors in a bad play."

Tiffany shrugged. "He looked like he felt sorry for me."

"Maybe he did. You know, with your mother—"

"He doesn't know about my mother. You heard Eve."

Ren nodded. "I forgot. But you did just have a flat tire. And you busted your pricey shoes. And you obviously have swallowing issues."

"And I don't have a significant other, like he does."

Ren raised her eyebrows. She took a drink from her soda. "You don't know Jeremy, Tiff."

"No."

"First of all, he's not that complicated. Nothing against Jeremy. He's fantastic and adorable, and I love him to death. But he does have that Y chromosome thing going on. He was probably already thinking about whether Eve would give him a goodnight kiss, not whether you were romantically fulfilled."

Tiffany tilted her head and regarded Ren. "I just realized what it is. You don't like Eve, do you?"

"What do you mean, 'what it is'?"

"You started blathering when she first came in here—"

Ren gasped, but she almost started laughing. "There was no blathering—"

Tiffany did laugh. "Believe me, there was blathering, and you haven't answered my question."

Ren took a long drink, never looking away from Tiffany. "Okay, it's like this. I really really really don't want Jeremy to get hurt."

"You think she's going to hurt him?"

Ren slowly put her soda on the table. "He's flitted from woman to woman for as long as I've known him. But at my wedding last year, he met one of Tru's fellow nurses—Brenda—and they started seeing each other. I think he was falling in love with her. I thought she was falling for him too."

"But?"

"Brenda moved to Colorado a couple of months ago. Kind of abruptly."

"Why? A better job?"

"For the skiing!" Ren gave Tiffany a crazed look.

Tiffany frowned, but she couldn't help laughing. "The skiing?"

"Don't laugh." Ren gave her a little smack on the arm. "She seemed like such a decent young thing—"

"He lost a girl to…snow?"

Ren snorted but caught herself. "He was crushed." She quickly sobered when she said that. "I've never seen him hurt like that." Ren looked down at her hands. "Jeremy and I have always felt pretty protective of each other. Even when I started dating Tru, who's about as noble as they come, Jeremy worried Tru would hurt me."

"Okay. So why do you think Eve is going to hurt Jeremy?"

"He's so smitten with her, and she…I could be wrong. I don't want to jump to any conclusions—"

"I think I jumped to the same ones, to tell you the truth." Tiffany looked seriously at Ren. "Is it okay to think someone's a phony if you're a Christian?"

Ren grimaced. "I don't think so."

Just then Ren's handsome husband, Tru, walked in. Tiffany stood and gathered her things. She quickly muttered to Ren.

"Then pray for me, sister, and I'll pray for you."

Five

The Friday-night crowd at Shearing's Restaurant had thinned down to late-dining couples and patrons at the bar. It was too late for family groups, who were no doubt home by now, snuggled in their beds or before their televisions. The pianist had livened up his musical numbers on the balcony upstairs, and a few of the drinkers joined in when the lyrics occurred to them.

Jeremy loved the nightlife, but he looked forward to joining the family ranks someday. Maybe that would eventually happen with Eve and him. He wasn't yet sure.

The waiter set the check in front of Jeremy. "Whenever you're ready, sir."

Eve placed her hand on Jeremy's arm the moment the waiter left. "Of course, you have to leave a decent tip for appearances' sake. But he was a horribly mediocre waiter."

"You think?" Jeremy made sure the fellow was out of hearing range. "He seemed all right to me. Nice enough bloke."

Eve sighed. "My mahimahi was lukewarm at best. And look. Our water glasses have been half empty for the past twenty minutes."

Jeremy winked at her. "Mine is half full."

She smiled back and shook her head. "What am I going to do with you, Jeremy? You let people get away with too much. You're too nice."

He leaned in to kiss her cheek. "But, look at who I got, being too nice. The prettiest bird in the place." He sat back in his chair and patted his hand over his heart. "And I have a surprise for that beautiful bird."

He pulled his wallet from his inside pocket and set his credit card on the dinner bill. When he replaced his wallet, he removed a small velvet-covered box and placed it on the table in front of her. "For you."

He wasn't sure what emotion lay behind Eve's gasp. Was that pleasure or fear he saw before she gathered her composure?

She looked from the box to Jeremy. "That's not...that's not a ring, is it?"

Now Jeremy was the one to gasp. "Oh!" He looked at the box as if he were surprised by it, too. "No! Oh, love, I...I'm a buffoon. Of course you would have thought that."

But did she *want* it to be a ring or not? Now he was fully flummoxed.

Before he could ask her anything, she opened the box. A single key sat on top of the white satin lining. Eve's eyes widened.

"Jeremy. Tell me this is *not* the key to a new car."

For a moment he simply froze. Was his face as ashen as it suddenly felt? A new car? Blimey, did Eve understand how little money elementary schoolteachers made?

"Uh, right. It is *not* the key to a car." Sweat seemed to burst through the pores of his forehead. "This isn't quite working out as I'd hoped. The key is, well, it's a symbol, actually."

Now Eve blushed, which at least helped Jeremy to feel they were on equal footing, but he hadn't planned for this moment to be an awkward one.

"Jeremy, you must think I'm awful and greedy." She placed her hand on his. "This was a sweet gesture." She took the key from the box. "So, is this the key to your heart? Is that what you're saying?"

Why did that make him laugh? Right out loud, as if she had said something ridiculous. Wasn't he just fantasizing about family, snuggling, the whole lot?

"Forgive me, love." He took the key from her. "Look, I'm not quite as poetic as that, I'm afraid. What I meant by a 'symbol' was that this key represents another key, which you'll have to retrieve when you take next week's trip with your mate Patti."

Eve frowned. "The San Diego trip? What do you mean?"

He leaned toward her and took her hand. "When I told Ren you were taking this trip to visit Patti, she positively glowed about the trip to San Diego she and Tru took recently. They stayed at a beach house right there on the beach. Nothing terribly fancy, she said, but they both loved every minute."

He placed the key in Eve's palm, which seemed uncharacteristically moist. "Rather than staying at Patti's wee place in the city and commuting each day to the shore, you'll be able to stay right there on the beach. I've rented the house for the entire two weeks. My treat."

She still looked flushed. "Jeremy, I don't know."

Blast. He'd have to pay for those two weeks, whether she and Patti used the place or not. He tightly rolled the edge of his napkin inward before he unwound it and started again.

"What is there to know? You said Patti's apartment was cramped, yeah? Ren says this place is plenty big enough for you girls to spread out and relax. And I trust Ren's judgment without question."

Something flickered in Eve's eyes. "Well. I must admit at least Ren seems to be one of your more stable friends."

"Yes, she is, rather." He frowned. "But, what do you mean? Which of my friends seems unstable to you?"

She laughed softly. "They're all fine, Jeremy. I didn't mean anything bad." Eve played with a lock of her blonde hair. "It's just that Tiffany girl. She's a little over the top, don't you think?"

He shrugged. "I don't really know Tiffany. But her attitude seems a good deal improved from when I met her a year or so ago. She was quite nasty to my friend Kara back when Kara introduced us. They worked together, you see, and—"

"Yes, nasty. In a number of ways, maybe." Eve pursed her lips slightly and raised her eyebrows.

"Oh, but I don't see that in her anymore, Eve. She seems to have, uh, softened a bit."

Now Eve shrugged. "Whatever. I don't really want to discuss her flaws tonight." She finally smiled at him. "Anyway, about the beach house. Thanks so much, Jeremy." She looked at the key in her palm. "You really are too nice."

The waiter had quietly retrieved Jeremy's credit card and now brought the charge slip for his signature before stepping away.

With a flourish Jeremy signed the slip. "Well, you'll understand then—since I'm so nice—that I choose to give our hardworking server here a generous tip. It's hardly two hours since I waited pizza tables, myself. This is a matter of empathy for a brother in arms, despite your lukewarm mahimahi."

"And my half-full glass." Eve held up her water glass and smiled.

He grinned in return. He had won her over. Surely by the time she returned from two lovely weeks at the beach house, she'd consider him the man of her dreams. He was sure of it.

Six

On Sunday Tiff came home from church encouraged. She had only started attending Christian Chapel with Ren and Kara shortly before leaving to care for her mother. Still, the church was such a comfortable breath of familiarity that she felt she had been attending there for years. She remembered some of the livelier worship songs and found Pastor Dan's sermon—about Christ and the men on the road to Emmaus—uplifting. She drove home hopeful about her future and appreciative of everything around her: the approach of spring, her friendships with Kara and Ren, and confidence about finding another job.

Yet, when she checked in with her father and heard his voice, her shoulders slumped, and she tilted her head against the phone receiver. There was unmistakable sadness in his "Hello?"

"Hi, Daddy."

"Well, hey there, kitten! How's my girl doing? You getting settled back in again up there?"

All for her benefit, this effort at cheerfulness. He had always tried to keep her from experiencing anything but sunshine and roses. If it hadn't been for Mama's view of life, Tiff would have grown up completely unprepared for the many disappointments she experienced in the real world. Thanks to Mama, she had come to expect people to let her down.

"Yeah, I'm settling back in pretty well." She put a whole-grain muffin in the microwave and zapped it. "My condo is in great shape, and I've already reconnected with some of my old friends."

"And when do you start back to work? Are you going to have a little time before then? You worked so hard down here, baby, with your mother and all. You shouldn't be in too big a rush, if you can help it."

She sighed and took a seat at her dinette set. "No, I won't be starting back anytime soon. That's the only drawback here. I can't get my old job back. I'll have to start job hunting—"

"What? Says who? I thought the manager—that Mickey fella—"

"Yeah, he thought he could give me back my job, but his bosses say no. I've been replaced."

She nibbled at the muffin and heard her father sputtering his anger before he spoke into the phone again.

"Replaced." He spat the word. "Replaced because you came down here and helped your mama and me the way you did? I don't know what I would have done without you here. I'm telling you, honey, I absolutely demand that you don't work for those no-good, callous—"

"It's okay, Daddy, really. I can get another job. I'll use Mickey as a reference. If anyone calls the gym, he'll explain everything. Don't worry, all right?"

"You need me to come up there and talk with them?"

She gave him a fond chuckle. "You're the best, Daddy. But, no."

She could hear the resignation in his sigh before he spoke.

"Well, I still think you should take your time before going back to work. I guess a job hunt might give you a chance to do that, huh? And if you need me to come on up there for anything, I'll be right there for you. You just say the word."

Finally, she got it. Daddy had always been there for her; but this was about more than his solid support. He was lonely.

Of course he was lonely. She had said as much to Ren the other day. With Mama gone, it was just Daddy and Boomer, Mama's sad-eyed Yorkie. And even Boomer had become a downer since losing his mistress. Sometimes he didn't even bother yapping at the mail carrier anymore.

Suddenly Ren came to mind, as well as the beach house she had mentioned. Tiffany gasped softly, considering the thought a blessing. She pushed the muffin aside.

"Hey, Daddy, I just got a terrific idea."

"What's that, kitten?"

"One of my friends told me about a beach house where she and her husband stayed a few months ago. In San Diego, California. Right on the beach. How about I call and see if we can get it for a couple of weeks?"

"*We?* You want me to go with you?"

"Daddy, I'd love that! You need a break as much as I do."

"But I've just gone back to work. Phil's likely to carp about having to fill in for me again."

She laughed. "Aren't you the man who just said he'd come up here if I just said the word?"

"Well, yeah. But I meant if you, you know, thought you were going to fall apart or something, out of fear about your employment prospects, or sadness over your mama, or—"

"Or frustration over my waffling dad? I think I could muster up some frustration if I had to."

He laughed. "Let me talk with Phil, honey. I'd really enjoy spending the time with you. I'll bet it will be fine for me to take a little more time. They're still being real nice to me because of your mama."

A sudden tightness in her throat made it hard for her to respond. "Oh, Daddy." She couldn't say more.

"You go on and make that call about the beach house. Call me back with the dates as soon as you have them."

⌢

The young man at the rental office sounded as if he'd had a head cold all his life.

"No, dude. I'm not the property manager. That's my aunt. She's out right now, but she'll be back soon. I got access to the computer, though, so let's rumble."

Tiff held her phone away and frowned at it. Let's rumble? And she couldn't stand being called "dude." Just a little too gender neutral for her tastes. But she plowed on. She clicked her pen off and on several times.

"I'm calling about a rental on—" She glanced at the notes Ren gave her before she left Ledo's the other night. "Thirty-four hundred Oceanfront Walk."

While she waited, she heard him muttering, presumably while he searched. "Hey, battah battah battah. Hey, battah battah battah. *Swing,* battah. Yeah, there we go. What dates are we talking?"

Tiff checked the calendar she had laid open on her kitchen counter. Next Monday would work. She put her finger on the spot. "March 24. For two weeks."

His muttering resumed in a rhythmic grunt. "Uh huh. Uh huh. Uh huh, uh huh, uh huh. Yep. Coming from Leesburg, Virginia, right?"

Tiffany suddenly straightened and cocked her head the way dogs do when they hear odd sounds. "Uh, what?"

"Gotcha down here, dude. Two people, two weeks. From Leesburg, Virginia. March 24 through April 6, just like you said."

"But—" She looked down, her face creased with confusion, and tried to put order to what he told her. "Who made the reservation?"

"Uh, hang tight. I don't see that. It should be on the page somewhere, but I'm brain cramping here. And this only shows the last four digits of the credit card."

"It's been *paid* for already?" Tiff scratched her head, as if her puzzlement itched.

"That's a big ten-four. Oh. Here we go. 'Referred by Ren Sayers.' That do anything for ya?"

Suddenly overwhelmed, Tiff felt the sting of tears. What an amazing thing for Ren to do for her. She really was a loving friend. "Um, yes. That does something for me. Thank you. Thanks very much." She almost felt as if the guy on the phone had performed a kind gesture toward her.

"Not a prob, dude. Pick up the key at the lockbox on the front door." He gave her the combination.

As soon as she hung up the phone, she started to call Ren. Then she realized it was probably too late at night. Ren was likely asleep already. She'd talk with her tomorrow. And she'd call her dad tomorrow, too, to give him the dates.

She smiled the entire time she got ready for bed, and she thanked God for her good friend Ren before dozing off. Mixed in with her prayers and thoughts, she remembered the "dude" mentioning that there would be two people at the beach house.

Weird. How in the world had Ren anticipated Tiff's bringing her father?

Seven

"No, wait! Ma'am? Lady?" Tiff tried, but failed, to stop the school secretary from paging Ren. She didn't mean to disturb Ren's teaching. She had placed her call while waiting for her order at the local salad bar. She hoped to catch Ren at lunch, but apparently she called too early. Now she was on hold, and there was no way to stop the interruption.

When Ren finally came to the phone, she sounded as winded as a fat man on a treadmill. Tiff pictured her poor pregnant friend waddling through the halls to reach the office.

"Hey, Tiff, how you doing? You all right?"

"Ren, I'm so sorry. I tried to keep her from paging you from class—"

"No, don't worry about it, really. My kids are with the art teacher right now. Your timing couldn't have been better. What's up?"

She was polite, but Tiff heard the busyness in her voice. "I just had to give you a call to thank you. *So* much."

"Sure, glad to oblige!" Ren's smile was audible. "What did I do?"

She paid for her salad and headed outside. "The beach house! I'm thrilled!"

"So you're going?"

Tiff laughed. "Am I going? Of course I'm going! I'd be a fool not to at this point."

"Wait, hang on a second, Tiff, they're asking me something here."

Tiff waited while Ren talked with someone in the office. She heard her say, "Okay, Peggy, would you please tell them I'll be right there?" When Ren spoke to Tiff again, she sounded even more pressed for time.

"Well, that's great, Tiff. I know you'll have a blast."

"Look, I'll get off. I can hear how busy you are. I just wanted to tell you thanks. And I'll pay you back, I promise."

"Great! You can babysit after the twins come so I can go out to dinner with my sexy hubby."

Tiff's eyes widened. Babysit? Actual babies? How many hours would she have to devote to Ren's screaming, pooping infants—*two* of them—in return for two weeks' worth of beach house rental? Before she could think it through, she heard Ren laugh.

"I'm kidding. I'm sure you'll return the favor one of these days. Take me out for a decadent dessert or something. Gotta go."

Tiff looked at the phone after Ren hung up. There was something off about that entire conversation. A fancy dessert in exchange for hundreds of dollars in rental fees? What was it Ren's husband did for a living? Tiff couldn't remember. But there was no way Ren could afford this extravagance on a teacher's salary.

She caught herself and sighed. She always looked for problems. Ren had done a generous thing. She needed to accept it, go home, and pack. She was about to have a perfect vacation. There was nothing to worry about.

Eight

They were surrounded by thousands of bustling people, but Jeremy focused on no one but Eve.

She brushed something from his shirtfront. "Now, don't be silly. There's nothing to worry about. I'll call you as soon as my flight lands in San Diego." She checked her ticket. "That will be around two o'clock your time."

Jeremy tried to give her a genuine smile. He wasn't prone to superstition, and he didn't have strong beliefs about premonitions. But this morning his stomach felt strangely unsettled about Eve's trip.

She reached up to pull his head down for a kiss, and she alleviated some of his concern. Maybe he just worried she wouldn't miss him.

She smiled sweetly. "Will you miss me?"

Relief rushed over him, and he laughed. "Love, you don't know how much. And I hope you'll miss me as well?"

Eve didn't answer because the swift movement of the security line distracted her. At least he hoped that was why she didn't answer.

"Whoops! I've got to go!" She grabbed her tote bag from him and slung it over her shoulder. She gave Jeremy one last peck on the cheek, and he breathed in that soft, floral fragrance she always wore.

He tried to give her a goodbye hug, but she moved farther along the line of passengers, and people filled the gap between them. He spoke to the back of her head. "Right, then. I hope you and Patti enjoy the beach house."

She turned back toward him. A blush quickly rose in her cheeks, and he was struck once again by how lovely she was. Porcelain skin, blue eyes, trim figure, and not one blonde hair out of place. *Immaculate* was the word that sprang to mind.

He watched her until she was too deep into the throng for him to see her. Just before she dropped from his sight, she looked back and blew him a kiss.

Jeremy grinned and waved. She did things to his stomach, that one.

He turned and walked against the stream of people heading toward the security check-in. So many people saying goodbye to loved ones or traveling to meet them.

He wondered if this was love. He had so often misjudged his feelings. Even now, he wasn't sure if what he felt was love, infatuation, or that same unease with which he awoke this morning.

Nine

March 24, San Diego, California

Later that afternoon Tiff and her father, Orville, faced the San Diego beach house. The clear air warmed them, and they were close enough to the water to hear the plaintive squeak of seagulls and occasional giggles from children chasing the waves. Yet the two travelers were distracted by their new living quarters.

Tiff double-checked the address on her notes. Without comment, Orville hiked his baggy shorts up on his waist, straightened his T-shirt over his generous belly, and returned to their rental car. Tiff turned to face him, squinting in the sun.

"Are you running away from this eyesore, Daddy?"

Orville chuckled and opened the trunk. "Just getting our luggage, kitten."

"Wait on that for a second." Tiff held up her well-manicured hand while she looked at the paper again. "This can't possibly be the house Ren talked about."

But the address matched. And Ren *had* called it the ugly child, compared to the houses around it. Tiff studied the orange red roof, the bug-eye effect of the windows on either side of the door, and the dreadful brown shutters. Ugly was an understatement. This thing looked like something straight out of a Dr. Seuss book, squished between two gorgeous, modern beauties.

Orville walked back to her side and draped his arm over her

shoulders. "It'll be fine. We're right on the beach and close to all the boardwalk shops and restaurants. Who cares if the house looks dull as dirt?"

"And as old." Tiff looked at her dad and couldn't keep the corners of her mouth from turning up. "Okay. Let's move in!"

As they pulled their bags from the trunk, Tiff saw the next-door neighbor about to enter his home. The man noticed them and approached. He appeared relaxed, tanned, wealthy, and good looking. Tiff thought he was about her father's age, somewhere in his fifties. But this guy had all of his hair, dark and curly, so he looked younger than her dad. He wore glasses, but she could see his kind, brown eyes, which crinkled when he flashed them a bright smile.

"Welcome to the beach house!"

And then Tiff remembered. The Scottish guy Ren mentioned. Deep, Sean Connery voice. Really classy, despite the cutoffs and faded T-shirt.

Orville reached out to shake his hand. "Thanks. Orville LeBoeuf. And this is my girl, Tiffany."

The man looked at Tiff, but he spoke to Orville. "Your...girl?"

"His *daughter*." Tiff was quick to clarify any confusion. Mercy. What had the world come to when someone might think she would date someone like her dad? Not that he wasn't the absolute greatest guy ever, but she laughed inside when she looked at her dad and imagined his dating a girl her age. Then she realized she couldn't imagine his dating *anyone* who wasn't Mama. In one brief moment her disposition switched from amusement to heartbreak, and her dad missed nothing.

"You okay, kitten?"

What was the matter with her? Was she more moody since Mama died or just more aware of her moodiness?

"I'm fine, Daddy." She put her hand out to the neighbor, who spoke first.

"I'm Julian, your neighbor this week."

"Tiff. Actually, we'll be here for two weeks."

"Marvelous. You'll feel like old-timers by the end of your stay, then. And your friend? Is she staying both weeks as well?"

Tiff and Orville shared a frown. Tiff looked back at Julian. "Our friend?"

"The young lady who arrived a bit earlier today. I didn't get a chance to meet her, but I saw her leave just as I did, a short while ago."

Orville lifted two suitcases. "Probably last-minute cleaning by the rental-agency staff."

"Ah, perhaps." Julian smiled at them. "I should let you get yourselves settled in. Please let me know if I can help you in any way while you're here. Enjoy!"

Tiffany grabbed her cosmetics case and carry-on bag from the flight. When she entered the code on the lock box, she realized the key had already been removed.

"What in the world?"

Orville tried the door and found it unlocked. "Hmm. You hang on just a minute, hon, while I take a quick look around."

Although Tiff didn't sense any danger—this place was too casual for danger—she still found this an odd beginning to their vacation.

Orville came to the door. "We're okay. But…"

"But, what?" Tiff walked in and looked around. "Whoa. Knickknack City." She looked at Orville and smiled. "But it reminds me of Grandma's a little." Doilies and trinkets cluttered every flat surface. Not a single chair or couch lacked an afghan or embroidered pillow.

Orville looked around as she had. "Yeah. You're right. But that's not what's troubling me."

Trouble? They weren't here for trouble. Tiff kicked off her platform-wedgie sandals and followed Orville down the hall, presumably to the bedrooms. The place smelled like lavender. That wasn't trouble. Nor were the fun, old-fashioned touches on the walls—apparent mementos from travel in the Alps, Paris, and Asia.

"So, what's the trouble, Daddy?"

Orville stopped in front of a bedroom decorated with a country theme. A suitcase lay open on the bed, and several neat piles of clothing suggested that someone had started to pack—or unpack—and left in a hurry.

"Well, *that's* weird." Tiff scratched her head. "It can't be the previous renter still here, because that Julian guy would have known, don't you think?" She noticed a soft-pink Michael Kors sweater set atop one of the piles. Where had she seen that before?

"Excuse me?" The voice behind Tiff was indignant and angry. "What exactly are you—"

Tiff turned. Her mouth gaped open, and more horror gripped her than had someone just announced she would awaken twenty pounds heavier in the morning.

"Eve!" Tiff didn't even have the wherewithal to mask her dislike. "What are you doing in our beach house?"

Ten

"*Your* beach house?" Eve had clearly broken her porcelain calm. "My boyfriend rented this place for me and—"

She hesitated.

"For me and my friend. We've got this place for two weeks." She pointed toward Orville but still ranted at Tiff. "I don't know what you think you and this old guy—"

"Hey, girl, you watch your mouth—" Tiff advanced, her right arm ready for a girl-fight.

Orville stepped between the two fuming women. "All right, ladies. Let's just step back and take a big breath here."

"That's my father you're insulting, you bloodless ice queen." Tiff could put her hands on her hips just as well as Eve could, and she did that very thing.

"All righty, then." Orville sounded more amused than uncomfortable. He turned to Tiff and placed his hands on her shoulders. "Sweetheart, why don't you sit right over there in that frilly little wicker chair." He turned to Eve.

"And…Eve, was it? Why don't you have a seat there on the end of the bed. We can talk this out calmly—it's not like this is the last corner of God's green earth to live on, now is it?"

Eve and Tiff both looked at him for several seconds before doing as he suggested. Tiff hated to have to back off, but she knew her father was right. She crossed her arms over her chest once she plopped into the wicker chair. Her skin was damp around her hairline, but she was doggoned if she'd let Eve see her sweat.

Orville remained standing. He said nothing for a few moments and appeared to be waiting for temperatures to cool, as if a pot had just boiled over and he had turned down the gas.

"Now then." He looked at Eve. "Why don't you go on ahead and fill us in, Eve? It sounds like there's been a mix-up, that's all."

Eve cast a sharp eye on Tiff. "Did Jeremy have anything to do with your coming here?"

Tiff's face registered disbelief. "Jeremy? He and I have spoken about ten words to each other since I got home from South Carolina."

She saw Eve relax to a small degree, so she continued talking.

"We're here because my good friend Ren reserved this place for us as a surprise. Ren and her husband stayed here a few months ago, and she wanted me to have the same opportunity for a relaxing vacation."

Tiff spoke with conviction and saw uncertainty creep into Eve's expression. Yet, something nagged her in the back of her mind.

Eve unpursed her lips long enough to speak. "All I know is my boyfriend told me the place was mine for two weeks. For my friend Patti and me." She gave the room a quick once-over. "It may be a dive, but it's a dive on the beach. *My* dive on the beach. Paid for by *my* boyfriend."

Orville leaned against the dresser. "And Jeremy is your boyfriend?"

Eve nearly closed her eyes in her expression of superiority and nodded once.

Tiff wondered how the two of them had gone so quickly from polite dislike to bearing claws and hissing at each other. She knew she should be the bigger person here, but she wasn't big enough yet. Maybe later.

Orville spoke up. "I think a few phone calls will probably clear this up. But without knowing for sure what's going on, I'd like to suggest the obvious possibility of all four of us using the house. It certainly has enough bedrooms and plenty of room. And no doubt we'll all be coming and going a lot—"

Tiff's wicker chair squeaked when she shifted to stare at her father. He stopped talking when she and Eve both looked at him as if he had suggested skydiving over the La Brea tar pits. Again, he chuckled.

"Oh, come on now, ladies. What has either of you done to the other to warrant this bellyaching? Huh? Eve? Let's give you the floor first. What has Tiffany done to you?" He cocked his head at Tiff. "And I'm going to ask you the same thing, miss."

Eve looked at the floor, a chastised child. "I don't really know her. We just met last week."

Orville straightened his back. "Last week?" He looked from one to the other. "That so, Tiffany?"

Tiff feigned distraction by something in the far corner of the ceiling. But she nodded.

Orville rested his hands on his hips. "Did you meet in the middle of a barroom brawl or something?"

Neither woman responded.

"A military coup, maybe?"

Nothing but crossed arms and pouting.

"A sale at Macy's?"

Tiff looked swiftly at him then. She was simultaneously insulted by, and impressed with, his estimation of things female.

He shrugged and looked at her. "Your mama was a big Macy's shopper."

Tiff cracked a minor smile and caught Eve doing the same thing.

"There we go." Orville broke into a full grin. "Now what I'd suggest is you both make a phone call or two and try to sort this out. I still think my idea to share the place is a good one, but we can talk about it once you both know something more. How's that?"

Tiff looked at Eve, who finally nodded.

"Okay, Daddy." Tiff stood and put her hand on her father's shoulder. "I'll call Ren."

Eve had already walked to her purse and retrieved her phone. "And I'll call my boyfriend."

Tiff willed her face to remain neutral, but it really grilled her cheese— and she thought it was meant to—that Eve continued to call Jeremy "my boyfriend" instead of saying his name. It felt as if there was a constant scoreboard between them, and Eve kept drawing attention to the boyfriend point on her side, which was glaringly absent from Tiff's.

Because the idea of prayer popped unsolicited into her mind, Tiff figured Someone was trying to get her attention.

Okay, Lord. I'll try to think happy thoughts. But did You bring me here to learn how to get along with really obnoxious people? If so, I'll do my best, but You might want to send down an angel or two to help. It would be good for one of them to kind of take over my every thought. And if that's not possible, maybe send one down with a big sword. Or at least a sloppy, face-sized banana cream pie.

Eleven

March 24, Northern Virginia

Jeremy wanted a shower the minute he got home that night, and he almost got to take one. He only managed to remove his sweatshirt—which was certainly an appropriate name—before the interruption.

His racquetball game had been more competitive than usual tonight, because he played against Gabe, his friend Kara's husband. Gabe was a great chap and perfect for Kara. Jeremy hoped he and Eve might get together with them sometime soon. Would Eve like Kara? He snorted. What a daft question. Who wouldn't like Kara?

Anyway, Gabe was tops as well. But he was too blasted good on that court, and Jeremy was unable to return a good many of his shots. In trying, he dashed around the court like a party balloon suddenly losing its air. Made him feel like a beginner, yet he'd been playing for years.

Jeremy smiled when he reflected on Gabe's postgame confession that he'd played for his Florida college.

"You bounder!" Jeremy had laughed right along with Gabe, as if someone else had been the brunt of Gabe's experience.

Jeremy could feel his muscles already tightening from tonight's overuse. It would be some time before he'd play against Gabe again. Or walk comfortably, for that matter.

He almost forgot to check his messages before heading to the shower. As usual, he had forgotten his cell at home. He had to admit to a bit of deliberation in that. After teaching ever-talkative third graders all day, he often needed freedom from conversation. He didn't mind a brief chat with any one of his mates, but most of the females he knew—well, now that wasn't quite right. He loved a heart-to-heart with Kara or Ren.

His cell reported three missed calls within the past two hours, and they all turned out to be from an especially angry Eve.

"Jeremy. I need you to call me immediately. Immediately!"

"Jeremy. Where are you? The arrangements here at the beach house are unacceptable. You need to call me *now*."

"All right, Jeremy. If you're too busy to take my calls, I'll have to take matters into my own hands. And I take back the nice stuff I said about your friend Ren. She must be as unstable as the rest of them."

Ren? How could Ren have possibly fallen on Eve's bad side from the opposite side of the country?

He nearly sat down to make his call, but he remembered how much he needed that shower. He grabbed a towel from the bathroom and threw it on the couch before he sat. He selected Eve's cell number and awaited her onslaught. She answered after one ring, and he could hear enough in the background to determine she was outside. He tried to speak before she could, to say something soothing, but she was quick.

"What in the world were you thinking, Jeremy? This is a ridiculous setup here, with that brazen redhead and her beer-gut father in the same house. How are Patti and I supposed to relax with *them* here?"

He didn't even know where to begin his response. Brazen redhead? Beer-gut father? Had he booked her into a San Diego beach house or in with the Beverly Hillbillies?

"Wait, love, wait. Calm down and tell me what's going on."

He heard her release a deep breath, but he could picture it happening between clenched teeth.

"Jeremy, I show up here just fine. I start to unpack. I realize I've forgotten to pack...well, deodorant, if you must know."

Jeremy raised his eyebrows. He didn't need to know, but no bother.

She continued. "I run down the road to the convenience store. When I get back, I hear voices. *Voices*, Jeremy, in my house."

Clearly she hadn't been harmed, so he didn't panic, other than for his own well-being with regard to Eve.

"I walk back to the bedroom where my luggage is, and there they are. Looking at my stuff! I mean, I had my underwear out and everything, Jeremy, and that old man—"

He sat up more rigidly. "Blimey, Eve. Who *are* these hooligans?"

"That girl. That *Tiffany* girl."

"Tiffany? My Tiffany?"

The silence that followed could fill a black hole, which is where Jeremy suddenly wanted to crawl. How could he fix *that* imbecilic outburst?

"I mean, *our* Tiffany?"

No. That didn't sound much better.

"Virginia's Tiffany, I mean. Tiffany of Leesburg." Tiffany of Leesburg? Blast, what was he, some medieval moron? *Please speak, Eve. Don't hang up.*

"Yes." A profoundly tight utterance. The smallest, yet angriest *yes* he had ever heard.

"And her father! Like a couple of gypsies, barging into my house. I want you to do something about it."

"Eve, I don't understand. I haven't spoken to Tiff since that one night she came to the pizza place, where Ren and I—"

Ren. This must have something to do with Ren. The now "unstable" Ren.

"Yes, where Ren and you made her feel so welcome she felt she could barge in on *me*. And yes, she said something about Ren setting it up for her to be here this week and next."

Jeremy rubbed his sweaty brow. The movement reminded him how desperately he needed a shower.

"Look, love, Ren knew I arranged for you and Patti to have the place these two weeks. She wouldn't have encouraged Tiff to come at the same time. I don't even know how that could happen with the rental office. Something's wrong."

"No kidding!"

He sighed. Eve's anger started to wear on him a bit. It was obvious he hadn't played a hand in this mess, yet she was as livid now as when she first answered the phone.

"Let me give Ren a call, love. I'll see what I can do, and I'll call you back."

"Fine."

He glanced at the clock. Nearly eleven.

"Oh, blast. Eve, it's eleven o'clock here."

"And eight here. I *know* about time zones, Jeremy."

He looked at the ground and frowned. Stay cool, stay cool, stay cool.

"Yes, but what I meant was it's a bit late for me to bother Ren and Tru."

"Oh, but it's fine for me to be bothered over here, is that it?"

He lost his grip on coolness. He pressed his palm against his forehead as he spoke. "Look, Eve. I'm terribly sorry this has happened. But it's simply a mistake. That's all. No one set out to harm you or even to inconvenience you. Ren is six months pregnant. It's beyond the point that she and Tru should be getting calls late at night, and I'd prefer to wait until tomorrow to call her about this. I gather you still have a private room, as does Patti, yes?"

No answer.

"So I would ask that you give me until tomorrow to straighten this out. I think you'll survive. It's not as if Tiff and her father are going to roast a possum in the middle of the living room or marry you off to cousin Jethro."

"What?"

He actually smiled. He knew his Beverly Hillbillies trivia. Clearly Eve didn't.

"Nothing, love. I'm hoping to lighten the situation. Please try to relax and trust me to make it right tomorrow. You don't honestly feel that Tiff and her father are going to bother you or go through your things, do you?"

No answer.

"Eve?"

"No." He heard her sigh. This was obviously difficult for her, the whole calming-down process. "Jeremy, I know you didn't plan for this to be such a disappointment to me...but it is a disappointment. And I want it fixed, okay?"

"Certainly. Has the reunion with Patti been enjoyable at least?"

"Oh. We haven't connected yet. Which is for the best at this stage.

I'll talk with Patti after you let me know exactly what we're dealing with here."

"Righto. I'll say goodnight, then, love. Talk with you tomorrow."

He hung up after Eve did and went directly to his room to strip off the rest of his sweaty clothes. Before he dropped them in the hamper, he muttered. "I might need to burn those."

Jolly good. Even though nothing had been resolved, he stood under the hot shower with a smile on his face. Eve wasn't the first girl with whom he had taken great pains to avoid conflict. Typically he caved to demands he considered unreasonable, or he simply backed out of the relationship. He wondered now if Eve would dump him for finally taking a firm stance with her and not calling Ren tonight. Perhaps he should always be of a mind that she would consider leaving him. For some reason he seemed to be a better man when he had that attitude.

It wasn't until the middle of the night, when he awoke, that the strangeness of that dynamic struck him. Probably not the healthiest facet of their relationship. Maybe he'd chat with Ren about that tomorrow.

Twelve

March 24, San Diego, California

Tiff and Orville had just walked out of the beach house to get a late dinner when her cell phone rang. She looked at the display.

"Daddy, I need to take this. It's Ren. Do you mind if I talk while we walk?"

Orville zipped his windbreaker halfway. "Better yet, hon, why don't you talk with her here so you can focus? We'll go when you're done. I wanted to walk out to the waves and have a little chat with God, anyway."

Tiff had answered Ren's call. But she froze at her father's comment. Then she heard a distant, "Hello? Tiffany?"

"Oh! Ren! Yeah. Hold on a minute." She nodded at Orville, who was already walking in the direction of the beach. "Okay, Daddy. I'll wait for you here."

She turned her attention to the phone, watching while Orville got out of hearing range. "Hey, Ren. I kind of didn't expect to hear back from you at this point tonight. Isn't it way past your bedtime, Mommy?"

Ren laughed. "Usually, yes. But Tru and I had dinner out tonight and—"

Tiff interrupted her the moment Orville got out of earshot. "Oh, my goodness, wait! You have to hear this. When your call came, Daddy was here, and he said while I talked with you he was going to go down to the beach and talk with God."

"Did he?" Ren didn't sound all that surprised. She sounded sleepy, actually.

"Yes! He did! With God!" She got a chill and wasn't sure how much of it was excitement and how much was the breeze coming off the ocean. She went back inside. This was the perfect weather for her Jared Ross cardigan, which she hadn't worn yet.

Ren said, "Hasn't your dad ever prayed around you before or anything?"

"Well, yeah. But not like this. Not walking on the beach, communing with the waves, seeking peace and wisdom from the Great Almighty. It's always been more like, 'Howdy, Lord, thanks for the meatloaf, amen.'"

She heard Ren's laughter again. "That's great, Tiffany. Maybe the loss of your mother has touched his heart that way."

"Wow, maybe. I have to get him to talk to me about this while we're here. I might be calling you again about that."

A stifled yawn. "Okay. I'll try to be here for you. But I take it that's not why you tried to reach me tonight. Your message sounded less…positive."

"Oh, that." Tiff landed, flat-footed, back on earth. "Something's wrong. Daddy and I got here, and guess who else was here."

"Um, Elvis?"

Tiff rolled her eyes. Why had she even approached this as a guessing game? "Yes, Elvis. Of course. But I mean here in the beach house—"

Suddenly Ren let out the most frantic gasp Tiff had ever heard.

"Ren? Are you all right?"

"Oh, my goodness, Tiff. You're at the beach house!"

Tiff put her free hand to her hip. "That's why we're talking about the beach house, girl. Have you been drinking or something? That's really bad when you're pregnant."

"But Eve's at the beach house right now!"

Tiff shook her head. "Duh!"

"No, now, wait a second. How did this happen? You're both there? Why are you there already?"

"What do you mean, already? You're the one who booked my reservation." Tiff pushed up the sleeves of her sweater and walked back onto the patio. She heard a voice in the background on Ren's end of the call.

Tru. No doubt he wanted to know why his wife was suddenly freaking out on the phone.

"Just a second, Tiff."

Tiff heard her say something in a much calmer voice before she talked back into the receiver.

"I'm not sure where we went wrong here, but I didn't book a reservation for anyone. Not you and not Eve. I didn't even book my own reservation. Tru did."

"But the rental agency gave me your name. I asked who made the reservation, and they found your name on their records as the referral."

"My name? That's just so strange. Oh. I'll bet I know why. Jeremy must have given them my name as the referral when he made the reservation for Eve and her friend."

Tiff thought about the dullard she spoke with at the rental agency. She remembered his head-clogged, surfer-dude approach to checking the agency's bookings for her. His inane *"uh huh, uh huh, uh huh."* "Uh oh. Does that mean you didn't pay for the two-weeks' rental either?"

"Me?" Ren sounded incredulous. "You *do* know I teach elementary school for a living, right? Got twin babies coming in three months? An underpaid nurse for a husband?"

Tiff flopped into one of the wrought-iron chairs on the patio. The brisk night air still chilled her, so she pushed her sleeves back down to cover her arms. "Mercy. That's what was bothering me before. I had a feeling something was off kilter here. I'm—oh, this is awful—I'm completely wrong, and Eve is completely right."

There was a quiet coo, and nothing more, from Ren's end of the line.

"I'm going to have to apologize to her. And she's such a—"

"Careful, now."

"No, I was just going to say she's such a hard person to apologize to. Ren, she's *mean!* Did you know that?"

A sigh from Ren. "I guess we've all been that at some point in our lives."

Ouch. Tiff knew she'd been plenty mean in the past. Ren could always be counted on to put a quick stop to gossip this way. But she always included herself in the conviction.

"And Daddy and I will have to find another place to stay. I think he really likes this place."

"You sure you have to leave? Maybe you could all stay there, if you reimbursed Jeremy for half of the cost. I'm sure he'd love to get some of that money back. And as I remember—that house is good sized. Maybe Eve wouldn't mind, even though she's an old meanie."

Tiff chuckled. Ren had a way of seeing humor within the mess. "I don't know. Daddy suggested our all staying here, but Eve didn't look terribly pleased with the idea."

She heard Ren yawn. Then she heard her own stomach growl. She stood and tried to spy her father beyond the sea wall.

"Man, it's late there, isn't it? I'm sorry. Give my apologies to Tru, okay? And thanks for clearing this up for me."

"So what you are going to do?"

"Daddy and I will talk about it. I see him walking back up here. We'll work something out. Thanks, Ren."

"No problem. Sorry I didn't pay for your trip. Maybe if my girls grow up to be rocket scientists or supermodels, I'll be able to treat all my friends to beach vacations some day."

"Well, if they turn out to be lazy surfer bums, I know a rental agency where they'll have no problem getting jobs."

Thirteen

"It's all my fault, Daddy." Tiff spoke as soon as her father walked onto the patio. "I completely misunderstood everything about this trip, and now I need to apologize to Eve, and we need to move out, or I need to pay Jeremy for half of the rental."

Her father put his arm around her, and she drew comfort from the familiar smell of Old Spice.

She glanced up at him and realized he had red-rimmed eyes. Yet his comforting smile looked genuine. "And Jeremy is Eve's boyfriend; do I remember that right?" he asked.

Why had he been crying out there on the beach? It was Mama. Had to be Mama.

"Yeah. Her boyfriend." She put her arms around her father and gave him a squeeze.

He squeezed her back. "Don't be upset, kitten. It will be all right."

"I know." She spoke into his chest.

"Let's walk down the boardwalk and find us some dinner, what do you say?" He nudged her enough that she had to release him and face forward with him. "And let's chat with Eve tonight or in the morning. I'll bet she and her friend will share the place with us. Especially if you apologize. A few humble words can be awfully powerful in circumstances like this. If not, I'm sure we can find another spot to stay."

They strolled down Mission Boulevard until they found Gringo's Cocina y Cantina. Tiffany thought the beautifully lit courtyard and enticing aromas were about as inviting as a restaurant could offer.

"Mmm, smells great." She looked at her dad. "What do you think?"

"I think I'm starving."

Gringo's was more stylish than they expected. The décor was modern and artistic, with beautiful fireplaces and elegant lighting throughout. The lofted ceiling towered above them and matched the stylish red wood furniture throughout.

Tiffany looked down at her knit top and jeans. At least she wore a nice cardigan. But she had rolled her jeans so they wouldn't drag on the ground, now that she was wearing comfortable sandals. It hadn't taken long to learn that high heels didn't work on the boardwalk, even though it was made of concrete, not wooden boards. "You think we're dressed too casually, Daddy?"

A young woman holding menus smiled at them. "Not at all. Just the two of you?"

At a comfortable window table, they enjoyed tapas, pollo placero, and herb-crusted pork loin. Near the end of their meal, Orville leaned back in his chair.

"Now, those are some flavors I don't believe I've ever tasted in good ol' Florence, South Carolina."

Tiffany looked at their empty plates. "It looks like we're going to fit in just fine here."

Orville put his hand on his stomach. "If we eat like this every night, one thing I won't fit into is the clothes I packed."

"Nonsense. We're going to walk the beach every morning and every evening."

"We are, are we?" Orville laughed. "That's what I get for going on vacation with a personal trainer."

"Yep."

He smiled at her. "This was a good idea, hon. After you went back to Virginia, I realized we were both so focused on your poor mama, and then on her funeral service…well, we just didn't have time for each other, now, did we? There aren't many grown women who would even consider spending free time with their old dads. Did my heart good that you asked me."

"I wouldn't have wanted to come out here without you, Daddy. We both needed this." She took a sip of her water. "I'm just sorry we got off to a bad start, thanks to me."

"What I don't understand is why you and this Eve gal are so fired up against each other. Especially since you barely know each other."

"We haven't spoken with each other much, no. I've just come across too many women like her. They act as if their feet don't touch the ground when they walk. And there was just something about her from the moment I met her. Like she suspected me of something, just because of how I look."

Orville squared his shoulders in a stretch. Tiff remembered that gesture as something he did when tired. But he didn't seem in a rush to leave.

"It's not a good feeling when you're mistrusted just because of how you look, I have to agree."

Tiff studied her glass before speaking again. "I admit I'm attracted—or I was, anyway—to her boyfriend."

"Mmm hmm." Orville stroked his chin with his hand. "And why do you say you *were* attracted to him? What happened?"

She shrugged. "I found out he was with Eve."

"Ah." He motioned for the check before looking at her again. "So, you backed off. Good girl."

"I guess so. I mean, there wasn't much backing off to do. I wasn't really...*on*."

She couldn't quite read his smile, but she saw teasing in it. Why did that make her want to explain herself more?

"Okay, so we had this, this *moment* a few days before I found out about Eve. That's all. I didn't even know who he was. No conversation, just, you know, eyes. Smiles." She sighed and looked at the table. "And a killer British accent."

"I thought you didn't have a conversation."

She affected a terrible British accent. " 'Six thirty.' That's all I heard. Someone asked for the time."

Orville leaned forward and put his hand on hers. "All right. So that answers a few questions, wouldn't you say, kitten? You probably envy Eve, and she's probably jealous of you."

"But why? I'm not after Jeremy. I don't do stuff like that anymore." She frowned. "I mean—"

He put up his hand. "You don't have to confess anything to me unless you need to talk about it, hon. I could see a change in you when you came home to help your mama. As if you started thinking about other people more than your own self. I'm real proud of you."

Her grin was huge. "Thanks, Daddy."

"But Eve doesn't know you, and she might not feel as confident as she acts. It would probably be a good idea to behave so she knows for sure that you don't have any interest in Jeremy." He waited a beat. "Even if you do."

She sputtered. "What? But, but I—"

Orville gently gripped her hand. "You said you were attracted to Jeremy but found out he was with Eve. So the attraction's still there. I'm just saying to be careful."

"But—"

"Hon, look at me."

She did.

"I know what I'm talking about here, kitten. You aren't the first person to have these feelings, okay?"

Well, *that* was a curious comment. Had *he* ever had such feelings? But she could tell he had finished with the topic for now.

She nodded. They had two weeks. By then she would surely find an opportunity to ask what that was all about.

The rich meal seemed to make a difference when they got outside. Now the cool air was a comfort. As they walked back to the beach house, Tiff looped her arm through her dad's.

"So who ended up inheriting Boomer while you're gone?"

"JJ from work." He looked at Tiff, and they both chuckled.

"Little Boomer and massive JJ, huh?" Tiff shook her head. "Poor JJ. He won't get a moment's rest with that little stinker yapping all night."

"Maybe. But, you know, Boomer's really toned down since Mama died."

She was surprised at how easily he said those last two words. He had refused to say them before, as if he could keep it from being a reality if he just avoided saying it.

She remembered walking into the hospital, seeing him sitting next to Mama's bed in the darkened room. He spoke to her as if she were awake. Now Tiff couldn't remember if that was before Mama slipped into a coma or after. Either way, Daddy spoke softly to her and even laughed about some of the news he shared with her, about JJ and Phil from work, about Boomer's latest stunt. True to form, Daddy's face masked his pain and fear. He was all smiles; his words full of promise. When Tiff saw a tear run down his face, he brushed it away quickly, as if Mama might awaken and see it. Tiff wasn't able to walk into the room. It felt like their moment, not hers, and she backed away and returned later.

The memory prompted her to give his arm a gentle hug. "You're such a good man, Daddy."

He looked at her with a mildly surprised expression. "Why, thank you, hon. And you're a good girl. Or, I guess I should say a good woman."

"At least I'm trying to be a better woman." She pulled back to give him a more appraising look. "Daddy, I don't get it. Why have I always ended up with men who are nothing like you? They're not unselfish and calm like you. They're full of themselves and nothing more."

He pulled his arm out of her grip and wrapped it around her shoulders. "Maybe you're reading your list upside down."

"My list?"

"Yes, your list. I'll bet if you think hard enough about it, you'll find it in there." He gently tapped her forehead.

She smiled. "Requirements, you mean? What I'm looking for in a man?"

"There ya go."

"Yeah, I suppose I've got a list in here. But I have things like 'giving,' 'faithful,' and 'kind' on the list. I'm sure I do."

"But I'll bet the things you saw in Jeremy when you first met him were something else, huh?"

She remembered. Long eyelashes. Smelled great. The perfect amount of chin stubble. Man, she wasn't the deepest chick in the world, was she?

Orville continued. "I'm not saying you should settle for someone you don't think is all that great looking. You need to be attracted to the one you love. But someone who's handsome probably already has you checking off some of the top items on your list, no matter what other qualities—or lack of qualities—he carries around with him."

She watched the boardwalk while they strolled. "Of course. But knowing that and avoiding that are two really different issues."

"Yep. Sometimes circumstances help there. If you can just take your time, hon, and get to know people before you invest any of your…intimate emotions in them, you might have a chance to read your list from the bottom up. I think that might be a good thing for you."

"Is that what you did with Mama?"

He nodded. "That's what Mama did with me. I was a goner no matter which direction I read."

She almost missed it, but just then he swiftly reached his free arm up and wiped at the side of his face. Just as she saw him do in the hospital room.

"I'm so sorry you're lonely, Daddy."

He squeezed her shoulders. "It's not that I'm lonely." Then he stopped. "Lonely is when you want the company of someone else, and you're waiting for it to come along. I actually look forward to feeling lonely. I'm not looking forward to anyone's company. I just miss your Mama. I miss my Sheila."

They were near the beach house now. Tiff could see no lights other than those they left on when they went to dinner. It didn't look like Eve had been home.

A man walked out of their neighbor Julian's home and passed them. He had a shock of dreadlocks and perfect black skin, his face only partially covered by his trim beard. He looked at both Tiff and Orville and smiled beautifully. "Hey, there." He was so upbeat, both Tiff and her dad broke into smiles.

After he passed, Orville stopped and turned. Tiff followed his movement and saw that the other man had done the same thing. He came back to Orville and put out his hand.

"You the new neighbors here at Faith's place? I'm Zeke."

Tiff spoke before Orville could. "Faith's place?"

Zeke pointed to the beach house. "Right there. Faith Fontaine, the original owner. Very sweet lady. A dear sister in the Lord."

"Yep, we're the latest renters." Orville shook Zeke's hand. "Orville and Tiffany."

Zeke closed his other hand around Orville's briefly before releasing it and shaking hands with Tiffany.

"Welcome to the family."

He walked away with a brisk step, and Tiff looked at her father.

"Daddy, why did you turn around after he passed us?"

"I did, didn't I?" He looked at the beach house. "I don't really know. When he smiled at us, I just sensed we were going to stay here at this house the whole time we're here. I felt a very strange certainty. Kind of drew me to him."

Tiff loved the look on her father's face. She thought about the things Zeke said: Faith was a "dear sister in the Lord," and "Welcome to the family." She wondered if it was Zeke or Someone else to whom her father had just felt drawn.

Fourteen

March 24, Northern Virginia

Jeremy jerked awake, or partially awake, in the dead of night. He immediately let his eyelids close again. Ah, his soft, warm pillow. The phone's insistent shrill startled him again. He grabbed blindly at the nightstand several times before knocking the receiver and a small glass of water to the carpet.

He remained hanging over the side of the bed, even after finding the phone and jabbing at buttons until the assault on his quiet room stopped. He would have dozed back off, had that tiny voice not called his name several times. He lifted the phone to his head. It was so heavy.

"'Lo?"

"Jeremy?"

"Hullo?"

Someone spoke to him, a woman, a lovely soothing voice, like a commercial, like the commercial about that pill for allergies, what did they call it again? And there were side effects, what were those again? He struggled to remember. Ah, yes.

"Indigestion." He could go back to sleep now, but the voice came back again, so he told her more.

"Diarrhea. Rare cases, death." Now would she kindly leave him alone?

"Jeremy, will you wake up, please?"

And the switch finally flipped. Blimey. He was on the phone. He righted himself and lay against his pillow.

"Hello? Who's that, sorry? I'm sorry, I was asleep."

"Oh, good. I mean, I'm sorry to wake you. It's Tiffany."

For no reason he could fathom, he did exactly as he had done when he talked with Eve.

"My Tiffany?"

And just as Eve had done, his caller answered with silence. Suddenly he realized he had also said something to her about diarrhea.

"Uh, I didn't mean—"

"It's Tiff, Ren's friend."

"Ah, yes." At least he hadn't lapsed into his inane "Lady Tiffany of Leesburg" routine.

"Look, Jeremy, I'm sorry to call you so late. It's about Eve."

Now he awoke fully. He sat upright. "Is there something wrong?"

"I don't know. She's not here. At the beach house."

He pushed the snooze button on his alarm clock to light it up. Five in the morning. That meant two in the morning there.

"Is Patti there?"

"No. She didn't show up here today. I was worried maybe that was why Eve wasn't here. Maybe something happened to Patti. Or to Eve. Or both of them. Do you know where Patti was flying in from? Daddy and I were out to dinner earlier, and I haven't really had a chance to talk with Eve about—"

"Patti's local, so she won't be flying in."

"Oh. Patti lives nearby? Do you think Eve's at her place? Man, I'm sorry I woke you. It's just…I woke up and saw that her room was still empty—"

"Yeah, I think Patti's flat is about an hour away from there. Lakeside, I think it's called." He grabbed the other pillow on his bed and tucked it behind his head. "She was supposed to be at the beach house by now, but Eve may be changing their plans. If she's not there, I'm sure she went to Patti's for the night."

He heard Tiff sigh. "That's because of me, isn't it?"

He didn't know what to say.

"Jeremy, I'm so sorry for spoiling your plans for Eve. The mistake was mine, and the house was reserved for Eve and her friend. My father and I will look for another place."

"I don't know if that will be necessary. Ren told me the place is quite roomy. I rather like the idea of your father being there for all of you."

"He'd love for us to be able to stay here. I'll talk with Eve tomorrow. And if we do stay, I'll reimburse you half the rent, okay? I originally expected to pay anyway."

"Righto, that's good of you. I may just take you up on that."

"Okay then, I'll let you get back to sleep."

"And you as well, eh? It's even late for you."

"Yeah, but I can sleep in. You have to teach tomorrow, don't you? Or, later this morning, I guess."

"It's no bother, really. I'll turn on the telly and let them watch cartoons all day. It's generally how I run the class anyway."

She laughed. She had a rather lovely laugh when speaking softly in the middle of the night like this. Actually, now that he thought of it, he quite liked her more boisterous laugh as well, the one he heard on the shuttle bus. He'd rather enjoyed that ride on the—

"All right then. Goodnight, Jeremy."

"Ah. Right. Goodnight." He almost hung up. "Oh, Tiff?"

"Yes?"

"That was quite sweet of you to worry about Eve and go to the trouble of tracking me down." Especially considering how Eve had probably gone ballistic over Tiff's scheduling mistake.

He heard her snort a little laugh. "To tell you the truth, I'm not so sweet. My first reaction was to dredge up my anger at how mean I thought she was. I didn't even care whether or not she needed help."

He laughed quietly. "Well, now." He reached for the glass on his nightstand and felt a puddle of water in its place.

"Yeah," Tiff said. "But then I couldn't go back to sleep. I kept listening for her to come back. I knew I'd never get over the guilt if she was in trouble and I could have done something. So I guess I had selfish motives, kind of."

"There's nothing selfish about listening to your conscience, love." He retrieved a T-shirt from the floor and wiped his nightstand dry.

Tiff smiled. "It sounds good the way you say it."

"It's the British accent."

She laughed out loud. "That wasn't what I meant."

"Goodnight, Tiff."

" 'Night, Jeremy."

He leaned back against his headboard and closed his eyes. He still had two hours to sleep, if he ate breakfast on the way to work. After allowing his body to sink back down under the covers, he quickly wiped his mind clear of anything that might keep him awake.

But a full hour later, he still struggled. He was sure Eve was at Patti's, but it bothered him that she hadn't made the effort to tell him or her "roommates," just as a matter of courtesy. And the fact that he was perturbed this much by her inconsideration also bothered him—a friend once called him an old lady for fussing so. He was just a little too in touch with his sensitive side at times.

What really unsettled him, though, was that he kept replaying in his mind his simple telephone call with Tiff. They hadn't spoken long, and they hadn't flirted, really. But he had immensely enjoyed something about the conversation. Her concern and her honesty. Her easy laughter. He liked those qualities in his friends, both male and female. He was typically comfortable having conversations with women, and Tiff had been no exception.

But it wasn't often he finished a phone call with a female friend and kept breaking out in a such a stupid, cheese-eating grin.

Fifteen

The next day Jeremy was in the teachers' lounge resting his head on the table. An apple, a bagel, and a packet of bologna sat next to him, untouched. He heard Ren when she rounded the corner and entered.

"I just got off the phone with the nicest parent of all time, and…hoo, boy, Jeremy, what happened to you?"

He looked up at his astute and amazingly pregnant friend, who stopped in the doorway. He gently rubbed at his eyes. "I couldn't go back to sleep."

"When?" She settled into the chair across from him at the lunch table. "I'm hoping you aren't talking about the first part of your teaching day."

He ran his fingers through his pale brown hair, but, as always, it flopped right back onto his forehead. "Last night. I couldn't stop my mind after talking with Tiff. It was as if someone shot caffeine straight into my brain." He took a bite of his apple.

Ren stopped unpacking her lunch. "Tiff? Tiffany LeBoeuf? What were you two doing on the phone together? This is a development I didn't see coming."

"No development. She called from the beach house—" He pointed at Ren. "You do know about the big, chummy family in San Diego, yes?"

Ren nodded. "Yep. That's why I called you all here today, as I'm sure you were wondering."

Jeremy looked around the room. No one was there but he and Ren.

She crooked her thumb toward the door. "Sandy will arrive shortly, so we'll have our quorum."

71

A small smile crossed Jeremy's lips. He opened the lunchmeat, broke off a piece of bagel, and fashioned a makeshift bit of sandwich. He didn't have time to make lunch this morning, so he grabbed what he could before running out the door. "I'm about to be counseled, I take it."

A plump, redheaded woman burst into the lunchroom, sporting a playful smile and a plastic tub of chocolate-chip cookies. "You got that right, Tex. Whoa. Our resident hunk is a little tousled this morning. Here, have a cookie, Jeremy." She walked straight back to the refrigerator and removed a bag of food, which she brought to the table. "I've been apprised of the sitchiation in San Diego, and I have my opinion, which I'll be *more* than happy to share with you."

Jeremy took a cookie from the plastic tub. "Sandy, I think the confusion between Tiff and Eve has been cleared up. Or it will be today, when Eve and her friend return to the beach house." He popped a piece of cookie into his mouth and leaned back in his chair. "Matters are somewhat out of my hands at the moment."

Sandy grabbed one of his hands and flipped it palm up. "Look at these manly hands, Jeremy. You are a good, kind man, and you're forever doing the gracious thing, do you realize that? We need more people like you in the world, honey. Now, you just need to take hold of your little girlfriend's hand and give her the guidance she doesn't realize she needs."

Jeremy looked at Ren, who grimaced, as if she were fearful of Sandy's next comment.

He addressed them both. "Look. If I don't hear from Eve before my lunch break is over, I'll ring her up. I wanted to give her and Patti a chance to sleep in. It's just past nine out there. I will recommend she and Tiff try to get along and go halves on the beach house, but the place is Eve's to share or not. All right with you helpful ladies?"

Ren looked about to speak, but Sandy laughed. "All I can say is this couldn't have happened to a better couple of gals. I would *love* to be a fly on the wall of that house, hearing those two prima donnas trying to be civil to each other."

Ren winced. "Sandy, one of these days you're going to come out of your shell and tell everyone what you really think."

Jeremy took another cookie. "I have to say I've seen a surprising change in Tiff from the woman I originally met. We actually had quite a nice conversation last night."

Neither Ren nor Sandy said anything. But they each raised a single eyebrow, in perfect synchronicity.

"What?" Jeremy rolled his eyes at their suspicions. "A *friendly* conversation, nothing more. She apologized about storming the beach house. She offered to leave and said she plans to apologize to Eve today, once Eve returns."

"From?" Ren frowned.

"From Patti's place. At least that's what I assume. It will be a real disappointment if Eve chooses to stay at Patti's place this entire two weeks, I can tell you that. The whole point of my gesture was to give them more time right there on the beach. And now I feel like I've put her in a bind, if she feels they simply can't stay there with Tiff and her father."

He looked at Sandy. "You say I'm always doing the gracious thing. Sometimes I wonder if my attempts at graciousness are appropriate."

Sandy pointed at him. "You ought to go out there."

Both Ren and Jeremy looked at her with surprise.

Jeremy frowned. "To California? Why?"

"Just a feeling I have." She shrugged. "A random hunch." She started eating from a plastic tub of macaroni salad.

Ren sat back and rested her hands on her rounded tummy. "A hunch about what?"

"Just that he should go out there."

"That's it?" Jeremy laughed. "That's your hunch. No insight or logic behind it?"

Sandy raised both hands, palms up, and spoke like a sage. "I do not question the hunches. I merely report them."

A young woman came to the door of the lounge. "'Scuze me, Sandy? You have a phone call in the office."

Sandy grabbed her salad and a cookie before she headed out the door. "Later, kids."

Jeremy looked at Ren and narrowed his eyes. "Has Sandy become, um, one of *you*?"

"One of me, what?" Ren frowned and put one hand to her hip.

"Are her so-called hunches a Christian thing?"

Ren chuckled. "I don't think so." She opened a Baggie full of grapes. But before she ate any, she tilted her head and looked at Jeremy with a more serious expression. "So, you're wondering how much credence to give her idea, huh?"

"Yeah." He shrugged. "Maybe. Why? Why does that make you smile?"

She looked away from him and seemed to focus on the grapes. "I find it interesting that you would consider Sandy's hunch more valid if she were a Christian. At least that's how it sounds." Now she looked him in the eye. "Why is that?"

His gaze remained fixed on hers while he thought about her question. Then he looked down at the table. "I'm not sure."

Ren ate a couple of grapes and smiled.

Jeremy returned a one-sided grin. He knew what lay behind her smile. She and Kara had often expressed hope that he'd ask Christ to take control of his life. Ren had finally told him she thought he was on the verge and was just waiting for him to come tell her about it after it happened.

"One of these days, Jeremy." Ren popped another grape into her mouth.

He smiled. "I haven't said no yet, love."

She leaned forward and rested her arms on the table. "Just promise me you'll let me know when you say yes."

Sixteen

March 25, San Diego, California

Tiff ran to the beach-house patio, two empty coffee cups in her hands. Her legs were still wet from wading in the waves. She brushed her hands down her T-shirt and cutoffs and kicked the excess sand from her feet before entering the front door. She started when she heard a sound down the hall. Eve and Patti must have arrived.

"Eve?" She set the cups on the kitchen counter and walked toward the bedrooms. Eve walked out of her bedroom, patting the back of her blonde hair, which was pulled back in a perfect ponytail. She held a small blue overnight bag. It matched her crisp, cotton sundress. She looked up and saw Tiff.

Both women stopped abruptly.

Eve spoke first, rather coolly. "Oh. Hello."

"Yeah, hi." Tiff pointed to Eve's bag. "You're not leaving again, are you? I thought maybe we could talk."

"Actually, yes, I'm going to stay out at Patti's again tonight, so feel free to stick around."

"Wait. Hang on a second." Tiff wrung her hands and glanced around the room. "Could we just sit for a second?"

Eve looked at her for a moment and then shrugged. "All right." She set her bag down and sat stiffly on the couch.

Tiff sat across from her. She glanced down at her feet and noticed she had managed to track in sand, regardless of her efforts before she entered.

75

She took a deep breath and shot a little arrow prayer for guidance up to God before speaking again.

"I...I want to apologize. This whole house thing was my fault. I misunderstood the guy at the rental agency when I tried to make reservations. Jeremy reserved this place for you and Patti—where *is* Patti, by the way?"

"She got called in to work for a couple of hours."

"Oh. Well, I just wanted to tell you that the beach house is officially yours. My dad and I walked down the boardwalk earlier this morning. He's waiting for me out there now, as a matter of fact—"

"So go."

"No, he's fine. He's just sitting there relaxing, waiting for a refill on his coffee. Totally loving it here. But what I wanted to say is we started looking for another place to stay. We didn't have any luck yet, but there are so many hotels out here, I'm sure—"

Eve interrupted. "Look. Since Patti is likely to have to stop in at her office a few times this week, I don't even know if it makes sense for us to stay here. We'll drive out here when we can, but why don't you two look for somewhere to stay next week? That should give you a little more time, and you can consider the house yours this week."

"Really?"

"Really. I'll probably stop by here on occasion by myself, when Patti's working. But other than that, I'll be in the city this week." Eve stood, bag in hand, and appeared ready to end the conversation.

Tiff stood, too. None of this was easy for her or even *like* her. She was used to being the short-tempered one. But she put out her hand and tried to keep a pleasant expression on her face. "Can we call a cease-fire, then? I don't feel good about how we started out. And when you do come by, we should try to get along, don't you think?"

Eve looked at Tiff's hand for such a long time. Tiff almost drew it back to her side. Then Eve lightly grasped Tiff's fingertips and moved them as vigorously as a butterfly would flap its wings.

Tiff nearly laughed. This was clearly even harder for Eve than it was for her. Knowing that helped. "Of course you and Patti can use the house any of the days this week you're able to come out. Daddy took the smallest room—the one with the wardrobe in it, so there's still a good-sized empty room for Patti." She chuckled. "Daddy joked about his disappearing through the wardrobe and entering a sandy version of Narnia. With hedgehogs on surfboards and a badly sunburned White Witch."

Eve's expression was mildly disdainful. "What are you talking about?"

"You know, Narnia. The book? The movie?"

"Oh." Eve barely moved a facial muscle.

Okay, so much for light conversation. "Anyway. I'll be sure to reimburse Jeremy for this week's rent."

"That's between you and Jeremy." Eve turned to leave.

"Sure. He already said he'd probably take me up on the offer."

Eve stopped and turned back to face Tiff. "When did you and Jeremy talk?"

Oops. "Oh, it was no big deal. I called him last night. I was concerned."

"Concerned?"

"About you. And Patti. Since you weren't here."

Lips pursed. "You called my boyfriend and reported that I wasn't home yet?"

"I didn't report anything. I asked him if he knew where you were. If he had heard from you. I thought something might have happened—"

"Did it occur to you that I might have stayed with my friend, since *you* two were here?"

"No, Eve, it didn't occur to me, since I had no way of knowing Patti was local. You and I hadn't spoken ten words to each other before you took off. I didn't know where Patti was from until Jeremy told me."

Eve emphatically set her bag on the counter. "Un-bee-lievable."

Tiff felt her body heating up. *Not good, Lord. Need some help here.*

"Eve, this isn't that big a deal. I'm not after your boyfriend—"

"Oh! As if!" Eve laughed without a modicum of humor. "Go after him all you want. You don't worry me."

"But—"

"All I ask is that you stay out of my business." She pointed toward the bedroom she had originally claimed. "I mean, am I even safe leaving my things in there? Or do you plan to rifle through my stuff when I go, just in case there's something you want to tell my boyfriend about?"

Oh, Lord. Not good at all. Lots of bad words boiling up here—

"May I be of any help here, ladies?"

Orville stood at the patio door, an amenable calm about him. Like an angel. In a Hawaiian shirt and Bermuda shorts.

Tiff exhaled. "Hi, Daddy." She gave Eve a sideways glance.

Eve was obviously working to regain her composure. She faced Orville and squeezed out a polite smile. "No help necessary. I was about to leave."

He stepped into the house. "But you don't mean for the day, do you? Tiffany and I are looking for another—"

"We've worked that out for now, Daddy," Tiff said. "Eve and Patti only want the place next week."

He nodded. "I see. So you won't be here tonight? My girl here was mighty worried about you when you didn't make it back last night."

Tiff couldn't help the smug smile she shot at Eve.

Eve's phone rang, and she pulled it from her purse. "That's my boyfriend. I've got to go." She nodded once at Orville and flipped her phone open. "Hi, Jeremy. Hang on just a second while I find some privacy." She walked out the door and didn't look back.

Once the door closed, Tiff widened her eyes at Orville. "That has to be the rudest woman I've ever met. If you hadn't shown up, I think the two of us would be rolling around on the floor right now, cursing and screaming and ripping each other's hair out."

He laughed. "Now, I don't believe that for a second. Not my little Tiffany."

She heard the tease in his tone and gave him a playful punch on the arm. "I would have been involved purely from a defensive standpoint, of course."

"Of course." He put his arm around her and sighed. "When I come across difficult people, I fume, like you did with Eve, but then I tell myself there must be some pretty big problems in the person's life for her to be behaving like that. I don't need to know what the problems are. It just helps me not to take it personally."

Maybe it was because her dad was the one saying this, but Tiff shuddered when her next thought occurred. She felt a little sick to her stomach, the sudden guilt was so strong. "How do you keep from taking it personally if—"

She couldn't look at him. "What about when the person is someone...someone close to you?"

Orville released her and gently forced her chin up. She had to meet his eyes, which reflected both hurt and understanding. "You're thinking of your mama?"

She looked down again. "I'm sorry. I loved her, Daddy, you know that."

He put his arms around her. "Honey, Mama dealt with some hard things in life, that's for sure. But not all of her sweeter moments were there at the end. If you think on it long enough, you'll remember other good times. She loved you too."

She nodded. "I miss her." She looked up at him. "Don't make me cry, Daddy. I don't want to cry today." Of course, her mouth quivered, and she cried a little just getting those words out.

He squeezed her gently and released her. "All right, no crying today." He stepped back and held his arms out, as if he were about to shout "Tada!"

"We have this beach house for the week! We have more coffee to drink! And we have the beautiful Pacific out there, just waiting for us. Let's walk the beach in the other direction from this morning. I'll tell you one of my favorite stories about your Mama and Wrightsville Beach in North Carolina. Involves a jellyfish, a baggy swimsuit, and some gyrations I'll never forget."

Seventeen

March 25, Northern Virginia

Jeremy stepped out to the school's courtyard while his students were in computer lab. Eve hadn't called by the end of his lunch break, so he reached her on her cell. She told him of her plan to stay at Patti's the first week and the beach house the following one.

"You're certain that's the way you want to work this, then?" Jeremy didn't feel she was being completely honest with him. He didn't want her sacrificing an enjoyable trip to make matters easier for everyone else.

"Really. This is what I want. Patti's schedule has forced us to be flexible, anyway, so it's not that big a deal. I told that Tiffany girl I expected to be able to stop by and use the place if I had time on my own, and she seemed okay with that. As she should be."

He heard her sigh.

"Are you horribly disappointed, love? Or is this at least better than being here, laboring away at work and catering to my every whim?"

She laughed musically. "Sweet Jeremy. You're the one who caters, I know that. As long as I know the down-home duo will move out next week, I'll be more comfortable using the place. This is a huge beach. There's no need for us to even cross paths next week."

"Right. Okay, then." Jeremy couldn't shake the heavy feeling he had, despite her affirmations.

The feeling stayed with him well after he hung up and went back to his class. It wasn't until he had to break up a fight at recess that the problem hit him. He knew in his gut that Eve had been harsh with Tiff again. Just the way she referred to Tiff and her father made Jeremy uncomfortable. "That Tiffany girl." "The down-home duo." He hoped she was only using those impolite terms when talking with him. But he felt associated with whatever behavior she demonstrated with people he knew, no matter how slightly. As soon as classes ended that day, he went home and found Tiffany's phone number on his caller ID.

"Hello?" She sounded uncertain when she answered.

"Tiff? This is Jeremy."

The lift in her voice brought a smile to his face. "Well, hi! Wow, you just would not believe it out here, Jeremy. Ren was so right. This is a fantastic place, and the day is perfect! Just perfect. Can you hear the waves? You should come on out."

He laughed. "You're the second person to make that recommendation this week."

"Well, sure, I would expect Eve to ask you to come out."

He shifted on the couch. "Uh, no actually, it was one of my coworkers."

"Oh. They're trying to get rid of you, huh?"

He laughed again. "Maybe. Are you with your father right now?"

"Nope. All by myself. But there are a couple of kids from a few houses down who keep coming by and showing me the shells they've found. I swear, kids usually hate me. This is very cool. Daddy's hanging out with Julian, the guy who lives next door to us. They hit it off right away. They're walking down the beach right now. To tell you the truth, I think Julian's talking with Daddy about faith and stuff."

"Ah." He didn't know what else to say to that.

"Oh. You're not...you're not...I just remembered Ren said you weren't a believer. Sorry."

"Ren told you that?"

"Oh, shoot, I'm saying something I shouldn't, aren't I? I do that all the time, just ignore me. I think I asked her about you once, that's all."

She asked about him?

"Jeremy? Please forget I said that about your not being a believer, okay? Man, I still haven't healed from my rude bug yet. I still say some pretty awful things sometimes."

"Actually, that was why I called."

She sighed. "Okay, tell me what I did. I'm getting pretty good at apologies these days."

"No." He laughed. "What I mean is I'm calling because I got the impression that Eve may have been rude to you the last time you two spoke."

"Just the last time? You're kidding, right?"

They both laughed at that.

He put his feet up on the coffee table. "I'm glad you're upbeat about it."

"Yeah, it's easy to shrug it off after the fact. But I'm just as rude as she is when we talk, I have to admit. She and I clash. My dad says we're too much alike, although I'm not thrilled with that idea."

He smiled. "Ah, so you have one of those honest fathers, as well, eh?"

"Yours too?"

"Mmm. It's been just me and my dad all my life. He's never used the soft pedal with me about any of my inappropriate behaviors."

"Where was your mother?"

"She died shortly after I was born. I never knew her. And dad never remarried."

"Wow. I'm sorry. What was that like, to grow up without a mother?"

"I never knew any difference. But I did get a crush or two on some of my mates' mums. I guess I was a bit envious."

"Hmm. So did you ever date older women?"

"No, Dr. Freud."

"Okay then, how about women who treat you like you're a little boy?"

He sucked air through his teeth. "You're treading just a little too close to home there, love."

"Really? Oh, man, I'm sorry."

"No, don't be. I think you may have touched on something there. Hmm."

"I need to shut up. Please don't repeat any of this to Eve. I feel like I've really intruded. And she and I are already practically snarling around each other. I should hang up."

"I know Eve can be harsh. But she has a kind side too."

"Maybe you bring that out in her."

That made him smile. "I'd like to hope so. But I worry sometimes when Eve and I talk, when she's *not* at her kindest, that I'm being unattractively…"

"…Wimpy?"

"Well, I say!"

Tiff's laugh was downright guttural in response. He pictured her head thrown back. That lovely long throat—

"I'm teasing you. You're a nice guy. I'm sure she appreciates you."

Now he sighed. "I don't know. I wonder if I shouldn't adopt a tougher persona. Maybe I should get a tattoo or a piercing or some such rot."

"Ew. No."

"No?"

"That is *not* you, Jeremy. No one is worth your marking up your body, in my opinion. You know, when I was taking care of my mom back home—"

"Uh, where exactly is 'back home'?"

"Florence. South Carolina. And—"

"And what was the matter with your mum, if you don't mind my asking? Was she ill?"

"Oh. You didn't know." Her voice dropped a few decibels. "I guess I assumed Eve would have told you. My mom died a few months ago. Breast cancer."

"Oh, Tiff. I'm sorry."

"Yeah, me too. You know, while we've been out here, I've almost picked up the phone a bunch of times to call her, and—"

She stopped talking so abruptly, he wasn't sure whether to speak or not. So that was one of the storms she had endured—probably why she had that Jesus book in the trunk of her car. "I'm sorry, Tiff," he repeated.

"Yeah. Thanks."

He heard the voices of children in the background and Tiff expressing appreciation for whatever they had brought to her. She sounded less emotional when she returned her attention to the phone.

"Sorry. A few of my adoring fans."

"Did you say Eve knew about what happened to your mum?"

"Yeah, I told her right after we met, at Ledo's. I can't remember why. She said you hadn't told her, and I said you probably didn't know."

"Right." He flashed back to his dinner with Eve that same night, when he said he suspected Tiff had been through some mysterious trauma recently. Why hadn't Eve told him what it was?

"Anyway, I didn't mean to get maudlin, Jeremy. What I wanted to tell you was when I was down there in Florence, I started flipping through some old photos of my parents. There was this entire era when my mother had her hair all teased up, spiked out, dyed ridiculous colors, you name it. They did the whole disco thing, you know?"

"Right."

"I mean, oh man, you should have seen my dad and his polyester suits. Macho, macho man, baby. Anyway, I see those pictures and crack up over what people did to themselves back then. It's all fine, because time goes by, and you stop doing stupid things to your hair or wearing stupid suits, and you look like someone's parent eventually. But a tattoo? Man, that's permanent. That's like having disco hair for the rest of your life."

He laughed. "Point taken. All right. No tattoos or piercings." He glanced at himself in the mirror across from his couch. "Perhaps I should start slicking my hair back and wearing leather."

He heard her start to laugh, but then she sounded more serious. "Actually, I think you'd look really good like that."

Neither of them spoke for a moment, and he suddenly felt heat around his ears. Had they just stepped into flirtation? He'd better say something funny straight away. But he couldn't think of anything.

"Um…"

"Yeah, I'd better go." Tiff sounded uncomfortable, too. "And don't worry about Eve and me. I'm sure we'll get along fine if we see each other again."

Right, maybe they would. Apparently Tiff was making an effort. What he was starting to wonder about was how well *he* and Tiff were getting along. Judging from the lift in his spirits, maybe they were doing a little better than they should.

Eighteen

March 25, San Diego, California

"Well, that's a pretty smile."

Tiff fought against a flash of guilt and closed her phone. She looked up from her beach chair. Orville approached with Julian, and a warm breeze brushed by.

"Oh!" Tiff laughed softly and shaded her eyes with her hand. "Hi, guys. I didn't see you sneaking up on me."

Julian looked at Orville. "I think we interrupted a phone call with Tiff's boyfriend."

"No, not a boyfriend. Just a friend." She looked at her dad. "That was Jeremy. So nice. He called because he knew Eve had been by. He wanted to make sure she wasn't too rude to me. And to you, of course."

Orville's eyes held that teasing twinkle he seemed to save just for her. "Of course. I'll bet he left a message on my cell phone too."

Tiff looked straight into her father's eyes. "I'm sure he would have, if you *owned* a cell phone."

Julian laid his arm across Orville's shoulders and addressed Tiff. "We're going to walk down to Kono's and have breakfast for lunch. Killer burritos. Party potatoes. Kono's is quite the hot spot here in Pacific Beach. Care to join us?"

"You bet. That sounds fantastic." Tiff rubbed gently at her temples. "I can tell I need to eat." She stood and tucked her phone into the pocket of her shorts. "And how about ice cream after? I'll bet they have sugar free somewhere around here."

Julian looked at Orville. "I thought you said she was a health nut."

Tiff laughed. "I'm on vacation."

"Anyway," Orville said, "we've only been here two days, and she already has me walking on the beach so much, I'm about ready for the Marine Corps Marathon." He puffed up his chest, which was still small compared to his stomach. "That's what comes from having a personal trainer for a daughter."

"And you walked even more with me," Julian reminded Orville. "Maybe we'll run that marathon together." He looked at Tiffany. "We can get ice cream and take a walk on the Crystal Pier after lunch. You haven't visited Pacific Beach properly if you haven't walked the Crystal Pier."

The threesome headed to Kono's, passing countless people on the boardwalk, some obvious tourists, some clearly homegrown.

"So what exactly do you do for a living?" Tiff asked Julian. He looked like one of the homegrown ones—laid back and in no hurry to go anywhere.

"I'm retired. I was in software design. My job was my god, you might say."

She pushed her thumbs into her pockets. "I take it you no longer approve of that attitude."

"No, as I was telling Orville earlier, that attitude nearly cost me my life. It *did* cost me my family. My wife left me many years ago. I didn't reconnect with my son and daughter until they were nearly adults."

"Wow. I'm sorry," Tiff said. Despite such a sad history, he appeared content. "You don't seem bitter at all."

"My bad choices were my doing," he said, looking straight ahead. "And I nearly made the ultimate bad choice."

Tiff's steps slowed to a virtual stop. "Are you talking about suicide?"

"Yes, I'm sorry to say. The lady who owned your place, Faith Fontaine, was the one who stepped in and did God's work with me. She and Zeke."

"Zeke? We met him last night, didn't we, Daddy?" Tiff asked.

"Yep. Just as he left your place, Julian. The fella practically glows, he's so cheerful."

Julian laughed. "He does glow. Yes."

"Does he work for you?" Tiff asked.

"No, but we work together at times."

No one said anything for a while. Tiff wondered if Julian had already given her father the answers to the questions she wanted to ask. Daddy didn't seem overly curious, and Julian wasn't terribly forthcoming. She decided not to press. She would ask her dad later about what he and Julian discussed on their walk.

"Oh, but I guess you got your wires crossed last night, Daddy."

"How's that, hon?"

"When we met Zeke, you were certain we'd end up staying at the beach house for two weeks. But today I promised Eve she and her friend could have the place to themselves next week. Not that I'm complaining—"

Without missing a beat, Julian said, "Well, why don't you two stay at my house, then."

"We wouldn't think of imposing, Julian," Orville said. "There are plenty of hotels—"

"No imposition at all. I rent out the upstairs apartment all the time. It's vacant next week, and I'd love to rent it to you."

"Really?" Tiff was thrilled. "Daddy, we *have* to take Julian up on this. I love it here!"

"I'll give you both a tour after lunch." Julian said. And then with a wink to Tiff, he added, "And after ice cream, of course."

"Of course."

Orville nudged Tiff. "You see, we're not going far from Faith's beach house after all. I wasn't so far off with the vibe I got from Zeke."

His vibe from Zeke. Tiff pictured her dad in his disco polyester pantsuit and suddenly felt an overwhelming rush of love for him. He was the cutest pot-bellied dad ever. She threaded her arm through his and gave him a squeeze. She couldn't remember the last time she and her father had spent such excellent time together.

Everything was falling nicely into place now. She relaxed and assumed the remaining twelve days would be conflict free. Why wouldn't they be?

Nineteen

March 26, Northern Virginia

Jeremy pulled up to the new Vietnamese restaurant in his Mini Cooper as dusk fell. He saw Sandy's minivan and Ren's SUV in the parking lot. Kara said she'd come with Ren, so he was last to arrive, as usual.

He found them the moment he walked into the dark, exotic room, thanks to boisterous laughter coming from their corner. Jeremy loved these outings with his female friends. He knew to appreciate them while he could, now that Ren's twins were due soon and Kara was a busy newlywed. Sandy had always been their wild card. She seldom joined them unless her husband and son had a boys-only event planned.

He recognized the strange music playing as Dan Bau. One of his students was Vietnamese, and her mother once brought a Dan Bau to play for the class. Only one string for all the notes. Unique and exotic, but Jeremy couldn't imagine listening to it longer than the amount of time it took to eat a meal.

"It smells great in here," Jeremy said as he sat next to Sandy and accepted her sisterly kiss on his cheek. "You birds haven't used up all the good stories, have you?"

"I lost a client today." Kara seemed oddly happy about her announcement. Like Tiff, Kara was a personal trainer. Her income depended upon how many clients she had.

"Why is that good news?" Jeremy smiled, anticipating a fun story.

Kara pushed her short, blonde hair away from her face. "This man made me so uncomfortable, Jeremy. I couldn't say boo to him without his finding some lame, double-entendre joke to make about it. So I always shied away from any comments having to do with the human body, or *any* body, for that matter, which isn't the easiest thing to do in my profession. But it didn't make any difference. I'd make a comment about the price of gas, and he'd manage to twist it into something sexual."

"Gas and sex?" Jeremy grimaced. "Sounds like quite a catch, that one."

"Well, my worries are over," Kara said. "Gabe made a point of coming in today when I was scheduled with the guy. And, well, you know what my handsome hubby looks like in a T-shirt and shorts, right?"

Jeremy looked at Ren and Sandy before answering her. "Oh, you're asking *me?*"

The women laughed.

"Well, then." He picked up his cloth napkin and fanned himself. "Everyone knows what Gabe looks like in a T-shirt and shorts, yes, of course."

Sandy laughed so loudly, people turned to stare.

Kara ducked her head and shushed everyone at the table, giggling. "Okay, so Gabe is all over the area in the gym where I am with my client. He's flexing his biceps and pumping iron as if he's Mr. Steroids USA. My client is so intimidated, he just shuts up and does his exercises like a normal human being. I think our problem is solved, but then Gabe can't resist. He pretends he suddenly notices us. He comes over and *lifts* me off the ground and gives me a kiss. He shakes my client's hand, introducing himself as my husband. And then he asks me all gruffly if anyone has been hitting on me today."

"Brilliant," Jeremy said.

"I hesitated in answering, just because I was trying not to laugh." Kara giggled, even as she spoke. "But I guess my client thought I was debating about whether to rat him out or not. He jumped out of the lat machine and mumbled something about a pressing appointment. He made a beeline for the locker room, and that was that. Later he called the gym to cancel his future sessions with me. He asked for another trainer."

The waitress's approach brought their laughter to a quiet pitch. After some deliberation, they all decided to order dishes none of them had ever tried before.

"But I have to watch it with the spicy stuff these days." Ren put her hand on her stomach. "My girls have made it clear they're not crazy about spicy stuff."

Sandy tapped Jeremy on the arm. "Hey, speaking of crazy girls, how's beach house bingo going?"

He shrugged. "To tell you the truth, I've had a hard time getting in touch with Eve. I don't want to be a nuisance, so I'm not calling often. But she never seems to have her phone on—you know how the message machine comes on right away when the phone is off?"

They all nodded.

"Yeah. It's like that. And she doesn't call back. I mean, I spoke with her yesterday, but I couldn't reach her today."

No one said anything.

"It feels a bit like she'd rather not talk with me right now. Perhaps she's just having too much fun to think of it. I can't imagine she's still angry with me about Tiff and her father staying at the beach house."

Ren raised her index finger. "Oh. I heard from Tiff yesterday. She and her dad are going to stay at the beach house right next door during their second week."

Jeremy lifted his eyebrows. "Next door?"

"Yeah. The guy who owns the house next door is this wonderful Scotsman." She looked at Kara. "I told you about him, right? Julian?"

"Yep. Voice like Sean Connery. And a Christian, you said."

Ren nodded. "Really a nice man. And his house is magnificent. He rents out the upstairs apartment. It sounds like he and Tiff's dad really hit it off. So they won't be far from Eve and her friend after all."

Jeremy's smile faded, and he rolled his eyes. "Ah. Yes, good."

He saw the women exchange glances. He sighed.

"The two of them don't seem to get along very well."

The server arrived with their appetizers, quietly naming each as she set it down. "Hue Stuffed Pancake. Spicy Squid. Fried Meat Puffs."

Sandy whispered the last three words, as if they didn't belong together. "Fried meat puffs. Hmm."

Ren spooned a pancake onto her plate and shrugged. "I don't know,

Jeremy. When I talked with Tiff yesterday, she mentioned Eve a couple of times. She didn't seem especially irritated with her. Maybe they've patched up their differences. Or at least reached détente."

"Or maybe *Tiff* is okay with Eve," Sandy said, "but Eve still has issues with Tiff." She gingerly bit into a meat puff and then smiled. "Well, this is just a little sausage burger in a fried bun, that's all."

Kara leaned in. "What's the big deal with Eve and Tiff? Am I missing something?"

Sandy snorted. "Kara, dear. We're talking about Tiffany. Remember, the one who had eyes for your husband?"

"But, hey, that's not fair, Sandy," Ren said. I don't want to get into a gossip thing here, but Tiff stopped flirting with Gabe once she found out he and Kara were...well, not dating, but...special friends."

"That's true," Kara said. "And, not to start a big religious debate, but Tiff is a Christian now. That's what led her to quit her job and go home to care for her mother." She sat back and shared a nod with Ren. "I think she's changed a lot."

"You even noticed that, Jeremy," Ren said. "You mentioned it at lunch yesterday."

Jeremy had just spooned several pieces of spicy squid into his mouth. He widened his eyes and grabbed his water. Before he swallowed, he pointed from the squid to Ren's tummy, shaking his head.

"Don't go there?" Ren smiled at his antics.

He took another drink of water before speaking. "Your girls will not be amused."

"My hero." Ren fluttered her eyelashes at him. "Okay, that means more puff balls for Mama. You nonpregnant people can have the squid."

Jeremy turned to Sandy. "Have you had any more of your hunches about the beach?"

"Nope." She shook her head. "Just the same one I had before."

"What's that?" Kara asked.

Sandy put her hand on Jeremy's shoulder. "I think he should go out there."

"To San Diego?" Kara said. "Oh, I like that. Wow, these little pancake thingies are great. Crab!"

Jeremy scooped the last two pancakes onto his and Sandy's plates.

"Mmm, yeah, all great starters, these. But why do you like Sandy's hunch, Kara?"

She shrugged. "I don't know. There's something romantic about it. Showing up unannounced like that, sweeping Eve off her feet. Running across the beach with her in your arms."

Ren broke into a delighted smile. "Oh, is that what you'd do, Jeremy? Arrive unannounced? Yeah I like that idea too!"

"I'm not going to San Diego!" he said. "It was just Sandy's crazy hunch."

The server then arrived with their entrees. While she named each dish and set it before them, Jeremy reflected. He got some kind of odd pleasure from the way these women gently bullied him into decisions at times. They seldom seemed to get it wrong.

But not only would Sandy's idea require some quick efforts at arranging a substitute teacher, he couldn't picture how it would actually play out on the San Diego end. He could picture arriving at the airport. He could picture arriving at the beach house. But when he imagined Eve opening the door and seeing him there, he couldn't for the life of him picture the expression on her face.

Twenty

Jeremy had no trouble picturing Eve's expression the next day, when he finally reached her by phone.

"Right next door?" Eve sounded less angry than dismayed. "That's as bad as having them live in the beach house."

"But why, Eve?" Jeremy pressed his palm against his forehead. She acted as if Tiff and her father carried a contagious disease. "You'll have nothing to do with them."

"But they'll—" She sighed. "Just never mind."

The woman made no sense. And his lunch break was nearly over. "Look, I've got to get back to my kids. Will I be able to reach you later?"

"Maybe. I don't know. Just call if you want."

Now, there was a fetching come on. He hung up and tidied up the table where he had eaten.

Ren walked into the lunchroom, and when Jeremy didn't speak, she said, "What's wrong?"

He looked at her for a moment before speaking. She was so very pregnant. So happy with her life. Yet he knew she had struggled with her relationship with Tru before they worked the kinks out. And she was one of his dearest friends, so he knew she'd be frank with him.

"Ren, did you ever feel that Tru was keeping secrets from you? That he wasn't being honest about everything?"

She rested her arms across her stomach and looked up in thought. "No. I can't say I ever felt dishonesty from him. He was extremely *polite* about things early on. You know, not telling me my mother drove him as crazy as she did. And he was unaware of a few facts for a while. Like the fact that *his* mother was a little too involved in his personal life." She smiled at him. "But you mean did I ever feel he was lying to me?"

"Yes. Either outright or by omission."

"No." She walked back to the refrigerator. "What's this about?"

He stood and tossed his lunch wrappers in the trash can. "Something's missing."

"With Eve?"

"I just got off the phone with her. She sounded all right until I mentioned that Tiff and her father would move into that Scottish bloke's place on the weekend. Then she got…"

"Mad?"

"No, not exactly. She sounded a bit cornered, as if she were trying to work something out that she didn't want to explain to me. I don't feel like she's telling me everything."

Ren sat at the lunch table. "What do you suspect?"

He shrugged. "Do you think she knew Tiff sometime in the past? Could there be some old conflict between them she doesn't want me to know about?"

"I kind of don't think so, Jeremy. I saw them when they met at Ledo's. If either of them recognized the other, she hid it really well."

He scratched his head. "Could there be any chance *Patti* and Tiff know each other? I don't think Eve has brought Patti by there yet. Maybe Eve doesn't want the two of them to meet for some reason."

Ren raised her eyebrows. "I guess there's a chance of that. But the fact that you're spending time trying to come up with excuses for Eve's weird behavior is really…well, puzzling."

He glanced at his watch. "Blast, I have to get back to class. But you're right. I'm being overly suspicious of her." He started to walk out the door, but Ren grabbed his arm.

"Hold on there, buddy. That's not what I meant."

"No?" He leaned against the door jamb.

"Jeremy, please don't take this the wrong way, and if everything works out beautifully between you and Eve, don't you dare hold this against me, because you know I want the best for you."

"Uh oh."

She sighed. "I could be wrong about Eve, but I've had a funny feeling about her for a while now. If you can't get her to be up front with you about why she's so dead set against crossing paths with Tiff, I think Sandy's hunch was a good one."

"Seriously?" He widened his eyes. "You think I should go out there?"

She nodded. "I know it's an expensive undertaking. And I don't know if the powers that be can fill your spot on such short notice. But that hunch is starting to feel more insightful the more you tell me about Eve."

Jeremy felt again the heaviness he experienced earlier when thinking about Eve. "Thanks. I've got to run, but I'll give this some thought."

He jogged down the hall to his class. Ren was right; taking time off and getting a last-minute flight could prove costly. The price he might pay for the trip troubled his stomach, indeed. But he knew in his heart that his concern had nothing to do with money.

Twenty-one

March 27, San Diego, California

Tiff and Orville waved goodbye to Julian and strolled back from the beach to the house.

"Should we have invited him over for lunch, you think?" Tiff laid her boogie board on the patio and loosened the neck of her wetsuit. She flopped comfortably into a chair at the wrought-iron table and pulled her wet hair back with her hands.

"I already did," Orville said. "He had other plans." He opened the storage shed, which housed a varied supply of beach toys, swim gear, coolers, and chairs. "I suppose we should let these boards dry before storing them in here."

"Yeah, I guess so." Tiff laughed. "Daddy, I never thought I'd see you boogie boarding again, let alone wearing that debonair wetsuit."

He looked down at himself and rolled his eyes. "I look like a big water beetle in this thing. But who cares. That was some kind of fun, wasn't it?"

She leaned her head back and relaxed. "It was the best. I love it here. I love the salty air and the gorgeous skies." She looked at her father. "I think I'll become a beach bum for a living."

Orville rubbed a towel over his head. "Yep. I hear the pay's not great, but the training is pretty bearable."

"You said it."

Orville walked around the corner of the house. He called back to

Tiff. "Here we go. I found the faucet. I'm going to hose off the boards and chairs before coming in for lunch."

Tiff unzipped her wetsuit. She stood and peeled the thick, black neoprene away from her body and wrapped a towel around her swimsuit. She poked her head around the corner. "Thanks for doing that, Daddy. I'm going in for a shower." She glanced down at herself. "I collected a lot of sand in that wetsuit." She pulled her shoulders up in discomfort. "Now I know what a snake feels like when it sheds its skin."

Then, as soon as she walked into the house, she saw Eve.

Speaking of vipers.

Please be with us Lord. Help us not to bicker.

"Hi, Eve." She glanced around. "You here alone?"

"Yes." Eve pulled a soda from the refrigerator. She wore a short green caftan and looked as if she were about to hit the beach.

"Is Patti at work again?"

"Yes. I assume there are beach chairs in that shed out there?"

Orville walked in. "Well, if the mystery girls haven't shown up!"

Eve gave him a polite smile. "Just me today."

"Welcome, 'just you.'" He chuckled. "I'm beginning to think your girlfriend doesn't really exist."

"Daddy!" Tiff's eyes widened. She had been thinking the same thing, but hadn't planned to bring it up.

"I'm just kidding." He looked from Tiff to Eve. "You know that, right?"

Eve headed for the patio. "Yeah. I know. I'll see you all later."

"Oh, wait! Eve?" Tiff walked to the patio doorway. "I wanted to let you know we're definitely out of here this weekend. We're going to be staying—"

"I know where you're staying." Eve looked over at Julian's house and then grabbed a beach chair from the shed.

"Oh. Okay." Tiff caught the stiffness in Eve's expression.

Eve turned and rushed away from the house.

Orville lifted his chin in the direction where Eve headed. "That young lady is hiding something. I remember your acting like that when you were a little scamp and you got into your mama's makeup bag. Didn't want to make eye contact, didn't want to talk, just took off for the playground, hoping no one was going to catch up with you."

Tiff gave him a wry smile. "I remember. Mama found my doll under my bed, completely covered in lipstick and nail polish. I still remember that spanking. Scared me to death, and she barely touched me."

Orville took some kaiser rolls from the bread bin. "You never went near her makeup again, did you?"

"No sirree. And I'm assuming I improved a little at applying makeup when I got older."

He walked up to her and gave her a quick kiss on her forehead. "Not that you need it, hon. This sun and surf agree with you. You ought to skip the makeup from now on."

She headed toward the far end of the house. "Only if I get that beach-bum job." She stopped before she left the room. "Hey, Daddy. What do you think—" She walked back toward Orville and checked out the front window to make sure Eve wasn't coming back. "What do you think is going on with Eve? Do you really think Patti is an imaginary friend?"

He shrugged. "Don't know, kitten. But she almost appears able to tolerate being around us as long as she's alone. It seems to me she's hiding the girlfriend. Either that or she's just a very strange gal."

Twenty-two

March 28, Northern Virginia

Jeremy slumped his shoulders, exhausted, when he got home from work. He normally had several hours left in him by nine o'clock, but this had been one of his busier Fridays. He zipped his suitcase open and flopped back onto his bed.

He had talked with Mary, his principal, at the end of the school day yesterday. Mary was an amazingly organized boss, and nothing seemed to trip her up. Yet this request for time off was quite last-minute, and Jeremy had inwardly cringed even to *ask* for a substitute teacher for his class next week.

He grinned now, remembering how Mary chided him as if he were her wayward son. "What am I going to do with you, Jeremy? Your chances aren't good, I have to tell you."

Still, she had pulled it off, finding Barbara Sneed, one of their more regular substitutes, who was eager to take Jeremy's class and earn the extra money.

He and Barbara got together after school and spent a couple of hours going over his lesson plans for the following week. She hadn't subbed for him recently, so he needed to bring her up to snuff on where the class stood in a few of their academic subjects.

Then, there were the flight arrangements, rental-car reservations, and the stopping of his mail and newspaper, all arranged. He would pack and go promptly to bed. But what else was there? Something nagged at his thoughts.

He went to the kitchen, where his wall calendar hung. There it was. Tuesday at four. A cleaning with his dentist. He would miss that appointment while he was busy sneaking up on Eve.

He called the dentist's office. The automated voice recited their business hours and requested he call back then. Jeremy sighed, knowing there was no way he would remember to cancel this appointment once he left town. He needed to call Ren.

He checked his watch and grimaced. Half past nine. A little late, but he didn't want to wake her before he left in the morning. Any later than that, and he may as well depend upon his own muddled sense of organization to remember to cancel. He walked toward his bedroom as he called.

Ren's husband, Tru, answered the phone.

"Ah, Tru, so sorry to bother you. It's Jeremy, calling for Ren. I hope you weren't asleep already?"

"Nope, not a problem, Jeremy. Ren's not even home yet. She went to her prenatal aerobics class with Kara, and they were getting a late dinner after."

"I see. Say, do you think you could have her give me a quick call when she's home? Will she be terribly late, do you think?"

"Probably another hour. Is there anything I can help you with?"

Jeremy hesitated. He didn't feel quite right asking such a stupid favor from Tru. Their friendship was growing, but Jeremy wasn't certain it had reached the stupid-favor stage yet. Still, he'd certainly like to cross this task off his list. "I don't suppose you could cancel a dental appointment for me, could you?"

There was silence from Tru's end. When Tru spoke, Jeremy could hear his amused confusion. "You have issues with canceling appointments, Jere?"

Jeremy laughed. "I didn't remember the appointment until my dentist's office was already closed for the weekend. I'm going out of town tomorrow for the week. I could call from San Diego to cancel, but I know myself too well. I'll get caught up in matters on the West Coast and forget. My dentist is rather finicky about missed appointments. I'll be liable for a bill if I don't show up."

"I hear you. Okay, give me the details. One of us will cancel for you."

After Jeremy shared the information, he meant to start packing, but Tru seemed particularly chatty. "So, you're going to San Diego? You going to that beach house where Ren and I stayed?"

"Uh, in a way. My girlfriend—"

"Which one is this, now?"

Jeremy could almost see the grin on Tru's face. "I say, you're in fine form tonight, aren't you? It's Eve. Hasn't Ren told you about her?"

"Yeah, I'm just giving you a hard time. Ren's mentioned Eve before. You two flying out there together?"

"No. She's already there. I hadn't planned on going."

"So, who's missing whom? Both of you?"

"Neither of us, actually." Jeremy scratched his brow. "I mean, perhaps we're both missing each other. I miss her, yes, certainly. I suppose."

"Now, don't get all mushy on me," Tru said.

"It's just…something's not right." Jeremy sat on the edge of his bed.

"Oh?" The tone of Tru's voice changed. "Something's wrong between you and Eve, you mean?"

"I think so." At this point Jeremy stood and started packing, one handed. He needed to keep moving in order to occupy his worried mind but also to make sure he could dash from home and catch his flight in the morning. He tried to count underwear while he focused on his conversation with Tru. Sunday, Monday, Tuesday. "Eve went there to spend time with a girlfriend." Wednesday, Thursday. "An old flatmate from college who lives about an hour away from the shore. Eve said they hoped to get a lot of beach time in." Thursday, Friday—wait, had he counted Thursday twice? "And, uh, what was I saying?"

"Eve. Friend. Beach time. You okay?"

Jeremy stopped trying to multitask. He didn't know how women did it. So he paced, because it made him feel better than standing there doing nothing. "Right. So, when Ren told me about the beach house, I decided to surprise Eve with a two-week rental so they could just stay there, rather than commuting."

"Generous of you."

"And she seemed happy about it, until Tiff showed up."

"Who's Tiff?"

"What, you don't know Tiff? The pretty bird who worked with Kara at the gym?"

"Oh, yeah. You mean Tiffany."

"Right, Tiffany. I started calling her Tiff, and I think she likes it."

Pause. "Uh *huh*. The pretty bird likes you to call her Tiff."

Jeremy stopped pacing. "Tru, do I sound too interested in Tiff?"

"I don't know. How interested do you *want* to sound?"

"Well, I...blast, now I don't know if this trip is such a great idea after all. Maybe Eve will think I'm going out there because Tiff's there, because I'm interested."

"So you *are* interested?"

"No!" He ran his fingers through his hair. "What do you think? Should I go?"

"Uh...what did Ren tell you to do?"

"She said I should go."

"Then you should go. My wife gets it right almost every time."

Jeremy nodded and looked at the pile of clothes he had strewn across his bed. "Right. Say, I'd better get off the phone. I need to recount my boxers."

"Of course you do. Hey, man, have a good trip. We'll pray for you."

"Yeah, ta."

No sooner had he hung up, than the phone rang again. He couldn't keep the exasperation from his voice when he answered. "Yes?"

"Jeremy! How's my lad?" The man's thickly accented voice immediately brought a smile to Jeremy's face. He sat back down on the bed.

"Dad! How are you? What a surprise!"

"You sound good, son. Keeping well, are you?"

"Pretty well, yeah. Juggling a few too many items, as always."

"Too busy for company, then?"

"Never," Jeremy said. "And who'll be my company, *you?*" His dad hadn't come back to the States since he brought Jeremy for his first visit, sixteen years ago.

"As a matter of fact, yes."

Jeremy stood up. "Honestly? That's marvelous, Dad! When can I expect you?"

"Hmm. Let's just take a look at the calendar, then. How about…how about tomorrow?"

Jeremy didn't say anything for a moment. He wasn't sure he had heard correctly.

His father's laughter rang in his ear. "That's got your attention, has it?"

"Are you serious, Dad? Tomorrow? Here?"

"Tomorrow. There. I thought you might like a surprise from your old man."

"Oh, Dad, this is rough. I'm leaving in the morning to spend a week in San Diego. In California."

"California! Well that's quite a trek for you, isn't it?"

"Yes, but, you see, my friend—Ren Sayers, I've mentioned her before—she and her husband recently spent time at a house out there on the beach. Said it was fantastic. And I rented the place for my girlfriend, Eve, for this week and next. For her girlfriend and her."

"But I thought you said *you* were going out there."

"I am, but I hadn't planned to. This was supposed to be just for the girls."

"Now, aren't you the gent? And are they enjoying their stay? Are you flying out to join them?"

Jeremy didn't want to go the same route he had just gone with Tru, so he simplified. "Yes, that's right. Going out to join her."

"I see. Hang on a bit."

His father muffled the phone and talked with someone briefly. Jeremy looked at the clock and his empty suitcase. He started pacing again. "Dad? You there?"

His dad returned, sounding calm and decisive. "Right, then. We'll just have to schedule for when you return, how's that?"

"You're aces, Dad." He could always trust his father to avoid complicating matters. "I'll be back no later than Sunday next. Quite possibly Saturday. Shall I call you then and make plans?"

"Yes, lovely, son. I'm looking forward to seeing you. I have a surprise to share."

Jeremy stopped pacing. "You can't tell me now? You know I'm not the most patient son in the world."

"That's true," his father said. "But you'll have to wait until I see you. That will be sooner than you think."

Probably so. Time would likely breeze by, and events could very well move quickly. By the time he saw his dad, his entire love life could be wiped away. He could imagine Eve mistaking his surprise visit as *I don't quite trust you!*

Or is that what his trip really meant?

Twenty-three

March 28, San Diego, California

Tiff sauntered back toward the beach house at perfect peace. She was loving Ren for suggesting she come out here. She was loving her dad for being such excellent company. And she was loving the people of Mission Beach—even the weird-looking ones—for being so much fun to watch and meet. She even had a few comfortable, casual conversations with total strangers while she walked along the boardwalk and did a little shopping. She held a bag of sugar-free fudge in one hand and a boutique tote with sundresses in the other. She stopped, closed her eyes, and turned her face to the brilliant sun. Life was good.

When she neared the house, she noticed a gorgeous red convertible parked in the beach house's carport. She was no car expert, but that looked like an old Jaguar. Wow. And the guy sitting behind the wheel— did he look hot simply because of the car?

She got near enough for a better look. Ooh la la. Maybe the car looked hot because of the guy. Even from this distance, she could tell he had thick, dark, wavy hair and a manly, rugged jaw line.

Tiff was suddenly attentive to how *she* looked. She grabbed her hair up and shook it over her shoulders. Her knit top and shorts weren't her most flattering, but they'd have to do. Her makeup—she wasn't wearing makeup! Then she remembered what her father had said about her natural look, and she shook off her insecurity. She was who she was. This was the beach, after all! And why was she still so focused on her looks? Or his, for that matter?

When he noticed her walking toward him, he smiled, and she focused on looks again. His eyes were so blue. Almost as blue as Jeremy's—

Now where did *that* thought come from?

"Hello." What a smooth voice he had. He got out of his car and extended his hand to her. He tilted his head toward the beach house. "Are you staying here?"

Tiff put down her bag and shook his hand. "Yeah. My dad and I. I'm Tiffany."

"Michael." He still held her hand.

She gently let it fall away from his. "Can I help you with something? Having car trouble?"

"No. Although this car does give me its share of troubles." He rested against the car and rubbed his hand along it, as if he felt affection for it.

Tiff held back from leaning beside him against the car, but she followed his example in stroking its shiny finish with appreciation. "It's beautiful. Is it a Jag?"

"Yep. A 1956. I'll give you ride in it, if you like."

Tiff laughed softly. "Who *are* you?"

"Oh!" He laughed, too. "Sorry. I'm a friend of Eve's. She's inside getting some of her things. I'm driving her back to my sister's place in Lakeside."

"Are you Patti's brother?"

"The very same," he said with a smile. "So, Eve's mentioned me?"

Tiff snorted. "Hardly."

Obviously, Eve understood her more than Tiff realized. If Eve wanted to keep her San Diego trip to herself, she certainly wouldn't want Tiff to get a load of Patti's brother. It was all she could do to not sit on his knee and call him Santa. But she tried to rein in those old impulses. "I mean, no, Eve and I haven't really spent much time around each other. She didn't get around to telling me about you."

"She told me a little about you."

"It's not true!" The words flew out of Tiff's mouth before she even gave them thought.

Michael flashed his beautiful smile and laughed out loud. "What makes you think she told me bad things about you?"

Tiff felt sheepish but broke into a smile about her outburst. "Come on, now. We can at least be *that* frank. I can't imagine Eve expressing a single kind thought about me."

"Well, there you are, Tiff!"

Tiff turned to see Eve walking toward them, looking shower fresh in a pale linen shift. She graced Tiff with a broad smile, but it didn't seem natural. Tiff wasn't sure she had ever *seen* a natural smile on Eve.

"Hi, Eve." Tiff narrowed her eyes slightly, trying to figure out this strange woman.

Eve spoke as briskly as she walked, on her way to the passenger side of the Jag. "I see you met Michael. He's been a dear, haven't you, Michael? Patti needed her car today, so Michael's been kind enough to chauffeur me around."

He looked at Eve. "Ready to go?"

"Ready. See you, Tiff. I'll be by tomorrow, but I'll probably stay at Patti's again tonight. So if you and your father want to wait until Sunday to move, that's fine."

Tiff lifted her hand in a wave. So. Today we're using our *happy* voices, children. "Okay, thanks. See you tomorrow." She headed to the house. They drove off, but she heard the car stop abruptly. She turned back and saw Michael jump out of the car and jog toward her. He held her tote bag from the sundress store.

"You left this on the ground."

Tiff rolled her eyes about her forgetfulness. "Thanks."

Michael panted slightly from jogging. He spoke quickly and quietly. "I'd love to see you while you're here. Maybe sometime when Patti and Eve are busy, we can get together."

She smiled and took her bag. She didn't have a chance to respond before he turned and ran back to the car.

As she walked into the house, her skin felt several degrees warmer than usual. Her thought before she first saw him returned to her: life was good. Yes, indeed!

Twenty-four

Saturday afternoon Orville and Tiffany relaxed on the beach house patio. Tiff had eaten her last bite of lunch and simply stared out at the waves. She loved the mesmerizing effect of their gentle, rhythmic wash upon the shore.

Orville set down his fork and sat back with a smile. "You amaze me, kitten. Here I made you a lousy cold-cut sandwich yesterday, and you were hiding your talent as a gourmet chef from me. All that hospital food when you were with us back home—you must have been miserable."

"It was just a salad, Daddy."

Orville rested his feet in the wrought-iron chair between them. "Nope. Iceberg lettuce and a tomato—that's just a salad. I never thought I'd be satisfied with a salad for lunch. What were those little peachy things in there?"

She nudged his calf with her foot. "Peaches, Daddy. You're teasing me now."

"Well, they were mighty good."

"I just wanted you to see you can have a tasty meal without *frying* everything. That chicken in the salad was good, right? And it was grilled. Much better for you."

"I know, you're right." He patted his stomach. "I'm telling you, even though we seem to be eating a lot on this trip, I feel like I might be dropping a pound or two. What with the walking and now eating this rabbit food, you're whipping me into shape. Your good habits might just rub off on me."

She got up and took his empty plate. "Diabetes will do that to you. I can't get away with eating too much junk. And if I miss more than a day or two of working out, I start to feel a little punk. It's not just about looking good."

Orville brushed his pinky across his eyebrow, affecting a mincing expression. "That's what I always say too."

Tiff gave him a kiss on the cheek.

Just then there was a knock at the side door. "I'll get that." Tiff brought the dishes into the kitchen and opened the door. Then she gasped.

"Jeremy?"

He looked wonderful. His tousled hair flopped onto his forehead as if the long journey had worn it out. His eyes were sleepy, and he had stubble on his jaw line. The shoulder strap of his suitcase pulled his golf shirt askew, revealing his collarbone and a little of his virtually hairless chest. All in all, he appeared to have been through an arduous trip, but Tiff thought he was the best-looking weary traveler she'd ever seen. And that was before he smiled.

"Come in!" Tiff finally said, collecting herself. "Here, put your bag on the couch."

Orville walked in, and the two men exchanged smiles. Jeremy reached for Orville's hand.

"You must be Tiff's father, eh? Jeremy Beckett."

"Orville LeBoeuf. And you're Eve's fella, right? This is a nice surprise."

Jeremy rubbed his hands against the sides of his jeans, as if his palms were sweaty. "Yes, well, that's exactly what this is. A surprise. I haven't talked with Eve yet. She doesn't know I'm coming."

Tiff and her father exchanged glances.

"I don't suppose she's here, is she?" Jeremy looked toward the bedrooms and back again.

"I, uh, think she's stopping by here later on today." Tiff wanted to take that sweet, worried look from his face. "But I'm not sure. She and Patti were going to move in here today, but she said yesterday that she was staying at Patti's again tonight."

Jeremy nodded and shoved his hands into his back pockets. "Ah. I see." He glanced back at the bedrooms again, as if he were hoping Eve might emerge, despite Tiff's claims.

"Hey, why don't you go back and freshen up?" Tiff pointed to the back rooms. "I know I needed to, after that long flight. And we just finished lunch, but I could whip up some more. It was only a salad—"

"A first-class salad—" Orville added.

She continued, "I'd be happy to put something together for you, Jeremy—"

"No, ta." Jeremy put up his hand. "I had a spot of food on the plane. But I will take your offer on that freshening up."

"And then maybe you'd like to join Daddy and me. We were just going to take a walk on the beach. I'm sure it will relax you and energize you at the same time."

He looked at her, and she saw something wonderful in his expression. Despite whatever was going on between Eve and him, she wanted him to feel good right now. And something in his eyes told her he knew that. Suddenly embarrassed, she glanced away.

Lord, what are You doing to me? Why can't I look at this guy for more than five seconds without blushing?

Jeremy spoke softly. "Thanks. I think I'll take you up on that."

Orville cleared his throat. "Let me take you on back, Jeremy. Bring your bag if you like. We can drop it in my room."

Jeremy scanned the living room and slung his suitcase strap over his shoulder. "It's just as Ren described it—she used the term *eclectic*. Looks as if several feisty dowagers pooled their bric-a-brac and had a right good time decorating."

"It grows on you." Tiff gave him a wry smile.

He smiled, a twinkle in his eye. He looked more relaxed already.

~

They hadn't walked far along the beach before they ran into Julian. When Orville introduced the two other men, Julian seemed to have expected Jeremy.

"Glad you finally arrived. You're Tiff's friend, I understand."

Jeremy stuttered his response. "Um, well, I—"

Tiff interrupted. "He's *Eve's* boyfriend."

"So you said. But your friend, too, right? At least I thought you said that, when Orville and I interrupted your phone call the other day."

Now why in the world would a comment like *that* make Tiff uncomfortable? For some reason, the way Julian said it, it sounded like she claimed too much attachment to Jeremy.

"Well, yes…" She looked at Jeremy and shrugged. "He's my friend."

Jeremy's smile put her at ease.

Julian turned to Orville. "And will you and Tiff be moving into the upstairs apartment today?"

"I think we might wait until tomorrow, if that's all right with you, Julian," Orville said. "Eve and Patti decided not to move in tonight. Oh, but now that I'm thinking of it, it might actually be best for us to go ahead today." He lifted his chin toward Jeremy. "That way you could make yourself at home there at the beach house, Jeremy."

"No, I planned to find a motel." Jeremy looked back toward the boardwalk. "I would imagine that wouldn't be too difficult, eh?"

"Jeremy, that's nuts." Tiff spoke without thinking. "You're paying for a week's rental on the beach house. *You* should stay here. Daddy and I will move out."

"Better yet," Julian said, "Jeremy, be my guest at the apartment tonight. If Eve and her girlfriend show up unexpectedly, you certainly don't want to be sleeping in the same house, right?"

Tiff couldn't bring herself to look back at Jeremy. She had no idea about Eve and him in that department. She knew what *her* status would have been, only six months ago, before she found Christ. Times had changed for her, and she wasn't ready to know too much about Jeremy's morals just yet.

Just yet? Why did she think that would ever be any of her business?

But Jeremy didn't skip a beat about Julian's question. "Ah, too right. Cheers, that's a great help, mate."

Tiff couldn't help but wonder about Eve and Jeremy. He'd flown all the way out here, and Eve didn't have a clue. Eve had been coming and going for a week now, and Jeremy didn't seem to know any more about her activities than Tiff and her father did. In this age of cell phones, how could two lovebirds be so out of touch with each other?

Twenty-five

But Eve didn't arrive as she said she would. Despite Tiff's assurance that she'd stop by, Jeremy had yet to see her by evening. And despite his sending Eve a text and leaving her two cell-phone messages, she even failed to make an appearance electronically. He didn't leave word that he was at the beach house, but at this point he wasn't sure that would make a difference. It was as if she had forgotten about the beach house. Worse, it was as if she had forgotten about him.

He sat on the beach wall just beyond Julian's home late that evening, his cell phone at the ready in case she called. He listened to the waves and took some comfort in the cooling breeze. The salt in the air reminded him of Bristol, back home in England. There were few people still milling about. He had begged off joining Orville and Tiff for dinner when they invited him. He told them he wanted to be here in case Eve stopped by. But there was something else.

That brief shuttle ride he took with Tiff several weeks ago had been inconsequential. A simple moment of harmless flirtation. But now every time he saw her, something seemed different about her. He couldn't believe she was that mean-spirited woman he had met at the gym nearly two years ago. And now he couldn't even believe she was the same woman he met again at Ledo's so recently. It was like watching those films of plants—flowers—shot in extreme slow motion, then played in rapid speed, showing the growth before your eyes. Every time he saw her or spoke with her, she seemed…better. He didn't understand what was happening to her.

Nor did he understand what was happening to him. But he knew instinctively he should keep some distance from Tiff, out of respect for Eve.

He breathed a heavy sigh. All of this reflection about Tiff was probably nothing more than his insecurity over Eve's apparent disinterest in him. He didn't trust his own judgment just now.

"Brother, you look like you got a load of questions and the answers are all out there, past the waves."

Jeremy turned to see a striking, dreadlocked African American man approach with a smile. He shook Jeremy's hand with friendly confidence.

"Zeke. Mind if I sit?"

"Jeremy. Be my guest."

Zeke sat down and exhaled, either in contentment or exhaustion. The two men stared off toward the ocean.

Jeremy wasn't sure he was up for polite conversation at the moment. But this bloke didn't seem all that eager to talk anyway.

Zeke gazed out at the dark shore and eventually said three words. "Assuring, aren't they?"

"Uh, come again?"

Zeke pointed to the shore. "The waves. The thing I find most relaxing about them is their consistency. Even in the dark you can hear the consistency." He gestured the movement of the waves with his hands as he spoke. "They always go out; they always come back. Assuring."

Jeremy looked back at the shore and closed his eyes. Yes, that was what he'd like right now. Some assurance. Some consistency. "I hadn't thought of that. But yes, I suppose that's one reason they're so soothing."

Zeke breathed deeply again and continued his thought. "Be nice if we could count on people to be that certain with us, don't you think?"

Jeremy glanced behind himself, at Julian's house, and then back at Zeke. "Are you a friend of Julian's, then?"

"Of Julian's? Yes, definitely. Why do you ask?"

This conversation was clearly heading in a more personal direction than Jeremy had anticipated. "Did he...uh, have the two of you discussed my situation? With my girlfriend, I mean?"

Zeke laughed. "Are you asking if we've talked with your *girlfriend* about your situation? Or are you asking if Julian and I have talked about you and your girlfriend?"

"Well, either!" Jeremy said, totally chagrined.

Zeke just smiled. "No, I don't know anything about you or your girlfriend. I just know about people. Sometimes we all let each other down, that's all. None of us is consistent, not even with our loved ones. Not as consistent as we should be."

Jeremy looked back toward the shore.

Zeke continued. "The only One you can count on all the time? Well, you know who that is, right?"

It took Jeremy a second to catch Zeke's meaning. "Ah. You mean God."

"You said it, Jeremy. The Lord. You just listen, you'll see. Sometimes, because of your situation, it seems He goes out." He gestured again, as he did while he described the waves going out. "But He always comes back." He brought his hands back and rested them lightly on his chest. "When you keep Him in here, brother, He's here for good."

For years Jeremy had listened to Kara and Ren talk about Jesus. Zeke was putting it in a different way.

"Assuring."

Nothing had changed with regard to Eve. But Jeremy felt his worry lessen. He lifted his cell phone, pressed the off button, and enjoyed the ebb and flow of the waves.

Twenty-six

The next morning Tiff and Orville talked Jeremy into joining them for breakfast at Kono's. He didn't need a great deal of coaxing. He preferred that Eve show up, but the night before he decided to enjoy his stay in San Diego regardless of the outcome with Eve. He had done all he could to reach her. His cell phone was back on, without a single message waiting from last night.

Orville brought Jeremy's attention to the present. "Now isn't that the tastiest breakfast burrito you've ever had? Wasn't it worth the long line?"

Jeremy finished his last bite. He wiped his hands and nodded. "Actually, it's the *only* breakfast burrito I've ever had. But I'm sure all future breakfast burritos will pale in comparison. I'm ruined for life."

Tiff tilted her head and regarded him. "Now look what we've done, Daddy. Have you ever seen a man look so satisfied and so distraught at the same time?"

Orville pushed the last of the potatoes toward Jeremy. "Finish those off, why don't you?"

Jeremy pushed back from the table and crossed his legs. "No, I've already had far more breakfast than I'm used to. Have you two been eating like this all week?"

Orville began to answer, but Tiff had adopted an odd, distant stare. She gazed beyond Jeremy's shoulder.

"Tiff?" He turned to try to discover the object of her interest, and she immediately reacted.

"No! Don't look."

Both Orville and Jeremy focused on her. She relaxed the glassy look in her eyes. She leaned in and spoke to them as if they were conspiring together.

"Those kids in line are going to smoke weed on the beach."

Orville groaned softly. "Tiffany, not again."

"What?" Jeremy looked from one to the other.

She refocused on the kids.

"She's reading lips." Orville said.

"*Is* she?" Jeremy grinned. "Brilliant!"

She stopped staring and smiled at him.

Orville cut in. "It's not so brilliant when people catch her doing it. Stop, Tiffany. You don't know how those kids will react if they know what you're doing."

She rested her hand on his arm. "Oh, they're harmless, Daddy. Stupid, but harmless. And they don't have a clue that I was watching them."

"Let's get going, anyway." Orville gathered up their trash and stood to go. "People need the table."

As they filed out, Jeremy tapped one of the teens in line on the shoulder and said, "Word to the wise: don't do the pot. They're watching you."

Tiff didn't laugh until they were out of earshot. "Daddy, between my lip reading and Jeremy's creativity—" She jutted her fist in the air like a superhero. "We could save the world."

Orville chuckled. "Oh, you're quite the team, all right."

They stopped on their walk back to the beach house to watch a saltwater-taffy sculpting contest outside a candy store. About thirty children of various ages sat at picnic benches on the boardwalk, each in possession of a paper plate, nuggets of taffy, and fifteen minutes to create. Tiff, Orville, and Jeremy watched them use their imaginations with the sticky pastel candies. Most of the children made flat, painting-like images—balloons, flowers, geometric shapes. But a couple of the kids actually crafted three-dimensional sculptures, which rose from their plates.

"I think as many candies are getting eaten as sculpted." Tiff nodded toward a little girl who simply stuck several pieces together on her plate and used the rest of her time to eat.

"I say, look at that one." Jeremy pointed to a boy who had fashioned a green dragon, complete with purple spikes along his back.

A bell rang, signaling the contestants to stop creating.

"Wow." Tiff nudged her dad to look at the dragon sculpture. "He did that in fifteen minutes. Amazing! It even has fire coming out of its mouth. Or…a carrot."

The boy didn't act as if his sculpture were better than anyone else's, and he didn't act surprised when a rather predictable, flat clown face was chosen as the winner. His mother, standing behind him, seemed equally unperturbed.

As people dispersed, Jeremy approached the dragon-boy's table. Mother and son tidied up the candy wrappers.

"Yours was the best." Jeremy nodded at the boy and gave him a thumbs up. He smiled at the boy's mother and then addressed her son again before he left. "Absolutely the best. You've a lot of talent."

Finally, the boy smiled. "Thanks." And then he looked humbly down at his artwork, which had already started to soften in the sun.

"That was nice of you," Tiff said. "I would never have thought of going over and telling him that."

Jeremy shrugged. "Occupational thing. You look for any chance to encourage kids. They're so open to suggestion at that age. It's important for them to hear good things about themselves."

Orville started them walking again. "That makes perfect sense. Of course kids need to hear encouragement like that." He glanced at Tiff. "You'd think that would be a no-brainer. But I can't say your mother and I thought that way when you were growing up. At least I know I didn't."

Tiff looped her arm through his. "You did what you could with what you knew, Daddy." She affected a stern posture. "And now I want no further confessions of your parental failings for the rest of our trip. I turned out all right, after being a completely insensitive lunatic for years."

As they neared the beach house, Jeremy noticed an older couple standing by the front door. "Friends of yours?"

Orville followed Jeremy's gaze. "Nope. Uh oh. I wonder if the rental agency has provided us with yet another personnel project here."

"Oh, please." Tiff laughed. "You don't really think they'd do that, do—"

"Blimey!" Jeremy stopped in his tracks. It couldn't be! "You crazy bounder!" He laughed and ran the rest of the way to the beach house, where he grabbed the man in a bear hug.

Tiff and Orville caught up to them. Before Jeremy could say anything, Tiff looked at Orville. "Daddy, I think Jeremy might know these people. What do you think?"

"He *is* a friendly fella, isn't he?" Orville said.

Jeremy beamed. "This is my dad! Sean Beckett." He put his head close to his father's and made a goofy grin. "Can't you tell? See the family resemblance?" He released his dad and put his hand on Orville's shoulder. "And Dad, these are my friends, Tiff and Orville, eh, I'm sorry, how do you say your last name again?"

"LeBoeuf." Orville shook Sean's hand. "It's not an easy name to remember. It's from my Louisiana roots. Nice to meet you, Sean."

"It means 'the beef,' doesn't it?" the woman next to Sean asked. Jeremy stepped back in anticipation of his father's introducing her. Had his father finally started dating again, after all these years? This woman looked kind. She was about the same height as his father, and probably ten years younger. Her eyes were dark and smallish, and her cheeks round.

Orville nodded. "Afraid so, ma'am. Means the beef. Not the most noble of names, eh?"

Tiff snorted. "Tell me about it. Not the most feminine, either." She put out her hand to the woman. "Welcome, um...?"

Sean spoke up and looked at the woman. "I'm so sorry, dear. This is Vera." He looked at Jeremy. "Vera is...my wife."

Jeremy knew his smile had frozen on his face, but he couldn't help it. "Uh, your *wife?*" Then he recovered his manners and gave Vera a welcoming grin. "Excuse my rudeness!" He gave her a polite hug. "Welcome."

His dad addressed Tiff and Orville. "I'm afraid I've kept a little secret from my boy." He put his arm around his wife. "Jeremy, Vera was the surprise I called you about."

Yes, just a bit of a surprise, after nearly thirty years of bachelorhood. Jeremy shook it off and tried to act normal. "Well, I say, congrats to both of you. You'll have to tell me all about it. As well as how you managed to show up here today, you scoundrel. You've completely flummoxed me."

Orville put his arm across Tiff's shoulders. "We should leave you three alone. Give you time to catch up."

"Oh, right," Tiff said. She lifted her hand in a brief wave at them and then added, "Hey, why don't you join us for lunch? We're having a late one and we're grilling. How about it?"

Sean regarded Vera and Jeremy before answering. "That would be lovely, dear. Tiff, was it?"

"Yes."

Vera tilted her head and spoke softly. "And where are you staying?"

Tiff pointed to the beach house. "Right here. My Dad and I are staying here."

Jeremy saw the confusion on his father's face. "I'm staying there, Dad." He pointed at Julian's beautiful stucco-and-glass home.

Sean looked behind himself. "I say! Quite a manor, eh? It looks as if teachers are paid a bit better in the States."

Jeremy laughed. "No, I'm in the upstairs apartment, as a guest. Julian, the owner, is extremely gracious. I'm actually paying for the beach house." He looked back at Tiff, who appeared unsure about whether or not to leave. He shrugged at her. "I guess we don't know who's staying where tonight, do we?"

Sean's brows creased. "Is Tiff your girlfriend, then, son? You didn't say."

"No!" Tiff spoke quickly. "His girlfriend is Eve."

She had supplied that clarification rather quickly, Jeremy thought. All for the best, he supposed.

Vera pointed at Julian's place. "And is Eve staying there as well? Where is she?"

Tiff turned to leave.

Jeremy was slow to answer. He didn't realize he had been watching Tiff leave until his father spoke.

"And *Eve* is the girlfriend, eh?"

"Yes. Eve. But there seems to be a spot of confusion."

"Indeed." His father had a twinkle in his eye.

Jeremy stood between his father and Vera and placed his hands on their backs. "Let's go inside. There's room for you two upstairs, but I'm not quite certain the place is available for any of us tonight. I need to chat with Julian."

"I must say, son, considering the fact that you've only been here a day, you seem to have made quite a few friends. Tiff, Orville, Julian—"

"And there's Zeke," Jeremy said. "You'll love Zeke."

"Zeke? Yes, we'll have to meet Zeke, as well." His dad patted Jeremy on the back. "You always were quick at making and keeping friends."

Perhaps. But girlfriends? That was another story altogether.

Twenty-seven

A few hours later Tiff carried a plate of burger trimmings out to the patio table.

Orville stood at the grill, flipping burgers. He glanced at Jeremy and Julian as they approached carrying two extra deck chairs. "Julian, you're joining us, right?" Orville asked.

"I'd love to, thanks. It smells like heaven over here."

"Thanks, mate." Sean walked up behind Julian. "That must be me. I've just had a shower."

"Well, if you're wearing hamburger cologne," Julian said, "maybe I *was* talking about you." He set down the chair he was carrying and asked Tiff, "Would you like some help?"

"Sure, thanks." She waved her thumb over her shoulder. "I left the rolls in the kitchen. Sean, where's Vera?"

"She'll pop on over soon. Something about her hair."

As Jeremy arranged the extra chairs around the table he asked Tiff and Orville, "I hope you two don't mind eating such a late lunch. We tried not to take too long before getting over here. If you were anywhere near as full as I was by that breakfast we had—"

"You bet." Orville turned and put a platter of hamburgers in the middle of the table. "I'm just now getting hungry again. I don't expect to bother with dinner tonight."

Tiff smirked. "We'll see about that, Daddy."

By the time Vera appeared, the table was full of food, and everyone was together on the patio. She fussed upon her arrival. "Oh, dear, I haven't helped at all, have I?"

Tiff waved her comment away. "Hey, you're our guest. Don't worry about a thing."

Once everyone sat, Julian flashed a smile at everyone. "Shall we say grace?"

Tiff quickly checked out the rest of the lunch guests. She hadn't been sure how to handle that part of the meal. She had taken to praying before her own meals but felt awkward doing it in restaurants or with people she barely knew. She still prayed at those times, but covertly. But Julian was right out there, asking everyone to join him.

She liked that. Better to feel awkward praying publicly than to feel guilty for slighting God. She hoped to be that confident some day.

Besides, no one seemed uncomfortable with the idea. They bent their heads as soon as Julian started to pray.

"We met through mutual friends and got on beautifully right from the start," Sean said. "The wedding was rather impromptu." He put his arm across Vera's shoulders. They had nearly finished lunch, and everyone relaxed and enjoyed Sean's story.

"We suddenly knew what we wanted to do, and we did it." He looked at Jeremy. "I'm sorry, son, that I didn't call you beforehand."

Jeremy shrugged one shoulder. "I've already told you, Dad, it's all right. It was just such a shock, that's all." He looked at everyone else at the table and added, "The man hasn't even shown interest in dating—let alone getting married—for as long as I've been alive." He grinned at Vera. "You awakened something in him, Vera."

She looked at Sean and got a teasing glint in her eye. "And vice versa, I must say."

Sean reddened. "We, uh, hopped on a plane straightaway to come surprise Jeremy here with our news. We called him Friday evening when we landed in Virginia. We thought we were so clever. And he tells us he's leaving for California in the morning!"

Vera laughed. "We never even left the airport area. We stayed at the Holiday Inn and grabbed the next available flight out here."

Sean grinned. "But we arrived too late last night to come to the beach house."

Tiff interrupted him. "How did you know where the house was?"

"I told them Ren recommended the place," Jeremy said. "They called her, and she gave them the address."

"And she kept her mouth shut." Tiff laughed. "I'm impressed. I don't know if I would have been able to keep from calling you, Jeremy."

Sean reached for Vera's hand and spoke to Jeremy. "It was hard for me to keep from telling you, too, when we called Friday night. But I wanted to handle it in a special way—we thought it would be fun to arrive on your doorstep."

Vera laughed and added, "We just didn't realize the doorstep would be on this side of the country!" She and Sean looked at each other and exchanged a light kiss.

Tiff got a kick out of the two of them, but when she looked at her dad, she saw a touch of sadness. She wondered if he would ever consider marrying again. She couldn't imagine it.

She glanced at Julian and was surprised to see he was looking at her. Normally that might have bothered her, but there was something "safe" about Julian. It appeared he had seen her studying her father, because he had such a kind expression in his eyes. It was as if he could tell she was worried about Orville. She looked away and stood. "I'll get coffee." She gathered a handful of plates and walked to the kitchen.

She heard someone follow her in. Then Jeremy whispered behind her. "Am I convincing, then?"

Tiff turned quickly. He was close, and she knew the flush that ran up her cheeks had to be obvious. "Uh, convincing? About what?"

He released a breath and his shoulders drooped. He ran his fingers through his hair, and he continued to speak softly. "Tiff, it's just odd that he didn't tell me about Vera. We don't phone each other often, but this truly was a huge event in his life. *Dating* would have been huge. I wasn't exaggerating about that."

She was surprised Jeremy was confiding in her this way. This was the type of thing he would discuss with Ren or Kara. She would have smiled, had he not looked so concerned.

"What do you suspect?"

He shook his head. "I don't know. It's just blasted odd."

"Are you feeling…replaced, you think?" She almost winced, fearing she sounded judgmental or inconsiderate.

"Well, maybe." He stroked his chin. "That could actually be what's bothering me. But the behavior seems so out of character for him. I hope Vera's good for him."

Tiff focused on the group outside. Vera and Sean laughed together about something Orville said. "They seem pretty happy, Jeremy. If he hasn't dated in years, and he suddenly fell in love, it could have done a real number on his normal behavior. That could account for why he made different choices than what you would have expected. Sometimes Cupid's arrow strikes the heart and then shoots right on up to the head."

He rolled his eyes. When he spoke he used a much thicker accent than usual. "And what are you going on about now, young lassie? Are you saying me dad has a hole in his head?"

She laughed and he joined her. Tiff wasn't sure if she was enjoying Jeremy as a friend or as something more, but she certainly *was* enjoying him. The entire afternoon had been enjoyable.

The next few minutes, however, were a little less so. In the midst of their laughter, both Tiff and Jeremy turned at the sound of the side door opening.

"Jeremy!" Eve stood in the doorway, her overnight bag in her hand, pale shock on her face, and Patti's brother Michael at her side.

Twenty-eight

For the briefest of moments, Jeremy flushed with guilt when Eve walked in on his laughing with Tiff. Then he remembered that she hadn't returned a single call since he arrived in San Diego. Not to mention that she was in the company of a bloke who looked like someone out of a men's fashion magazine. Patti's brother or not, he looked like competition.

But then she nearly screamed with delight and ran into Jeremy's arms, right in front of the chap. She wouldn't do that if he really was competition, would she? Jeremy hugged her too, but his heart wasn't quite sure with the embrace.

She did look lovely, though. Despite the fact that she had spent so little time here at the beach house—and presumably, the beach—her skin glowed, sun-kissed. Her blonde hair shined brighter than ever. And he hadn't seen this particular sundress on her. Some vivid version of pink. He tried to remember his students' crayon colors. Magenta? Whatever the color, it suited her.

"You horribly naughty man, flying out here without telling me!"

"But I called you a number of—"

"Oh, don't tell me. You've been calling my cell." She looked at Michael. "See, didn't I tell you, Michael? Stupid phone." She looked back at Jeremy. "I forgot to pack my charger, like a ninny. So I only turned the phone on those first few times you and I talked. Then I only used it when Patti and I needed to touch base. You know, when she was at work. I *told* Michael I needed to give you a call. I thought you might worry. And then my phone battery died. I'm sorry, Jeremy, but I always use my speed dial to call you. I couldn't remember your number at *all* on my own."

As he listened, Jeremy avoided eye contact with Tiff. She knew how concerned he had been by his inability to get in touch with Eve. And if Tiff had a "what*ever*" expression on her face right now, regarding Eve's feeble excuses, he'd be hard pressed to speak politely to Eve or her Adonis friend. He didn't like the fact that Tiff had that much influence on him, but he wasn't going to deny it either. He was starting to enjoy her as much as he did Ren and Kara when he first met them. And her opinion of him mattered.

Plus, he was unable to ignore the fact that Tiff had tracked him down at home quite easily, when she called him about Eve's absence that first night. Why hadn't Eve experienced the same ease in reaching him, assuming she actually tried to?

"Jeremy, I need to introduce you to Michael here." Eve stood beside Jeremy and presented Michael as if she were a magician's apprentice. "He's been so sweet to drive me around when I needed him to. You know, like when Patti's been at work and needed her car."

Michael shook Jeremy's hand, a comfortable smile on his face. "I've heard a lot about you, Jeremy. It's a real surprise to meet you." Then he turned his gaze on Tiff, and the nature of his expression struck Jeremy uncomfortably.

So did the way Tiff smiled at Michael when they greeted each other. Jeremy wasn't sure, but he thought he detected some sort of attraction going on between Michael and Tiff, which for some reason disappointed him. Tiff deserved…what? Someone less handsome? The guy's looks couldn't be what bothered him. Jeremy didn't really know anything about Michael, but he simply didn't trust him.

Eve interrupted his thoughts. "Now you've gone and done it, Jeremy. Tonight's going to be a mess. If I had known earlier—"

"He can take my ticket." Michael reached into his jacket's inside pocket.

Eve put her hand at the same spot, to stop him. "No. Let me give a call to the box office and see if I can get another ticket."

"What tickets are you talking about?" Jeremy shot a glance at Tiff, who had already turned toward the kitchen.

"Patti and I—and Michael, too—have tickets for the San Diego Opera. *Pagliacci*. Michael just drove me out here so I could change into a more formal dress." She looked at her watch. "At this late hour, I'm afraid I won't be able to get another ticket." She looked at Michael. "And I know Patti had her heart set on your seeing *Pagliacci*, Michael. You can't give your ticket away."

"What a crock." Tiff walked past them. She carried a tray of coffee cups and sugar and cream. She looked innocently at Jeremy, Eve, and Michael. "Just look at this sugar crock. The lid is a windmill. Isn't that hilarious? And the creamer is a fat little cow. From Holland, maybe?" She looked pointedly at Jeremy for an extra second before addressing them as a group. "If any of you would care to join us for coffee on the patio, grab a mug and come on out."

"I'll be right out," Jeremy said. He turned back to Eve. She made no comment, but her smile was absent when she looked back at Jeremy.

"I haven't even had a chance to tell you, Eve. My dad's here."

"Your dad? Goodness! How did that happen?" She acted as stunned as Jeremy was by the news, her palm against her chest.

"He surprised me—"

"Like you surprised *me*."

"Uh, yeah…But my dad brought his new wife."

She gasped. "Jeremy! You never told me he had a new wife!"

"I didn't know about her until this morning," Jeremy said, replaying the disbelief.

Eve sighed. "Wow, this has been a crazy week." She looked from Jeremy to Michael. "Okay, so who has a phone I can use?"

Michael handed her his.

"Thanks. Let me give a call to the box office and see if I can get you a ticket, Jeremy. Then I'll come out to the patio and meet your dad and his wife." She looked at Michael. "Why don't you go on out there with Jeremy?"

"Will do."

Jeremy and Michael turned to exit, and Michael bumped directly into Tiff on her way back in. He caught her to steady her, holding her a bit longer than he really needed to, or so it seemed to Jeremy.

Tiff laughed softly. She pointed to the kitchen. "Got to get the coffee."

"I'll grab it." Jeremy turned around before he realized he had just left Tiff in Michael's care. He heard Michael speak while they walked outside.

"Tiff, maybe you can show me around this interesting little house. I'd like to see what other funky knickknacks you've discovered."

Jeremy retrieved the coffee pot and muttered under his breath. "What a crock, indeed."

Twenty-nine

When Eve joined them on the patio, Jeremy made the introductions.

"Ah, you're every bit as lovely as my son said," Sean said as he kissed Eve's hand.

"And I see where Jeremy gets his penchant for surprising people!" Eve said brightly. She then turned her attention to Julian. "I gather you're the gentleman I need to thank for giving Jeremy a place to stay."

"Yes. It's been my pleasure for Jeremy to use the flat upstairs," Julian said.

"You bring up a good point, love." Jeremy scratched his head. "What are our living arrangements this evening? I imagine you and Patti will want to come back here after the opera tonight."

"Oh." Eve put her finger to her chin. "Hmm."

Orville spoke up. "Julian, if you can accommodate Jeremy and his folks another night, we certainly have room for Eve and Patti. And Tiff and I can find another place tomorrow. It's what we agreed to—the place is technically yours, Eve."

"The apartment is available," Julian said. "For whoever needs it."

Michael looked at Eve. "I'd be happy to drive you back here tonight, but I know Patti has to work in the morning."

"Good grief." Tiff set down her coffee cup. "Has that poor girl had a *single* day off during her vacation?"

Eve shrugged. "She expected to work a little during my visit. It's just been more than she anticipated." She then turned to Michael. "I guess I could come back here tonight. Especially since you'll be right next door, Jeremy." She gave Jeremy a sweet smile, then turned back to Michael. "You're sure you don't mind?"

"Not one bit." Michael was emphatic.

Finally, Eve affected a pout and turned to Jeremy. "You sound like you've already accepted the circumstances tonight, Jeremy. I wasn't able to get you a ticket for the opera. Are you sure you wouldn't prefer I stay here and let Patti and Michael go without me?"

Of course that's what he would prefer. He wanted this Michael bloke as far as possible from his girlfriend. But he answered, "Don't be silly, love. It's only one more evening, and it's to be expected that my coming unannounced might have interfered with something. Besides, I have excellent company here."

Eve leaned down and gave Jeremy a kiss on the cheek. "You're so understanding." She turned to Michael and said, "Just give me a few minutes to change." She scurried off to the bedroom.

Sean leaned back in his chair. "So, Michael, you've been quite the chauffeur, I take it."

Michael smiled. "It's been fun. Eve and I met each other before, when she and Patti went to college together. I've enjoyed getting to know her better."

No doubt. Jeremy kept his expression blank.

Vera sipped her coffee before she spoke. "Did I hear you say your name was O'Shea when you introduced yourself?"

"Yeah, that's right. My family hails from Ireland, actually."

"Is that a fact?" Sean smiled.

"Oh, aye." Michael said it with a lilt. "The O'Sheas of County Cork. Sure an' I was named for me father's father, Michael Padrick O'Shea." He chuckled and switched back to his real voice. "I haven't had a chance to meet my Irish cousins yet, but I'm hoping to go next year."

Eve returned just then wearing a beautiful, sleek black dress. Her hair fell softly around her shoulders. And she had put on a bit of that lovely, powdery fragrance of hers that Jeremy liked so much.

Jeremy noticed Tiff shift uncomfortably in her chair. She glanced down at her own clothes and frowned. He often saw women doing this kind of thing—comparing themselves unfavorably to other women.

Jeremy thought Tiff looked just fine in her faded jeans, bare feet, and T-shirt, but now was not the time to say so.

When Jeremy looked back at Eve, she resumed her sad puppy face. "I'm so sorry about this, Jeremy. Are you *sure* you're not mad at me?"

He stood and gave her a kiss. "Of course not, love. You couldn't have known I was coming. And you did your best at trying to get me a ticket on such short notice." He looked at his father. "I have plenty of catching up to do with my surprising father here."

Michael shook hands with everyone before they left. When he shook Tiff's hand, Jeremy saw him give her a quick wink.

Tiff's face lit up. "'Goodbye, Michael. Maybe we'll get a chance to meet again before I leave. We'll do that knickknack tour." The tone of her voice confirmed what Jeremy suspected. She was attracted to Michael.

"I hope so." Michael said in an unmistakable tone.

Eve interrupted sharply. "We need to get going." She headed for the door, and Michael followed. As did Jeremy.

"That's quite a car," Jeremy said with a whistle when he saw the Jaguar in the carport.

"Yeah, she's a beauty," Michael said. "And a beast. Keeps me busy with engine work."

Jeremy opened the car door for Eve and gave her a kiss. As he stepped away, Michael stopped him. "Say, Jeremy...do you know if Tiff is already involved with anyone?"

Jeremy faltered. "Uh, actually, I don't know much about her personal life. You'd have to chat with her about that."

Michael nodded. He gave Jeremy a warm smile. "Maybe the four of us could go out to dinner or something before the week's end."

Jeremy smiled back. Why was he so suspicious of this bloke, anyway? He wasn't so bad, really. And it was none of Jeremy's business if Michael and Tiff hit it off. "Maybe, yes. We'll chat tomorrow."

He rejoined the group on the patio. Julian had gone home.

"He said to give you his regards." Orville stood and removed the cooking utensils from the grill area. "Said he'd see you back at the house."

Jeremy nodded.

Tiff went to the kitchen to refill the creamer. Jeremy followed casually, and said, "Michael suggested maybe we could try a double date while we're here. Would you be interested?"

Tiff looked at him with an expression he couldn't quite read.

"That would be fun, yeah. So, you think he's interested in me?"

"Um, yes, I believe so. I'll ask Eve to put in a good word."

Tiff laughed. "You do that."

Sean's voice drew them back out to the patio and into the discussion. "I was just saying, kids. We've got a regular British Isles contingent at the beach house, eh?" He settled back and smiled at everyone. "We've Julian from Scotland, Vera, Jeremy, and myself from England, and young Michael Padrick O'Shea from Ireland."

Vera gave Sean a sly glance. "My first boyfriend was a Padrick."

"Was he now?" Sean gave his wife a crooked grin.

"Oh, yes. Quite a scoundrel he turned out to be, actually. But he was a lovely lad. We all called him Paddy. A real ladies' man, he was."

She stopped. "Long time ago, of course," she added with a blush.

"Paddy, eh? I'll have to remember that," Sean said in mock suspicion.

The room fell silent, and then all of a sudden Jeremy stood abruptly. "Blast! It's not Patti. It's *Paddy!*" He ran back toward the carport.

By the time he slogged back to the patio, he could see Tiff had figured out the same thing he had.

Eve was gone for the evening, spending her time as she had been since she arrived in San Diego.

With Paddy.

Thirty

Tiff had figured out that "Michael" was Paddy as quickly as Jeremy had. Sympathy for Jeremy washed over her as the realization dawned on his face. As he ran out after Eve, Tiff started toward the carport along with him. But her father gently stopped her.

"This is between Jeremy and Eve, kitten."

Tiff's cheeks burned when she turned to look at her dad, Sean, and Vera...but all of them matched her distraught stare. They all wanted to run out with Jeremy too.

"I didn't know," Vera said, on the verge of tears. "I didn't mean to suggest, that is, I wasn't insinuating anything about Michael, when I mentioned calling Padrick by his nickname."

Sean put his hand on her knee. "Not to worry, darling."

But she remained clearly upset and confused. "So, Michael goes by Paddy too? Is that it? Jeremy's girl has been seeing Paddy?"

Sean sighed. "This whole arrangement sounded strange to me right from the start, when Jeremy explained it to us. He said this Patti was to spend two weeks on vacation from her job, as Eve was doing. But when you—Tiff and Orville—showed up, the plans supposedly changed, and Patti was suddenly too busy to come to the beach house. Rubbish. What kind of person plans a vacation with a friend and then works the entire time? It sounded like a ruse to me, straightaway."

Tiff fumed as she reviewed some of the events and excuses of the past week. She ached to dish about Eve and the extent of her lies. But she held back, knowing she wouldn't help matters at all.

Her father was the more rational speaker. "I have to agree with you, Sean. It was clear she was hiding something from Jeremy. From all of us."

As Jeremy walked back onto the patio, they all fell silent. The sound of the waves and seagulls seemed suddenly clear. Jeremy didn't have tears in his eyes, but he looked close to it. Tiff wanted to go to him, but that, too, seemed inappropriate. She was relieved when Vera, of all people, stood and went to him, as if he were her own son.

At first he seemed embarrassed by her affection, but then he hugged her briefly. He pulled away and looked at Tiff, even though he spoke to everyone in the room. "Was I the last one to get this horrible joke? Did anyone else figure it out before now?"

Tiff spoke up at once. "Jeremy, you know any one of us would have told you if we had figured it out."

Words of agreement filled the air.

Jeremy wiped his palms along the sides of his jeans, as he had done when he first arrived. "It just seems as if it was so obvious, now that I realize she came out here for that bounder. But, I don't understand why she didn't just break things off with me."

He sat in the chair next to Tiff. "She went to considerable lengths to hide this from me. What did she think I'd do if she broke up before she came out here?"

"Jeremy," Tiff said gently, "I don't think she plans to break up with you." She shrugged, and a shiver ran up her arms. "I don't know what's going on in Eve's mind, but I have a pretty good idea. I'm not happy to admit it, but some of my past behavior wasn't much better than Eve's."

"Now, I don't believe that," Sean said.

"Believe it, Sean," Tiff said. "It's possible to become a new person and walk away from living like that, I'm here to tell you."

Her father winked at her. His smile gave her courage.

"You know how men mess around on their wives—or wives mess around on their husbands—sometimes for years and years? But they never actually leave their spouses if they can help it?"

She didn't wait for their response.

"I think the same kind of thinking is what's driving Eve right now."

"But why? We're not married," Jeremy said. "Or engaged. I haven't even talked with her about marriage yet. I mean, I never *will* now, of course."

He looked so dejected that it took all the restraint Tiff could muster to keep from wrapping her arms around him. How could Eve be so stupid to risk losing such a good man?

"But, Jeremy, Eve's behavior has nothing to do with you. The girl has issues! She's trying to feel…I don't know…desirable. Or mysterious, or daring. She probably doesn't even know that. But that's why she's doing this thing with Michael. Or Paddy, whoever. But she wants what you offer, too, probably more than what she gets from Paddy. So she hopes you won't ever find out. You're a terrific catch, and she knows it. Everyone knows it. You're…you're—"

Jeremy looked up at her. When their eyes met, she forgot what she planned to say next. How could someone in pain be so gorgeous? She couldn't look away from those big, passionate eyes. She felt absolutely exposed to Jeremy and everyone else on that patio. Her entire being broke out in heat, and there was no stopping the color that rushed to her face. She needed to start speaking again right away, but she could only stammer.

"It's why…see…Eve knows—" *Oh, please couldn't someone else say something right now?*

"Tiff is spot on." Vera spoke with authority, no longer confused. "This was a fling for Eve. Some women are like that. *Many* men are like that. Maybe you don't know how she knew this Paddy character in the first place, but since he carried on the charade with her, he obviously wasn't trying to break the two of you up. This was a fling for him too."

Sean, who looked angrier by the minute, spoke so quietly he sounded frightening. "Disgusting. Both of them. When you think how she pretended to seek a ticket for you for tonight, son. And how Michael—Paddy—said he'd bring Eve back here tonight but his *sister* had to work in the morning. They were downright evil about it. I'm telling you, Jeremy, when he brings Eve back tonight, I'll be here with you if you want. We'll have a right old punch-up with Mister Michael Paddy O'Shea, how about that?"

Jeremy laughed sadly. "No, Dad. Much as I'd love to pound the stuffing out of him, that's not my way. Had anything happened to Eve without her consent, I'd hammer him within an inch, that's certain. But she wanted this. And she'll have it."

He stood and looked at them all. "I'll have a chat with her tomorrow. She doesn't know any of us are onto her, so there's a good chance she'll come back here tonight. I'd appreciate it if no one said anything to her about this before I've had a chance to talk with her."

They all nodded.

He turned toward the beach. "I hope you'll all understand if I need a bit of time on my own. I think I'm going to take a walk."

As he left a million thoughts flooded Tiff's mind. What if Eve *did* return tonight? Would she and Tiff cross paths tonight or tomorrow morning? It would be difficult to keep quiet about what a creepette Eve had turned out to be—even worse than Tiff originally thought.

And Tiff knew herself. She would have a hard time with feelings of vengeance on Jeremy's behalf. She wanted to tell Eve about Paddy's discussing a double date with Jeremy, that he wanted to take Tiff out. Or was that part of the lie? All that flirting Paddy did with her—was that genuine? Or did he pretend to be interested, so he and Eve could fool everyone? Or did he do it to make Eve jealous? Ugh! Who cared? Horrible people.

And what would happen the remainder of the week? Would Jeremy be depressed and inconsolable? Would she be able to be his friend, and nothing more? He needed a friend right now, not another woman running after him.

Still, they had five more days at the beach house, and she had one overriding concern.

Would Jeremy even be here after tomorrow?

Thirty-one

In the middle of her dream that night, Tiff awoke so suddenly that she thought a noise must have been the cause. Yet the house was peaceful and quiet. The gentle roll of the waves outside was far too soothing to have awakened her.

It was a blessing, really, to have had that dream interrupted. Jeremy was flying away on a huge white bird. He was crying, and the bird was singing opera. Tiff shook her head to clear the bizarre image.

The clock on the nightstand read two twenty. Tiff got out of bed to get a bottle of water from the kitchen. The house was dark, save the occasional spots of moonlight smattered across the living room.

Eve's bedroom door was still open. She must have decided against coming back tonight. What new lie would she tell to explain that change of plans?

Tiff retrieved a bottle from the refrigerator and took a long, cold drink. She heard footsteps at the side door and then a key in the lock. Oh great. Eve was back, and she and Tiff would cross paths, after all. Tiff bounced from one foot to the other, considering whether to try to blend with the kitchen's darkness or sprint back to her bedroom. But she was too late; the door opened. She stepped deeper into the kitchen and hoped Eve would fail to notice her on her way to the back of the house.

Paddy was at the door with Eve. He spoke quietly, intimately. Eve whispered something in return, and they laughed together like conspirators. The ensuing silence between them suggested a goodnight kiss was in progress. Tiff got ideas about what she could do with her bottle of cold water, but she stayed put, as still as a cardboard cutout. Eve started slowly, nearly on tiptoe, back to her room.

But before she got too far, Tiff's stomach growled like an old porch dog. Eve spun around, squinted in Tiff's direction, and locked eyes with her as if *Tiff* had been the one running all over San Diego with the wrong man.

Tiff knew a time to pray when she saw one.

Lord, this is one angry schemer coming my way, and I want to rip into her like a monkey's last banana. Please help me honor Jeremy's request and Your wishes about my behavior!

Surprisingly, Eve spoke in quiet tones, as if she didn't want to wake Orville. But her seething added more menace than had she yelled. "What do you think you're doing, hiding in the dark like that?"

Tiff held up her water bottle. "I think I'm getting a drink of water. What are you doing, sneaking in the dark like *that?*"

"Well, excuse me for being considerate of others."

Tiff snorted. "Yeah. That's you, Eve. Considerate." She took another drink from her bottle in order to make herself shut up.

Uh oh, Lord. Not good. Help me help me help me.

Eve put her hand on her hip. "What are you insinuating? If you think I've done something inconsiderate, let's hear it."

No, no, no, they weren't going to go there. Tiff had promised Jeremy. She tried to affect nonchalance by taking another long drink.

Fantastic, now she had to tread carefully with Eve *and* she needed to use the bathroom.

She finally looked back at Eve, and goose bumps erupted on her arms.

Oh, no, Lord, is this You? Please let this just be my imagination. Please.

This was definitely not what Tiff wanted. She looked at the awful, deceitful woman in front of her, and...she felt sorry for her.

Now, hang on there, Lord. Please don't make me go that route. Diplomacy, fine. But sympathy?

Yet there it was. Like lightning, sympathy—no, *empathy*—struck her. She had been a similarly awful woman at times in her dark past. Did anybody's snippy judgment ever improve her choices?

She sighed. "You know what, Eve? I'm cranky at two thirty in the morning. You're right. It was thoughtful of you to try not to wake my father and me."

Eve opened her mouth but looked at a loss for a good comeback.

Tiff drained the last of her water bottle and tossed it into the recycling bin. "I'm going to use the facilities and go back to bed. Goodnight."

Before Tiff closed the bathroom door, she heard Eve's reluctant mutter. "Night."

Tiff despised what Eve and Paddy had done to Jeremy. But tomorrow Jeremy would rectify that situation, she assumed. And he would eventually heal, no doubt.

But the emptiness Eve tried to fill by manipulating men? No one was likely to rectify that tomorrow. Tiff remembered that emptiness. She realized it had gradually disappeared from her life, even though she hadn't been involved with a man for more than—

She counted back on her fingers. Several months before Mama got so sick. Wow. She'd been uninvolved for more than eight months and hadn't suffered for it. Of course, she wasn't made of wood. She had noticed plenty of men, not to mention that sleazeball Paddy and...

Jeremy's eyes came to mind again. Those sad, gorgeous blue eyes looking for something in hers when she encouraged him earlier in the day. And that playfulness she had first seen in his expression when they took that airport shuttle together.

Yep. She had definitely noticed Jeremy.

Still, she was quite prepared to be nothing but a friend to Jeremy. That might not be easy, but she knew it was possible. That, too, was surely a God thing.

She smiled when she returned to her room and crawled back into bed. She pulled the soft covers up to her neck and stared at the ceiling. That empathy hadn't struck like lightning. It had struck like a blessing. She had prayed, hadn't she? What did she expect in response, the ability to make Eve disappear? Or even change at all?

All right, Lord. I'm listening. And while You've got me all mushy and open to Your will, I'll go ahead and ask You to transform me for the rest of the time I have to be in contact with Eve. Or Paddy, for that matter. And maybe you could keep me from flirting with Jeremy. Oh, wait. Maybe not.

Or maybe yes. Okay...how about I leave that ball in Your court, and You could give me unbelievably obvious guidance? But, wait. He's not a believer, is he, Lord? Was that just guidance? Please don't let that be guidance! Yeesh. I'm going to sleep, Lord, okay? Guidance. That's the ticket. I need guidance. I love You, Lord. Goodnight.

Thirty-two

Later that morning Jeremy stood at the side door of the beach house. He rubbed his sweaty palms against his cargo shorts. When had that started? Was it only here in San Diego? One thing was certain. His nerves had been dodgy since his relationship with Eve began. He just hadn't wanted to see that before.

Here he was: thirty years old, comfortably established in his work, self-sufficient for the most part, and not without social possibilities. Yet every time he dated an interesting woman he became a gullible, blind choirboy.

He couldn't help but wonder if Eve had *ever* been faithful to him. He'd never known anyone to become deceitful overnight. Not this deceitful. So had she always pretended with him? Granted, they had only been together a couple of months, but still, why hadn't he picked up on Eve's true character?

Jeremy rubbed his palms against his pants pockets once more before knocking.

The moment his knuckles hit the door, it swung open.

Tiff stood there in jean shorts and a T-shirt, her long auburn hair pulled up in a ponytail. She wore little makeup and looked more like a teenager than the woman she was.

"Well?" she said with a sly grin. "Aren't you going to come in?"

"You saw me walk over?"

"Yep." She looked over her shoulder at the back of the house. "Eve's in the shower. She had a late night. I was up when she came home."

Jeremy started to speak, but Tiff put her hand up.

"Don't worry. I kept my mouth shut. And Daddy and I are going to run down to Kono's for breakfast, so you two can have some privacy."

He rubbed his palms on his pants again. "Actually, I thought we'd walk on the beach."

She nodded, then cocked her head. "Listen, are you okay?"

"There are better ways to spend a beautiful morning in San Diego, eh?"

He looked away from her as Eve emerged from the bathroom, fresh and beautiful. She was dressed more formally than Tiff, wearing a linen shift and heeled sandals.

"Jeremy! Nice and early. Just give me a minute to tidy up in here." She glanced at Tiff and made a minimum effort at politeness. "Morning."

"Hey." Tiff grabbed her purse from the kitchen counter. Eve had already walked back to her bedroom, so Tiff said, "Daddy's out on the beach, waiting for me. We'll be gone at least an hour." She looked at her watch. "The line at Kono's will be crazy at this time of the morning."

"Right." He looked at the floor. "Ta."

"You want us to bring back something for you?"

"No, thanks. I'm not terribly hungry right now."

"Understood." Tiff walked past him and turned before she closed the door. "Jeremy, I don't know how you feel about this, but I want you to know I'm praying for you."

He tried to give her a smile. That was such a sweet comment.

She closed the door and then opened it again. She spoke quietly. "Oh, and remember you're totally in the right here, and she's totally in the wrong. And you're...well, she's just *stupid*, that's all."

He smiled at that. "Ta."

He was still smiling when Eve emerged, armed with an air of confidence and glamour. Jeremy's palms were still sweating.

⁓

Eve carried her sandals in her hand, swinging them as they walked along the shore. "And then, they finally got to the Vesti La Giubba—you know, that's the really famous part, when Canio puts on the clown makeup and starts to cry while he's singing. You know which part I mean?"

Jeremy nodded. He had seen *Pagliacci.* He looked pointedly at her. "Remind me. Why was he upset?"

"Oh, you don't remember? He found out his wife was..." She looked toward the waves.

"Yes?"

"She was in love with another man."

Jeremy let that hang in the salty air.

"Anyway. When they got to that part, Michael—who had seemed bored to death for most of the opera—actually got teary."

"Did he?"

"Yeah. I knew he would like it more than he expected to."

"And what was Paddy's reaction?"

A brief hesitation. "Well, she loved it, of course. I told you she was the one who wanted Michael to see it, right?"

"Yes, you said that last night when he tried to give me his ticket."

Jeremy was amazed at how different their conversation felt from this new, informed perspective. She was really something. Something that could have destroyed him, had he gone so far as to marry her.

"All right, handsome, what should we do today?" She took Jeremy's hand, and suddenly he couldn't put it off any longer.

"Uh, you haven't made plans with Paddy?" He had to give her one more chance to come clean. "Maybe we should meet."

She wasn't fazed a bit. "No. She's been too busy for me so much of the time I've been here, I decided today was just for my man and me." She flashed him a smile that appeared so genuine, Jeremy's stomach turned. "But tomorrow might be a different story. I mean, I *did* come out here to visit her, and I'm sure you and your father want to spend some time together, right?"

He studied her lovely face. He was amazed at how pointless her perfect features were now. "Right. Tomorrow will be a different story."

She looped her arm through his and gave him a gentle squeeze. "But today! Today we could enjoy the beach together—I haven't really had much time on the beach. Or we could go into town and shop. I've done a bit of that since I've gotten here, and I saw a number of things you might—"

"Say, Eve, we need to talk."

Her steps slowed almost imperceptibly. Her soft laugh was musical and false. "I thought that's what we were doing, silly."

He stopped, and she followed suit. He faced her. "Eve, I think you need to tell me the truth."

The flash of fear that crossed her face almost made him pity her. But she caught herself quickly and seemed to dig her heels in the sand.

"The truth?" She tilted her head and put her hand up to shield her eyes from the sun. Or from his gaze, perhaps.

"Eve. I understand now who Michael is."

She smiled with condescension. "What does Michael have to do with anything? He's nothing more than a glorified chauffeur."

"Last night he slipped up, Eve. He told us his middle name was Padrick. I might have missed that clue. But Vera innocently said something that helped me realize—"

"Vera? Are you actually going to put store in anything some total stranger says to you?"

He sighed. "This isn't about Vera. This is about your flying out here to spend two weeks with a *man* named Paddy. This is about your lying to me and continuing to lie, right up to this moment."

She pasted on a smile of mock disbelief. He watched her try to decide whether to continue lying or to simply give in.

He spoke gently. "Could we just speak the truth for a moment or two?"

And then she started to cry softly. He didn't offer any consolation but waited for her to talk. When she did, it was with a victim's whine.

"You have no idea what it's like for a woman my age, Jeremy. I'm almost thirty, and I'm nowhere near getting married or starting a family." She looked him in the eye. "Consider my biological clock for a moment, will you? I'm scared!"

He couldn't believe what she was saying. "But how will your being unfaithful to me bring you any closer to getting married and starting a family? If you wanted those things with this Paddy bloke, why didn't you simply break off with me?"

Now she spoke passionately and defensively. "Look, Paddy and I dated each other years ago, when we both went to UCSD out here. I thought he and I would marry, but there were things he wanted to do before settling down. Then, out of the blue, he called me a few months ago. We made these plans for my visit right before you and I met." She raised her eyebrows. "So, actually, *you're* the one I'm being unfaithful with, since Paddy contacted me first."

Jeremy just stared at her for a moment. Then he glanced toward the beach house. They hadn't gone far. "Would you like me to walk you back to the beach house? I'll keep you company until Paddy can come move you out, if you like."

Her mouth opened, but no words emerged for a moment. She didn't even blink. Then the outburst began.

"You're kicking me out?"

Her angry indignation touched a chord. He felt he had spoken with respect until now, and yet she was attacking. It was difficult to hold his emotion in check. "There isn't a great deal of kicking involved, is there, Eve? You've barely been there since you arrived. It's simply time for you to throw the few remaining items into your luggage and stay where you originally planned to stay during this trip."

She raised both hands to her waist. "And once we return to Virginia? What are your plans then?"

"I plan to get back to work. To hang out with friends. I'll go on with my life, just as you will."

"I *mean* what are your plans regarding *us*?" Her lips had become tight and thin.

"Eve, have you been listening to our conversation? We're not *us* anymore. We're you and some stupid berk who was nothing but a hedged bet. You'll have to bet all your chips on Paddy now."

He walked away from her, and she started to cry again. He heard her behind him, running to match his stride.

"But that's just it, Jeremy. Being here with Paddy has made both of us realize we're not right for each other. Jeremy, you're the one for me. The only one."

He stopped and turned. She wiped her tears and tried to smile, apparently thinking he had stopped to reconsider.

"I'm sorry to hear that, Eve." He sighed. "I've reached the same conclusion about us that you and Paddy have. Now, let me walk you back to the house so you can ring Paddy. I'll get my cell from Julian's."

Eve drew herself up and pouted. "I can use my own phone." She then stomped—as well as she could on sand—back toward the beach house.

Jeremy watched her angry, crooked march through the sand and almost laughed at himself. After all the lies, he had still believed her story about the dead phone battery.

So many lies to sort through.

He turned and watched the waves.

He was tired. He hadn't slept well last night, and the stress of the past week was settling down on him like a heavy, damp blanket. He wouldn't sort through anything just now. He had plenty of time for that, now that he was alone again. And it would be a long while before he'd take a chance on being made the fool again.

Thirty-three

"You were spot on there, Orville," Sean said as he leaned back in one of the chairs outside Kono's. "That was a jolly good breakfast."

"Yep." Orville devoured a few more potatoes and winked at his daughter. "Tiff, we should own shares in Kono's by now."

"Or a potato farm," Tiff said.

Vera looked up at the clear sky. "Such a beautiful place. California, that is. I've never been to the States. I was especially pleased when Jeremy's change of plans brought us here." She took Sean's hand. "Although I'd love it if we could visit him when he goes back home to Virginia as well."

"Yeah. So would I, if he'll have us." Sean stared at the table. "He was so quiet last night. I don't know what to do for him."

"Just be available for him, dear." Vera looked at Sean as if he were the one Eve hurt.

"Do you think we've given them enough time?" Tiff pushed her chair back. "What do you guys think?"

"He might need some moral support right about now," Vera said.

"Yeah, he might," Orville said.

On their walk back to the beach house Sean seemed intent on talking about anything *but* Eve and Jeremy's relationship. The others followed his lead.

"And what is it you do for a living, Tiff?" Sean asked. "Are you a schoolteacher too?"

"Wow, no," Tiff said. "I don't have nearly enough patience for that.

That's a career for tolerant people like Jeremy and Ren. I'm a personal trainer."

"So you train individuals, is that it?" Vera asked.

"Yep, that's right."

"To do *what*, exactly?" Vera's eyes, though small, were delightfully childlike and inquisitive.

"To be healthier. And in better shape." Tiff instinctively flexed her bicep. "I work at a gym, and I design a workout routine to suit each client's particular needs."

Vera quickly glimpsed Tiff's body. "I can imagine people place a great deal of value in your advice. You've a lovely figure."

"Thanks. I do enjoy the work. But I don't actually have a job at the moment, which I'll have to remedy as soon as I return home."

"Is it a difficult position to find, then?" Sean asked.

"She lost her job unfairly," Orville said.

Tiff put her hand on his shoulder. "It's all right, Daddy."

"What happened?" Vera asked.

"You got *sacked?*" Sean looked incredulous. "What ninnyhammer would sack you? You're perfect for work like that. You're the very image of good health."

"You'll see, kitten." Orville put his arm around Tiff. "Those clowns will be sorry they lost you." He looked at Sean and Vera. "She came home to South Carolina to tend to her mama during her last months. When she went back to Virginia, they told her she couldn't have her job back."

Tiff shrugged. "It's not that big a deal, really. I know God has something better for me. I'm not worried anymore. Besides, if they had given me my job back, I wouldn't be here now. God knew best."

Tiff noticed a brief twinkle in Vera's eye. Amusement? Pleasure? At least it wasn't scorn. Then Vera simply said, "Faith is a wonderful thing to have."

"Yes." Sean took Vera's hand. "Vera and I made that discovery together."

"Oh?" Tiffany wanted to hear more. Could they possibly be believers?

Vera looked to Sean, apparently leaving him to answer.

He looked slightly uncomfortable. "We haven't talked with Jeremy about our...new discovery yet, so we'd best not touch on the subject further just now."

Tiff simply nodded.

Orville took the cue to shift subjects. "I met my wife at a firehouse spaghetti dinner. I've been a volunteer firefighter for thirty years now. Or, rather, I was until just recently. I quit when Sheila got sick. I still worked for the trucking company some, but I quit the volunteer work."

Orville paused in his reflection, then continued.

"This one night, when I was still pretty fresh faced, we had one of our fundraising dinners at the firehouse. In walks this wild-looking redhead with a couple of her girlfriends. She thought she was something." He smiled at Tiff. "And she was. She had such attitude! Cocky, smart-mouthed, and a heart of pure gold."

"Mom?" Tiff said. "A heart of gold?"

"You bet, honey."

"Oh, I didn't mean—" Tiff stumbled in her walk and caught herself, just as Orville caught her arm to steady her. "It's not that I didn't think Mama had a good heart—"

"I know." Orville looked at Sean and Vera. "Life threw a few rocks at Sheila, before the ultimate one that took her down." He looked back at Tiff. "So sometimes her delivery was a little strong. But your mama had a good heart. She just tried to hide it so it wouldn't get hurt again."

"Like what, Daddy? What rocks did life throw at mama?"

Orville put his arm around her. "I'll tell you about it some day. Just not today, all right?"

"Sure, Dad," Tiff said, accepting his hug.

As they approached Julian's house, he came out to greet them.

"Morning, all," he said. "Say, I don't suppose I could solicit some help? I've had a new dresser delivered, and the thing weighs a ton. I've decided I prefer it in the back bedroom, and I'd like to move it without destroying any of my internal organs."

"Sounds like a plan," Orville said hitching up his waistband.

He and Sean followed Julian while the two women waited.

"I wonder where Jeremy is?" Tiff asked.

"I was wondering the same thing," Vera said.

"Maybe Jeremy and Eve haven't returned yet." Tiff looked at the beach house. "I think I'd like to freshen up a bit and then maybe look for him. You want to come over while they move that dresser?"

"You go ahead. I'll do the same thing—freshen up—and we'll check on Jeremy together."

"Are we being busybodies?" Tiff couldn't help a small smile when she asked.

"Yes, of course we are!" Vera turned on her heels and headed into Julian's house.

Tiff laughed. She quickly sobered as she realized that she might never see Vera again after this week. And she seemed like such a potential friend—and maybe a sister in the Lord.

Thirty-four

The moment Tiff walked into the beach house, she heard Eve—and she was *not* in a good mood.

"I don't *care* what your schedule is like. This is totally *your* fault. I expect you to come get me immediately!" Pause. "What? No, I can't stay here, are you kidding? And the original plan was two weeks at your place, anyway. If you expect me to stay here with these…these…these people—"

Eve stormed out of the bathroom carrying a bottle of shampoo in one hand, her cell in the other. She stopped abruptly when she saw Tiff.

Tiff had frozen upon hearing Eve on the phone, and now she was so startled she actually raised her hand in a feeble wave.

Eve's eyes narrowed like a cat's. "Paddy, I have to hang up. I expect you to pick me up. *Now.*" She didn't wait for Paddy to speak before she shut off her phone.

"And how long have you been standing there eavesdropping?"

"Uh, I just—"

"Well, you certainly got your way, didn't you?"

"Pardon?"

"I'd love to know how much help Jeremy got from you in figuring out what was happening with Paddy. You've had your claws bared ever since I met you. You must be thrilled."

Tiff wanted to laugh, but she felt no humor. "What claws? I've never done anything to you, Eve. You brought this on yourself."

Eve pointed the shampoo bottle at her. "There! Like that! Why don't you just scream 'I told you so' at me?"

"I'm not screaming, and I *didn't* tell you so," Tiff said. "You and I never got close enough to have a civil conversation. That was your choice. And I had no idea what you were up to until last night."

"What I was 'up to,' you say. What I was 'up to.' You make me sound sneaky."

Tiff closed her eyelids once and then spoke slowly. "I think we need to *not* have this conversation. This is between you and Jeremy." She turned to leave the house.

She could hear the sneer in Eve's next words. "Well, don't get your hopes up about him, that's all I can say."

Tiff turned. "What are you talking about?"

"I've seen the way you look at him. But you can forget about *ever* having a chance with him. He told me you were nasty. Mean and *nasty*, were his exact words."

"I don't believe you."

Just then there was a quick knock on the door, and Vera and Jeremy entered. They both appeared startled to see Eve still there.

Tiff looked at Jeremy. "Jeremy—"

"Just *ask* him." Eve still held the shampoo bottle, and she used it to point at Jeremy. "Just ask him if he didn't tell me you were nasty. Mr. Honesty won't dare lie about it. Will you, Jeremy?"

Jeremy's face paled. He looked first at Eve and then at Tiff, who stood as still as a post, searching his face.

"Tiff…"

"Ha!" Eve stomped back to her bedroom. "There you go, Tiff. That's what he thinks of you."

Tiff felt the sweat on her forehead, above her lip, everywhere. She knew she was about to cry.

"Darling, don't let her do this to you," Vera said.

But Tiff couldn't stay another second. She ran out the patio door toward the shore, to try to blend in with the strangers on the beach. She'd jump into the waves if she had to, shorts and all, to hide the tears already running from her eyes.

Thirty-five

"Blast!" Jeremy started after Tiff, but Vera stopped him.

"Wait, Jeremy." She put her hand on his arm. "I'm sure she'd appreciate your effort. But she wouldn't have run from here if she was comfortable with your seeing her so upset."

"Vera, that's insane!" Jeremy said. "I don't care what she looks like. I just want to make her *not* upset."

"And you will," Vera said. "But let me go after her and calm her down. She won't mind so much if *I* see her falling apart."

They heard Eve curse about something back in the bedroom. Vera cocked her head in Eve's direction. "Besides, you have another task at hand."

Jeremy's lips tightened. "Right." He looked from Eve's bedroom to the patio. "And you'll go to Tiff? Honestly, Vera, I only made that 'nasty' comment to point out—"

She patted his arm. "You needn't explain to me, Jeremy. I can tell you think the world of Tiff." She headed for the patio door. "I'll find her."

From the bedroom, Eve cursed again.

What could be arousing such anger in her back there? All she was doing was packing.

Jeremy neared her room and rapped on the door jamb before he looked in. She spun around, fire in her eyes. But when she saw him, she teared up.

Jeremy tried to speak calmly. "What's got you so worked up, Eve?"

She was a mixture of wrath and self-pity. "Jeremy, are you a total idiot?

154

You dumped me! That's what's got me worked up. On my vacation! You dumped me while I was on vacation!"

He laughed, incredulous. "Eve! You were on vacation with another man. I don't think my reaction is terribly out of line."

She turned her back on him and tried to close her suitcase. She had packed too much and needed an extra pair of hands.

Jeremy walked in and approached her. "Let me help." He pressed down on the case hard enough for her to get it closed. When they finished, they stood rather close together. Jeremy glanced at her, and she watched him, her eyes moist and doelike.

He could read her intention immediately and stepped back.

"Jeremy, you don't really want me to go, do you?"

Jeremy picked up her suitcase. "The answer is no, Eve."

"No, what? You don't really want me to go?" She took one step toward him.

"No, you asked if I was a total idiot. The answer is no. Now, let me give you a ride to Paddy's."

She glared at him. "He's already planning on picking me up."

"When? Because if he hasn't left yet, I'll take you there straightaway."

She pulled out her cell phone. "Well, aren't you charming?" She pushed one button and waited a moment.

"Where *are* you?" She nearly barked into the phone. Then she heaved a grunt of exasperation. "Fine. Don't bother. Jeremy will bring me over."

She started toward the side door, and Jeremy followed her. Just before they reached the door, Eve stopped abruptly, as if a last-minute thought had occurred to her. "You go ahead, Jeremy. I just remembered something."

He nodded. "I have to get my keys and wallet from Julian's place. I'll meet you at my car."

⁓

The drive could have been less comfortable, Jeremy supposed. Say, if a badger were gnawing at his hindquarters the entire trip.

Eve alternated between caustic comments and bitter crying. Then she would take a moment to tend to some part of her appearance before she started the cycle again.

"I never should have given you a chance, Jeremy. I knew Paddy wanted me to come out here, and I should have turned you down flat the moment you first asked me out. What a waste this has been." Then she burst into tears, put her face in her hands, and whined. "What a waste! A total waste." Moments later, she produced an emery board from her purse and perfected her nails, until she resumed her carping. "A schoolteacher! What *ever* made me think I'd be happy with a schoolteacher?"

Through it all Jeremy attempted to distract himself by calculating his gas mileage for the trip. He knew otherwise he'd allow Eve to engage him during one of her taunts, and the bottom line was that none of her comments mattered now. What mattered was that he had blown a good deal of his savings trying to make this a special trip for a woman who didn't deserve his efforts. What mattered was that plenty of people loved and respected him, even if none of them was *in* love with him. What mattered was that he was getting what looked to be 25 miles to the gallon, which wasn't nearly as good as he got with his Mini Cooper stick shift. Good to know. He had done well in buying that Cooper.

Moments later, both sighed with relief when Paddy's place came into view.

Thirty-six

All Tiff could think of was getting away. Away from Jeremy. And especially away from Eve.

Had she ever been so mean-spirited as Eve?

But then she was flooded with memories of the woman she used to be. Not the least of which was the time she had tried to break up a man's family. That alone put her in Eve's league—if not worse.

And if that memory weren't painful enough, perhaps worse was the knowledge that Jeremy had thought negatively enough about her that he shared his opinion with Eve.

Tiff knew he must have made his comment early on. She and Jeremy seemed to be getting along fairly well now. Still, how could she look him in the eye when she knew he had talked about her that way? And with how many people? Had he said that to Vera and Sean too? To Julian? Ren? Kara? Had they discussed her behind her back?

The depression that descended upon Tiff dragged down everything about her. Even her face felt drawn. Her tears threatened to turn into sobs. She ran straight toward the water and plunged in, shorts and all.

The cold shocked her, as she had hoped it might. But not enough to dull the pain. After only a few moments she waded out of the water and lost her footing as a wave hit her from behind. She unceremoniously plopped on all fours in the gritty sand of the shore. She stood in a stagger, trying to brush away pebbles and broken pieces of shell from her skin. Her knees stung where she had cut them. And on top of everything, she lost her favorite scrunchie.

She shivered and headed back toward the house, her arms wrapped around herself. She hadn't walked far before she regretted wearing her denim shorts that morning. The stiff, wet fabric began to rub against her inner thighs, and in no time she grimaced with each step.

At least her tears were less obvious, since water continued to drip down her face from her tangled wet hair. She reached up to wipe her eyes, and her hands revealed that her mascara had enthusiastically dripped all over her cheeks.

She mumbled to herself. "Waterproof, my foot." She wiped her hands on her shorts and continued to hobble forth, legs stiff, knees bleeding, her entire body shaking.

And then, as if she were an angel, Vera appeared.

"You poor lamb!" She enveloped Tiff in her jacket and put her arm around Tiff's shoulders. "What happened? You look like you nearly drowned. Did someone attack you, dear?"

Tiff couldn't help but laugh, even as her teeth chattered. "Nope. I managed to do this all by myself."

Vera obviously worked to keep a straight face, but a laugh worked its way loose. "Oh, I'm sorry, Tiff. I shouldn't laugh. Don't make me laugh. It's just that your mascara…"

"Vera, I'm such a mess. You were right. I shouldn't have let Eve hurt me like that. But, honestly, right now my thighs hurt more than my feelings, I think."

Vera loosened her grip on Tiff's shoulders. "Your *thighs?*"

Tiff waved her hand. "I just need to get out of these jean shorts. It was just the timing, I guess, of what Eve said. I didn't expect her to make an issue of Jeremy and me at that moment. I was caught off guard."

"You were innocent," Vera said firmly.

"I…I was? But, Vera, you only heard her accuse Jeremy of calling me nasty. Did you know she also accused me of running after him?"

"It doesn't surprise me," Vera said. "I've seen my share of Eves. She's sharp and observant, as many women are. But she puts a demeaning twist on what she sees, when it suits her fancy. She sees a kind, beautiful, single woman who gets along just fine with Jeremy. She's well aware she's destroyed her own relationship with him. She knows the possibilities, whether you and Jeremy pursue them or not. Eve reminds me of a schoolyard bully who's been banned from the playground for his behavior. Just before he leaves, he gives a swift kick to the child least expecting it, hoping to retain some of the power he's just lost."

As they neared the beach house, Orville and Sean approached them. "Good golly, kitten, what happened to you?" Tiff's father asked.

Tiff hoped to stave off detailed explanations. "I took an impromptu swim, Daddy. Just a stupid stunt."

Sean pointed to her still-bloody knees. "Are the piranhas out this early in the morning, then?"

Tiff chuckled. "I fell."

Orville still looked concerned. "What can I do for you? Want me to come in and help you clean up those cuts? We came out here to look for Jeremy and thought maybe you two found him. Then we thought you might have taken your morning walk without us."

"Nope." Tiff stood still, the skin on her thighs burning. "I think I might bag the walk this morning, Daddy."

"I should say so," Orville said. "Come on, let me help you."

"Actually, I can clean up on my own, Daddy. But…do you think you'd be able to carry me the rest of the way?"

Orville put his hands on his ample waist. "Do I think I can carry you? Honey, I've been a volunteer firefighter for years. I've carried a few women in my day."

He scooped her up easily, but she heard him grunt as he straightened.

"Are you sure, Daddy? It's harder when you're walking on sand."

"Nonsense." He walked unsteadily over the sand and they both started to laugh when he staggered sideways and nearly dropped her.

Sean lifted Tiff's feet in the air until Orville could right himself. "All those breakfast burritos might be taking their toll, mates. I think the Missus and I may just go ahead and take that walk without you."

Orville grunted his words out. "It's a plan."

Tiff looked over her dad's shoulders and waved to Vera. "Thanks, Vera. Thanks for everything."

Orville set Tiff down at the patio door. "There we go. You going to be all right, hon?"

She nodded. "Yes. *After* I shower and change into dry clothes."

As Orville turned to go, Tiff reached up and gave her dad a kiss. "Thanks, Daddy."

"Sure, hon. I'll check in with you later."

As soon as her father left, Tiff waddled like a toy soldier back to her room. She peeled off her wet shorts before she noticed a note on her bed.

It was obviously written in haste. Either that or Eve had appalling handwriting.

> Tiff,
>
> Just wanted to take a minute to apologize. I've been unkind and unfair to you. It's not about you. It's about me and Jeremy. I messed up really bad, and I took it out on you. After you left, I told him I was harsh with you because I feared he was interested in you. He assured me you were nothing but friends and had no romantic chemistry whatsoever. I'm sorry I suspected you.
>
> Jeremy and I have gone for a drive to try to patch things up. He says he wants to forgive me and try to make this work. I think we can. Maybe I'll see you again, here or in Virginia. We'll keep in touch.
>
> Eve

Tiff sat on the bed and read the note again. She tried to remember how Jeremy acted toward Eve when he and Vera walked in earlier. He seemed surprised to see her, but he wasn't unpleasant toward her.

She read the note a third time. There was no way. Jeremy wasn't brainless. He was certain about breaking off with Eve.

Still. Would Eve actually write a note like this, just to mess with Tiff's emotions? There was something about that woman—even about reading this note from her—that made Tiff want to shower for an especially long time.

Thirty-seven

When Jeremy and Eve arrived at Paddy's house, Jeremy opened the trunk to get out her bag. By the time he had closed the trunk, Eve had already stormed into Paddy's house.

"I've a good mind to leave this blasted bag here for whomever happens by," he muttered.

Instead, he decided to bring the bag to the front porch and leave it.

Just then the front door opened and Paddy came out. Jeremy's heart suddenly raced as he considered how satisfying it would feel to give Paddy a punch in the eye.

But Paddy walked toward him with his hands up, palms forward. Jeremy saw it as a gesture of peace.

"Look, Jeremy, I'm sorry for being such a jerk."

"That makes two of us," Jeremy said. "I'm sorry you're a jerk, too. But we all make our choices."

Paddy grimaced. "Yeah, see, that's just the thing. I really regret the one I made." He crooked his thumb over his shoulder, toward the house. "Especially now. She's gone ballistic on me. I don't remember her being like that when we were in college together."

Jeremy set Eve's luggage down. "She's your problem now."

Paddy took one step closer. "Problem. You said it."

Jeremy turned to go.

"But—" Paddy scratched the back of his neck. "I don't suppose she could stay at that beach house the rest of the week? You *did* pay the rental on it, and those yokels have been kind of freeloading the whole time they've been there—"

Jeremy turned, his face burning with anger. "You haven't the first notion of what a yokel is. How you can look down your suspiciously perfect nose at anyone after the way you've behaved is completely beyond me."

"Fine, fine—"

"And as for freeloading, not only did Eve freeload—allowing me to rent a place she merely flitted through when you were otherwise occupied—*you've* performed the ultimate in freeloading by how you treated my girlfriend. And now that you've wised up, you want to pawn her off on me."

"Lighten up." Paddy tilted his head and seemed intent on drawing Jeremy in as a fellow cad. "I was just having fun. I never promised Eve anything after this trip. And I didn't mean to insult that other girl—Tiff, was it? I don't really think of her as a yokel." He grinned conspiratorially. "I really meant it when I said I'd like to take her out."

Jeremy stepped closer to Paddy. "She's too smart for you. And far too good. You've hurt enough people, and clearly you're about to hurt Eve as well. But I'll tell you right now. You take one step toward Tiff, and I *will* pound the stuffing out of you."

Paddy put his hands back up in mock surrender. "Okay, okay, I get it. Hands off Tiff."

Jeremy said nothing more and hoped Paddy wouldn't make any further insinuations. He had tried to keep his fists unclenched through their exchange. He turned to go and caught his foot on the sidewalk. He broke his fall by smacking his eye against the side-view mirror of his rental car.

Paddy swore, then grabbed at him.

Jeremy thought Paddy was about to take advantage of the situation and give him a belt in the other eye. He tensed in anticipation of a knockdown brawl.

But Paddy only helped him to his feet. "Man, sorry, dude." He pointed to Jeremy's eye. "That's going to be a total shiner. You want to come in and get a bag of ice?"

Jeremy dusted his hands against his pants. "No. I've got to get back."

As he drove off, he looked at himself in the rearview mirror. Now he looked like a hothead. And a poor fighter.

Thirty-eight

Halfway through her shower Tiff realized she hadn't prayed all day, save the short, private plea she made for Jeremy when she and Orville had breakfast. No wonder she was wound up, trying to figure this out on her own. Her mind quickly reached out to God in prayer.

Lord, on a logical level I know everything is in Your hands here. I know Jeremy's welfare is even more Your concern than mine. I know You can handle Eve, whether she's lying or not. And I know You love me and want the best for me. But on an emotional level, I'm really spazzing here. Help me not to worry or be stupid with my emotions. Please help me to trust that You'll work everything out just fine. And please help me to accept whatever Your plan is.

She stood under the warm water and imagined God's blessings flowing over her. Then, as she emerged from the shower far more relaxed, her cell phone rang, and she recognized the number. Ren!

"Wow, Ren, are you ever the answer to prayer!"

Ren laughed. "Hello to you, too. That's a nice way to answer the phone."

"What made you call?" Tiff asked, knowing full well her call was God's answer to her prayer.

"I don't know. You just came to mind, and I realized I hadn't talked to either you or Jeremy since he left. Did he surprise Eve? Did his folks find him?"

Tiff sat on the bed and sighed. "Oh, honey, you won't believe what's been going on here. I can't believe it's only been two days since Jeremy arrived."

She filled Ren in on everything that had happened since Jeremy first knocked at the beach house door Saturday afternoon.

"And then I came in to find this message from Eve."

As soon as Tiff finished reading the note to Ren, Ren hooted. "She is amazing!"

"How do you mean?"

"I mean, I think Eve might be short for Evil. That chick is sick."

"So I'm not paranoid to suspect another lie with this note?"

"Tiff, if you believed that note, I'd worry that the old Tiff was just too far removed for her own good. You have to hang on to at least a healthy amount of suspicion. I mean, in this case, we're talking simple discernment. And God's blessed you with that—you're absolutely right in discounting that note. Poor Jeremy. What a nightmare she turned out to be."

"That's what you were afraid of, isn't it? That's what you said when we talked at Ledo's that night."

"You got it. How is he doing? He was pretty worried when he left here."

Tiff laid back on the bed, her wet hair pressed against her head. "I only saw him for half a minute this morning. I don't know where he is right now."

"And how about the new stepmom, Vera? Does Jeremy like her?"

"I know *I* like her. But I think Jeremy was a little put off by the fact that they got married and didn't even tell him they were dating."

"Yeah. That's weird. Pretty inconsiderate, actually. Why did they do it that way?"

"We don't know yet. They're kind of secretive about their relationship."

Ren sighed. "You have to give Jeremy a hug for me. It sounds like this trip is running him ragged."

Tiff didn't respond.

"Tiff?"

"Yeah?

"What haven't you told me yet? And don't waste my cell phone minutes acting like nothing's bothering you."

"I should wait until I talk with Jeremy, I guess. But at one point today, Eve announced that Jeremy had told her I was nasty. And Jeremy didn't deny it. He looked embarrassed, but he didn't deny it. I haven't talked with him since then. I mean, we haven't seen each other."

Ren didn't respond right away. Tiff actually thought the connection might have been dropped. "Ren, are you there?"

"Yeah, sorry. I was just thinking about a couple of nice things he said about you to me, right before he left."

Tiff's heart lightened at once.

Ren continued. "So, think about how he's acted toward you since he's been there. Has he acted like he'd rather not share your company?"

"No. To tell you the truth, we've been completely comfortable around each other."

"Okay, then Eve's either lying or distorting something Jeremy said. He probably said you *used* to be nasty."

Tiff gasped. "But that's awful too." She felt like Ren had just stabbed her with a small but sharp dagger, to say such a thing so blithely.

"I'm sorry, Tiff. I didn't mean...hey, listen. Before I decided to honor Christ with my lifestyle, anyone who knew me would have said I was materialistic. And obsessive about money and partying. Even cutthroat in the business world. But when people from my old lifestyle meet me now, I can tell they see a difference. Don't you think Jeremy might see a change in you?"

"I guess. It just hurts to think he told her that."

"So talk with him about it. Give him a chance to explain. Whatever you do, don't take Eve at face value. She has too many faces for you to do that."

"Okay. Thanks." She noticed she was starting to get shaky. "Oh, Ren, I haven't eaten enough today. I have to fix something or I'm going to get sick. I can tell my blood sugar's getting too low."

"Go, go. And once you're comfortable enough to do it, give Jeremy that hug from me."

"Okay," Tiff said. "I'll try to get that comfortable."

Ren laughed. "Fine. Just remember. He's a great guy and usually very open to talking. He's almost like a woman in that regard. That's why he and Kara and I are so close."

Tiff got off the phone and chuckled. She flushed when she thought about that original exchange with Jeremy on the shuttle bus. Almost like a woman, huh? Not the Jeremy *she* knew.

Thirty-nine

For hours Jeremy tried literally to drive off his frustration. He deliberately lost himself in the city. He passed signs for a number of attractions and events he would have loved to attend, had he and Eve been together. The drive simply accentuated the fact that he *was* alone again. Every hand-holding couple on the street kept him painfully aware of his unwelcome return to singlehood.

And speaking of pain, his eye throbbed as if he carried his battered heart right there on his face, where it pulsed in agony for all to see. Each time he checked himself in the rearview mirror, his eye had turned a deeper color and a larger size. He sported a sharp purple line diagonally across the wound, apparently where he hit the edge of the mirror. After he drove for a while, he realized his knees were torn up from his fall as well.

He thought about what awaited him when he returned to Julian's. He had clearly crushed Tiff with his careless chatter to Eve. No doubt her father would now be less than fond of him.

Yes, indeed. He was the king of self-pity when he walked into the apartment at Julian's. With relief he saw that his father and Vera had gone out. They had left a note on the coffee table for him, suggesting that he might "need some space." That must have come from Vera. His dad never said things like that. Also apparent from the note was that he had missed lunch. And it appeared Sean and Vera might not make it back before dinner, since they left word he should meet them at the Turquoise Café if he was up to it.

Just as well. Better not be around anyone until he could pull his attitude out of the gutter.

He made some toast and tea, ate with little awareness, and headed for the bathroom to repair whatever body parts he could.

Then he heard Vera and Sean come in. *Blast.*

"Ah, thank heavens you're back, lad." Sean came up behind Jeremy, who was bent over to wipe the blood from his knees.

"Hi, Dad." He turned to look at his father. "I thought you two weren't—"

"Son, what happened?" Sean stepped back to get a better look at his son's colorful eye. Vera was quickly at his side.

"Oh, Jeremy!" She held her hand out and clearly wanted to nurse his wound. "Did that blighter of Eve's do that—"

Jeremy turned back to the mirror. "No, no. Paddy and I didn't fight. I just fell."

"Now son, don't hold back the truth. If he got in a good one, there's no shame—"

"Dad, I'm telling you. I fell against the mirror on my car, that's all." He turned to look at them again. Vera's grimace confirmed he looked as bad as he thought he did.

Sean was insistent. "Because he hit you, eh? That's why you fell? Tell the truth, now."

Jeremy lost patience. "No, Dad. Why are you so sure I'm holding back information? That's *your* thing, not mine."

Immediately Jeremy regretted his choice of words. Both Sean and Vera looked shocked.

"I'm sorry. That was uncalled for." His shoulders slumped. "Look, I slept horribly last night, and I've been driving for hours. I'm utterly chinstrapped."

"Of course you are." Vera played the diplomat. "You just need a bit of a kip, dear. We'll let you rest."

Sean nodded and patted Jeremy once on the shoulder. "Yeah. That's all right, lad. You get some rest. Sleep in the bed, not the couch, eh? We'll bring you something home to eat, how's that?"

Jeremy would have preferred a rock to crawl under. "Right, Dad. Ta. I'm sorry."

"Not at all, son. Not at all."

After they closed the door behind themselves, he heard them talking softly before they left. He was unable to keep from eavesdropping.

"Of course he's miffed, Vera. That Paddy bloke has off with his girl, we show up unannounced, married—"

His father was actually being understanding. Now Jeremy's self-pity took on a self-loathing aspect. He lay back on the bed and welcomed the drowsy fog that descended faster than any further thought was able.

A tinny version of the "William Tell Overture" brought him back to awareness. He frowned as he realized his cell phone was ringing. He brought his hand up to his eye, which felt like a pillow full of pain.

He rolled off the bed and wandered around trying to remember where he had left his phone. The ringing, which had now stopped, had come from outside the bedroom. He scanned the living room to no avail, but when his phone alerted him to a message, he was able to follow the beep to the potted plant just inside the doorway. Of course. Why wouldn't he have dropped his phone into the potted plant upon arriving home? Doesn't everyone?

Ah, good. It was Ren. He could use a chat with someone whom he hadn't managed to offend yet today. He hit her number.

"Ah, so you do have your phone with you!" Her voice was a breath of fresh air.

"Actually, I had it in the potted plant. How are you, Rennie?"

"Huge, as always. But I don't want to talk about me. I called Tiff earlier today, and I wanted to find out how *you* are. I'm so sorry about Eve."

"Yeah." He gingerly touched his eye. "I'm glad that you and Sandy thought I should come out here. Otherwise I might never have found out what she was up to."

"Tiff's arrival was a big help in outing her, too, I guess," Ren said. "If she hadn't accidentally gone out there while Eve was there, no one from Virginia would have been any wiser, you know?"

"And now I've managed to hurt Tiff, on top of everything else."

"What do you mean, on top of everything else? Sounds to me like everything was done *to* you, not by you."

"That's my girl," he said. "Take my side all the way."

"No, really. Tell me. All I know so far is you said Tiff was wicked."

He moaned. "Nasty."

"Right. But, don't worry, you two can patch that up easily. I talked with Tiff about it."

"Thanks, love. You're the best." He looked at his knees. They had stopped bleeding. "Is it too late to put ice on a black eye..." He looked at his watch. "Four hours later?"

Ren gasped. "Tiff *hit* you? But she didn't seem all *that* mad—"

"No, Tiff didn't hit me. It was my car."

"She hit your car?"

He laughed. "Tiff didn't hit anything or anyone, as far as I'm aware. I fell and slammed my eye against my car's sideview mirror."

"Poor baby. I think it's too late, yeah, for cold compresses. You have to do it right away. Takes a couple of weeks for the bruising to go away, I think. That's going to cause quite a stir with your third graders. You can bring your eye for Show and Tell."

"Just doing my part to further Virginia's educational process." He noticed he was hungry. Talking to Ren was good for him. He walked into the kitchen and scrounged around while they talked.

She continued. "Okay, so tell me what else you did."

"Well, I snapped at my dad about getting married without telling me."

"Aw, Jeremy. I know how much you love him. So you're feeling all guilty about that, huh?"

"Mmm." He found some cold calamari in the fridge and ate it straight from the Styrofoam container.

"Did he explain himself to you at least?"

"No. They went out to dinner alone. I mean...that wasn't meant to sound as pitiful as it did. They came to get me for dinner. I snapped at them and scared them away so I could take a nap."

Ren laughed. "You sound like an eighty-year-old man."

"That's about how I feel right now."

"Is that all? You spoke about Tiff, you snapped at your dad?"

"I made a fool of myself in front of Eve's...boyfriend."

"I can't imagine your doing anything worse than what that jerk did to you."

"No, I didn't say I was a jerk. I was a fool. He made a fool of me, and then I put a cherry on top."

"I doubt it, but let me hear it."

"I spoke quite forcefully to him and turned to make a stunning exit. Then I tripped and executed a lovely pirouette, smashing my face on the aforementioned mirror. I landed on my hands and knees, which required Paddy to lift me like a child—or like an eighty-year-old man—from the concrete. Before I realized he was helping me, I thought he was about to pound me. It's all a bit of a blur, but I may have emitted a Bruce Lee scream and attempted to kick him like a little girl."

Ren failed to stifle a laugh. "Okay, maybe you put a cherry on top, just a little. But it doesn't matter. You'll never see that creep again."

"I *hope* not." He found a bag of baby carrots in the vegetable bin. They appeared fresh enough to eat, so he set them on the counter and munched away.

"So, you told him off about Eve?"

He shrugged. "A little. Sorry, I'm eating. I sounded off at him more about Tiff, actually."

"About Tiff? What's up with that?"

"He's already tired of Eve. He thought he might take a shot at Tiff."

"Yeesh. He just gets better and better. But I don't think Tiff would give him the time of day now."

"No. I don't either."

"Did she tell you about Eve's note?"

He stood upright at that. "Note?"

"I swear, Jeremy, Eve's like one of those super viruses. Just when you think you've found a cure, she mutates into something even worse!"

"Tiff and I haven't talked since she ran out of the beach house this morning. Was the note since then?"

"Yep. It was waiting for her when she came back, apparently."

Ah. So that's what Eve went back to do, right before he drove her to Paddy's. "Oh, great. What did it say?"

"It was some sort of fake apology and said you wanted to get back together with Eve."

"Tiff didn't believe it?"

"Not by the time we finished talking. Oh, and the note also said you told Eve there was no romantic chemistry between you and Tiff."

"Blast!"

Ren said nothing. She seemed quite deliberate in saying nothing.

He needed to say something. "Where does Eve come up with these ideas?"

"Hmm. I don't know, Jeremy." He could hear her smiling.

"Ren, I, uh, I've got to get something to eat." He walked to the door, as if he could escape Ren's scrutiny by leaving. "It's getting late, and there's nothing but rabbit food in here."

"Okay, Popeye. You take care of yourself. Will you stay the rest of the week?"

"I suppose. The rest of the week can only be an improvement, unless we have an earthquake or something."

"I'll pray against that. Say hi to Tiff for me." She was smiling again.

"Righto. Ta, Ren."

He turned off his phone and dropped it back into the potted plant before he stepped out. The door shut behind him before he realized he had left his key inside. Now he was locked out until Sean and Vera returned. And Julian's lights were out.

On second thought, an earthquake might just be an improvement.

Forty

Jeremy walked out onto the boardwalk and glanced over at the beach house. There were a few lights on, but he just didn't have it in him to socialize right now.

Instead, he stopped at a hot-dog stand and ordered a couple of dogs, some chips, and a soda. He took a seat on the seawall and tried to relax. People passed behind him, and he listened to their random conversations. It was a pleasant diversion and gave him perspective about his small place in the world.

At one point he was sure he noticed a familiar voice. He looked over his shoulder and locked eyes with Zeke, the bloke he met his first night there.

Zeke's face glowed with pleasure, as he recognized Jeremy. He pointed in his direction. "I know you, brother! Was it Jeremy?"

Jeremy nodded. "You've a good memory for names, Zeke."

"I don't always remember names, to be truthful," Zeke said as he joined Jeremy. "But yours stuck with me for some reason." He pointed to Jeremy's eye. "Ouch. How did you get that shiner?"

"I got clumsy. Tripped over my own feet and got up close and personal with my car's sideview mirror."

Zeke grimaced. "So sorry. But at least it was an accident, right? Nobody hurt you."

That last was said more as a statement than a question, and Jeremy chose to treat it as such. He reached into his bag of food. "Hot dog?"

"No, thanks," Zeke said. "I've had my dinner."

"Do you live near here, Zeke?"

"No, brother. I live in East County. That's a ways from here."

Curious fellow. "So you simply like the beach?"

"I simply like people!"

"You don't have people in East County?" Jeremy asked around a bite of hot dog.

"This beach is where the Lord seems to draw me," Zeke said. "I come across so many different people here, and I just wait to see who the Lord wants me to minister to."

Jeremy wiped his mouth with a napkin. "Are you ministering to me?"

Zeke regarded him for a moment. "Do you need ministering?"

He looked toward the ocean. "I need *something*."

"We all do, brother." Zeke nodded as if he listened to music no one else could hear. "Things got worse for you since I met you the other night, maybe?"

Jeremy gave a sardonic laugh. "You might say that."

Neither spoke for awhile. Jeremy appreciated that Zeke didn't need details. He was sick of the details.

Zeke looked at the waves. "You have a number of friends who are believers, right?"

"Believers?"

"Right, *believers.* You have friends who follow Christ, I think."

"How can you tell?"

"You understand everything I say. You've heard it before." Zeke touched his temple. "Up here you understand."

Jeremy shrugged. "Kind of. You put things a little differently than my friends do. But yeah." He tapped his own temple. "I understand."

Zeke simply looked out at the waves, stretched his arms outward, and breathed in deeply. When he exhaled, he gently brought his hands to his chest, just for a moment, before he reached out to shake Jeremy's hand. "Jeremy, it's been a pleasure. I'm going to see you again soon."

"I've enjoyed it too," Jeremy said. When Zeke was out of sight, he looked back out at the waves. He remembered what Zeke said the other night. About the waves. And about God and His consistency when you had Him in your heart.

An awareness slowly dawned on Jeremy. Zeke said he could tell Jeremy understood what Ren and Kara believed. He had pointed to his head when he said that. But he had wanted Jeremy to consider his heart.

Well, he had a good heart, comparatively speaking. When he thought about people like Paddy and Eve, he was certain he had higher morals than they did.

Jeremy had never been much for praying. But he supposed he did believe in God. You'd have to be daft to think life and nature just fell into place without God running the show. So slowly he began...

So, God, if I spoke to You, would You have time to listen, eh? I truly am sick of the details, You know. I don't suppose You have time to do anything about the details—my piddly issues in life. But I wouldn't mind a nudge. You know, something to show me You hear me. And to help with whatever Zeke's talking about with regard to the heart. Eh, yours very truly—

"Jeremy!"

Jeremy jumped out of his prayer to see Julian approaching. "Julian! Perfect timing." He stood up from the wall and dusted the sand off of his shorts. "You know, I locked myself out of—"

He stopped. He stood still and heard nothing but the waves. Was Julian's arrival a coincidence or the nudge he requested? His arms broke out in goose bumps.

Julian breached the moment. "You're locked out of the apartment? That *is* perfect timing. I'll let you in. Are you ready?"

Jeremy nodded. Yes, maybe "ready" was exactly what he was.

Forty-one

Later that night Tiff repositioned herself in bed, again, and waited for sleep. Her mind buzzed. She tried to shut down her thoughts, to see nothing behind her eyelids. But it was like a movie screen back there. No matter how black she tried to imagine the night, before she knew it, events kept rehashing themselves before her.

Finally, when it was obvious sleep would continue to elude her, she felt twitchy enough to surrender to alertness and get out of bed. She wrapped her flannel robe around herself and sighed.

Warm milk. Maybe that would do it. She walked to the kitchen and could hear her father snoring in his room. She pulled his door closed so she wouldn't wake him.

The fire her dad had built earlier had been a nice touch. The beach got brisk in the evening, just like the East Coast beaches did. Still, soon as her warm milk was ready, Tiff grabbed one of Faith Fontaine's many afghans off the sofa and went outside to sit on the patio for a while.

She quietly shut the door behind her and curled up in one of the chairs at the wrought-iron table. The night was gorgeous and still, and the rhythmic waves provided a natural lullaby. Tiff knew she was in no danger of dozing off out here, though. She'd have to be more exhausted than she'd ever been to fall asleep out in the open like this.

She sipped her milk and looked upward. The moon wasn't terribly bright, so the sky was black enough that Tiff started to see more and more stars as her eyes acclimated to the dark. She liked knowing the stars were out there, even though she hadn't seen them without staring incessantly at the sky. They were like God and His blessings and guidance. Ren had called it discernment.

So the more I focus on You and watch for Your blessings and guidance, the more discernment I'll get, is that it? I like that.

The murmur of quiet voices interrupted her thoughts. She recognized the British accents.

It was Jeremy. And Vera.

She got up to investigate. She looked around to the side of the house and saw them outside. They both seemed agitated, even while they spoke in subdued voices. Tiff didn't know whether or not she should make her presence known. But when she stepped back, she bumped into one of the chairs, which jolted on the flagstone. The noise was enough that both Jeremy and Vera looked over at her.

Well, she certainly wasn't going to sneak away now. She wrapped the afghan more securely around herself and walked over.

Jeremy spoke first, in a quiet voice. "I'm so sorry we woke you."

"No, I was wide awake," Tiff said, a little embarrassed. "I was sitting on the patio with a cup of warm milk, trying to get sleepy." Her eyes were so used to the dark by this point that she could see Jeremy's injured eye once he got close enough.

"Oh, Jeremy, what happened?"

"It's my dad."

"No, I mean, your eye." Then she gasped and looked at Vera, who had been crying. "What's happened to Sean? Where is he?" She looked back at Jeremy's eye. "Were you guys mugged or something?"

Vera wiped her eyes with a handkerchief. "No, dear, it's not as bad as that, thank God."

"I hurt my eye earlier," Jeremy said. "That's not important. But my dad…" He looked at Vera, as if he needed her permission to speak further.

"He's out there somewhere." Vera opened her hand toward the expanse of boardwalk. "I expected him home by now. I was about to go looking for him."

Tiff looked puzzled. "But, didn't he go with you to dinner?"

Vera looked down the beach, straining. "Yes. We had an argument, and I came back without him. I thought he'd be back shortly after me, but it's three o'clock in the morning and still no sign of him."

"I'm going to find him." Jeremy started toward his car and spoke to Vera over his shoulder. "You wait here, in case he returns."

She nodded.

"Jeremy, wait." Tiff caught up to him. "Give me a second to put on my jeans, and I'll come with you."

He thought for a second, and then said, "That's nice of you, Tiff, but you don't have to do that. You should go back to bed."

"Nothing doing!" she said. "I already have insomnia. That's why I was up. You think I'm going to be able to fall asleep now?"

Jeremy looked at her, clearly debating.

She put on her pleading face. "I want to."

He nodded. "All right. But hurry."

She turned and ran back to the beach house. She would need to leave a note so Orville wouldn't worry if he awoke.

Just before she opened the beach house door, she heard Vera tell Jeremy, "You'd best look for him in the local bars."

Forty-two

"We're almost to the Turquoise Café, where they had dinner," Jeremy said as he navigated the streets. "I figure we go that far, then we'll work our way back in the direction of the beach house."

"What if he went in the other direction?" Tiff said. "I mean, I hate to be a pessimist—"

"Yes, he could have gone in the other direction. He might have gone deeper into the city too. But we have to start somewhere. And I think most of the bars are closed by now. He could be on his way home already. Vera took the car back, so he'd have to walk."

"Unless he got a ride. Or a cab."

Jeremy shifted slightly in his seat. "Listen, about what Eve said this morning—" He glanced at his watch, although it was too dark to read it. "Or, rather yesterday morning. I want to explain, but no matter how I phrase it, it's still going to sound bad."

She turned in her seat to face him better. "Give it a try."

"Well, you see," Jeremy began, weighing his words. "You see, Eve mentioned you in a negative light shortly after she met you—"

Tiff expelled a breathy grunt of indignation. "I was the picture of nicey nice when I met that girl—"

Jeremy held up his hand. "Don't you think, this far along, we should consider the source? Eve hasn't panned out all that well in the nicey-nice realm."

Tiff folded her arms across her chest. "So you just jumped on her mean little bandwagon and said, 'Yeah, that's one nasty chick'?"

"Not at all," Jeremy countered. "On the contrary, I said you seemed to have changed quite a bit from the woman I met at the gym, with Kara. I said you were no longer that woman."

"That *nasty* woman."

He cringed. "You know, I believe I've heard that word enough to last a lifetime. I will never utter that word again. The bottom line is I'm sorry, Tiff."

"Okay. Apology accepted." She zipped her sweatshirt jacket closed. "So are you ever going to tell me what happened with your eye? Does it have anything to do with Paddy?"

"He was only a bystander," Jeremy said. "I did this all by myself."

"Oh, that's funny!" Tiff laughed. "That's exactly what I said to Vera yesterday when she found me all bedraggled on the beach. I fell and tore up my knees—"

"I tore up *my* knees too!" Jeremy said.

"We're sure a couple of klutzes, huh?" Tiff smiled.

"I think we established that at Ledo's a few weeks ago, eh?"

"Ugh. Don't remind me!"

Jeremy's eyes were casing the sidewalks as they approached the Turquoise. "This is the block Vera gave for the café," he said. "Let's take one block at a time."

"Looks like most of the bars are closed."

"Yeah. I suppose there's not much point in getting out of the car. Let's just circle each block and keep our eyes open."

In this way they slowly worked their way back toward the beach house. They passed the occasional drunken straggler, but Sean wasn't among them. Jeremy shuddered to think of his father in that kind of condition.

"There!" Tiff grabbed Jeremy's arm. "Is that him?"

Jeremy followed her gaze. Sean stood under a streetlight with two other men. The scene didn't look sinister. But it looked unsteady, to say the least.

Jeremy pulled the car up, and he and Tiff got out.

Sean laughed at something one of the men said before he caught sight of Jeremy. He opened his arms wide and spoke too loudly. "Jeremy, my son!"

"Hey, Da. Time to go home now."

"So soon? The night is young."

Sean turned to Tiff and gave her a big, goofy smile. "Ah, lads, this beauty is me boy's sweetheart…uh, what was your name again, love?"

Tiff gave him a confident smile. "I'm Tiff, Sean. I'm Jeremy's *friend*. Come on, let's go home. Vera's worried about you."

The two other men mumbled something to Jeremy and Tiff and then headed down the street.

Jeremy and Tiff stood on either side of Sean and put his arms across their shoulders. Jeremy bore the bulk of Sean's awkward weight, as they guided him to the car. When he entered, he bumped his head against the door frame and flopped onto the back seat. He seemed unaware of the thump.

They drove back toward the beach house in silence for a while—except for Sean's light snoring.

Jeremy tried to say something to Tiff, but what could he say? That he had seen his dad like this before? Once again, the old feelings from his past returned. Embarrassment, anger, helplessness.

"He was like this sometimes when I lived at home," Jeremy finally said. "I don't know how often it happens now."

Tiff glanced at Sean in the backseat. "Well, this is the only time it's happened since they got here, isn't it?"

"Yes. And Vera seems pretty shaken up, so my guess is she doesn't tolerate his drinking."

Sean awoke when they arrived at Julian's house, and Jeremy helped him out of the car. Side by side, the three of them were too broad to fit up the steps, so Jeremy carried most of Sean's weight. Vera awaited them at the door.

As they entered, she pointed to the bedroom. "Do you think you could help him to the bed?" She turned toward the kitchen. "I'm going to fix some tea."

Tiff slipped into her previous position, to support Sean's right side, his arm across her shoulders. They got as far as the couch before Sean slinked away from them and flopped face first onto the cushions.

"No, Dad, that's where I sleep." Jeremy managed to turn him face up.

Tiff looked at Jeremy. "You want to just leave him here?"

"No, we can't. I can't exactly share the bedroom with Vera."

"Oh, mercy." Tiff put her hands on her hips. "See, this is why Daddy and I should have stayed here. There are plenty of beds over there. You want to just stay at the beach house tonight?"

He hesitated. "I know this sounds old-fashioned, Tiff, but if it were just your dad, that would be fine."

She blushed. "Oh. Right. Okay then, let's move him before he becomes one with this sofa."

Jeremy pointed at Sean's feet. "You take his legs. I'll get the shoulders."

They grasped their respective parts of Sean.

Jeremy said, "At the count of one, two, three."

They worked as one, but to no avail.

"I'm losing him!" Tiff grabbed more furiously at Sean, and his right foot pressed her hair up and over her face. She started laughing, and Jeremy couldn't help laughing with her.

"Hey." She blew her hair out of her face. "Where are his shoes?"

Jeremy looked at Sean's stockinged feet. "Did he have shoes on when we put him in the car?"

"I don't know, but we'd better progress here, or I'm going to lose him again."

They shuffled toward the bedroom, not without the occasional bump of Sean against a piece of furniture.

Jeremy tried to guide her. "Watch. Bookshelf on the starboard bow."

"Which is starboard?"

"Right."

"My right or your—"

And Sean's rear end swung against the bookshelf.

"Whoops, sorry," Tiff whispered to Jeremy. "I'm not much of a sailor."

As they reached Sean's bed, he broke into a mumbled version of a drinking song Jeremy remembered vaguely from the past. When they dropped him onto the bed he accentuated the moment by emitting a sound, presumably a belch.

Jeremy rolled his eyes at Tiff, who was trying unsuccessfully not to laugh.

They were nearly out of the bedroom when Sean burst out in song again. Something about a musical frog. Tiff laughed aloud and threw her hand over her mouth. Jeremy did the same thing to her, a twinkle in his eye. Then he quickly removed his hand. "I'm sorry. I shouldn't have done that."

"It's okay. I shouldn't be laughing."

They stood there for a moment, just outside Sean's room, and simply smiled into each other's eyes. At once Jeremy was aware that he wanted very much to kiss her.

Just as he moved closer, Vera approached. "Oh, I'm so sorry," she said, flustered.

"No!" Tiff's face was flushed. "Don't be. I was just leaving."

Vera put her hand on Tiff's arm. "Maybe you could stay a bit longer? I know it's terribly late. But there's something I need to tell Jeremy, and maybe he'd like you here, as well."

Jeremy nodded. "Please stay."

Forty-three

"I thought you might be hungry," Vera said as she set out tea and cookies on the small Formica table in the kitchen.

Jeremy and Tiff sat down opposite one another. Vera silently poured tea, and then she sat between them and briefly touched their hands with hers.

"Jeremy, I'm going to talk to you and Tiff without your father's permission, and for that I apologize. But I know why he's remained silent, and frankly, it's nonsense and rubbish."

Jeremy nodded.

"Now, when we first arrived here Sunday, your father was utterly chuffed, you know that."

Jeremy saw Tiff's puzzled expression. "Happy," he told her.

"But when that Eve woman's horrible treatment of you came to light, and you looked so dejected, he...well, he took it quite to heart."

"Yeah, that's Dad," Jeremy said. "In cases like that, sometimes he hurts even more than I do."

"And after you went for your walk on the beach that night, he went for a walk of his own. Down to the pub. Some bar down the road."

"But I saw him that night." Jeremy tried to remember clearly. "He wasn't tipsy at all."

"No. He was fine. He stopped after one drink and came right home. He wanted to be here when you came back." Vera sat back. "I was proud of him for that."

Tiff set down her teacup. "Are you saying Sean has a drinking problem, Vera?"

184

"Yes. And you see, he thought he could do the same last night. He was quite depressed when we went to dinner. He was heartbroken that he kept you in the dark about our wedding, dear."

Jeremy sighed. "I knew I set him off with that mouthy comment I made."

"What comment?" Tiff asked.

"I gave him a hard time about the wedding. I criticized him for not telling me about anything significant. I don't remember exactly what I said, but it wasn't kind." He looked at Vera. "So this binge was my fault."

"Now, listen to me, Jeremy." Vera leaned forward, emphasizing her words. "Your da made the choice to drink tonight. He'd be the first to tell you he doesn't want you on eggshells when you're with him. He's a grown man, not a helpless child."

"But—"

"Dear, you're not the only person with whom your father will have conflict in life. You can't control how your dad reacts to adversity any more than I can. He has to make his own choices there."

Jeremy didn't argue.

"So I attempted to influence him when he started drinking at dinner," Vera continued. "But he'd have none of it. That's why we fought. And that's why I left." She took a sip of her tea. "Actually, it was indirectly because of the drinking that you didn't hear about me earlier. Or the wedding."

"How so?" Jeremy asked.

"Part of the problem is that we haven't been going to our AA meetings regularly, since we were so wrapped up with the wedding and then with coming out here to surprise you."

"Are you saying he's a full-blown alcoholic, Vera?" Jeremy asked.

He looked at Tiff, embarrassed. But she had caught on to something he still hadn't. He could see it in her eyes.

Vera rested her hand on his arm. "Dear, Sean and I are both full-blown alcoholics."

"*You?*" Jeremy asked. But…you're a sweet woman, Vera."

"And your dad is a sweet man," she said. "It happens to the best of us, darling."

"I would never have guessed," Tiff said.

"Sean and I met at an AA meeting two years ago," Vera said. "I had been sober for several years. Sean struggled to attend regularly at first, but once he found a sponsor, he made great strides. He hit his first year's anniversary six months ago."

"He never told me," Jeremy said. "Not about his sobriety, nor about you."

"It was hard for him, Jeremy. Please try to understand. Sean and I were interested in each other right from the start. But it's usually recommended to not get romantically involved during your first year in AA. Too complicated."

Jeremy laughed softly. "That's certainly true. Maybe I would have resorted to drink these past couple of days if not for...such supportive friends."

"Really, Jeremy?" Vera said.

"No, not really, I guess," he said. "I've never been fond of alcohol. Maybe those memories of Dad's drinking scared me off. When he drank, it was...not fun. He was never violent. He just wasn't Dad."

"It's important that you understand something about your father," Vera continued. "He didn't tell you anything about dating me or marrying me because of how tangled our story is with AA. He planned to tell you while we were here—"

Jeremy nodded. "I understand. He felt he needed to protect himself."

Vera took his hand. "No, darling. He didn't have a thought for himself. He felt he needed to protect *me*." Vera grabbed a napkin and dabbed at tears that formed in her eyes. "You see? Nonsense and rubbish."

They were all silent for a few moments, then Vera stood and said, "Jeremy, your father is a good man." Then she came around behind Jeremy's chair, put her hands on his shoulders, and gave him a kiss on top of his head. "And you're a fine man, as well. Just lovely." Finally Vera walked over to Tiff's chair and squatted down to hug her. "And *you* are nothing short of a gift from God. God knew where you were needed. He sent you here, to San Diego, at this exact point in time. No accident, that." She gave her a pat on the arm and said, "You remember that... And now, I'm going to get some sleep." With that, she left the room.

Jeremy glanced over at Tiff. Her expression concerned him. Something had obviously triggered a thought she didn't like. Tears formed in her eyes and she rose to leave.

"I think I could sleep now, too," she said.

"Right." Jeremy followed her to the door. She nearly walked out without turning around. "Tiff? Is something wrong?"

She turned but hesitated to look at him. Certainly that "kissable" moment had passed.

"Just tired, I guess." She had withdrawn.

"Have I done something wrong?"

"No, not at all." She pasted on a smile. "I'm just really sleepy. We'll talk later, okay?"

And she left. He watched her, hoping she'd look back at him. But she seemed intent on avoiding that very action.

Once she was out of sight, he closed the door. He thought about Vera's comment that romance was too complicated during that first year attending AA. From what he could tell, it was complicated no matter *where* you were.

Forty-four

Orville was still asleep when Tiff slipped back into the dark, silent beach house, so she crumpled up her previous note and replaced it with another.

> Daddy,
>   There was a minor crisis with Jeremy's dad last night. Everything's okay now. But I helped out and didn't get back to bed until early this morning.
>   I need to take my morning shot by 8:00. Would you make sure I get up for that? I can always go back to sleep after.
>   Love you!
>
>   Zzzzzzz,
>   Tiff

~

When Tiff lazily rolled over and awoke well into the next day, she barely remembered Orville waking her earlier. But she knew she had gone through the motions with her shot and a small snack before flopping back into bed. She checked the clock on the nightstand. Past one o'clock in the afternoon.

"Yikes." She knew she needed that sleep, but she always felt cheated when she woke up with the day half over. She felt she had missed important events. A quick glance out the window confirmed her suspicion that she was missing another beautiful San Diego day out there.

Minutes later, she stepped into the welcoming warm shower. Thinking about her day ahead—or what was left of it—she realized she needed desperately to talk with Ren. Once out of the shower, she didn't even bother to dry her hair or put on makeup.

She counted on her fingers as Ren's phone rang. "Two, three, four-thirty in Virginia, good."

"Hey, Tiff!" Ren greeted her on the third ring.

"You're out of school, right?"

"Yep. Well, I'm leaving any minute. You're not interrupting anything. What's shaking at Mission Beach central?"

"Good grief, so much." Tiff ran her fingers through her wet hair. "But I don't know what's appropriate to talk about, to tell you the truth. I'm trying to do like you and not be a gossip. But I really want your advice about something."

"Okay. That's cool," Ren said. "Here's my rule of thumb. If you want to tell me something about a person and you realize it would honestly be better for that person to tell me—rather than you—you're probably stepping into the wonderful world of gossip. Does that help?"

"Hmm." Tiff reviewed what had happened last night through Ren's personal sieve. "Yeah, I think that cuts a lot of it out, but not what I really wanted to ask you about."

"Great! Hang on, I'm in my car now. Let me put my headset on before I start to drive."

At that moment Orville walked in through the patio. "Hey, sleepy-head! Oh!" He saw she was on the phone and brought his finger up to his lips.

Tiff gave him a peck on the cheek and whispered. "Hi, Daddy. I'm on with Ren. I'll be off soon."

"Okay, I'm ready for you, Tiff," Ren said. "What's the non-gossip stuff?"

"Remember you asked me about Jeremy's stepmother? Well, I really like her, Ren."

"Is *that* what you called me about?"

"Sort of. But it has a part that might be gossip, so I'll just say she's cool."

"Got it. So, let me guess. You *really* want to talk to me about Jeremy."

"And how did you know that?"

"You didn't want to talk about it in front of your dad, for one. And I can't imagine your thinking that talking about Jeremy would be gossip. So, what's up with you and our beloved Brit?"

"I kind of like him."

"You mean you *like* like him, or you just like him?"

"Ren, don't make fun of me or I'll call Kara about this instead."

"Okay, I'm sorry. Well, he's certainly not seeing Ms. Evil anymore, so he's unattached again. What's your take on his feelings? Do you think he's interested too?"

Tiff looked around, as if someone else might hear. "Ren, I think he almost kissed me last night."

Ren made a little happy scream. "That's exciting, Tiff! What happened? Why *didn't* he kiss you?"

"Vera walked in on us."

"What do you mean she walked in on you? Where were you?"

"In his dad's bedroom."

Ren gasped. "*What?* Good golly, Tiff, what's going on over there?"

"Nothing's going on," Tiff gave her an exasperated sigh. "We had just put Sean—oh, wait. Stepping into the wonderful world of gossip there. But Jeremy and I were perfectly innocent, trust me."

"So you have what...five days, counting today? You could do some serious groundwork, girl. I like the idea of you two together, I really do."

Tiff wanted to reach across the country and give Ren a big hug for saying just what she wanted to hear.

"Okay, so there's one glaring problem," Tiff said.

Ren was silent a moment. "I don't see it."

"Um, shouldn't I be concerned about the fact that he's not...a believer?"

A long intake of breath followed on Ren's end of the line. "Oh, Tiff. I can't believe I forgot about that. You're right."

And Tiff's heart fell. She knew the truth of the situation. But the fact that Ren didn't mention it right away had given her hope. Now she watched that hope disappear.

"So, what do I do?"

"Let me think." Ren's frustration was tangible. "I've talked with him about this a bunch of times."

"You have?"

"He's complained to me about the women he dates. They don't all turn out as amazingly horrible as Eve did. But, you know, he meets these women at bars and stuff and then expects them to be wholesome and longsuffering."

Tiff grimaced. "Well, I can't say I'm exactly wholesome and longsuffering."

"Honey, you're Mother Teresa stacked up against Jeremy's past dates."

They both sighed at the same time.

Tiff repeated her question. "So, what do I do? Just give up? Avoid him? Stop brushing my teeth and wearing deodorant? Ren, he's so sweet. And when he says something in that cute accent and looks at me with those long-lashed blue eyes and those dimples and that cleft thingy in his chin, and have you noticed how perfect his *nose* is?"

"Your point?"

"I find him hard to resist, and he hasn't even flirted outright with me yet."

Ren groaned. "Okay, here's the plan."

Finally. Tiff looked for a piece of paper and something to write with. "Ready."

"We have to pray."

"Right. And then what?"

"That's it. That's all I've got."

"Ren! That's it?"

"Hey, don't underestimate prayer. Really. And I'm going to need your prayer power of attorney."

"My what?"

"I try not to gossip either. So, if I'm going to enlist Kara and our husbands in prayer about this, you have to let me tell them what's up."

"Not your husbands!"

"Okay, but those are two particularly excellent—and gorgeous, I might add—prayer warriors who could be working for you."

Tiff sighed. "Oh, all right. But tell the guys the bare minimum. Don't tell them what I said about his eyelashes and cleft thingy."

"Yeah, like they'd listen to that stuff anyway."

Tiff sat down on the sofa and rested her head in her hand. "Okay, so we're on a prayer mission. When do we start?"

"Hey, let's go," Ren said with confidence. "Dear Lord—"

Tiff closed her eyes and listened as Ren prayed firmly and insistently for Jeremy. And then for Tiff. "…Amen."

"Amen." Tiff echoed. Ren had hit it on the head with her prayer. "Gosh, you're good at that, Ren."

"Practice makes perfect. Now, don't forget to call me and let me know what's up, okay? And I'll keep in touch with Jeremy too."

After they hung up, Tiff looked at herself in the mirror. Her long hair was a little disheveled for not having been blown dry, but she looked like her natural self. She remembered Jeremy's complimenting her on that look when he arrived. She was going to run a brush through her hair and leave it at that. If he liked natural, that's what she'd be.

Forty-five

Sea foam lapped around Jeremy's ankles as he and his father walked together along the shore.

"Do you think you drank more from loneliness, Dad?"

Sean watched the sand ahead of them, his hands in the pockets of his windbreaker. "Perhaps. I'm still not sure of my reasons."

"Did I make a huge mistake in leaving you alone? Should I have put off Kings College?"

Sean squinted in the sunshine. "Ah, no, son. You were a young man when you left for London. I was well prepared for your leaving." He paused. "Not happy about it, but prepared."

Sean bent to pick up a smooth rock, which he turned gently in his hand. "You seem to be looking to blame yourself. I hope you know better than that."

Jeremy shrugged. "I suppose it's natural to wonder if there was any way I could have helped."

"You were always a wonderful son, Jeremy," Sean said. "But, to be honest, I drank before I met your mum. I drank more often after I lost her. And I just took a long, slow ride downhill over the years. That's all. No great heartbreak brought it to its crashing climax. I just arrived there one day. Or one night, I should say."

"When was that?"

"The worst?"

Jeremy nodded.

"A little more than two years ago. You might remember from when you lived at home that I could go days, sometimes weeks, between drinking bouts."

"Yeah, that's the way I remembered it."

"Although there were a few times when you were a wee lad. You came home from school and had to call your Aunt Sarah to come get me off the floor."

"No," Jeremy said. "I don't remember that."

Sean continued. "I didn't notice it happening, but eventually there were no days between bouts. Took a long time, as I said. But several years ago, going to the pub just became a part of my day. And I didn't drink ale much after awhile, I drank whiskey." He tossed the rock into the waves. "I'm amazed at how long I was able to go before it started to hurt my work."

"Dad, I had no idea. Why did you keep that from me? *How* did you keep it from me? You were never drunk when I visited for Christmas."

"That's just the thing, son. I was able to control it when I needed to." He chuckled. "Of course I didn't need to very often, so I thought I'd always be able to control it."

"So you mentioned one night, when the drinking finally caught up with you."

Sean scratched behind his neck. "Yeah. That would be the night I ended up in hospital. Nearly killed myself. Drank too much too quickly. Alcohol poisoning."

Jeremy stopped in his tracks. "Dad! Why didn't I know about this?"

Sean pulled his shoulders up and gave his head a tilt. "I didn't want you to know. I was mortified. And scared." He kept walking, so Jeremy took a few steps to join him.

"But I would have come home straightaway."

"I knew that, yeah. That's another reason I kept me trap shut."

"Da, this is insane," Jeremy said. "We're family. I love you. I should have been there for you."

Sean seemed unable to speak for a moment. "I got through it just fine, don't you worry. I have friends, you know, and your Aunt Sarah and Uncle George. And now Vera. And my AA sponsor and friends. This doesn't need to rest on your shoulders. You have enough going on in your own life from the looks of it."

Jeremy put his arm around his dad's shoulders. "I want you to promise me, Dad. I want you to promise to call on me if you ever need help again. It breaks my heart that I wasn't there for you. That I might have lost you while I was over here, ignorant of what was going on."

Sean reached up and gave Jeremy a pat on the cheek. "You're a good son."

"Promise me, Dad."

"Right. It's a promise."

They were almost back to Julian's place. Jeremy didn't feel like going inside yet. The day was simply too beautiful.

Sean took off his windbreaker. "Vera and I are going to a local AA meeting in an hour or so."

"They have them during the day, eh?"

"Oh, all times of the day. Julian told us about this one."

"You told Julian about last night?"

"I don't think we could have kept it secret even had we tried," Sean said. "He heard you and Tiff dragging me upstairs early this morning. I think he wanted to make sure you hadn't knocked your old man off or something."

Jeremy smiled. "I'm afraid Tiff and I came pretty close when we tried to carry you back to your bed. You have any new bruises this morning?"

He put his hand to his hip. "Just a wee one here. And maybe here." He touched his head, where he had hit the car door. "But my real problem is that I can't seem to find my shoes."

Jeremy grimaced. "If we can't find them in my car, I think you left them behind somewhere."

"Ah well. Vera hated those shoes," Sean said with a shrug.

Just then Julian approached, wearing his wetsuit. "How are my favorite tenants doing?" he asked.

"Going surfing, are you?" Jeremy said as he removed his sunglasses.

"Bodysurfing. Want to come?"

"I'd love to. But I don't have—"

"There's a full supply of gear in the storage shed at Faith's. Come on, we'll suit you up."

"You don't mind, Dad?"

"Not at all. Vera and I need to get going to that meeting."

"Blessings with it," Julian said. "You've got the directions, right?

"All set." Sean cocked his head and winked at Jeremy. "We'll meet for dinner, eh?"

"Righto." Jeremy started to walk away with Julian. On impulse, he stopped and ran back to his dad. He gave him a kiss on the head. "Love you, Da."

Forty-six

Tiff stretched like a cat and sighed with pleasure. "I haven't done enough of this on our trip, Daddy." She relaxed in her beach chair and dug her feet into the sand until she felt the cool, damp layer under the surface.

Orville looked up from his fishing magazine. "Just relaxing, you mean?"

"Yeah. I feel like I could go right back to sleep."

"Go ahead. We have no obligations today."

"I suppose I should start thinking about work." She sighed. "We *are* going back in four days."

"So think about work in four days. You still want to do the personal training, don't you?"

"Yep. That's one thing I thought about since we got here. I wondered if maybe I should go back to school and learn something else. But I really love doing the training. And I think it's good for me, personally. I mean, when I'm working with fitness and health, I think about it more for myself. I've almost forgotten my shots while we've been here, just because I haven't been focused on health as much as usual."

"We *did* miss our walk this morning, thanks to your long sleep-in."

She swatted him lightly on the arm. "And don't think you've gotten away from it, mister. We can take a nice walk before dinner."

He nodded and returned to his magazine, emitting an amused grunt.

Tiff looked out at the waves. The dinner hour was approaching, and there were fewer people out, even fewer in the water. But there was a healthy handful of people in wetsuits clustered where the waves were best. Most of them used boogie boards, and one or two simply floated on surfboards and relaxed.

Her attention was caught by one of the guys bodysurfing. He looked great from here. He seemed to be with a buddy. Or was he more than a buddy?

What did it matter, anyway? What was she thinking? It wasn't like she was going to meet someone in the next four days here in San Diego with whom she'd spend the rest of her life. She was amazed at the way her brain worked—like a thirty-minute sitcom. Meet 'em, love 'em, walk off into the sunset together before the credits roll.

She knew, though, what she was doing. There was a fantastic, kind, absolutely beautiful man staying next door. He was available, and he seemed attracted to her. And he was obviously going to be in her circle of friends for quite a while in the future. But she had this *nonbeliever* thing hanging over her head, and she was trying to think about other men. Other possibilities. So it was easy to fantasize that the handsome surfer was all of those things Jeremy was *and* he was a believer who just happened to be planning a move to the Northern Virginia area shortly. And then—wait, what was that?

She bolted upright in her chair.

Had he just waved to her?

"Oh. My. Goodness." She took off her sunglasses.

"What?" Orville put his magazine in his lap.

"That's Jeremy!"

"What's Jeremy?" Orville brought his hand to his forehead and looked toward the water. "Oh, yeah, look at that. He's with Julian, I think."

"He is *so* flippin' gorgeous."

Did she say that out loud? She looked at her dad, who was staring at her with a grin. "I'm not sure how to respond to that, kitten."

"Oh, Daddy, be nice to me," she said. "I'm all confused."

"What's the matter? There's nothing wrong with your being interested in Jeremy."

"It's just not that simple."

"Why not?" He set his magazine on the sand and leaned forward, more attentive. "Too soon after his breakup with Eve?"

She tsked. "There's that, too, I guess, but that's not why I'm bewildered." She looked in Jeremy's direction again. "I am *totally* riddled with temptation."

Orville's features froze. "Oh. Maybe I don't want to hear this."

"No, that's not what I mean. He's a great guy. But…well, did I ever tell you about my Jesus thing?"

"Your Jesus thing."

"Yep."

"Uh, no, kitten. I'm quite sure I'd remember if you had." Orville sat up in his chair.

Goodness. She was about to witness to her father in order to talk about a romantic complication.

Could use some help here, Lord.

"Okay." She rubbed her hands together. "When Mama was first diagnosed—"

"This is about Jeremy?"

"Don't interrupt me, Daddy, I'm going to have to roll through this or I'll mess it up."

He nodded. "Yessum."

"Okay. So, when Mama was diagnosed, I needed something. I started going to church with some of my friends. Kara and Ren. You met them a couple of years ago when they drove me down home, remember?"

"Oh, yeah, sweet girls."

"Right. So, while I was going to church, I realized I needed guidance. And I prayed for it, Daddy. And I got it. From Jesus. I asked Him to take control of my life, and one of the first things that happened was He told me to go home and take care of Mama."

"What do you mean, He *told* you?"

"He…spoke to me. Through the pastor, kind of. Don't ask me how I knew. I just did."

"Okay. Well that was a good thing, kitten. That was a really good thing."

"Yes, it was. So I prayed like the dickens when I was with you and Mama. First, I prayed, 'Lord make her well.' Then I prayed, 'Lord take her from her misery.' But finally I just prayed 'Lord, help me accept whatever You have planned for Mama.' And that was when I had peace about her."

Orville looked away from Tiff out to the shore.

"Daddy, it hurt so bad when Mama died," Tiff said. "And I miss her every day. But I know His plan for Mama was what was best for her. I *know* it. And it gives me peace."

He nodded, still watching the sea.

"So I...I've given my whole life over to Him, Daddy. I lean on Him for everything. And He comes through. All the time."

Tiff looked back out at the shore and saw Julian and Jeremy were headed their way. "Shoot!" She wiped at her eyes.

"It's okay, honey. You take your time."

She pulled her hair back with her hands. "It's just that I can't be getting involved with anyone who doesn't feel that way about Jesus. If I fall in love with someone who doesn't love the Lord, we'll never make it. I know that."

Orville looked out and waved at Jeremy and Julian, who were just outside hearing range. "Are you sure Jeremy doesn't feel that way? About Jesus, I mean."

"No. I'm not sure. But I don't think he does."

"Okay, then. I'll do what I can for you, kitten."

"What do you mean?"

He spoke under his breath. "I'll run interference. I'll keep my eyes open. I'll make sure you're never alone with him." He turned and smiled at Julian and Jeremy. "Hey, gents! Looked like you two were having a great time out there."

Tiff turned and looked at Jeremy, who was James Bond in the flesh. Unbelievably, the black eye made him look mysterious and manly. He was smiling at her and clearly trying to read her eyes.

"Hi. I didn't realize that was you out there." She tried to make her voice sound confident and casual, but she felt like a wallflower, and her voice still shook a little with emotion. And now she was acutely aware of her father's assessment of the situation, as if he were a one-man SWAT team, ready to defuse any heat that might arise.

"You two should join us," Julian suggested. "We're going out for a few more waves before calling it a day."

"Oh, no, we couldn't do that." Her dad sounded so false. "We've got to get ready for dinner."

"Ah." Jeremy looked at Tiff. "I hoped you two would join us tonight. I'm meeting Dad and Vera later."

"Yes!" Tiffany blurted it out before her dad could fabricate an excuse. She looked at her dad as if he were a German Shepherd who needed to chill. "Let's do that, Daddy." She looked back at Jeremy. "That would be terrific. It's a plan."

Jeremy beamed. "Brilliant. I'll get back to you as soon as I hear from them."

He was his old self again. Tiff wanted to hug him, especially while he was covered in black neoprene. It was definitely a look that worked for him.

Still, she figured it was good she alerted her dad. There was a new accountability at work here, and it was something she probably needed. Her dad wasn't even a believer, but he could serve the Holy Spirit here, to some extent.

And there was no telling how this could work out. If she represented the Lord well enough here, she might win Jeremy over. She might even win her dad over.

She needed to get on the phone to Ren. That prayer thing needed to go into overdrive tonight.

Forty-seven

Ren answered Tiff's call on the first ring. "Wow. Two calls in one day. Either you're bored or freaked out."

"The latter." Tiff paced in her small room. "Well, not really freaked out. Just nervous. Have you talked with Jeremy?"

"Since you and I talked this afternoon? Nope. I put in a call to him, but he hasn't called back. What's up?"

"We're going out to dinner tonight."

"Awesome! Just the two of you?"

"No, Ren, remember? I'm trying not to let things get romantic. Just the two of us going out to dinner would qualify as romantic." She flipped through the few sundresses she had in the closet and pulled out the peach shift with spaghetti straps. "We're all going. Jeremy, his folks, Daddy, and me." She stood before the mirror and held the dress in front of herself.

"So that sounds safe enough."

"Right. As long as Jeremy doesn't show up dressed in that wet-suit."

"He's been wearing a wetsuit to dinner?"

"I *wish!* I mean, I don't wish. Has he always been this attractive, or is my judgment getting distorted?"

After a moment of silence, Ren answered. "Don't get me wrong, here. Jeremy is almost like a brother to me. And my husband is *the* most hand-some man I've ever met. But Jeremy runs a fairly close second. Your good judgment is just kicking in, sweetheart."

"So that's why I called. I need you to get that prayer thing going for tonight."

"It's already in force. Kara and Gabe—even their families—are keeping you all in prayer. And Tru's on the night shift tonight at the hospital, so he's even enlisting some of his fellow nurses."

"Oh, no, he's not mentioning names, is he?"

"Mentioning names, addresses, he even brought in eight by ten glossies of you and Jeremy."

Tiff sat on the bed. "Now you're just being mean."

"Don't *worry*, Tiff. We're praying fairly generically. It's all in God's hands."

Tiff snorted. "And my dad's."

"Your dad's on board? Cool!"

"Not with the praying. He's not there. *Yet*." She smiled. "But he's…how did he put it? Running interference. I'm afraid he might tackle Jeremy tonight if he comes within ten feet of me."

Ren cracked up. "I love your dad."

"I do, too, but maybe pray for discernment for him tonight too. I talked with him about why it was important to me that I not date someone who wasn't interested in living for Christ. And I guess he understood. A little too well, maybe."

"He likes Jeremy, though, right?"

"Definitely. He was all for my dating Jeremy before I talked with him today. He's just doing this interference thing for me."

"Gotta love 'im."

"I do. So pray for Daddy to be cool. And for me to be a good rep for Christ somehow and not be a total wackozoid around Jeremy."

"Check, check, and uh, could you spell wackozoid, please?"

Tiff sighed. "God knows how to spell it."

"Love you, Tiff," Ren said. "Now go have a great time and don't *worry*."

Tiff turned off her phone and almost cried. She used to be so mean to Ren. And to Kara. God had done such a number on her attitude. But not in a million years did she ever expect to be so touched to hear Ren say "Love you."

If He could soften her heart and endear her relationships like that, he could certainly reach Jeremy, who was already one of the nicest men she'd ever met.

Just that one step, Lord. Please guide him to take that one, awesome step.

Forty-eight

The moment Jeremy, Tiff, and Orville walked into the Costa Brava restaurant that evening, they were greeted with the aromas of garlic and grilled steak, and live flamenco guitar music filled the air. Tiff loved the casual but wonderfully European atmosphere. White walls, dark wooden ceiling beams, and arched doorways hinted at country getaways in remote Spanish villages.

"Feels like we've stepped into Don Quixote's hometown," Jeremy said.

Tiff saw Sean and Vera across the room, and told the maître d,' "I see our party over there."

Jeremy had ridden over in the car with Orville and Tiff, since Sean and Vera's AA meeting had been just down the street from the restaurant.

As they were seated, Tiff made a point of not sitting across from Jeremy so she wouldn't be tempted to stare at him or wink or get otherwise twitchy. Unfortunately, her efforts led to their sitting right next to each other. So she was painfully aware of his presence, whether she looked at him or not.

Nevertheless, once the conversation got rolling, she was able to relax and enjoy everyone's company, including Jeremy's.

"And how was the bodysurfing, son?" Sean asked Jeremy.

"I loved it," Jeremy said, pretending a shiver. "I've never done it in such cold water before. The wetsuit was an absolute gift from heaven."

Tiff remembered him out there on the beach, all in black. *An absolute gift.* She was in total agreement with that.

"Julian had Tiff and me out there when we first arrived," Orville said. "That water will really wake you up in the morning, huh?"

Jeremy turned to Tiff. "I didn't realize you enjoyed bodysurfing. Maybe we could go together tomorrow."

Before Tiff could speak, Orville answered. "That's a great idea. Let's all go!" He took in everyone with his eyes and then gave Tiff a cagey wink.

Vera laughed softly. "I'll beg off, I think. I'm not a big swimmer."

"Well, *I'll* join you!" Sean said. "Are you in, then, Tiff?"

"Love to," she said.

"Brilliant! It's a date," Jeremy said.

He presented his palm to Tiff in a gimme-five gesture, and Orville coughed. Normally Tiff would have felt comfortable returning Jeremy's gesture, but her father's cough distracted her. Was he warning her about flirting? She looked at her father while she absently presented her hand to Jeremy. Rather than smacking his palm, she rested her hand on top of it, as if she actually meant to *hold* his hand.

Orville coughed again, louder this time. And then Tiff realized what she had done.

Jeremy looked momentarily puzzled. He started to gently close his fingers around her offered hand...but then she pulled it away as if she had put it in a flame.

When she looked at Jeremy, he searched her eyes, clearly confused.

"Orville, you catching a cold there?" Sean asked. "I've noticed you've been coughing quite a bit tonight."

Tiff looked pointedly at her father. "Yes, Daddy, you've been doing a lot of that. Too much of it. I'm getting *nervous*."

The waiter arrived with plates of different tapas—imaginative Spanish appetizers—as well as paella, fresh seafood, and grilled chicken and steak dishes.

Halfway through their meal, two women in traditional flamenco dress danced while two guitarists accompanied them. Tiff loved how intensely they performed. The guitarists were strong and virile in their playing, the women feminine and passionate. Tiff considered the beauty in their differences. She loved that God had created men and women to complement one another. That's what she wanted—to complete someone and have him complete her. *Partners.* She didn't crave the manipulative domination Eve had attempted. Where was the beauty in that?

Tiff somehow became aware that Jeremy was watching her. When she looked at him, he caught himself, smiled, and looked back at the dancers.

Tiff flushed with...what? Nervousness. Embarrassment. But good things too. Pleasure that Jeremy found her interesting.

Suddenly she was aware that her lips burned. No doubt from the spicy food. She opened her purse and had to pull her comb free in order to reach her lip gloss. Before she was able to stop it, a panty liner, which had attached itself to her comb, flew out of her purse as if from a catapult. It arced high with the momentum, then plummeted directly onto the dance floor.

She froze. Clearly not every patron had noticed it yet. No doubt some of them saw where it came from, but—

Before she could think about what to do, Jeremy was up and into the fray. He advanced to the dance floor and tossed his cloth napkin on top of the panty liner. His unexpected presence brought the dancers to a standstill. The music broke down to a few strums, then stopped. Jeremy stepped forward and picked up his napkin and what it covered. All eyes were on him. A baby's playful yelp was the only sound in the room.

"So sorry." He bowed slightly to the dancers, in courtly fashion. "Very sorry. Carry on."

And then he walked out and headed toward the restrooms.

The music started up, and the dancers got back in step.

Tiff was up and after Jeremy in seconds. She left the table, ignoring the unmistakable and unrelenting coughing of her father.

Forty-nine

Jeremy tossed Tiff's…lady thing into the trash and set the table napkin on the restroom counter.

As he exited the men's room, he saw Tiff leaning against the wall in the foyer, waiting for him. After an awkward pause, they shared an embarrassed smile about what had happened.

"I believe you owe me," he said.

"Jeremy, you are my absolute hero."

He put his hand on the wall behind her and feigned smugness. "Hero. Yeah, I think I like the sound of that." He looked back toward the dining area and tilted his head as if he were searching. "Although I can't say I made a stellar impression on anyone else." When he turned back to Tiff, his face was close to hers.

He was close enough to notice a few lovely freckles across her nose. And her eyes were an amazing shade of blue. "You know," he began, "we'll all be going home in a couple of days, getting back into the rush of regular living." Then on impulse he reached up. She had a lock of hair he wanted to brush back from her eyes. "And I don't know if I'll have a chance to—"

"You two all right out here?" Orville's voice boomed at them as he approached.

Jeremy stood upright and shoved both hands into his pants pockets.

Tiff stopped leaning back on the wall and began fussing with her hair.

"Righto, sir, just fine." Jeremy nearly saluted.

Orville smiled harmlessly at both of them. "Just want to use the facilities."

They moved farther apart to allow him to pass. When the door closed, they looked at each other again.

"I don't know why I'm acting so guilty," Jeremy said. "It's not like we—"

"Right. We were just talking. We didn't—"

"We didn't do anything." Jeremy's hands were still in his pockets. He glanced at the door to the men's room.

Tiff laughed nervously. "No! Not at all! We didn't even come *close* to kissing or anything, for goodness' sakes."

"Right."

What if he just went ahead and grabbed her and gave her a quick one? What harm would it do? She was looking at him as if she wanted him to.

He took hold of her at the exact moment Orville walked out of the men's room.

Jeremy released her and ran both of his hands through his hair, as if he were going a bit mad. Maybe he was.

He stepped back from where Tiff stood.

"You kids still here?" Orville put his arms across both of their shoulders and stood between them. He planted a kiss on Tiff's forehead.

"Still here, Daddy." Jeremy heard a touch of sarcasm in her tone.

"Well, looks like you both have perfect timing." Orville looked toward the dining area, and Tiff and Jeremy followed suit. Sean and Vera walked into the foyer.

"Ah, good, all ready to go, then?" Sean smiled and placed his wallet into his back pocket.

Vera held up Tiff's purse. "I hope you don't mind my bringing this for you, dear?"

Tiff stepped out of her father's embrace to approach Vera. "No, thanks—"

"Dad, you didn't pick up the whole tab, did you?" Jeremy reached back to pull out his wallet.

Sean waved him off. "Orville and I took care of everything. Not to worry."

"Yep." Orville squeezed once on Jeremy's shoulders. "Took care of everything." Then he looked at Tiff. "Don't worry about a thing."

There seemed to be some underlying communication going on between Tiff and Orville, but Jeremy wasn't quite sure what it was. Orville hadn't seemed the overprotective type before, but perhaps he felt Jeremy was getting too forward with his daughter now.

Was there something in Tiff's past that colored Orville's feelings about her romantic life? Jeremy certainly didn't know a great deal about Tiff. But he knew he wanted to know a great deal more. He was, without question, attracted to her. And that hadn't happened before this trip. Well, there was that steamy little ride on the airport shuttle bus, but this was a different kind of attraction. She was delightful. He certainly hadn't expected that. As a matter of fact, he remembered once telling Kara he thought Tiff was blasted awful. And she *had* been. She was a completely different woman now.

"Jeremy, son, would you mind driving?" Sean took Vera's hand, and handed Jeremy the keys.

And there went Jeremy's chance of riding alone with Tiff. What was his alternative? *Say, Orville, how about you drive Dad and Vera, so I can be alone in the car with your daughter?* Not likely, not the way Orville hovered.

"Sure, Dad."

He turned to share a resigned smile with Tiff, but Orville stood between their line of vision. How appropriate.

Once they were outside, it was too dark to make eye contact with Tiff. It didn't look as if she were trying, anyway. She called out a generic "Good night" to everyone and got into her car. At least she sounded disappointed.

He bucked up once he started driving, though. They still had a couple of days. He made *some* headway in the few things he managed to say before the chaperones descended. He simply needed to find out what Orville had against him, if anything, and make that right.

After all, Jeremy and Tiff were both unattached—absolutely perfect timing. They lived in the same general area of Virginia—quite convenient.

They shared a number of friends—lovely social environment. It seemed they were developing something between them that might be more than a friendship.

What could possibly get in the way?

Fifty

"Okay, kitten, I think we need to have a talk," Orville said as soon as they drove away from the restaurant.

She sighed. "All right."

"'All right,' as in 'that's enough from you'? Or 'all right,' as in 'yes, let's talk'?"

"Let's talk."

Orville held the steering wheel with both hands. "Okay, then. Now, you know I think Jeremy's a fine young man. I could see you two dating, and as long as he treats my daughter with love and respect, I'm right there in his corner."

"Uh huh."

"But, honey, you told me you wanted to steer clear of Jeremy because of your religion, didn't you?"

"Well, it's not really my religion—"

"But you said you preferred not to get involved if he didn't believe the same as you, right?"

Her shoulders slumped. "*Ver*-doggoned-*batim*."

She shifted in her seat and glanced out the window. "You're right, Dad. Completely right. He's just so terrific. And such a gentleman. And so adorable."

"But the religion thing is more important to you?"

She drew in a deep breath, tilted her head back, and groaned. "Yes. When I put my emotions aside and think on a realistic level, my faith is more important than the fact that I want to give him a big old kiss on the smacker."

"Then I did the right thing back there? Coming after you two when you didn't return right away?"

"I thought you had to use the facilities."

He snorted. "Right."

"Please don't tell me you enlisted Sean and Vera in that effort? They didn't leave, thinking they'd help you tear me and Jeremy from a passionate embrace, did they?"

"Nope. That was just a bonus."

She lifted and then dropped her hands in her lap. "I guess you should keep on being the bulldog."

"Now, see, that's one of the things I wanted to talk with you about."

"Yes?"

"We have, what, three more days here? Four? And then you'll head back to Virginia, and I'll head back to South Carolina."

"Right."

"And from what you and Jeremy have said, you have a few mutual friends. You're likely to cross paths. And I assume you want to be friends, regardless of whether or not romance ever plays a part."

"All true."

"So, who's going to be your bulldog when I go back home?"

She paused for a moment. "I guess I hadn't thought that far ahead."

"And that's fine, since you're on vacation. You're not supposed to be too focused on life back home when you're taking a break. But in this case you have a bit of home right next door, don't you?"

Despite the context, Tiff liked to think of Jeremy in that light. A bit of home right next door. Somehow she didn't think Daddy was shooting for that effect with what he said.

"Sometimes, honey, you just have to be stronger than temptation, all by yourself. You have to make a firm decision beforehand, so when the temptation occurs, you're ready to stand strong. No struggle."

Tiff stared at her lap and sighed. "You know, Daddy, I just realized what I've been doing."

"And what's that?"

"Even though I said I needed to be just friends with Jeremy since, you know, we believe differently—"

"Yes."

"In the back of my mind I think I've just taken it for granted that eventually he'll change his mind. He'll accept my beliefs as truth. But the truth is, he may never change his mind."

Orville tilted his head. "That's true."

"Ren and Kara told me about women at church who married men who didn't share their faith. Then, later, when that caused problems, they prayed for their husbands to change their minds. Some never change."

"Why don't you just tell Jeremy about your concerns? What's the big secret?"

She shrugged. "I'd never want to pressure anyone that way about such an important decision. This is between Jeremy and God, not Jeremy and me. I'd never want him to make that kind of decision just to please me."

"And so this issue is big enough for you to take this stance with Jeremy?"

"Yes." She turned and looked out the side window.

"Well, then stick to your decision. Going back and forth is going to frustrate you both."

Tiff rolled down the window and let the cool air wash over her face. She closed her eyes and recommitted herself to the painful decision she had already made. There was one thing Daddy had wrong—she didn't have to fight the temptation alone.

You know what I need, Lord. Please.

She put her hand on her father's arm. "You are hereby relieved of bulldog duty. I'll treat Jeremy as a friend. No more flirting."

She looked back out the window. She'd have to call Ren. She wasn't going to give up on Jeremy's faith. But that's all she was going to pray about regarding Jeremy anymore. And in order to stick to that, she'd need Ren to pray for *her.*

Fifty-one

The next morning, Jeremy tapped on Sean and Vera's bedroom door. "You decent, Dad?"

Sean came out, straightening his shirt. "I've been accused otherwise, from time to time."

Jeremy held up his coffee mug. "There's coffee ready in the kitchen. I thought I might run next door and ask Orville and Tiff if they'd like to join us at Kono's this morning."

"I just assumed they were coming," Sean said with a grin. "Feels like a regular family thing at this point."

That was true. So funny that Jeremy's initial plan in coming to San Diego had been to join Eve. And look at the scenario now. Staying with Dad and Vera in a totally different house, as guests of a generous Scot he never expected to meet, and spending most of his time with Orville and Tiff as if this were the plan all along. No doubt everyone involved was a tad surprised by the turn of events, but none of them *seemed* surprised anymore. They had all settled in quite comfortably.

And wasn't there something positive in that? Didn't this prove that he and Tiff might relate to one another quite well on a more serious level?

He headed next door where Orville greeted him, a glass of orange juice in hand.

"Come on in, son. What are the Becketts up to this morning? Tiff and I were just about to head over to Kono's for breakfast."

"But, that's exactly why I came over. So were we. We hoped you'd join us."

215

Tiff walked out of the bedroom, her head down as she pulled her long hair out from under her shirt collar. She spoke without looking up. "Daddy, you think it's safe to ask Jeremy and them to join us for—"

Then she looked up and saw Jeremy. She took a barely audible gasp. "Uh, good morning. Another beautiful California day, huh?"

The weather? No. He refused to resort to discussing the weather with her. He looked at her fresh face and thick auburn hair. "Lovely."

Orville set down his glass and said, "We're all heading to Kono's."

Tiff smiled more genuinely. But Jeremy still sensed her withholding something.

"Great," she said.

During breakfast Jeremy paid closer attention to Orville. He seemed just fine, and Jeremy couldn't detect any feelings of ill will from him. In fact, Orville was the ringleader in planning the day's activities.

"So everyone but Vera is game for bodysurfing, right? I haven't seen Julian, but maybe he'd like to join us too."

Tiff looked at Vera. "Are you sure you don't mind our doing this without you, Vera?"

"Ah no." Vera smiled. "There are a number of physical activities I love. Dancing, hiking, even occasional exercise classes at the community center. But bodysurfing is a bit more rowdy than I can handle. I fully intend to relax on the beach and watch all of you get tossed and turned out there."

Orville said, "Sean, you mentioned something last night about another meeting today. We need to plan around that, I guess?"

Jeremy's ears perked up at Orville's mention of an AA meeting. Could that be the problem? Was Orville worried that Jeremy might be headed in the same direction?

He needed to volunteer some casual comment to let Orville know he wasn't a drinker. But what? Especially in front of Vera and his dad, Jeremy couldn't think of a way to work that particular point into the conversation.

"Our meeting isn't until five o'clock," Sean said. "Maybe we could get together on the beach shortly before lunchtime. Surf for a couple of hours."

"That sounds lovely," Vera said. "And that would still leave us enough time to return the rental car before our meeting."

"Already?" Orville asked.

"We don't need it," Sean said. "We'd just as soon get it back early and save a few quid."

Tiff gathered up her things. "Well, breakfast was delightful, but maybe I should head back ahead of you all. I need to pick up some more sun block."

"I'll go with you." Jeremy spoke so quickly even Sean and Vera looked at him. "I'm done here, after all. I'll keep you company, Tiff—"

Vera reached for her purse. "We have sun block you can use."

"Waterproof?" Tiff asked.

"Ah, no, I don't think so," Vera said. "I don't remember, exactly."

Tiff stood, prompting everyone else to rise. "I have to use waterproof if we're in the waves. Really important. I had that microdermabrasion stuff done right after getting back to Virginia, after caring for Mama. My skin looked so...what's the word? Sallow?"

As they all left Kono's, Jeremy sensed that Vera and Tiff were entering a women-only conversation. Still, he felt a ridiculous need to get in there and stake a claim. "So that's why you had that book in the boot of your car!"

Sean and Orville were walking ahead of the other three. They had already removed themselves from the conversation, clearly having read—and accepted—the women-only sign. But Tiff and Vera looked at Jeremy as if he had crashed a party around which they had already begun building a wall.

"Boot?" Tiff asked.

"Your trunk." Jeremy nodded at her. "When I changed your tire, I saw a couple of books in the trunk. One was about not having bad skin, or trying to keep your skin from looking so old, or some such thing."

Tiff spoke more to Vera than to Jeremy. "Glad I didn't have anything *really* embarrassing in there."

"Oh, I didn't mean to pry. Actually, I remember wondering why you had the book, because your skin is...well, so beautiful."

"So what was the microdermabrasion like?" Vera asked. "I've wondered about doing that, myself."

Jeremy saw that party wall rising again. Like a child fussing with a sore, Jeremy couldn't make himself stop. What was wrong with him?

He was torn. He could join Sean and Orville—and possibly ingratiate himself with Orville. But he felt compelled to stay with Vera and Tiff, hoping...

"The technician was, I don't know, maybe South American," Tiff said. "Her accent and the ritzy atmosphere of the salon made you feel like you were doing something special. But then she started with her little suction tool on my face."

Both Vera and Jeremy grimaced, although Tiff didn't seem to notice Jeremy.

"She tells me, 'It will feel like erasing with a pencil, see?'" Tiff spoke with an exotic accent using her hands as she spoke, as if she were the technician. "And then she starts stroking it across my skin, harder and harder. Erasing. Yeah. Like when you—have you ever tried to erase *ink* with a pencil eraser? You know, and the paper shreds from your rubbing it to death, until this big hole appears and you have to throw the whole thing out and start over?"

Neither Vera and Jeremy answered.

"Well, it was like that. And she kept going at my chin—which always looked pretty normal to me. It was as if, I don't know, as if she thought she could get to China if she just hung in there long enough."

"Oh, that's done it," Vera said. "No microdermabrasion for this old dame."

Jeremy piped up. "You're not old, Vera."

"Ah, well," Vera said with an appreciative smile, "Aging is simply something that happens. Not much one can do to prevent it, I guess."

"Well, I can tell you take good care of yourself," Tiff said. "My poor Mama, I can hardly remember her ever looking very young."

"Because of the cancer?" Jeremy asked.

"Even before the cancer," Tiff said. "She lived kind of hard—"

She glanced ahead at her father and then lowered her voice.

"Although I'm not sure why. I mean, Daddy didn't smoke, and he didn't drink much, that I can remember. But Mama did both, and it played out in her appearance."

Jeremy straightened up and looked ahead at Orville. *So Tiff's mum was a drinker.* Maybe not to the extent of his dad and Vera, but enough that her daughter was aware of a problem. That would probably make Orville more sympathetic to Sean and Vera. But if Orville suffered a lot of pain, or if his daughter did, because of the mum's drinking, that could definitely give Orville pause in considering Jeremy's chances of becoming a drinker, himself.

Yes, he needed to make sure Orville knew where he stood on that subject. He would watch for a moment alone. If he had to, he'd create a moment alone.

Fifty-two

The waves drowned out their elated screams, but Jeremy could tell everyone else was having as much fun as he was. He loved the exhilaration of watching a wave mount and trying to catch it just so. And the experience was doubly fun when others caught the wave with you. Regardless of any undercurrent of tension that might exist between Tiff and him, or Orville and him, this activity washed everything clean and undeterred. They were all like unabashed children.

Julian had joined them, and when he took a break from the fun, Jeremy joined him.

The two men stood on shore and watched the others.

As Julian toweled off his curly hair, he said, "You know, Jeremy, I never got a chance to tell you how sorry I was about what happened here with your girlfriend. Dishonesty in a loved one can be devastating. Makes you question your ability to tell fact from fiction."

"Exactly," Jeremy said. "I felt such a fool once I figured it out. And I don't want to ever feel that way again."

"My guess is you'll have to make a special effort to keep cynicism at bay. At least for a while. Eventually you'll be willing to trust another woman."

Jeremy spotted Tiff out on the waves. "'Eventually' may come sooner than I had expected. Perhaps I'm healing faster than normal."

Julian followed Jeremy's line of vision to Tiff. "Ah. You'd like to take your friendship with Tiff in a different direction, maybe?"

Jeremy kept watching Tiff and said, "I suppose I'm trying to move on a bit quickly."

"Possibly." Julian's eye crinkled at the corners. "You two do seem to get on well. Does she share your interest?"

"I'm not sure," Jeremy said. "There are moments that are astonishing. When we both seem to...*click*." He looked at Julian. "You know what I mean?"

"Sure. It's a great feeling when that happens."

"But then there are moments when she's quite guarded," Jeremy continued. "Of course, that may well be because of Orville."

"Oh?"

"I think he's figured out that Tiff and I are attracted to each other, and there may be something he doesn't like about that. He keeps stepping between us."

"Are you sure Orville is the one with reservations about you and Tiff becoming a couple?" Julian asked.

"Well, Dad and Vera certainly don't have any problems with the idea." Jeremy did a double-take at Julian. "Oh. You mean Tiff?"

Julian just lifted his eyebrows.

Jeremy watched her again. She and Orville stood in thigh-deep water. Orville said something to her that made her throw her head back and laugh. Jeremy had never seen her so relaxed. Certainly not when she was with him.

"But that doesn't quite fit," Jeremy said. "As I said, sometimes the air is simply charged with the attraction between us."

"There's more to a relationship than sparks." Julian draped his towel across his shoulders. "She may be waiting to learn more about you. To make sure the two of you have something more than a vacation romance brewing. Or there may be other areas of her life that need attention before she can indulge in romance. She may even feel there are areas of *your* life that need attention before a romance is in order."

When Jeremy remained silent, Julian patted him on the back. "Or *not*. Perhaps this *is* about Orville. Either way, both you and Tiff will return to Virginia soon. Don't be in a panic to make things gel here. If it's God's will, it will happen, whether here or there." He smiled at Jeremy. "I've got to run. Maybe I'll see you later tonight."

"Oh, right." Jeremy lifted his hand in a quick wave goodbye. "Thanks."

Jeremy picked up his boogie board and walked back toward the water. Julian had a point about God's will. Here Jeremy was, trying to figure out how to bend Orville's will. Or determine Tiff's.

Hmm. How could he possibly hope to influence *God's* will?

Fifty-three

They all took turns hosing the sand off each other once they returned to the beach house. While he toweled off, Sean asked Jeremy, "Why don't you and Tiff run down to the market and pick up something for lunch?" He turned to Tiff and Orville. "You *will* join us, eh?"

Tiff hesitated, then said "Sure. Okay with you, Daddy?"

"Works for me," Orville said. "Kitten, you want me to go to the market with Jeremy so you can go shower or something?"

She gave him an appreciative smile, but said, "No, I'll shower after lunch. Thanks."

As they drove to the market, Jeremy said, "You were right at home with that boogie board. I was surprised."

"We lived only about an hour from Myrtle Beach in South Carolina when I was a kid," Tiff said. "By the time I could drive, my girlfriends and I would go nearly every weekend, when it was warm enough."

"I grew up right *on* the beach, in Bristol," Jeremy said. "But the shore was far more rocky, so we didn't surf quite as much as you can here in the States."

"So how much do you miss home?"

"Home England, or home Virginia?"

She laughed. "It's only been about four days for Virginia, Jeremy."

"Well, I love Virginia," he said. "Especially after four days sleeping on a foreign sofa, four days away from my own personal coffee pot, four days without TiVo—but, sure I miss England. Especially with Dad and Vera here, reminding me so graphically of Bristol."

"Would you ever move back there?"

They had just pulled into the market's parking lot, and Jeremy turned the car off.

"No. That is, I love England, and I'll make a point of visiting in the future. But I consider the States my home now. I wouldn't move away or expect anyone to do that with me."

"Okay then." She pointed at the market. "Should we…"

He broke out of his intense expression. "Oh. Right."

They walked up and down the aisles, trying to reach a decision about lunch.

"No more lunch meat," Tiff said. "I'm completely burnt out on ham-and-cheese sandwiches."

A moment later, Jeremy held up a large can. "How about tuna—or have we banned all foodstuffs in the sandwich realm, as it were?"

"Yes, let's do put a ban on sandwiches," she said. "But we could do a salad Niçoise kind of thingy."

Jeremy nodded primly. "Do let's. I have always been a big proponent of all kinds of thingies, niçoise and otherwise."

"Okay." She began ticking off items with her fingers. "So, we need another couple of cans of tuna, and some green beans and new pota-toes, and tomatoes and, oh, you think they might have eggs here, already hardboiled?"

She stopped when she saw his expression. "What?"

"Are we actually planning to combine those things in the same meal?"

"And *you*, a European," she said. "This is a dish from *your* side of the world."

"Why do you think I've decided to live on *this* side of the world for the rest of my life?"

"Oh! I'd use fresh tuna if they had it." She gasped. "Maybe they do!"

Jeremy surveyed the store. "I don't see any signs advertising seafood, Tiff. I think we may have to go with the canned—"

Tiff almost didn't notice the abrupt halt in his talk. "That's fine. It will still…"

And then she saw what Jeremy saw. At the front of the market, Eve and Paddy appeared to be arguing over fruit.

Tiff stood mesmerized. She muttered to Jeremy. "You're just as pig-headed as ever."

"I beg your pardon?" Jeremy gasped.

She shushed him, still staring at Eve and Paddy, and then she spoke again. "And you're just as spoiled."

"Ah, you're doing it again, aren't you?" Jeremy said with a grin. "You're reading their lips?"

She made a quick curtsy before him. "I did."

"Brilliant!" They both glanced back at Eve and Paddy.

Eve thrust a large grapefruit into her shopping cart. Paddy rolled his eyes. Eve turned her back on him and then locked eyes with Tiff. She halted, looked at Jeremy, and then adapted a superior smirk, as if she had caught Jeremy and Tiff at something illegal.

"I vote we ignore her," Tiff muttered.

Jeremy picked up a jar of peaches and studied it, as if rapt with interest. "So moved, seconded, and unanimously ratified."

But two aisles later, the inevitable happened. Tiff wondered if Eve hadn't deliberately come after them.

"Well, look who's here," Eve cooed. "You're still in California, Jeremy? I thought you'd have run on home by now."

Jeremy gave Eve a polite smile. "Hello, Eve." He nodded once at Paddy, who didn't seem to have much interest in the exchange either way. But he nodded back and gave Tiff a wink.

Tiff turned their cart around and headed in the opposite direction.

Eve talked at their backs. "You were right, Paddy. You did give him quite a nasty black eye." When both Jeremy and Tiff looked back at her, she looked more intently at Tiff. "And I do mean *nasty*."

"Man, *I* never told her I gave you a black eye," Paddy said. "Come on, Eve, let's go." He reached for her arm, but she shook him off.

"I suppose I should thank you, Jeremy, for trying to fight over me. But obviously Paddy was the better man."

Tiff couldn't stand hearing her talk so falsely about Jeremy. She spoke just loudly enough for the four of them to hear. "What a dark little world you live in, Eve."

Jeremy spoke quietly behind Tiff. "I thought we voted—"

"I change my vote," Tiff said, looking back at Eve. "Jeremy is too much of a gentleman to respond to your petty sniping. And I'm too good a Christian to voice some of the thoughts you keep provoking in my head."

Eve laughed, but Tiff kept talking. "There are a lot of really bad people out there in the world. Why do you want to be one of them? I don't know what happened to make you so hateful, but it's hard to see how beautiful you are behind all that *ugly*."

Eve's face tightened as Tiff continued. "Now, all four of us know that Jeremy really got that black eye by—"

She looked at Jeremy. "You never did tell me how you—"

"Fell. Hit my eye on my car's sideview mirror."

"Ewww." She turned to Eve. "All four of us know he got that black eye by *falling*, all by himself, and smacking his eye on his car's mirror." She glanced back at Jeremy for approval. He gave her a thumbs up.

"And all four of us know he didn't raise a single angry fist to fight over you. So to whom are you directing this nonsense, Eve?"

Eve glowered at Tiff.

"Take it from an old, retired pro," Tiff continued. "If you're going to lie, don't bother lying to people who already know the truth."

Tiff and Jeremy turned to leave, and Eve started to follow. Jeremy turned to Eve, one eyebrow raised, as if she were one of his errant third graders and said, "That's enough, now."

"Yeah, Eve, let's go," Paddy said as he took their cart and pushed it in the opposite direction. For a moment Eve stood alone in the middle of the aisle and then turned to follow him.

Once they were apart from Eve and Paddy, Jeremy said, "A nice efficiency of words, that. Not too many, not too few. Jusssst right."

Tiff snorted. "Yeah, well, I have a lot more right on the tip of my tongue, so if she swings back around here, you might have to call in the riot police to break us up."

"No, I don't think we'll see them again," Jeremy said. "Looks like all they really needed was that grapefruit that caused a rift between them."

"Really," Tiff said. "What kind of fight can you wrap around a grape-fruit?"

Jeremy spoke in a haughty voice, "Well, I don't know about that. I happen to be *emphatically* anti-grapefruit."

"You *cad*. You know fully well I am decidedly *pro*-grapefruit." She pointed from him to herself. "No wonder this will never work out."

Regretting the end of her statement, Tiff changed the subject. "Now, I'll go find the veggies, and you find the olive oil."

"Nope." Jeremy remained where he stood.

"No?" Tiff said. "No salad Niçoise?"

"Oh, the salad's fine. But I'm having fun. We'll find the ingredients *together*."

"Okay," Tiff said, pleased with that answer. "But maybe we should see if there's olive oil at the beach house or Julian's place. Do you have your cell?"

Jeremy felt his pocket, then said, "You know, I can't remember the last time I used my cell phone. Huh. I wonder where I left it. The battery's probably dead by now."

"Mine's in the car," Tiff said. "I'll get it."

"Blast!"

"What's wrong?"

"I think my phone's still in the potted plant at Julian's apartment."

"Since when?"

He shrugged. "A couple of days ago, I suppose."

"Oh…so you never returned Ren's phone call."

"Ren called me? Why?"

"Why did you put your phone in the potted plant?"

"I asked first," Jeremy said.

Tiff grinned. "Well, I'm not telling."

"Me neither."

"Well *obviously* Ren called you because of your witty repartee," Tiff said. "I'm going to go get my phone from the car. Please stay here and don't embarrass yourself. Don't smash anything with your face if you can help it."

She waited until she left the store to sigh. He was so much *fun*.

But friends could be fun couldn't they? They were supposed to be fun.

And it was all right to be attracted to a male friend. That didn't have to go anywhere, did it?

She muttered to herself. "He's my friend. He's my friend. He's my friend."

Fifty-four

The umbrella on Julian's patio table tilted at the perfect angle to keep direct sunlight from baking everyone assembled for lunch. A gentle breeze blowing in from the shore was a welcome guest for the group.

Jeremy took up the large serving spoon on a nearly empty platter and asked, "Does anyone mind if I take the last of this smashing salad?"

There were no objections, so Jeremy filled his plate with the last of it.

"Salad...what was it, now?" asked Vera.

"Niçoise," Tiff said. "I think it's French. Did you like it?"

"Just delightful. Thank you both for putting it together."

"I was a mere lackey." Jeremy shrugged. "But I've been proven wrong. You actually can throw a number of disparate ingredients together to create a culinary masterpiece."

"Well, not just *any* ingredients," Tiff said. "I love chocolate, but I think it might have been out of place in this particular dish."

"Ooooh, chocolate!" Vera stood from the table. "I found some lovely chocolates at the candy store on the boardwalk. I'll run get them, shall I?"

Sean answered. "I thought you'd never ask, love. Would you like me to go get them?"

"Ah, but you don't know where they are," Vera said. "I've hidden them from you."

"Ah. Right, then. You go on ahead." He shot a quick wink at Tiff as Vera left.

"Does that wink mean you've unearthed her stash?" Tiff asked.

"I did, indeed," Sean said. "You know, I was never a big one for chocolate before Vera. But she's always got the stuff around."

"I guess chocolate is considered mostly a chick thing," Tiff said. "But I know plenty of men like you who have been taken down by the woman they love."

"Yes, that's me," Sean laughed.

"Tiff's mama was a chocoholic," Orville said.

Jeremy pushed his now empty plate away. "I haven't really seen you go at the sweets that much, Tiff. You completely ignored them at the market."

"Has to be sugar-free for me. You know about my diabetes, right?"

Did he? Jeremy couldn't remember if anyone had ever mentioned it to him. "I don't know if I knew, to tell you the truth. How long has that been going on?"

"Since middle school. The good thing was they diagnosed me so quickly. I was fine once they got me going with my insulin shots and gave me some help with my diet."

Sean grimaced. "You take the shots every day, then?"

"Twice a day," Tiff said. "But I've done it for so long, I really don't think about it anymore."

Vera entered with the chocolates. "I see a wee mouse has already nibbled at my supply, Sean. You know anything about that?"

Sean feigned surprise and said, "Looks like they've got the same chocolate-eating mice here as we've got back home."

"Apparently so," Vera said with a raised eyebrow. "We'd better eat them up before they all disappear, then." She set the opened box on the table.

When the men were slow to move, Tiff said, "Don't hold back on my account. I get plenty of sweets, believe me."

Vera looked puzzled. "What's happened?"

Orville said, "Tiff just explained to Sean and Jeremy about her diabetes."

Vera brought her hand to her chest. "Oh, great heavens, I'm sorry! And me with my silly chocolates!"

"It's not a big deal. Really." Tiff reached into Vera's box of chocolates, grabbed one, and faced Jeremy. "Open!"

Like a trained puppy, he opened his mouth.

Tiff popped the entire chocolate in. "Close!"

Jeremy chewed the chocolate with obvious pleasure. Sean and Orville eagerly joined in.

"But you're the very picture of health, Tiff," Vera said as she sat at the table. "I can see you haven't held back from exercise and taking care of yourself."

"Actually, the diabetes was indirectly responsible for my becoming a personal trainer," Tiff said. "Once I got used to eating healthy, I became more interested in working out. Then I found I *loved* working out. Eventually, people at the gym started asking me for advice. I was about a year out of high school when the manager of the gym asked me if I'd be interested in getting licensed to be one of their trainers. I jumped at the chance. I quit my other job as soon as I was able to train full-time."

Jeremy took another chocolate. "What was your previous job?"

"I worked in the office of Daddy's trucking company." At that, Orville shook his head and pressed his palm against his forehead.

"What was wrong with that?" Jeremy asked.

Orville said, "She was the only young woman there, with all of those truckers coming and going."

"But I wasn't the *only* woman," Tiff said defensively.

"I repeat." Orville gave her a sideways glance. "The only *young* woman. Gert, the office manager, was ancient and tough as horsehide. If she hadn't been there, I would never have let Tiff work there. I was a nervous wreck as it was."

Sean spoke up. "And now you say the gym no longer has a place open for you? Will you go back to the trucking company, then?"

"No!" Tiff and Orville answered simultaneously.

"No," Tiff continued. "I still love personal training, and I'm comfortable with it. There's bound to be a position at another gym somewhere. I just have to get cracking and find it as soon as I get home. My friend Kara and the gym's new manager, Mickey, both promised to ask around for me. Mickey used to be one of my fellow trainers, and he knows my work. He just couldn't get the big boys to give me my job back."

Jeremy pretended to scratch at something on the table. "But, you don't plan on moving out of the area, do you?"

"Not if I can help it," Tiff said. "I guess you should never say never, but I have the condo, which I'd rather not sell, and I love Northern Virginia." She beamed at Jeremy. "All of my best friends live there."

Fifty-five

That evening Vera and Tiff wanted to make dinner at the beach house, so they shooed the men out to take a walk on the beach.

The sunset streaked copper and scarlet across the sky and turned the ocean a rich shade of purple. Sean, Jeremy, and Orville hadn't walked far before they stopped to face the horizon.

"That has to be one of the most magnificent sights I've seen in a long time," Sean said, crossing his arms against his chest.

Grunts from the other two men echoed their agreement.

"Funny," Orville said. "I took these two weeks to relax with my daughter and get to know her better. I think I've done that, but I never expected to fly to the other side of the country to spend so much time with a couple of men. And Brits, to boot."

"You never know how you're going to make new friends, eh?" Sean said. "I've seen quite a few changes in my friendships over the past couple of years. Used to be I didn't hang out with other blokes if we didn't have fishing poles or pints of ale in our hands." He scratched the back of his neck. "It's been hard to give up the pub part of my life. But Vera's been a big help there, keeping me occupied otherwise."

"Yeah," Jeremy added, "aside from my racquetball mates, I tend to make most of my male acquaintances through the women in my life. My friends Ren and Kara are both married now, so I've gotten to know their husbands a bit. That kind of thing. Or, if I'm dating a bird, I get to know her friends' boyfriends."

"Must be an epidemic," Orville said. "Sheila withdrew from her friends a little during her final years, although I didn't pay attention at the time. But one day it dawned on me that my own friendships were kind of sparse too. I mean, I hung out with the guys at the firehouse when I was on duty, and I spoke in passing with people at work. But, yeah, I guess my friendships came from Sheila's efforts." He glanced at Sean and Jeremy, and the three started to walk again. "And now I'm especially aware of the emptiness."

Jeremy was surprised Orville spoke so frankly in front of him. He must have judged him incorrectly. Unless Orville was pretending for Sean's sake, he didn't seem to feel any animosity or discomfort toward Jeremy. Quite the contrary.

"How long ago did Sheila pass on?" Sean asked.

"Almost four months ago. December ninth."

"That's not long at all," Sean said. "When Jeremy's mum died, I completely shut down. I didn't give it great thought; it just happened. Deeply depressed, I was. I didn't eat much. Barely slept. Jeremy, you were but a wee one, so I don't think you remember that."

"No."

"My sister and her husband helped a lot with Jeremy, and she brought me food at times, to get me to eat more than beans and toast."

"I guess I got over that part," Orville said. "You've both seen the way I've been eating on this trip. Apparently I don't carry my grief the same way."

Sean nodded. "Yes, but you can't be sure how your grief will show up. I eventually came to, and took better care of myself. But you hear the cliché about numbing pain with alcohol, don't you? Well, I became that cliché. At first I couldn't look away from yesterday and all I lost when Ellie died. Then, once I was able to consider what was going on in the present, I found I couldn't do anything but live for the day. I took *carpe diem* and beat the living daylights out of it. More than anything I was convinced I'd never love another woman again. And I didn't even realize how much I needed to love another human being like that."

"I can't imagine it," Orville said.

"It's still so early, though, eh?" Jeremy said. "Certainly Dad didn't rush. Almost thirty years he stayed a bachelor."

"I didn't think of myself as a bachelor," Sean said. "I thought of myself as a widower."

Orville gave Sean an almost imperceptible nod. "Yes. It feels like a betrayal to call yourself a bachelor under these circumstances."

Jeremy thought how shallow his own romance life was, given what his dad and Orville had suffered. Still, he craved the depth of love these two men expressed. He had just turned thirty. It was time for him to take his dating life more seriously. He didn't want to wait as long as his father had, but he didn't need to rush into romance without doing more groundwork. It wasn't a matter of time, necessarily; it was a matter of depth.

Perhaps he needed to talk to someone like Ren or Kara about this.

An image came to mind of his cell phone in that blasted potted plant. He would retrieve his phone and call Ren. She had taken great care about her relationship with her husband, and he could see how well that had worked out. And maybe he should call Kara and get her input, as well. Blimey, she had even refused to date Gabe, opting for a virtually romance-free courtship prior to their wedding.

Jeremy had seldom thought about marriage. But Sean and Orville certainly saw value in the institution. Perhaps it was time he started to learn more about how that kind of love begins.

Fifty-six

"What a fabulous aroma!" Sean said as he entered the beach house ahead of Orville and Jeremy.

Perfect timing. Tiff poured another spoonful of batter into the hot pan and watched as tiny bubbles popped all along the surface. "Oh, good, you're here. Are the others with you? We're just about ready."

Orville breathed in deeply. "That smells great, ladies."

"It's all Tiff's doing," Vera said as she removed a pitcher of iced tea from the refrigerator. "I think she's topped even herself this time. We have Ethiopian fare tonight, gentlemen."

"I love Ethiopian!" Jeremy said. He came up beside Tiff, but then backed off when she quickly folded what looked like a thick crepe in the pan and transferred it to the oven. "You're even making the little wash-cloth things. Smashing!"

"They *do* look kind of like washcloths, don't they?" Tiff said. "They're called injera." She poured another spoonful of batter in the pan. "So you've had Ethiopian?"

"Yeh, at Fasika's. Have you heard of it?"

"In Adams Morgan, right?" Tiff said. "I love that place!" She returned her attention to the pan and gently lifted the edge of the crepe before she released it again. "I hope this stands up to Fasika's."

"Well, we'll just have to compare when we get back home, that's all," Jeremy said.

Had he just asked her out on a date? What was she supposed to do with that? Had her dad heard Jeremy's offer? She then folded the next injera and lifted it from the pan.

"Uh, Daddy, there's a bowl of yogurt in the fridge. Would you please bring that out to the table?"

"Yogurt. Washcloths." Orville walked to the refrigerator. "I want to know where that *real* food smell is coming from."

"Dad, you're going to love this stuff, I promise," she said as she pulled a large bowl from the oven. Then, in a deep caveman voice, she said, "Look! Meat!"

"There you go!" Orville grabbed a towel and used it to carry the bowl to the patio.

Jeremy started for the door along with Orville. "I'm going to pop over to Julian's apartment for just a sec and get my cell phone."

Tiff had just poured the last of the batter into the pan, so she didn't look at him as she asked, "Do you have to go right now, Jeremy?" She looked over her shoulder at him and pointed at the pan with her spatula. "This is the last one, and they cook so quickly. Everything else is ready to go on the table."

"No, it can wait," he said. "Only don't let me forget about my phone. It's still in the potted plant." He looked at Vera and Sean, who each carried a bowl of food toward the patio door. "No one's watered that plant near the front door in Julian's apartment, have they?"

"Oh dear, were we supposed to?" Vera asked. "I'm horrible with plants."

"No, no, that's great," Jeremy said. "I've just got my cell phone in there, that's all."

Vera laughed. "Oh, of course you do. How silly of me!"

"Okay! Last one's done!" Tiff announced as she removed the final crepe and added it to the warm platter in the oven. "Everybody out to the patio!"

⌒

As she knew it would be, the Ethiopian meal was a great success. After the diners spooned portions of everything onto their individual plates, they tore off handfuls of the crepe-like injera and used them to pick up meat, yogurt, and legume and vegetable mixtures and scoop them into their mouths.

"Not only does this hit the spot," Sean said, "but I never thought I'd be encouraged to eat with me fingers at such a fine meal."

"That's part of the fun, isn't it?" Tiff said. "Sort of like being little kids again."

Sean winked at her. "Not my Jeremy. He was the cleanest child I've ever had."

Jeremy frowned. "What do you mean, the cleanest you've ever had? I was your only child." He made an exaggerated grimace. "Wasn't I?"

Sean nodded with a laugh. "Sorry. Yes, I meant you were the cleanest child I'd ever *seen.*" He looked at the others. "Hated being dirty. He'd roughhouse like all the other boys, but as soon as he was done, he'd be in the house to clean up. Didn't even like walking on the sand when we'd go to the shore."

"I can be a neat freak, I'll admit," he said.

Tiff decided "neat" was far better than some of the slobs she'd dated in the past. Not that she was dating Jeremy, but still.

Vera turned to Jeremy. "Do you have a streak of the perfectionist about you, then?"

"In certain areas," Jeremy said. "It's one of the reasons I like being an elementary teacher. My heart goes out to perfectionist kids. Sometimes the parents create them—" He raised one eyebrow at Sean. "But it doesn't take much for a child to believe he has to overdo his efforts until someone notices him. I try to notice my little students' efforts right away and let them know they're doing well, even when they're not perfect. I try to help them gain confidence without having to stress so much about being perfect."

Orville, who had been eating silently until now, said, "There should be more teachers like you, son. In fact, there should be more *parents* like you."

"It's just one of my hot buttons." Jeremy spooned more beef and yogurt onto his plate. "I can remember to this day when I was learning to read at school. First year, was it? Maybe early second. Anyway, I remember I caught on quickly. Reading was easy for me, and not everything was. So when the teacher put words on the board and asked us to try reading them, I constantly had my hand up. And I was always right when she called on me. But, of course, she called on other students, too, which drove me crazy if I knew the answer. One time I just couldn't get her to call on me, even though I was the only one in the class with my hand up. She waited for someone else to get it. Finally another boy did. And do you know, I actually prayed for the kid to be wrong. And when he got it right, I raised my hand anyway. The teacher called on me, and I announced, 'I knew that.'"

"So you actually prayed that the boy would be wrong?" Vera asked.

Before Jeremy could answer, Tiff said, "I remember doing that when I was a girl. What a little snit I was. Thank God, He didn't listen to me. Or, I mean, I know He listened to me, but sometimes He must just shake His head and—"

"And love us even though we're imperfect." Sean said. "Imperfect kids. Imperfect parents. Imperfect all of us."

"True," Orville said.

"Only one perfect Being ever walked this earth," Sean continued. "And I let Him down two nights ago. And probably a hundred times since then. Yet I know He doesn't expect me to be perfect. He just expects me to be His."

Tiff wondered if Jeremy was uncomfortable with the conversation's turn. Certainly, Orville looked uncomfortable. But all Tiff noticed about Jeremy was the slightest glistening in his eyes.

Fifty-seven

Jeremy rescued his phone from the potted plant the moment he got back to Julian's apartment.

He dusted off the phone, and turned it on. He recalled the thoroughly delightful evening. Despite the horrible beginning of this California trip, he was enjoying every moment now. He couldn't have handpicked a more pleasurable group of people. He appreciated Julian's advice to back off with regard to Tiff—hadn't that been what he advised? It was something like that. He and Tiff seemed more at ease with each other this evening, and he thought their behaving as friends—rather than romantics—had contributed to that.

Even his black eye was pain free, as long as he didn't touch it.

He checked his watch. He didn't think it was too late to call, despite the time difference. And he was sure they'd be home. He remembered Ren saying she had become quite the homebody, that her energy levels had petered out considerably during this last trimester of her pregnancy. And she'd have to be up to teach in the morning.

"Ren?"

"Yes?"

"It's Jeremy. How are—"

"I'm sorry, who was that again?"

He laughed and took a seat on the couch. "Right then. I realize you called me two days ago, but I didn't know."

"Don't you have some kind of caller ID on that thing? And I left a beautifully worded message, too, bucko."

"You were in the potted plant, love. I couldn't hear you calling."

"You had your phone in the potted plant the last time I called. Don't you people have flat surfaces over there?"

"Actually, I dropped the phone right back into the planter after our last chat. I wasn't quite myself—my eye was throbbing and I was starving. I couldn't think straight."

"How's the eye now?"

"Quite attractive, actually. The women are positively swarming around me, rugged he-man that I am. I've been telling them I'm a pirate, and you know how well that goes over."

"Mmm."

"So, listen, are you all right over there, Ren? Are the babies being kind to you?"

"Jeremy, the babies are making me eat so much ice cream, I don't think I'll ever forgive them. They'll accept nothing but full-fat Häagen-Dazs." Ren paused and spoke away from the phone. "Don't roll your eyes at me, Tru, or you know what fate awaits you. Jeremy, he's put his hand around his plate, guarding it from me."

"Oh, I'm sorry. I didn't expect you'd be dining so late. Let me call you later."

"No, you called late enough. Tru's eating a Danish. It's his nightly post-dessert snack. We're getting fat together."

"Yes, but a good deal of your weight is actually other *people*," Jeremy said. "And they'll be vacating the premises in a couple of months. Tru'd better be careful."

"That's what I told him! But it's no use. He knows full well I'll still think he's hot stuff even if he gets tubby."

"Uh, too much information, Ren."

"Sorry. So, how are things in sunny San Diego? Has Eve reared her pretty little head since the big Paddy discovery?"

"Tiff and I ran into her at the market today."

"Ran into her as in, you saw her? Or did you actually run her over?"

"No, I've tried to cut back on those shallow displays of ill temper, love. You know that."

"Was she civil, at least? Did she talk to you? Was she with Paddy?"

"No, yes, and yes. She was quite ugly when she spoke to us. Paddy was rather…impotent in his behavior."

"You mean he's letting her push him around?"

"I prefer impotent, thank you."

She sighed. "Well, just so long as you're not bitter."

"You probably realize who was quite the killer in her behavior toward Eve, don't you?"

"Are you *kidding?*" Ren laughed. "Tiff used to leave tread marks on people she laid into. I would imagine someone like Eve would bring out the old Tiff in a flash."

"She wasn't vile at all, really." Jeremy said. "I was actually proud of how she behaved. She actually gave Eve some advice."

"Oh, boy. I'll bet!"

"No, it was something along the lines of living in a dark little world and being one of the mean people out there and lying to people who already know it's a lie. And to stop doing those things. Something like that."

"Okay, enough about Eve. What's happening between Tiff and you?"

She caught him off guard.

"Jeremy? You there?"

"Uh, what do you mean, what's happening?"

"I get the feeling something's brewing. If I'm wrong, just tell me now, and we'll move on."

Ren was his best friend. He was going to dive in. "Uh, yes. That's partially why I was eager to talk with you. I mean, I know I waited two days to call, but now I have more fodder for your excellent mind to consider."

"Well, then, let's get cracking, mister. So you're interested in Tiff. Is all the fodder about Tiff and you?"

"No, I wanted to ask you about a couple of bigger things."

"Bigger things?"

"I had a talk—or rather, I was on the sidelines of a talk—between my dad and Tiff's dad. They talked about losing their wives. And grieving. And finding love again."

"Yeah, those are big."

"Right. But I honestly question whether I'll ever feel so profoundly about a woman that way. I mean, I've always figured I would, of course, but I'm *thirty,* Rennie. And I've been involved with so many different women and never reached that level of intensity. Certainly not with Eve. And even Brenda and I didn't get to that level—before she took off for Colorado."

"Obviously not, if the girl chose the ski slopes over a fantastic guy like you," Ren said. "Depth requires the efforts of two people, Jeremy. You have amazing potential for developing a deep love with the right woman."

"Ren, do you remember Julian out here?"

"Sure, the guy next door. He's great. He and Tru hit it off especially well."

"Yeah. I talked with Julian for a while. About Tiff, in particular, because I've been a mite confused. His advice was to relax and take it easy, not to rush. He said something about God's will."

"Did he?"

"Right. So there's one of the things I thought you could advise me about, as such a good church girl."

"Okay. The good church girl is all ears."

"The thing is, I'm not quite sure how all of that works. I have a question about God's will. I know He's out there, right? I assume He occasionally takes time away from huge world events to notice a few of the things going on in each of our lives as our final tallies mount—"

"Wait, wait. Final tallies?"

"Right. The goods. The bads. The bottom line."

"Um, okay, we'll talk about that in a minute. What's your question about God's will?"

"How do I change it?"

She was silent for a moment. "Uh, Jeremy, why would you want to?"

"Well, love, isn't that why people pray?"

"I'm sure that's why some people pray, but it doesn't make much sense. It makes more sense to pray to accept His will. Or to pray for help to live within it."

"What does *that* mean?" He sat back and propped a throw pillow behind his head.

"Take your interest in Tiff, for example. And whatever you're confused about. If Julian brought God's will into the conversation, he probably said your relationship with Tiff was up to God."

"Something like that, yes."

"Okay, so I've always found that when I've done everything I can about a situation, I need to make sure I've surrendered the outcome to whatever God has planned. Because that's how it's going to turn out, anyway, in the long run."

Jeremy scratched his eyebrow. "So why bother to do everything you can about the situation? If God's completely running the show, no matter what I do, should I bother even *trying* to develop something with Tiff?"

"Actually, Jeremy, I should have said that the other way around. Surrender *first*. Decide to accept whatever God has planned. I mean, you're *part* of His plan. So surrender, and then do what you can. He'll help you. And He'll guide you. It's far less stressful, since you accept that whatever happens is the best for you and Tiff, even if you don't end up together."

"So, I'm supposed to pray, eh?"

"That's a great place to start."

"But—" He stood, suddenly nervous. "I don't know any prayers. Dad and I never—"

"You can talk, right?"

"Huh?"

Ren laughed. "I mean, other than right at this moment, you can speak. You can put one word after another and express the thoughts in your head and the feelings in your heart."

He grinned crookedly. "Yes. I've done that on occasion."

"So you can pray. Just talk to Him. Then shut up and listen."

"For how long?"

"How long to pray? Or how long to listen?"

"Both."

"As long as you want. Anytime you want. It's so simple. But it's so deep, too, when you consider you're actually communicating with God and He's answering you back. He's always listening, even while those huge world events are going on."

"Oh." Jeremy tried to imagine it could be so. *Could it?*

"And, about that final tally—the good, the bad, the bottom line?"

"Yes?"

"Ain't no such animal."

He sat back down. "What do you mean? You and Kara are constantly volunteering and contributing to charities and such."

"But…oh, I don't want to throw too much at you at once. We do those things to say thank you, not to say please."

"I think you may have lost me there."

"We can talk more about that later. It kind of ties in with the whole surrender thing. You say Kara and I volunteer. We don't do that to try to change God's heart. We do that because He changed ours."

"Oh, I think I understand."

"Good."

This seemed quite enough information to digest in one call. They soon signed off with "Goodnights." Jeremy then made up the couch and crawled under the covers. But he found he couldn't bring himself to sleep without giving it all a shot.

Uh, hello, God. Jeremy Beckett here. So sorry to have given You so little notice in the past. I'm still not quite sure what to do or say. To You, that is. But I just want to let You know I do believe in You. And Ren's idea sounds easy enough and makes a bit more sense to me now. So I'm asking You to help me to accept Your will about Tiff. Or everything, I suppose. But maybe we could start with Tiff? Yes, please. Let's start with Tiff. Unless, of course, that's not Your will.

See, now? I'm getting the hang of it already.

Um, amen. And goodnight, Sir.

Fifty-eight

Tiff showed up at Jeremy's door the next morning, a bacon-and-egg sandwich in her hand.

Jeremy answered her knock wearing a T-shirt and baggy flannel pants, and his hair formed a lopsided point on his head. He looked like a ten-year-old in a grown man's body, and Tiff's heart melted at the sight. So early in the morning too.

"I'm sorry. Did I wake you?" she asked.

"No, no. I was just about to get up."

"Good." She took his hand and turned it palm up. She slapped the foil-wrapped sandwich into it. "Eat that first, and then throw on some clothes and meet me downstairs."

"Smells good."

Tiff looked at her watch. "You've got fifteen minutes." Then she turned and walked down the stairs.

Not only did he show up on time, he had clearly showered. He wore a pale gray Henley and army green cargo shorts. His hair was damp and combed back, although drying strands slowly fell forward onto his forehead.

Tiff was amazed at how quickly he had transformed himself. "I'm impressed!" she said.

"You should have seen me eat that sandwich in the shower. You'd be doubly impressed."

"Okay, smarty pants, let's go." She walked to the carport, her keys in hand.

"Where are we going?" he asked as he got in on the passenger side.

"Not telling."

"How about the others?"

"They're not coming." She pulled into traffic. "They all went to breakfast. They refused to accompany us on this trip."

"Us?" he asked. " How did you know I'd be willing to come along?"

"I knew." Five minutes later Tiff announced, "We have arrived." She pulled into the parking lot of Belmont Amusement Park, the visible highlight of which was a massive roller coaster. "Jeremy, you don't get sick on rides, do you?"

"No," he said, taking in the towering ride. "But I might scream like a little girl."

"Me too." She reached for her door handle. "So, are you game, fella?"

"Uh, how about we work our way up to the roller coaster? I think that breakfast sandwich needs a bit more digestion time. Plus, I'm just a tad anxious about coasters, truth be told. I always feel like a statistic waiting to happen."

"Well, we can do miniature golf first," Tiff suggested. "I just like the idea of doing something a little different before our time here is up."

"I agree," Jeremy said. And with that, they both got out of the car.

"I must warn you, though, Tiff…"

She tilted her head. "About what?"

"I am *unbeatable* at miniature golf. This could get embarrassing for you."

"Uh huh. We'll see about that"

As it turned out, Jeremy was absolutely horrible at miniature golf, but he had Tiff in tears with his excuses.

"Yes, well, you see, I would have had that stroke, but I'm concerned about global nuclear proliferation. I can't be expected to focus on *everything* at once."

"That child ahead of us distracted me by making a face. Right there, you see, where my ball went askew? Clearly I had a hole in one before my shot was so rudely disturbed."

"But you didn't warn me that the course would be indoors. My footgear is completely wrong. I'm far more familiar with the outdoor courses. And everyone knows a pirate theme is bad feng shui. Very bad."

Next, they moved on to the bumper cars, the Tilt-A-Whirl, and the Beach Blaster, which slowly rocked like a pendulum, increasing the height of the lift with each swing.

Tiff had always enjoyed amusement parks, but she couldn't remember the last time she had laughed so hard. Jeremy didn't take anything seriously here, and she had never seen him so unguarded. He acted like Snidely Whiplash in the bumper cars, arching a villainous brow every time he approached her car and referring to Tiff as "Nell." On the Tilt-A-Whirl, he exaggerated the effects, acting as if he were about to be thrown from the car, and then acting as if he couldn't help but squish against Tiff when the sway thrust them in the opposite direction.

She especially enjoyed that ride.

It was nearly lunchtime when they had exhausted all of the adult rides other than the Giant Dipper Roller Coaster. They passed the carousel on the way.

Jeremy put his hand on Tiff's shoulder to stop her. "Are you sure you wouldn't rather ride on a horsy?"

"Later, scaredy cat. First the coaster, *then* the carousel. And if you're good, I'll buy you an ice cream."

"Right," he grumbled. "That's what they told me right before they ripped out my tonsils."

As they stood in line, they passed a sign that Jeremy read aloud.

"Built in 1925." He looked at Tiff. "Well, that takes a load off. This thing is only eighty plus years old. And here I was concerned about safety."

"Look." She pointed to another section of the sign. "Recently restored."

He nodded. "Yes, but that sign is sixty years old."

She smacked his arm. "Oh, stop."

When their turn came, they brought down the safety bar and braced themselves.

As they began their slow incline, Tiff said, "These things are always more fun if you aren't terribly tense and rigid. It feels great to be lifted right off the seat."

"Righto." Jeremy peered over the edge of their car. "My favorite part is when the car sails off the rails and plummets into the ocean."

At last the slow climb had brought them to the top of the rise. The clicking of the track stopped. Then a second later they were swiftly pulled into a frenzy of falls and hairpin turns, quickly rising and dropping several times. True to their promise, each one screamed like a giddy child.

As soon as they reached the calmer final portion of the track, Tiff realized she had leaned hard against Jeremy without thinking. And at some point he had thrown his arm around her, as he might have done to shelter a child from harm.

Their faces were mere inches apart, before Jeremy released her and Tiff pulled back, embarrassed.

"I guess I was more scared than I expected to be," Tiff said. "Thanks for being protective of me."

"I wasn't being protective," Jeremy said. "I was hanging on for dear life."

They stepped out of the car when it was their turn, and Tiff dusted off her shorts as if she actually needed to. "There. That wasn't so bad, was it?"

"Bad? I'm ready to go again!"

And they did.

They rode the coaster twice more before leaving the park. To Tiff's disappointment Jeremy was less "protective" during the final two rides. He obviously no longer felt the need to hang on for dear life.

Fifty-nine

"Are you hungry, Jeremy?" Tiff asked on the drive home.

"*Ravenous.* Cotton candy doesn't last very long. Shall we stop for something?"

A minute later Tiff pulled into the parking lot of the Mission Beach Seafood Grill. The restaurant didn't look too pricey, and it appeared clean and decent.

"Seafood Grill," Tiff said. "Is that okay with you?"

"Sounds perfect. I have a craving for fried shrimp. You think they fry anything here?"

Tiff shrugged. "If they don't, someone else will."

But they did. Tiff opted for grilled coho salmon, and Jeremy ordered a fried-shrimp basket large enough to satisfy two men. After their food arrived, Jeremy turned to catch the server's attention.

Partially to be funny and also because Jeremy's shrimp looked and smelled so delicious, Tiff grabbed one from his plate and popped it into her mouth. The hot shrimp scalded her tongue so quickly her eyes watered. She seized the beverage menu and held it in front of her face so she could open her mouth and move the shrimp around with her tongue in an effort to stave off too bad a burn.

By the time Jeremy had spoken to the waiter and looked at her again, she was still holding the menu up as a mask.

Jeremy peered around the menu and did a double take. Then he asked, "Tiff, are you crying?"

She closed her mouth and lowered the menu. She had to finish the shrimp before she could talk, but she shook her head.

Jeremy wagged his finger at her. "You bad thing. You stole one of my shrimp, didn't you?"

She pulled the tail from her mouth as daintily as she could.

"Those babies are hot!" Her face flushed more from embarrassment than from the heat of the shrimp. "Sorry. I couldn't resist."

He pushed the basket toward her. He said softly, "I don't want you to resist."

She darted her eyes up from the basket. Their locked gaze seemed to add significance to Jeremy's comment that maybe he hadn't intended.

The server interrupted, breaking the magic of the moment. Tiff relaxed, and the server asked if they were pleased with their meals and whether they needed anything else.

Once they were alone again, Tiff tried to regain an attitude of nonchalance. She leaned forward and rested her chin in her hand. "I'm not terribly eager to start job hunting in—" She counted on her fingers. "Friday, Saturday, Sunday, four days."

"When do you head home?"

"Saturday afternoon."

"I'm early Saturday morning," Jeremy said. "Dad and Vera leave tomorrow. They're staying in D.C. for the weekend, sightseeing and such, before they visit with me a few more days in Virginia."

"Let me know if they need any company while you're working," Tiff said. "I might have some free time between job searches, and I'd love to see them before they head back to England. I'm going to miss them."

"Me too." He sighed. "What I dread most about going back to Virginia is that I'll have to see Eve one last time to return some of her things. I certainly hadn't planned this to be the breakup trip it turned out to be."

Tiff had to ask. "Were you two, um, living together, kind of?"

"Oh, blimey, no. We weren't even…well, our romance hadn't gone beyond kissing, frankly. That's one reason this trip's illumination was such a shocker."

She took a sip of her water. "I have to say, you handled yourself really well through the whole breakup thing. Even at the market. You were a pretty cool customer, considering what Eve did to you. I mean, Ren and I talked briefly right after I met Eve, and Ren thought you were lovestruck with Eve."

"Yeh, I guess I was. After I dropped her off at Paddy's that last time, I was anxious about having to contact her back in Virginia. I assumed I'd crumble as soon as I saw her again. I've always thought her so beautiful. But when she walked into the market, she looked different to me. It was a bit like admiring a gorgeous butterfly and suddenly realizing it had fangs. Just not quite the same." He bit into a shrimp. "Now I only dread having to listen to her talk rubbish as she does."

Tiff set her fork down. "You know, Jeremy, I have a pretty extensive resume when it comes to trash talk. I'm not proud of that. But I think for most people who talk rubbish like that, it has a lot more to do with being insecure than anything else. More than how you really feel about the person you're yammering at."

"You think?"

She nodded and took a small bite of her salmon. "I'm just starting to realize it. I think maybe I'm getting a little more sure of myself. I can tell I'm thinking differently about people than I used to. Before, it was as if I needed to hurt someone before he or she had a chance to hurt me." She thought a moment. "Remember when we met each other—or met each other again—at the pizza place? Our crash into the wall?"

"Not a graceful encounter, was it?"

"No," she said. "But I remember you called yourself an idiot or klutz or something—"

He sat up. "And you thought I was calling *you* that name."

"Yeah. And I got all angry and upset because I just assumed you would say something mean to me. See, that's what I'm talking about. If I had more confidence, that whole episode would have been funny."

"I hate to break it to you, Tiff, but that whole episode *was* funny as far as everyone else was concerned."

"See?" She pointed with her fork. "But now I know that. And I know you. I know how nice you are." She paused a moment, then gently touched the area around his black eye, and said, "And I know you *are* a klutz."

He laughed.

Wonderful. *He* had confidence.

Jeremy prodded further. "So, when Eve starts her yammering, as you put it, I should feel pity for her? If she calls me a useless blighter, I should tell her I feel sorry for her?"

Tiff laughed. "Only if she's nowhere near any sharp objects, honey. Seriously, Jeremy, she's not going for pity. She's going for power. Just let her have her dark little moment. That's what I planned to do at the market, but then I got all defensive on your behalf and couldn't keep my mouth shut." She shrugged. "I still have my moments."

He tilted his head. "I loved that moment. I've never been so certain of your friendship."

Tiff felt a slight lift all over her body. Until then she hadn't been aware of how important Jeremy's friendship had become.

Later, as he paid the bill, Jeremy said, "Maybe we should do a little shopping. Maybe I could find something San Diego-ish to put in my classroom for the kids. Do you fancy a bit of shopping?"

"Oh, I'm always ready to shop!"

They walked out to the car, and while she unlocked her door, Tiff said, "Should we make sure no one needs us back at the beach house yet?"

"We could," Jeremy said. "Or not."

She laughed. "Or not, it is."

He chuckled and leaned forward, just for a moment—as if he sensed a natural opening for a kiss and almost acted upon it before he stopped himself.

Tiff straightened, shocked at how comfortably she had responded, as if she and Jeremy gave each other kisses all the time.

But no, this was a wonderful friendship. They both knew that.

She and her *buddy* would go shopping. They would fully enjoy each other's company. And she would continue to bottle up those moments of extreme attraction. Maybe before they all went home, she'd be able to toss that bottle out to sea.

Sixty

Jeremy and Tiff dropped off her car at the beach house and walked leisurely down the boardwalk, browsing as they went. For the most part, they didn't see anything they hadn't already seen on the East Coast.

But when they came across the Coastal Charms jewelry shop, Tiff oohed and aahed at a couple of colorful necklaces in the front window.

"They're so unusual," Tiff said. "I can't tell if those are gems or stones or what. Would you mind if we went in for a minute?"

"Not at all," Jeremy said.

A middle-aged woman with short, vivid red hair was ringing up a sale for another customer. She nodded to Tiff and Jeremy and said, "I'll be with you in a second."

"There are more over here, Tiff," Jeremy said, looking in a display case.

Tiff sighed softly. "So pretty!"

Each piece was clearly handmade. The colors were predominantly pastels, and the stones each had a different, asymmetrical shape.

"Ah, you like the sea glass," the red-haired woman said as she approached them.

"That's glass?" Tiff stared into the case. "But it all seems so opaque."

"Yes. That's what happens to it after it rolls around for a long time in the sea." She pulled a necklace from the cabinet and rested it on a small flannel-covered board on the counter. A handful of flat, pale blue chunks of glass were set across the length of the necklace.

Jeremy touched one of the pieces. "How do they make it? You said it rolls around in the sea?"

"Right," she said. "All of these pretty pieces are actually someone's trash from sometime in the past. Discarded marbles, medicine bottles, beer and whiskey bottles, even old telephone insulators."

Jeremy looked again at the jewelry. "They're all so beautiful. It's hard to imagine them as trash."

"Yes, it is," the woman said. "But at some point in history, someone tossed their glass into the sea. Then it broke into pieces, got tossed around, weathered storms, and was beat up by the sand and grit on the ocean floor."

She took a few more pieces out of the case. A rose-colored set of earrings sat beside a silver bracelet embedded with light green glass. "Eventually, shards like these wash ashore. They usually have softer edges, and their appearance is…well, perfected. Then collectors find them. Even the waves and the wind play a part in turning someone else's litter into our treasure."

"Well, I think this stuff is gorgeous," Tiff said. "A little pricey, but beautiful."

Jeremy noticed a poster on the wall behind the woman. Photographs of sea glass were grouped by shade, to form a natural color chart.

"Do you have copies of that poster available, by any chance?"

The woman turned around. "Yes. Would you like one?"

"Please."

"Hang on." She returned the jewelry to the case and walked to the back of the store.

"That poster's probably the only thing from here I can afford to bring to my class, eh?" Jeremy said.

"And you have a nice little lesson to tell them, about how the glass comes about."

"I'm not sure if I can fit that information into the S.O.L. requirements, but it will be a fun aside."

"S.O.L.?" she asked.

"Standards of Learning. Just stuff I'm required to teach each year. My students get tested at year's end, to show I've taught them specific information. If they don't test well, my school—my job—suffers."

"You mean, you don't get to teach your class the way you want to?"

"Not much, no."

Jeremy paid for the poster, and they left. But outside, Tiff continued the discussion as they walked back in the direction of the beach house.

"I think that's terrible," she said. "I'd hate to be under strict guidelines with something I was teaching in order to keep my job."

"But you are, don't you think?" he asked.

"What do you mean?"

"You must be under legal regulations of some kind as a trainer. If you taught your clients something that didn't improve their health status, or worse, if you taught them something that hurt them physically, don't you think the gym could be in trouble? And couldn't you lose your job?"

"You mean the job I already lost?"

"Whoops. Righto."

"Oh, I'm confident I'll get a job at another gym in the area," she said. "And if I don't, I'll just have to figure out something else to do with my life."

"And you said you don't expect to move right away, right?" Jeremy asked.

Tiff paused as they approached a snack bar. "I'm thirsty. You want to share a bottle of water?"

"Sure," he said.

Tiff bought the bottle, took a drink, and handed it to him. "Anyway, I really don't want to leave Virginia. There's no reason the job market would be better anywhere else. And I've finally made the right kinds of friends. I mean, Kara and Ren have turned out to be so sweet. I just needed to be open to them, which I'm better at now."

"Now that you're more secure."

"Yeah, I suppose that's it," she said. "And even though you and I don't know each other all that well, yet, I consider you a good friend too."

They were barely moving. He took a deep breath. "Say, could we sit down for a minute?" Without waiting for an answer, he took her hand and walked her to the seawall.

He had no idea what he was going to say, but he began anyway. "Tiff, I consider you a good friend too. I can't believe we've known each other for such a short time."

"Considering our proximity this past week," she said, "we've probably spent more time together than other people do in a few months."

"Yes. And you've been such a delightful surprise."

Tiff gave the side of his foot a gentle kick. "You mean, because I'm not as nasty as you remembered?"

"Yeah." He grinned.

"I know my edges were a little rough before."

He glanced down at the rolled-up poster from the jewelry shop. "You're…you're like sea glass."

She smiled at him. "How do you mean?"

"This week you talked about a few things from your past—your experiences with your mum in particular. They sounded like the tossing about and the storms that woman mentioned back in the jewelry shop. You may have had rough edges, as you say, when we met before, but they're gone now. And…"

She waited while he found his words.

"…And now you're lovely."

Tears formed in her eyes. "Jeremy, that's one of the nicest things a man has ever said to me. Yeah, I went through some storms—I guess we all get tossed around in rough waters from time to time." She paused before continuing. "But if I emerged from my experiences as someone 'lovely,' it isn't thanks to the storms. It's thanks to the Collector. You know? The One who thinks I'm a treasure and waited for me to come to shore."

Ah. This was the kind of thing Ren or Kara might say. She was talking about Christ. He understood.

She stood, and Jeremy grabbed his poster and joined her. She quickly wiped at her cheek.

He put his arm around her shoulders. "Are you all right?"

She nodded but didn't speak.

She really was lovely. Although Jeremy kept his arm around her, he didn't feel like he should kiss her. Even though he was aware of how much he wanted to.

Rather, he looked straight ahead, moved by everything he had witnessed this week. The unexpected arrival of Tiff and Orville here at a time Eve might otherwise have deceived him. The discovery that his father had found both love and salvation through the same Person Tiff embraced.

The well-timed encounters with Zeke and Julian whenever he was particularly troubled.

And now, one day after he had offered his meager prayer for guidance about Tiff, she makes a point of crediting Christ with everything about her that he finds lovely.

So he didn't kiss Tiff, and he didn't move his arm. He simply spoke quietly to her.

"I want what you have."

Sixty-one

It wasn't hard for Jeremy to suggest a walk on the beach with his father. He knew that the questions he had could not and should not be answered by Tiff. Simply put, she was too much of a distraction from the issue at hand. A pleasant distraction to be sure...but a distraction nonetheless.

And so the two men strolled along the beach as the late-afternoon sun eased closer to the horizon and the crowd of beach lovers thinned. Before Jeremy and Sean reached the shoreline, Sean rested his hand on his son's shoulder.

"What's on your mind, Jeremy?"

Jeremy tilted his head. "Last night you said something that stayed with me. About God. Or, about Christ, I suppose."

"Did I now?" Sean smiled. "I'm happy to hear that. That it stayed with you, I mean. What did I say?"

"That only Christ is perfect. And He doesn't expect perfection from us. Then you said He expects us to be His."

"Oh, yes. I remember that."

A moment of silence stretched between them. Jeremy began again. "How, exactly, does one do that? Become His?"

Sean stopped walking.

"It's all about recognition, son."

"How do you mean?"

"Well, if you recognize the Bible as God's Word, you believe what it says. And it says we humans are a special part of God's creation. We're

259

the only ones to whom He gave souls. We're the only ones to whom He gave *choice*."

Jeremy nodded. "Choice."

"Right. The other night I chose to wear those shoes Vera hated."

"The ones you lost, you mean?"

"Those would be the ones." Sean shrugged. "A relatively harmless choice, although Vera might argue that point."

Sean faced the horizon and continued. "But just about everything else I did that evening was the result of harmful choices. The Bible calls that sin." He paused. "So there's your next point of recognition. You need to recognize your sin." He looked into Jeremy's eyes. "We've all sinned, you know."

Jeremy had no trouble conjuring up a few of his own harmful choices. He pressed the ball of his foot into the cool, wet sand. "Right. I've no trouble recognizing some of my sins."

"Good. And the Bible tells us our sins have separated us from our perfect God. Forever. We might not recognize the separation yet, because there are so many blessings here on earth. So much good amid the evil. But if we don't discover the way to God—the way to bridge that horrible separation—forever will begin the moment we die. The Bible describes that as eternity."

Despite the warm sun, Jeremy's skin erupted in goose bumps. "And the way to God, then?"

Sean thought for a moment, then began. "When Jesus hung on the cross, He suffered. He died. But the worst thing He experienced, son, was when He was separated from God. That's when He cried out, 'Father, why have You forsaken Me?' He did that for us. He took our punishment to give us the choice to escape it. And the way we do that is to recognize what He did for us and say thank You. That we *believe* He did that for us and we accept His amazing gift of forgiveness."

"But you said last night He wants us to be His," Jeremy said. "It sounds as if you've told me how to accept Him as *mine*."

"And that's the whole point of recognition, Jeremy. You need to recognize that you *are* meant to be His. Make Christ yours—your way to God, your savior, your friend, your advisor—by giving your life to Him, and you're choosing to be His. Your recognition of Him as your savior, makes you His. You'll never be separated from God again. Forever won't begin when you die. It will start today. Right now, even."

Despite the depth of what his father had just told him, the choice seemed so simple.

"Da, I thought I came out here to be with Eve. But when I think of some of the people who have surrounded me this week—you, Vera, Zeke, Julian—and Tiff…"

Sean nodded. "He brought them here. And He brought you here for this moment, son. Do you recognize that? Do you recognize the choice you need to make?"

Jeremy nodded, and then he looked at the sand. "What do I do, Dad?"

Sean put his arm around Jeremy's shoulders, and they stood, side by side, facing the horizon. Sean inclined his head toward Jeremy. "Well, I'm not very good at this sort of thing. But here's what I did. Close your eyes, son, and pray this with your heart. Father, I believe I need You. I believe my sins have drawn me away from You. Jesus, I believe You're the Son of God and You suffered pain, separation from God, and death—all for me. I don't deserve such love, Lord, but I accept it. In exchange for Your life, I give You mine. Holy Spirit, please fill my heart and show me how to live. Amen."

There was a brief silence after which Jeremy, his eyes still closed, whispered, "Amen." Then he looked up at Sean with a puzzled look. "Should I feel different?"

Sean simply smiled. "That will come. Every day, that will come."

They started to walk back toward the beach house, and Sean repeated his earlier words. "It's all about recognition."

Sixty-two

That evening Tiff sat cross-legged in front of the bookshelf in the beach-house living room. She read the titles of the few CDs Faith Fontaine—or a former renter—left behind. She wasn't all that familiar with them, but she could tell from the cover photos the music would be closer to her dad's era than hers. Or maybe even her grandparents' era. That was fine. She was in the mood for something other than the contemporary songs she had heard *ad nauseum* while on the beach and boardwalk these two weeks.

She read the artists' names: Nat King Cole. Tommy Dorsey. Ella Fitzgerald. She shut her eyes and shuffled a few before picking one at random. Les Brown. She plugged in the small CD player, and seconds later the sounds of big-band music filled the house. She recognized the song, but couldn't place the title. Whatever it was brought to mind the old Fred Astaire movies she used to watch with Mama.

Orville stuck his head in from the patio and said, "That's great! I didn't even know we had music here."

She called back to him. "You recognize this stuff?"

But he had already stepped back out to the grill.

Tiff turned the music down slightly, but she couldn't keep the bounce out of her step when she headed for the patio. She smiled when she saw her father from behind, bebopping in his own fashion. She stepped onto the patio and spoke up so he would hear her above the music.

"Hey, Daddio, how soon do you expect that chicken to be ready?"

Still moving to the beat, he said, "About fifteen minutes. You're hungry?" He stopped dancing and boasted, "My secret barbeque sauce brings out the starved savage in everyone."

She rolled her eyes. "There's nothing a girl likes more than having her father call her a savage. Actually, I'm trying to time the veggies."

"I thought the Brits were bringing the veggies."

"I volunteered to do them, because Vera decided to treat us to crème caramel."

"Crème who? What's that?"

"Trust me, you'll love it," Tiff said. "It's a custardy dessert with a sweet sauce on top. Really yummy and fattening. She's experimenting with a sugar-free version for me, so I didn't want her to have to do anything else. Sometimes recipes don't adapt well to fake sweeteners. She wasn't sure she'd be successful."

Orville pointed his spatula in the direction of Julian's house. "We'll soon know. Here they come."

Sean, Vera, and Jeremy entered the patio area. Vera carried a square, glass pan.

"Vera, that triumphant smile on your face is a good sign," Tiff said.

"Well, this is the second one I've done," Vera said. "The first was just to make sure I could do it with the different sweetener." She then nodded toward the music. "Love that era. Makes me feel young!"

"Here, let me put that in the fridge for you, love." Sean took the dish from her and winked at Tiff. "I was happy to serve as her guinea pig for the first custard." He gave Vera a quick peck on the cheek before he headed for the house. "Dee-licious, darling."

"Thank you, dear. So are you." She followed him toward the house.

Jeremy leaned against the patio wall and watched Sean and Vera. His eyes met Tiff's, and he smiled easily at her.

Tiff broke the moment to slip back into the house and shoo Vera and Sean out. "Go relax out there. I have to toss these veggies into the micro-wave for a couple of minutes and we'll be all set."

As Sean and Vera obeyed, a tinny snippet of a Bach prelude sounded from Tiff's purse.

She opened her cell to hear Ren's enthusiastic voice. "Tiff! I'm so glad you have your phone on!"

"I'm happy to talk with you, too, girl," Tiff said, "but we're going to be having dinner soon. Can I—"

"No! You can't call me back. You have to call Kara right now. I promised her I'd get you to call her as soon as possible."

"Why didn't she call me herself?"

"She needs *you* to call *her* where she is right now."

"Where is she?"

Ren released a groan of exasperation. "No more questions, young lady! Just jot down this number and call her before you sit down to dinner."

Tiff looked for a pen and paper. "Okay."

Ren gave her Kara's number. "You promise you'll call right now?"

"Promise."

She hung up and walked out to the patio. "Hey, guys, I need to make a quick call." She looked at Jeremy. "Something about Kara."

He tilted his head. "Something good?"

"I...think so. I'll try to be quick." She retreated to her bedroom with her phone and sat on the edge of her bed.

Kara answered her phone on the second ring.

"Hey, Kara, it's—"

"Oh, Tiff, what a wonderful coincidence that you're calling right now."

"Not really, Ren just called and—"

Kara interrupted her again and spoke to someone else. "Mickey, you'll never guess who's on the phone. Tiffany LeBoeuf."

Kara was being weird. Something was up.

"Tiffany, is that you for real, girl?" said Mickey, her former boss at the gym.

"Hey, Mickey, what's up?"

"What's up? Girl, you just don't know how crazy things have been here. You couldn't have called at a better time."

"Um, okay."

"Please tell me you haven't taken a job at another gym."

Her stomach flipped. "Uh, no, Mickey. I'm in San Diego with my dad right now. On vacation, kind of. I haven't even started looking for another job yet."

"Awesome!" Mickey sounded as if he were pumped up on stress and caffeine. "Hang on a second, Tiffany." She heard him speak to someone else in the room, and it clearly wasn't Kara. "Okay, David, I've got to put my foot down about this. I can't run the gym without hiring power, and we need someone immediately. Considering the circumstances, either let me hire this tried-and-true trainer or you can look for another manager too."

Tiff gasped. "Mickey! Don't—"

He shushed her quietly, and she heard David answer Mickey. David sounded calm. Tiff didn't know whether that was a good sign or not.

Mickey came back on the phone. "You still interested in coming back to American Gym, Tiffany?"

"Absolutely!" She stood from the bed and started pacing.

"When can you start?"

"I'll be back in town late Saturday. Is Monday too soon?"

"You're on, girl. Come see me at nine sharp, and we'll get your papers on file. You totally rock, Tiffany. Here, I'll give you back to Kara."

"Thanks, Mickey!" She almost screamed with excitement. Kara came back on, and spoke softly. She sounded as if she were exerting energy, maybe lightly jogging.

"Hold on a minute, Tiff. I want to get out of the office so the guys can talk." Tiff heard the sound of a closing door. "Okay." Kara squealed as quietly as one can squeal. "Can you believe that? Am I a genius, or what?"

"Kara, you stinker! How did you know to have me call?"

"Oh, you know how impulsive Mickey is. I knew he was going to be freaked out during this meeting with David."

"Who's David, anyway?"

"One of the corporate guys. One of the guys who told Mickey he couldn't hire you back. I wanted your call to come in when Mickey was pumped for this meeting. He's always more assertive when he's wired like that. And I hoped he'd demand having you back if you called before he could think about it too much."

Tiff couldn't stop walking back and forth in the small bedroom. "Well, you know him better than I do, obviously," Tiff said. "You were completely right. But what was the meeting for, anyway?"

"It's been *nuts* here the past week or so. That girl they hired to take your place? She stole the petty cash right out of Mickey's desk. *Stole* it!"

"So they fired her?"

"You bet. They're going to prosecute too. So that was strike one for the employee pool. And strike one in your favor."

Tiff finally sat back down on the bed. "Strike one. You mean there's a strike two?"

"Yep. They're going to be short another trainer in about eight months, so they need you back more than ever."

"Who's leaving?" Tiff asked. "And who gives eight months' notice, anyway?"

Silence.

"Kara?"

"It's not forever," Kara said. "At least that's not the current plan. American Gym allows three months' maternity leave, and we'll see what's happening after that."

Tiff jumped up from the bed and gasped. "*You?*"

Kara laughed. "Why should Ren have all the fun and morning sickness?"

Tiff finally screamed. "Kara! Congratulations! Gosh, I leave town for two weeks and look what happens. Petty theft, impregnation, religious conversion—"

"Religious what? What are you talking about?"

Tiff paused. "I shouldn't say anything too soon, really. But Jeremy's been showing some really good signs. He said he wanted what I have."

"Oh, Tiff. Whatever you do, don't push him. He's been resisting Ren and me for years now."

"I'm being very hands-off, Kara. This has to be between Jeremy and God."

Kara agreed, then asked, "When are you all coming home?"

"Jeremy leaves early Saturday morning. Daddy and I leave later the same day."

"Well, have a safe trip. And I'll see you at the gym Monday morning."

Tiff sighed. Such relief. "Kara, I don't know how to thank you for helping me like this."

"Hey, we need you. And I look forward to working with you again, now that you don't, you know, hate my guts and stuff."

"You're awful," Tiff said. "I never hated your guts. I was just…confused." She grimaced. "I guess that's an understatement, huh?"

"Been there, Tiff. 'Amazing Grace.' That's my theme song. Hey, I've got to go. My client just arrived."

As soon as Tiff closed her phone, she looked heavenward.

I can never thank You enough. And You'll never cease to amaze me. Thank You, thank You, thank You.

Sixty-three

Jeremy stepped into the beach house. He recognized the song playing on the CD player. This version of "Stardust" featured the soft, muted sounds of several clarinets playing the melody. Jeremy owned the Willie Nelson version, but he liked this old-fashioned, big-band style even more. Struck by a simple urge to compliment Tiff on her musical tastes, he glanced toward the bedrooms.

And there she was. Beautiful, beaming, and running straight toward him.

Her expression immediately brought a smile to his face, just before she threw her arms around him and shrieked with joy.

He was no fool. He threw his arms right back around her.

Tiff laughed while she spoke, which made him laugh too. But he couldn't understand a word she said. He pulled back to look at her.

"Wait, Tiff, slow down. What are you saying? Something about your job?"

She stopped talking, breathless. She still wore a radiant smile, but when she looked into his eyes, her expression relaxed.

They still had their arms around each other and now Tiff seemed to become aware of how close they were.

And that was one mighty romantic song in the background.

"Jeremy."

She simply said his name. The least he could do was return the favor.

"Tiff." He leaned in.

"What is it?" Orville stepped into the house, followed closely by Sean and Vera.

Jeremy pulled away from Tiff, but she looked at him, smiling, for a moment longer before she included the others in her circle.

"I got my job back at the gym!"

Everyone reacted with a cacophony of cheers and questions that drowned out the last stanzas of "Stardust." In a fitting change of atmosphere, an upbeat, celebratory song played next, complete with a horn section to accompany the happy chatter of the group.

Orville's voice finally emerged above the din. "So, they came to their senses."

Tiff stepped over to turn the music down. "It's more like they were forced back to their senses. Kara knew exactly how to time everything, and—" She looked at Jeremy. "Kara's pregnant!"

"Brilliant!" Jeremy cheered.

"Was *that* part of the timing?" Vera asked. "She *is* an organized planner."

"No," Tiff laughed. "Maybe's *God's* timing, but not necessarily Kara's. Either way, it really helped me. She's one of their best trainers, and she'll take maternity leave in about eight months."

Jeremy put his hand on Tiff's back. "Say, why don't you all head out and start serving yourselves. I'll grab these vegetables—"

"Oh!" Tiff dashed into the kitchen. "No, you go out. I'll tell you the rest in a minute." Her excitement was palpable. Jeremy didn't think he'd ever seen her this happy. He watched her, wishing he could somehow be responsible for that kind of happiness in her life.

"Uh, son?" Sean interrupted his thoughts. "You coming?"

As they stepped outside, Sean spoke quietly to his son. "Remember, now, to listen and watch for God's guidance. If she's the one, He's going to keep showing that to you. If she's not, He'll close some doors. Just pay attention."

Jeremy nodded but subtly brought his finger to his lips to signal for Sean to change the subject in front of Vera and Orville.

Earlier, Sean and Jeremy had talked about Tiff after Jeremy had prayed to receive Christ. Now, with his conversion a reality, the question of Tiff loomed large. Was she part of God's plan? Could He guide Jeremy in sorting out his feelings for this charming "friend"?

He loved the way they related to each other. She made him laugh, and she seemed to appreciate funny things about him, even when he wasn't trying to be funny.

It happened again at dinner that night as Tiff related to everyone their experiences at the amusement park. The moment she mentioned she had to cajole Jeremy into riding the roller coaster, Sean piped up.

"My Jeremy? He was always wild for roller coasters. Always had to ride up front, arms flailing, over and over again. A complete madman."

The comment stopped Tiff in her tracks. She looked at Sean to see if he was joking and then slowly turned to Jeremy.

Jeremy, who had clearly gone to great lengths to manufacture a fine excuse for holding on to Tiff for dear life, mustered a smile meant to beg forgiveness.

Tiff simply said, "Oh, *really?*"

And when she looked away from him, he knew by her expression that she appreciated his charade.

Yes, he loved that about her. She was a good sport, and he realized that was something that had been missing from his past relationships. His female friends, Kara and Ren, were good sports and had excellent senses of humor, but they were truly just friends. His romantic relationships had always involved women like Eve, who found his humorous side too silly, or who didn't seem to care or understand at all what was humorous about him.

Until now, he hadn't even appreciated how important a sense of humor was. Perhaps this was one of those bits of divine guidance his dad had mentioned. When he turned his attention back to the group, Tiff reacted to something Vera said. She threw her head back and laughed with abandon. Then she looked at him, wanting to bring him into the moment. He didn't even know what Vera had said, yet he laughed easily because of Tiff.

If what he felt about Tiff *wasn't* divine, he was going to need some significantly closed doors mighty soon.

Sixty-four

When Jeremy, Sean, and Vera had left, Orville turned to Tiff and said, "Fancy a walk, kitten?"

"The Brits finally made their mark on you?" she smirked.

"Mark? What mark?" he asked, feigning ignorance.

"Daddy, I suggest you delete 'fancy' from your vocabulary before you go back to the trucking office." She took him by the arm, and they headed for the boardwalk.

Orville glanced at Julian's house as they passed. "I'm going to miss them."

"Me too."

He patted the arm she looped through his. "But you and Jeremy will cross paths still, right?"

"Yep. I'm not sure about the course of our paths, but I'm sure they'll cross." She studied his face. "Daddy, will you be horribly lonely back home?"

He shrugged. "Not always. You know, I realized during this trip that I need to make more of an effort to spend time with people. We talked about that, Sean and Jeremy and I. We men just don't typically make friends the way you women seem to. But I'm going to do something about that. Phil and JJ from work have asked me to hang out with them before. I've always said no, because I wanted to stay home with your mama—"

"Oh, Daddy."

He reached up and wiped at his eyes. "Well, now. That caught me by surprise. I suppose I've managed to think of other things these two weeks. I guess I'm not ready to go back to the real world just yet."

Tiff fought her own tears. "We just have to accept that tears are a part of the real world." She squeezed his arm. "But these two weeks have been real-world weeks too. I feel like our friendships with the Becketts are already rich, and we've barely gotten to know them." She gave him a smile. "Daddy, how about we start planning a trip to England sometime soon. Wouldn't that be fun?"

There was sadness behind his smile, but he said, "Kitten, that's a great idea. The Becketts were one of the highlights of this trip. So was Julian."

"Yes."

"And...Zeke!"

"Yeah. Zeke too."

"No, I mean, Zeke!" Orville pointed dead ahead. Zeke was approaching them.

He flashed his trademark smile at them and said, "I thought maybe you two had gone home by now!"

"One more day," Orville said.

"And is that why you're sad, brother?" Zeke asked. It was clear he had easily pegged Orville's mood.

"Oh. Partly."

"We were just talking about my mother," Tiff said. "We came out here to San Diego to try to relax a little after the struggle of her last days. She died a few months ago."

"Ah, no," Zeke said. "I'm so sorry."

"And it's hard to go back home and get back to regular life, knowing she's gone," Tiff said.

Zeke sat on the beach wall and said, "If you don't mind my asking, have you found any solace in God?"

"That doesn't seem to be in the cards for me," Orville said. "I've tried praying, but I just get angry." Orville turned to Tiff and continued, "I'm sorry, kitten, but I just don't believe the way you do." Then he addressed Zeke. "How could I ever embrace a faith that says my wife isn't in heaven now because she didn't 'accept Christ' as her savior?"

Tiff recalled her mother's last days. Tiff had prayed, she had whispered to her mother about Christ, and she had felt a sense of peace about God's will when her mother died. But her father's question brought fresh fear to her heart.

Zeke spoke softly. "May I ask what your wife's name was, Orville?"

"Sheila."

"And do you remember what Sheila's last words were, by any chance?"

"To me? Nothing much," he said. "She asked for ice chips. Answered yes when I asked if she wanted me to adjust the pillow under her head. Nothing important."

Tiff remembered the last words her mother had said to her, but they had nothing to do with God, and she didn't want to discuss them here.

Zeke nodded. "So you're certain her last words weren't about Christ? She didn't say she rejected Christ as her savior."

"Of course not. She was heavily medicated. It wasn't the time for a theological discussion. And then she was in a coma for two days before her body just gave up."

Zeke put his hand on Orville's shoulder. "Brother, I'm not saying this to argue with you or to try to sway you in any way. But I've never died and neither have you. We don't know what Sheila saw or thought or did before her last breath. We don't know whether or not she had a conversation with the Lord." He paused, then continued. "But maybe she did. Maybe she realized something beautiful in her final moments here on earth. There's great hope in that, don't you think?"

Orville took a deep breath but couldn't reply.

Zeke stood. "I won't be around over the weekend, so I won't see you again before you leave."

Orville extended his hand. "It's been a pleasure, Zeke."

"For me, too, Orville," Zeke said.

He turned to Tiff, who put out her hand, but he gave her a quick hug instead. He spoke softly, "And I'll see you again for sure, sister. Until that day, we'll just keep praying, okay?"

He pulled back and Tiff nodded. "Okay."

As Zeke walked on, Tiff threaded her arm back through her dad's.

"He told you to pray for me, didn't he?" Orville asked.

"Actually, Daddy, he just encouraged me to keep praying," she said softly. "I might include you in there if I think of it."

He patted her arm. "You do that, kitten." They walked a few silent steps before he spoke again. "Yes, please. Do that."

Sixty-five

The following morning Jeremy sat by the seawall facing the ocean, and let the sun soak him with warmth. The weather would still be brisk when he arrived home in Virginia tomorrow. For one last day he wanted to enjoy this glorious weather.

He looked out toward the ocean and noticed Tiff among the early beachcombers. Her empty beach chair blocked most of his view of her, but he'd recognize that light auburn hair anywhere. He grabbed a folding chair from Julian's porch and walked out to join her.

She didn't appear to notice his approach. She gazed at the horizon deep in thought. He was only able to see her profile, but from his vantage point, she looked less than content.

Jeremy cleared his throat, and she started before she turned to see him.

"Jeremy! How long have you been standing there?"

"Just a moment." He opened his chair next to hers. "Do you prefer privacy?"

"From you? No! Sit." She moved her chair an inch, as if she needed to make room for him on the beach.

He sat and glanced briefly at her bright yellow sundress. "You look stunning as always. But I sensed you had a case of the mulligrubs when I walked up."

She sat next to him and said, "I just have so many things going on in my mind." She didn't look away from him. Rather, she seemed to study his face—his eyes, his mouth. Her scrutiny actually moved him to look away. He couldn't remember the last time a woman regarded him like that. It was unnerving.

He pushed his bare feet into the sand. "Do you want to talk about anything? I mean, would it help to discuss whatever you're thinking about?"

"Maybe." She sat forward and stretched her arms over her legs. "I'm a little nervous about starting back at work. I know I'll do fine, but I hate feeling like the new kid. And I will, even though I've worked there before." She shrugged. "That'll pass."

"Well. Glad I could be of help with that."

"And there are your folks," she continued. "I'm going to miss them. Especially Vera." She looked at him quickly. "I mean, I love your dad. He's terrific. But Vera just came along—"

"When you were missing your own mum."

"Yeah. These two weeks would have been totally different for me if Vera hadn't been here."

"They've decided to stay with me in Virginia a full week, you know, before they go back home. I know they'd love to see you. We could all go out together."

"I'd love to do that," she said.

"And make sure you come to Julian's to say goodbye to them before I take them to the airport. We leave in an hour or so."

She sat back. He rested against the arm of his chair, still watching her. "What else?"

"Oh. My dad. I'm concerned about his being lonely after he goes back to Florence. I guess he just has to go through this. He has to learn to live without Mama in his life." She opened her hand, as if she held her next concern there. "And, of course, Mama is one of the people I've been brooding about too. She and I always had a strained relationship, and now I realize it was more than just the way I was acting as a teen. I made plenty of awful decisions in my life, but I don't think that's why Mama was disappointed with me. I think some of my bad decisions were actually *because* she was disappointed in me."

"Why are you so certain of her disappointment?"

Tiff teared up. "Even the last thing she said to me was about that."

"What did she say, Tiff?"

She paused, then said, "You can't tell Daddy, okay?"

"Not if you don't want me too."

"She said, 'Your father would have been so proud of you...'"

Again, he waited. But she didn't complete the sentence. "Proud of you if what?"

"Exactly my question. What did I fail to do to make him proud of me?"

Jeremy sat up. "But your father's ecstatic about you, Tiff! Anyone can see that. You have to talk with him about this." He took her hand. "Please promise me you'll talk with him. Something's not right there. Your mother wasn't well. Maybe she wasn't thinking straight. I want you to promise you'll talk to him about this."

"I'll try."

He released her hand. "Good."

"You're quite the problem solver today," she said.

He shrugged. "It's a guy thing, I guess. I know I'm simply supposed to nod and try to understand. Ren and Kara have counseled me about that before. And I am trying to understand. But you have these things floating about in your mind making you worry. I simply *don't* understand why you would want them left floating there if you can do something about them." After a moment he added, "So, is that all...or is there more?"

"What?"

"Was there anyone *else* wandering about in your thoughts?"

"Hmm, anyone else. Anyone else."

He couldn't hold back. "I think you're the meanest girl in the world...I know I'm plug ugly with this blasted black eye—"

"Oh, stop." She spoke like a strict schoolteacher. "If you're going to start fishing for compliments, Mr. Beckett, you'll have to stand closer to the water."

"Fishing, eh?" he said, "You *are* cruel."

"Just make sure you wear that wetsuit."

"The...the wetsuit?"

She nodded. "Yessiree."

"You like that?"

She pointed to herself. "*Big* fan of the wetsuit."

Without thought he looked up and said, "Thank You."

"My pleasure."

"Uh, actually, Tiff, I wasn't talking to you."

"Huh?"

"I was...praying, sort of. You know, to my...savior."

She looked out at the waves and sighed. "Finally."

"Finally, what?"

"Actually, Jeremy," she continued. "*I* wasn't talking to *you.*"

He gently knocked her knee with his. "I say. Let's take your father to dinner for our last night, eh?"

"Oh, he'd like that," Tiff said. "What do you think? Should we go casual or dress up a little? Since it's our last night, and all."

He shrugged. "I don't know about you, love, but I plan to wear that wetsuit."

Sixty-six

As Tiff and Jeremy walked into the guest apartment, Vera dashed past in a whirlwind. She stopped, middash, just beyond Tiff and turned around. "Tiff! Come give us a hug, darling!"

She complied, remembering that during this past week she had overcome a personal hurdle in her life thanks to Vera. The hurdle of hugging, of all things. Now she could actually envision comfortably accepting hugs from Ren when she returned home. Maybe even *giving* one. That was a giant leap for the woman who stiffened under Ren's affectionate squeeze just a few weeks ago in Ledo's pizza parlor. But Vera was so easy to hug. Sweet smelling, a little squishy, and so many things Tiff had never experienced before in a mother figure.

That made Tiff a little sad, but she was starting to appreciate whatever it was each person in her life offered. And she was starting to wonder what she could offer each person in return. Everyone had their own needs and gifts. It was all about paying attention and appreciating. And not expecting what can't be offered.

Jeremy quickly disappeared into Sean and Vera's bedroom where he could be heard talking with Sean about their schedule.

Vera interrupted her eavesdropping. "I was just throwing together some quick sandwiches—we're going to eat on the way to the airport. Would you like something?"

"No, no, don't mind me," Tiff said. "I won't add to your work. I just wanted to come say goodbye. Jeremy tells me you're going to stay with him for a week in Virginia?"

Vera sliced into kaiser rolls and threw roast-beef sandwiches together like a pro. "Sean and I plan to stay in Washington for the weekend. I'm quite excited about that. So much to see there. And then we'll stay at Jeremy's condo for the week, before we head home." She shot a glance toward the bedroom before she spoke to Tiff, as if in confidence. "I hope we'll be seeing you some, eh?"

"I think so," Tiff answered. "Jeremy said something about that."

"Oh, and have you no say in the matter?"

"No, I mean, he's inviting me to join you all," Tiff said. "He's leaving it up to me. He's very gentlemanly that way."

Vera took an open bag of potato chips from the cupboard. "He is, isn't he? He's his father's son in that regard. And did he tell you about his chat with his dad?"

"After he and I came back from shopping?"

"Yes," Vera said. "Very good chat, that."

"He hasn't told me about it, but he seems to assume I know about it."

"And do you?" Vera's grin was positively gleeful.

Tiff found Vera's delight contagious. "He mentioned his savior a while ago. He's *there*, isn't he?"

Vera gave a pat to Tiff's hand. "I think that was your doing, dear! He's quite taken with you."

"Well, I hope it's more than his being taken with *me*."

Vera put several items into a shopping bag. "Oh, yes. But you've been quite a good example for him this week."

"I think I had company there, Vera."

Vera set the bag of food by the front door and motioned to Tiff to join her on the couch. "I want to tell you something, Tiff." She patted the seat beside her.

In the back room, they could hear Jeremy and Sean laughing about something.

Vera said, "Your father was over here to say goodbye a little earlier. He's a good man, your dad."

"Yes, he is."

"I don't know if you have any idea of the impact you made on him when you ministered to your mum during her final days."

"Oh, I guess so. I did my best."

"Of course, yes." She put her hand on Tiff's arm. "But I'm talking on a more grand scale, dear. You absolutely amazed him by your self-sacrifice during your mum's last days. I hope this doesn't come out the wrong way—but your father said it was as if you were an entirely different girl from the one he had always known. And loved, by the way."

Tiff said nothing. It was the reformed nasty girl all over again. Interestingly, this time she saw the comment through Ren's eyes. *I once was lost and now I'm found,* and all that.

Would wonders never cease? She was actually serving as a good example to her own father, the man who had always been her hero. Amazing grace, indeed.

Vera broke through her thoughts. "Anyway, it's important you know that. Your father might still balk at some of the things you tell him about your faith. But you're doing the right things around him."

"You don't know how much it means to me to hear that. Thank you for telling me." Tiff leaned over and gave Vera a hug just as Sean and Jeremy walked out of the bedroom rolling several pieces of luggage behind them.

"Ah, Tiff, are you riding to the airport with us, then?" Sean asked.

She stood up. "No, actually, I need to talk with my dad about some stuff. But I wanted to say goodbye."

As Sean gave her a big hug, Tiff glanced at Jeremy over his shoulder and received a delicious wink.

Vera interrupted them. "Sean, we need to get moving. Jeremy?"

"It's goodbye, then Tiff," Sean said. "We'll see you next on the *other* coast."

Tiff gave Sean one last hug. "Yes, see you in Virginia, Sean."

As they left, Tiff felt like the most wonderful time of her life was drawing to a close. Would she ever be this happy again?

Sixty-seven

"Daddy, are you here?" Tiff stepped into the beach house from the patio.

"Back here, honey."

She walked back to his room, where he had his suitcase open on the bed. He looked around and said, "I saw you out there talking with Jeremy. Everything all right between you two?"

"Yeah, great!" she answered. "You're packing already?"

"Already? We have to leave in twenty-four hours. I'd just as soon have most of this out of the way."

"Vera and Sean just left. They told me you said goodbye earlier."

"Yep. Really fine people, those two. I hope I get to see them again sometime."

She started to fold some of his shirts. "As I said before, now you have a good excuse to travel to England…and I might even go with you."

"I like that idea."

She sat on his bed. "We want to take you out to dinner tonight."

"We? Who's we?" he asked, a twinkle in his eye.

"You know, Dad," she said, "you're going to miss having me around to tease."

"That's for sure."

After a moment in which neither of them spoke, Orville said, "So, really, kitten, what's happening with you and our man Jeremy? I thought you needed to avoid getting too involved with him."

"I did." She sat back on the bed. "And we're not actually involved.

That's just become a better possibility. 'Our man' and I are on the same track now."

"Your Jesus thing, you mean?"

"Yep. My Jesus thing."

Orville grabbed a handful of socks from the dresser and dropped them into his suitcase. "Well, I'm happy for both of you. Jeremy's a fine young man."

Tiff tried to work up her courage for what she had to say next. She just didn't know if she was ready to hear about how she let her father down. But if Mama thought it was important enough to mention at the end, Tiff had to ask.

"Daddy, I need to talk to you about something."

He seemed distracted by the way he arranged the clothes in his bag. "Shoot."

"Mama said something to me...it was actually the last thing she said to me that I was able to understand. And I need to ask you about it."

He abruptly stopped what he was doing and looked at her. He pushed the suitcase farther up on the bed so he could sit next to her.

"What did she tell you, honey?"

Tiff couldn't look him in the eye while she asked. "Mama said, 'Your father would have been so proud of you.' But that's all she said." Tiff forced herself to look up at Orville. "She didn't tell me how I failed you, Daddy."

And then Tiff had to choke back a sob. "I have to know what I did wrong. Was it because I didn't go to college? Because I was such a run-around? What?"

He put his arms around her. "Oh, Tiffany, no. No, baby." He stroked her hair. "You've got it all wrong. That wasn't—"

He stood and grabbed a box of tissues from the dresser. He presented it to Tiff before he pulled some for himself.

"Look." He grabbed a small stool from the corner of the room and settled himself down on it opposite Tiff. "Look at me, kitten."

Tiff looked up at him.

"I never planned to tell you this, Tiffany. I'm selfish that way. But I can't have you thinking I'm not as proud as I can be about you. You're the best thing that's ever happened to me. I mean, I loved your mama, but, honey, you are the jewel in my life."

"But, then—"

"You remember what I said about the first time I saw your mama?"

"At the firehouse, you mean?"

"Yeah."

"You said she walked in with her girlfriends, and you were smitten."

"I was, absolutely." He wiped his hands on his pants. "But your mama wasn't smitten with me. She fell head over heels for Franklin."

Tiff had seen pictures of Uncle Frank, but she had never met him. "Uncle Frank? He was alive then? But you said he died really young. Didn't you say he was killed—"

"In Vietnam, yes. Your mama only dated him a month or so before he shipped out. And he was only there a few weeks before he was hit by sniper fire."

Tiff had a ball of tension in her stomach. "Daddy, what are you telling me?"

He paused. "The day Franklin died, I lost my only brother. Your mama lost her first love. And you, honey—" His voice shook. "You lost your father."

She felt as if she wasn't even there, in that room, hearing what he said.

"No. *You're* my father," she said firmly.

He moved to sit next to her, but she turned so she could face him.

"You're my father," she repeated.

He nodded and reached for her, but she kept her distance.

"*You're* my father." She sobbed and curled forward. She hugged herself, her head near her knees.

Orville wrapped his arms around her. "Honey, Frank didn't even know. Your mama didn't find out she was pregnant until after he was killed. She confided in me. We were good friends by then, and we were already leaning on each other because of Frank's death. We didn't plan to fall in love. But we did."

Tiff sat up enough to lean into him. "You loved each other?"

"Completely."

He held her and rocked her, and she remembered his doing that when she was little.

"I don't know why your mama decided to mention Franklin to you, kitten. But obviously it was important to her that you knew he would have been proud of you. She wasn't saying I would have been proud of you if you had done something different. She meant Franklin would have been proud of you—just as you are—if he had lived."

He lifted Tiff's chin and kissed her on the forehead. "She was telling you *she* was proud of you, honey. And she was."

Tiff sat up and put her arms around her father's neck. She had to say it once more, as if she needed to lay a claim. "You're my father."

Sixty-eight

Tiff walked along the beach allowing the waves to wash around her ankles. Each cold splash served as a reminder that she wasn't dreaming. She was wide awake and needed to come to grips with this new aspect of her life. She wasn't even sure what this feeling was—what was she battling, exactly?

She didn't think she felt betrayed. She understood why her parents would keep this news from everyone, including her. Despite the physical intimacy Mama shared with Franklin, she obviously barely knew him before he died. Once Orville stepped in, Mama clearly felt the best course would be to let Orville become Tiff's dad. And Orville certainly loved Tiff as if she were his own.

She also didn't feel the emotional draw some adopted people had—that compulsion to meet their biological parents. Her curiosity about Franklin was definitely piqued, but it was a detached curiosity, not a need motivated by self-discovery.

"Tiff."

She turned around to see Jeremy approaching her. Had Daddy already told him? The concern on his face seemed to indicate so.

"Are you all right, love?" He put his hand on her shoulder and studied her eyes. "What's happened?"

"Daddy didn't tell you?"

Jeremy glanced back toward the house. "Actually, I did stop in when I got back from the airport. I could see your father was upset. He said

286

you'd gone for a walk but would probably like the company if I wanted to look for you."

Two small children came running back and forth around them, laughing and screaming over a wayward beach ball. Jeremy moved his hand to her back and guided her past them. He leaned forward and searched her face. "Did the two of you quarrel, then?"

"No." She almost laughed at the idea. "I can't remember the last time Daddy and I quarreled."

She told him the news without tearing up again until she had to say the sentence that bothered her the most. "So Daddy's not really my father."

He put his arm across her shoulders. "I'm sorry, Tiff. What did you…I mean…how do you feel?"

"Awful." She shrugged. "Well, I'm not sure. I know I'm not mad about it. It's just such a shock, and I feel…confused." She looked at him. "You know, the strongest feeling I had at first was that someone was going to…I don't know…take Daddy away from me."

"Orville?"

She nodded. "Yeah. I mean, when I thought he didn't have a choice about being my father, I just felt more secure." She paused. "I know that's stupid, but—"

"No. I know what you mean. Choice changes things."

Tiff stopped walking and faced him. "You think so?"

"Well, to tell you the truth, Tiff, I experienced something similar this morning when I thought about God."

"I don't follow."

"When I talked with my dad yesterday and prayed to Christ, I felt like I had finally figured it all out. I could feel a connection between God and me."

"I know that feeling. You became a new creation."

"A new creation." Jeremy smiled. "I like that. But for a moment when I woke up this morning, I worried a bit. As if I would lose that connection." He waited. Then he continued, "It was just for a moment. Then I remembered that I had made that choice. It wasn't made for me. So if I didn't choose to lose my connection with God, I wouldn't lose it. Ever."

Tiff put her hand on Jeremy's chest. She didn't look up when she spoke.

"That's it, Jeremy. That's what bothered me. I suddenly realized Daddy chose to be my father. So I supposed he could choose not to be too."

Jeremy put his arms around her, rested his head against hers, and spoke softly. "But you know he'd never make a choice like that, Tiff. No more than God would. As long as you consider Orville your father, he will be."

"You're right. I know that."

He gave her a kiss on the forehead, and she closed her eyes.

He kissed her eyelids and gently cupped his hands around her head.

Until now, she actually hadn't thought about how close they had come to each other. Now she opened her eyes and looked at Jeremy's face. He had a couple of small smudges of black on his lips.

She reached her fingers up to his mouth. "I guess I didn't cry away all my mascara, after all."

As she wiped the smudges away, Jeremy kissed her fingertips. She barely had time to move her fingers away before he drew her closer and kissed her.

The thoughts that came next were a wonderful untangling of truth. He's Christian. He's single. He's the sweetest man ever. And mercy, mercy, mercy, these lips are some of the Lord's finest work.

She put her arms around him and kissed him right back.

Sixty-nine

Tiff could see her father sitting on the couch through the front window. When she opened the door, she realized he had fallen asleep. She closed the door quietly behind her.

He had put on another one of Faith's CDs. A classical song was playing, featuring a lovely but solemn piano solo.

Tiff carefully sat down next to him. She snuggled up and rested her head on his shoulder. He stirred and put his arm around her before he dozed back off. She wasn't sleepy, but she decided she'd enjoy this moment while she had the chance.

But he stirred again and awoke.

"Are you okay, kitten?"

"I'm just fine," she said.

"I was dreaming about my brother." He rubbed his eyes. "We were in the middle of a snowball fight, and he started playing a piano right in the middle of the field."

"Did he play piano in real life?" Tiff asked.

"Not a note."

"Must have been the music from the CD."

Orville nodded. "The snowball fight brings back memories, though. We spent a couple of Christmases at our grandparents' place in Pennsylvania when we were kids." He laughed. "This one fight, oh man. We teamed up with some of our cousins, and Franklin and I were on opposite teams. Franklin really nailed me with a snowball imbedded with this huge chunk of ice." Orville pointed to a scar over his eyebrow. "Five stitches." He paused. "He got in so much trouble with your grandma." Another pause. "Frank was only two years older than I was, but he grew up faster. I really looked up to him. He was—"

And he stopped abruptly, as if he had said too much. Or maybe he felt awkward suddenly discussing Franklin with Tiff.

It dawned on her that she had heard very little about Franklin before. Now she understood why. The subject must have been difficult for Mama and Daddy to discuss with her, considering their secret.

Then something else occurred to her. "Daddy!"

"Yeah?"

"When we first got here, and I told you I was attracted to Jeremy, you warned me to be careful how I behaved. Because of Eve. You told me to make sure Eve could tell I wasn't running after Jeremy."

"I believe I told you to let her see you weren't interested, even though you were."

"But that's what *you* went through, isn't it? When Mama dated Franklin. You had to act like you weren't—"

"Yep. She was my brother's girl. I had to do the right thing. Just about killed me, but to this day I don't regret how I handled that situation. If I had interfered and then lost Franklin like I did…"

"Daddy," Tiff sighed. "Was there ever a time you *didn't* do the right thing?"

Orville laughed. "I don't think I want to take our discussion in *that* direction, honey." He stood and hitched up his shorts. "Anyway. Guess I should get back there and shower. You and Jeremy still planning to treat me to a fancy dinner?"

"Yep." She arose and embraced him from behind. "We're taking you to a Persian restaurant. You'll love Middle Eastern food." She rested her head against his back and sighed. "Daddy, I hope you know that I can't ever think of anyone but you as my father. That's okay, isn't it?"

Orville turned and caressed her face. "That's more than okay, honey."

"Good." She walked into the kitchen and pulled two coffee cups from the cupboard. "Now, we have time before we have to get ready for dinner. So how about I fix us some coffee?" And then she added, "And what else would you like to tell me about your brother?"

Seventy

Tiff opened the door at Jeremy's knock. He paused before entering, taking her in. She was such a stunner naturally, but now she was like something out of a movie. Her dress, the color of the Caribbean Sea, made her eyes appear the same color. The top was strappy and exposed her lovely shoulders. The sun had deepened her skin tone and lightened her auburn hair.

"Tiff, you look positively like a mermaid...except for the leg thing, of course."

"Thank you...I think!" She laughed. "Jeremy, that's what you wore on the shuttle bus!"

He looked down at himself. Blast. Was it a good thing to be wearing the same thing again? He didn't own that many suits. Did she care about such things?

But when he looked back at her, he sensed she approved.

"So it looks all right?"

She moved aside so he could walk in. "That's an understatement. You're *gorgeous*."

Just then Orville walked out from the bedrooms in dress slacks and a colorful collared shirt. "Why, thank you, kitten. I do try."

Jeremy reached out to shake Orville's hand and said, "I don't know why, Orville, but when I'm dressed this formally, I feel awkward not shaking hands."

Orville returned the gesture. "That's because you're a gent. Should we go?" And then he patted his back pockets. "Oh, you two go on out. I forgot my wallet."

"Okay, Daddy," Tiff said. "But remember we're treating you tonight."

With Jeremy behind her, she muttered to him. "I notice you didn't feel like you needed to shake my hand."

"Forgive me." He planted the lightest kiss on her shoulder.

He heard a quick gasp as she said, "Oh yeah. That works too."

~

They went to the Bandar Restaurant and enjoyed stuffed grape leaves, lamb shanks, charbroiled chicken, and beef kabobs. The restaurant boasted modern décor more typical of an artsy Manhattan eatery than what Jeremy originally pictured for a Persian restaurant. He liked it.

"I never would have expected to enjoy something called Barg Kabobs," Orville said as he finished off his last bite with satisfaction.

"I guess barg is steak, Daddy," Tiff said. "Now we know, huh?"

"Yep. I can see myself back home, ordering up a big slab of barg, medium rare," Orville said. "I'll impress my friends with how cosmopolitan I've become."

"What sorts of things do you do with your friends, Orville?" Jeremy asked. "Or, rather, will you do? After that conversation we men had on the beach, I'm curious."

"You mean, will I get off my keister and do things with my buddies, or will I sit at home and shrink down into a small, pathetic lump?" He winked at Jeremy and took a sip from his water glass.

"Daddy, don't even joke like that," Tiff said. "I'm worried about you. Should I come down there and stay with you a while longer?"

"Kitten, what in the world are you thinking?" Orville said. "You just got your job back."

"Oh, I know," she groaned. "But I remember your default answer was always no, when your friends called you about doing things."

"But that was before. I'll be fine now." He reached over and squeezed her hand. "I'm not completely against socializing. I'll get out there. I told you, Phil and JJ always used to press me about golfing with them or watching the games on Sunday. Those two are so sick of telling each other the same stories over and over again. They're dying for a new set of ears. And there's always something going on at the firehouse."

"Well, if you're *sure*," Tiff said.

"Yes, I'm *sure*, kitten," Orville said.

Tiff excused herself to go to the restroom. When she was gone, the two men were silent, until Jeremy said what was on his mind. "Orville, I think I'm a bit taken with your daughter."

Orville cleared his throat. "Yes, I've noticed. I believe I had the same lost-puppy-dog look on my face when Sheila walked into our firehouse some twenty-nine years ago."

"That's reassuring," Jeremy said. "I'm not always the best judge of my own emotions. But I'd like to think I've got a good handle on what I'm feeling for Tiff. She's just surprised me in so many ways this week. She's had an amazing influence on me. And she makes me laugh." He smiled and felt sheepish. "And she's beautiful, of course."

"That she is, son." Orville looked in the direction Tiff had gone. "She always was. Lately she's been so beautiful she breaks my heart."

Jeremy figured this was as good a time as any to bring up his other concern. He sat up straight and spoke as if he were pronouncing a new government edict.

"Orville, I am *not* fond of alcohol."

Orville looked at him with a baffled frown. "I see. Are you…of the impression that I *am*?"

Jeremy gasped. "No! That wasn't my impression at all. I simply thought you might be concerned that, well, like father like son, you know? That I may have inherited an addiction that could lead to future problems."

"Did I say something to make you think that, son?"

Jeremy leaned forward and rested his arms on the table. "No, you didn't. It's just that for a while there, I thought you didn't want me to have anything to do with Tiff."

"Did you?" Orville sat back in his chair. "Why is that?"

Jeremy shrugged. "It seemed like you made a point of interrupting us anytime we had a private moment together. I mean, there's nothing wrong with that, she's your daughter, and I would expect you to feel protective of her. But I figured you didn't like me."

"Oh, *that*." Orville said with a laugh. "That was Tiff's idea."

Jeremy didn't like the sound of that at all. "What do you mean?"

"But now that I think of it, the interference thing was my idea." Orville scratched his head. "I must have been driving both of you crazy."

"Orville, what *are* you talking about? You're driving me crazy right now."

Orville leaned forward. "Well, I guess it's okay to tell you now that she was mighty attracted to you—said you were, uh, flipping gorgeous, I believe were her words."

Jeremy grinned.

"But she had her Jesus thing—"

"Jesus thing?"

"Right. She didn't want to get involved with someone who didn't believe the way she did."

Ah. He had heard this from Kara and Ren.

Orville continued. "So for a while I stepped in when it looked like she needed me to." He scratched at the table. "I think she tried a couple of times to make me stop, but I didn't catch on."

"But, why didn't she just tell me herself? About her, uh, Jesus thing, I mean."

"See, that's what I said, but she said she didn't want you to make such a big decision for the wrong reasons."

That sounded right. Had he known about the reason for her hesitation, he might wonder today about his motives for embracing Christ. "You see, Orville, that's exactly what I like about her. She thinks about things that don't occur to me. I want so much to find out what else she has going on in that head of hers. It's not just because she's beautiful."

Orville tapped the table a few times when he spoke. "It all boils down to respect, Jeremy. I always felt that for her mama. If you don't respect a woman, don't even begin to think she'll respect you. How could she? And if you don't respect each other, ain't no amount of love that'll hold you two together."

Jeremy thought about respect. He had never had to struggle to respect women. The concept must have been hammered into him as a child. He thought they were fantastic and fascinating. He loved how mysterious they could be and how unfathomably intuitive. His female friends were smart and funny and utterly worthy of respect.

Still, when he saw Tiff walking back, Orville's words replayed in his mind. He realized some of his behaviors with women in the past weren't exactly respectable, by some standards. He was a Christian now. He was no lover boy, but chances were he needed to make a few changes in his romantic habits.

As he stood to welcome Tiff back, he noticed Tiff's long, shapely legs, and he thought this might be a tad more difficult than he originally imagined.

Minutes later they left the restaurant and walked to where the car was parked. Tiff walked between Orville and Jeremy. Her hand accidentally brushed against his, and he felt the kind of thrill he typically got with a romantic embrace. He gently looped two of his fingers with hers. When she responded by curling her fingers against his, it was as exciting as if they had kissed. And when he enveloped her entire, lovely hand in his and felt her gentle clutch, he may as well have died and gone to heaven.

Seventy-one

Tiff groaned with disappointment when she awoke abruptly from her dream. It was a good one. She and Jeremy were with a group of people, all friends and coworkers. They were running, taking part in some group activity, when he suddenly grabbed hold of her and kissed her, right in front of everyone. The romantic action in the middle of such an unromantic setting was surprising and thrilling. And now it was over.

She rubbed her eyes and took a drink of water from the glass on the nightstand.

Then she heard a muffled sound outside. She snapped to attention. Every time she'd been interrupted from a dream this week, something significant was about to happen: Eve sneaking in with Paddy; Vera looking for a drunken Sean.

She got out of bed, threw a light robe on, and walked quietly into the living room.

She started when she saw movement through the windows. Someone or something was on the patio. She stayed still until her eyes were able to make out what was going on. She almost knocked on her father's door, but then she caught a glimpse of the figure outside and realized it was Jeremy. What in the world was he doing?

She carefully approached the patio and gently unlocked the door.

He whipped around at the sound, and she saw his shoulders drop. Either she had startled him, or he had been trying hard to keep from waking Orville and her.

She opened the door as quietly as possible and whispered.

"What are you doing out here, crazy man?"

He turned his back to her for a moment. When he turned back around, she saw he held a bouquet of flowers.

"I was hoping to leave these here for you to find when you woke up," he said softly.

"Well, I woke up and I'm finding them," she said. "And it's all the more delightful finding them with you attached."

Jeremy handed her the bouquet of lovely yellow roses, some of which were tipped in red.

"I realize you probably won't be able to take them home," Jeremy said, "but I wanted to give them to you, even if for a few hours."

"They're beautiful! Come in, I'll put them in water."

"No, I don't want to wake Orville."

"Dad'll sleep through just about anything," she said. "If we whisper, he'll be fine. What did you do, go to an all-night florist?"

He followed her in and stood at the kitchen counter. "I bought them before dinner last night and propped them in a big glass of water while we were out. I couldn't decide on the best time to give them to you, so I ended up bringing them now."

She glanced out the window. "With the dawn."

"Right." He smiled. "What time do you and Orville arrive in Virginia today?"

She carefully rummaged around in Faith's cupboards until she found a vase long enough for the stems. "In the evening, I think. Nine-ish. How about you?"

"Actually, I've got to leave in a few minutes. I'll be home by five or so."

"Oh, look at that. They removed the thorns for us." She held up the flowers. "That's full service!"

He glanced down at the counter briefly and said, "Oh. I did that."

"Well, that's the sweetest thing in the world," she said. "You didn't have to do that."

He shrugged. "It was a bit of an impulse. I did it because of something I read in the Bible last night."

"You were reading the Bible?" She spoke before she realized her words were probably a little insulting. She slowly opened drawers and looked for shears to trim the stems. Then she noticed Jeremy said something she couldn't hear. She cocked her head to direct him. "Come over here so I can hear you."

He came around and stood closer to her. "Julian keeps a couple of Bibles in the guest apartment. He's like those hotel Bible people."

Tiff didn't look up when she spoke. "Comes in handy if you happen to figure things out while you're on vacation, huh?"

Jeremy nodded, a wry smile on his face. "I suppose."

Tiff found the shears and whispered triumphantly. "Eureka!" She held them up and then began to trim the stems and arrange the roses as she talked. "So what did you read in the Bible that made you think to trim the thorns away?"

"It was near the beginning, in Genesis." He laughed softly. "I didn't get terribly far into it. To be honest, I got distracted in my reading when I got to the part where Adam named his wife Eve."

Tiff looked up from her work. "Well, you *knew* what her name was going to be, right?"

"Certainly. I just found it hard to concentrate at that point."

Tiff went back to her trimming. "Poor Eve. Branded forever for making the absolutely wrong decision."

"Which Eve are we talking about now?"

Tiff said, "I guess that applies to both of them, doesn't it?"

She filled the vase with tepid water and set it on the coffee table. "Gorgeous." She turned to find him directly behind her, watching her. She sat on the couch. "So tell me the thorn thing."

He sat in the chair adjacent to her and spoke quietly. "There was the part when they were in trouble, Adam and Eve, for eating the fruit from that one tree. God's telling them what their punishment will be. Very sad. And He tells them, or rather, He tells Adam, I suppose, that now he's going to have to work the ground in order to get by. And He said they'd have to deal with thorns and thistles while they worked."

Tiff nodded.

"So, before I brought these over, I remembered that part about the thorns. I know they serve a botanical purpose. You know, protecting the roses. But I still had that biblical connotation—punishment—in my mind."

Where was he going with this? She couldn't imagine.

"I really liked what you said on the beach yesterday, about becoming a new creation. That was quite lovely."

"I can't claim credit for that," Tiff said. "Ren and Kara told me that one, and I'm pretty sure they got it from the Bible."

"Still." He glanced at the roses and then back at Tiff. "I appreciated what the colors of these roses meant—the florist told me. That's how I decided which ones to give you. And I didn't think you should be given thorns. It didn't seem to fit that there was any hint of punishment about these. Not for a new creation." He shrugged again. "So I knocked all of the thorns off."

She took his hand in both of hers, brought it to her lips, and gave him a gentle kiss. "You are the dearest man." She took a yellow rose from the vase. "So, what does the yellow rose mean?"

"A number of things, actually. But the one I liked particularly was—" He looked into the distance, obviously trying to remember the precise wording. "The promise of a new beginning."

She handed the rose to Jeremy. "Then I want you to have one too." Then she pulled a red-tipped yellow rose from the vase. "And this one? What does it mean?"

He glanced down at his hands. "Friendship."

She smiled. "Perfect."

"And, uh, falling in love."

She drew in a deep breath and placed the red-tipped rose in Jeremy's hand too.

They were mere inches from each other, but when he whispered, "Come here, Tiff," she absolutely loved how they bridged that short distance together.

She was thrilled he had awakened her tonight. With reality like this, who needed dreams?

Epilogue

One year later.
The Beach House, San Diego, California

Jeremy and Tiff drove up to the beach house and parked the car.

"It's just as ugly as I remembered it," Tiff said. "I love it!"

They got out of the car and walked around to the trunk. While Jeremy unlocked it, Tiff faced the house. "This time last year it was just Daddy and me." She looked at Jeremy and ran her hand over his back. "I'm so glad I stuck around long enough to come across you."

He stepped up to her and kissed her. "That's two of us, love."

She saw him clench his jaw and sigh as she had heard him do so many times over the past year. He focused on the car again and turned the luggage in the trunk so they could access the zippers without removing their bags.

"Only take enough for the one night, all right?" he said. "We have to leave fairly early in the morning for our flight to Kauai."

"Right." She took out her cosmetics bag and a change of clothes for tomorrow while he waited for her. She looked at him over her shoulder. "Step away for a minute, Jeremy. I don't want you to see what I'm...what I'm wearing tonight." She had no control over her blushing, still amazed at the way God had brought back her innocence.

She packed her things into her carry-on bag from their flight. Then Jeremy opened his suitcase. He looked over his shoulder at her. "All right, then, you have to look away as well."

She gave him a shove. "Don't tease me, Jeremy."

"But I'm serious," he said in mock sincerity. "I have a surprise for you. Be a good girl and step away."

She walked toward the front door and Jeremy called out, "Don't go in without me, Tiff. Threshold and all that, you know."

He wanted to carry her over the threshold. That was so like him, to want to do the traditional things.

He shut the trunk and jogged up to her, carrying his clothes in a bundle under his arm. He had a big grin on his face, and that same lock of hair fell onto his forehead. As she had many times in the past year, she reached up to brush it back, knowing it would fall right back down again.

He took the key from the lockbox and unlocked the door before he turned to her. "Right. Wait here for just a moment." He pointed at her as if she were one of his students. "Don't walk in under any circumstances."

"Yes sir," she said with a mock salute.

He closed the door behind him, and she heard him rummaging around. At one point she heard him say "Blast!"

Finally she heard music. Big-band music—but a slow song. And Jeremy opened the door.

He stepped out and swept her off her feet and carried her into the beach house. When he set her down in the living room, she kept her arms around his neck and pulled him down for a kiss before releasing him. He rested his forehead upon hers and said, "I love you, Tiffany Beckett."

She sighed and looked up at him. "I remember this song. We played that when we were here last year, right?"

"'Stardust.' It was playing when you ran out of your room and jumped into my arms."

She pulled back feigning shock. "Did I do that? What a hussy!"

He laughed. "You were just happy. You had gotten your job back."

"Oh, that's right." She glanced around the house. "What a lot of fun memories."

"Like bodysurfing," he said.

"Breakfast at Kono's."

"The roller coaster."

Tiff laughed at that. "You big faker. Trying to get me to let you ride the carousel instead of the roller coaster, as if you were scared."

"And you were heartless! Do you remember? 'Later,' you said. 'First the roller coaster. You can ride the carousel later.'"

He took her by the hand and brought her to the couch. "Have a seat. I have something for you."

He unrolled the bundle of clothes he had brought in and revealed a small rectangle box in the center. He sat next to her and put the box in her hands.

Tiff opened it slowly. A gold necklace stretched across its length, with pale blue pieces of sea glass hanging like jewels.

"Oh Jeremy! This is the necklace we saw at the jewelry store last year! How did you get this?"

"I bought it last year, the same afternoon I bought the roses. But it felt like an extravagant gift—bordering on strange, actually—considering the fact that we weren't even dating yet. Then, once we were dating, I wanted to give it to you for a special occasion. Once we got engaged, our wedding day seemed like a fairly special occasion."

He paused.

"Then I realized I wanted to give it to you here. You're right about there being so many memories here. I don't know if you remember our conversation outside that jewelry store. But this necklace reminds me of when you helped me understand how much God loves me."

Tiff touched his cheek with her hand.

He continued. "And it reminds me of when God helped me understand I was falling in love with you."

Tiff looked down at the necklace. "Jeremy, I'm never going to be able to wear this without tearing up."

She took the necklace out of the case and said, "Will you put it on me?"

They walked back to the bedroom and she faced the mirror. He stood behind her and fastened the necklace before he rested his hands on her shoulders.

She reached her hand up to feel the sea glass. "I love it."

"It matches your eyes."

She turned and kissed him again. He wrapped his arms around her, but she pulled back and gave him a playful smile.

"Hey, we could probably get in a ride on the carousel now. I'm sure the park is still open."

Jeremy smiled at her crookedly. She knew that particular smile. He did it when he most appreciated her, when he got a kick out of something she had just said or done. He gently ran his hands through her hair and cupped her head as he did on the beach before their first kiss. He kissed her softly. "We'll do that, love." He kept kissing her until he nuzzled her neck and raised a tingle across her skin.

He repeated himself. "We'll do that." Finally he whispered in her ear. "Later."

Questions for Discussion

1. *Beach Dreams* touches upon a number of mistaken or altered first impressions between various characters. What impression did Tiff make on Jeremy when they met at the gym? On the airport shuttle? At Ledo's? And Tiff's first impression of Eve was that she seemed perfect. How accurate was that? Jeremy even suspected something amiss when he met his father's new wife, Vera. Why? Was his impression right or wrong?

2. Can you think of a specific person about whom you formed a mistaken first impression? What later changed your impression?

3. Jeremy comments that he tends to give in to demanding girlfriends. He also says he becomes gullible and blind around interesting, beautiful women. Is that the way you see it? Did Jeremy show growth in that regard?

4. Do you identify at all with Jeremy's self-critical attitude, mentioned above, with regard to interesting, beautiful people? Have you found yourself compromising your beliefs, intuitions, or judgments when challenged by someone you find attractive or charming? How do you stand firm when challenged by someone like that?

5. At several points in the story, Tiff refers to strained relations with her mother. How do you think that relationship might have influenced Tiff's pre-salvation behavior?

6. Although still far from perfect, Tiff has clearly improved in her outlook on life, love, morality, and people because of her faith. Have you seen such a transformation in anyone in particular (maybe even yourself)?

7. Jeremy's father deliberately chose not to tell Jeremy about his new wife, Vera, in order to protect her from exposure about her past. In the process he hurt his relationship with his son, albeit temporarily. Was that the best choice?

8. Jeremy is unsure how to behave when Eve walks into the beach house with Michael. He chooses to believe Eve, and he sits by while she leaves for an evening with Michael and his "sister." Did he have any other choice? How would you have handled that situation if you had been in his shoes?

9. Does your impression of Paddy change at all as the book progresses? Why or why not?

10. Is the attraction between Tiff and Jeremy purely physical? Regardless of your answer, how can you tell?

11. For part of the story, Orville is on "bulldog" duty between Tiff and Jeremy. Did he help Tiff achieve her stated goal of forestalling romance with an unbeliever? How did Orville's efforts affect Jeremy?

12. How did Zeke influence people in the story? Julian? Ren?

13. How did you feel about Zeke's comment to Orville with regard to Sheila's last thoughts and her eternal status?

14. What did you think of Tiff's reaction to Orville's news about Franklin? How would you have reacted, getting such news as an adult?

15. Jeremy booked a night at the beach house a year later in our story. Why there? Do you have a specific place that represents a significant turning point in your relationship with a loved one? With God?

Meet Trish Perry

Trish Perry is the award-winning author of *The Guy I'm Not Dating* and *Too Good to Be True*. She serves on the board of the Capital Christian Writers organization in the Washington, D.C. area and edited its newsletter, *Ink and the Spirit,* for seven years. She has published numerous short stories, essays, devotionals, and poetry in Christian and general-market media, and she is a member of American Christian Fiction Writers and Romance Writers of America.

Says Trish:

"I live in Northern Virginia with my brilliantly funny son, whom I love and can embarrass with one hand tied behind my back. I have a gorgeous adult daughter who has become my most intuitive friend, and an amazing grandson who sweetly calls me MayMay instead of...the G word."

Trish loves to hear from her readers. Please feel free to contact her via mail at:

Trish Perry
c/o Harvest House Publishers
990 Owen Loop North
Eugene, OR 97402

or

via her website at:
www.trishperry.com

or

via e-mail at:
trish@trishperry.com

If you enjoyed Beach Dreams *by Trish Perry,*
be sure and read her other fun novels featuring
Tiffany, Rennie, Kara, and Jeremy.

"Yowza!" exclaims Kara Richardson when she sees the handsome proprietor of the new delicatessen in town, Gabe Paolino—who soon expresses mutual interest. This would be the start of a perfect love story, except for one thing—Kara has vowed to stop dating until she feels God's leading.

But when humorous circumstances send Kara and Gabe on a road trip to Florida, hope springs anew. Even with Kara's flirtatious coworker Tiffany—"a hyena in heels"—along for the ride, the *un*couple begins a lively journey that could change their paths forever.

This memorable, charming story of love's persistence captures the honor of waiting on God's timing and the adventure of finding the perfect guy to not date.

Rennie Young, heroine of *Too Good to Be True,* meets the gallant Truman Sayers after she faints in the boys' department of the local superstore. Despite this unromantic introduction, Tru Sayers, a handsome young labor-and-delivery nurse, seems like a gift from God. But a recent divorce and other life disappointments cause Ren to question whether she can trust her heart and God.

This clever novel encourages readers to lean on God's leading and to be open to life after the hurt—even when it seems too good to be true.

To learn more about books by Trish Perry
or to read sample chapters, log on to our website:
www.harvesthousepublishers.com

HARVEST HOUSE PUBLISHERS
EUGENE, OREGON

Praise for
Like Always

"*Like Always* is proof that God's finest miracles are wrapped in hope and tears."

—DiAnn Mills, author of *Leather and Lace*
and *When the Lion Roars*

"Robert Elmer has proven his genius in his latest novel, *Like Always*. He combines the gentle touch of a poet with the astute intelligence of a skilled instructor to delve into the heart-tugging story of one woman with an agonizing choice to make. Very powerful."

—Hannah Alexander, author of the Hideaway series

"What a tender, moving, triumphant novel! Robert Elmer delivers another perfect love story…like always."

—Deborah Raney, author of *Remember to Forget*
and *Leaving November*

"With style and prose reminiscent of Nicholas Sparks, *Like Always* weaves a tender thread of love and faith, and offers an intimate glimpse into the depth and breadth of one couple's devotion…and heart-breaking conviction."

—Tamera Alexander, bestselling author of *Rekindled,*
Revealed, and *Remembered,* Fountain Creek Chronicles